PATH TO ASHES

A VAMPIRE ROMANCE WITH FANGS, FEELINGS,
AND A FEW CORPSES.

RHITA MORITZ

1

MEETING THE DEVIL

I had never intended to become a murderer. It was an accident.

At least, that's what I told myself as I stared into the clouded eyes of my husband's mistress. But perhaps destiny never cared for personal intentions. The NYPD certainly wouldn't. I doubted "oops, she swan-dived three stories onto construction steel" would go over well with a jury.

Though I'd never seen a corpse before, I was also fairly sure they weren't supposed to wither before rigor mortis had a chance to set in. A brittle crackling filled the air as her milk-white skin drew impossibly tight, shrink-wrapping to the bones beneath.

Maybe it was shock, perhaps madness, but when her fingers curled in on themselves, the tips blackened and crumbled away. A cold gust swept through the unfinished skyscraper, lifting her into the night in a scattering of fine dust.

The metallic clattering of the rebar pole spearing through her chest crashing to the floor coupled with the cooling spray of blood across my face, made a liar out of both my self-proclaimed innocence and reality itself. For frozen in her death scream had been two monstrously long canines stretching past ruby lips. The image seared itself into my mind long after the rest of her had disintegrated.

I could have screamed—opened my mouth, shredding my vocal cords until someone dragged me away in a straitjacket, raving about the fangs of a woman who moved too fast to be natural. Still, that didn't feel like the proper reaction. My mind remained bent on her teeth, on the sharp pricks they'd left against my neck when she pressed her mouth to me. That was, of course, just before I managed to trip her over the unguarded edge of what would eventually become a third-floor mezzanine.

Twisting the simple ring on my wedding finger, I tried desperately to piece together how I'd ended up here. How the worst day in my life had culminated in watching a tattered, blood-soaked dress flap in the wind from the haphazardly placed rebar she'd fallen onto.

My thumb circled the gold band.

Twist. Twist. Twist.

I could see myself on the plane to New York City from Savannah. The beer in my hand grew warm as I pressed the cold glass to my temple, wishing it could numb more than just my skin.

Twist, twist, twist.

I was standing before an unfeeling skyscraper. Black metal framing darkened glass stretched high into the sky. Luke's office suited him, all harsh angles with no warmth.

Twist, twist, twist.

I was trailing behind them, Luke and the woman with fiery hair that was several shades brighter than my own. My steps felt heavy, my heart heavier still. It might have fallen right out of my chest, plopping onto the ground to scrape along the unforgiving asphalt until it was a beating, shredded mass.

Twist, twist, twist.

My reflection in the window of the restaurant stared back at me, a dead-eyed ghost of the woman I used to be. Behind that ghost, I watched my husband get tangled up with this woman. His lips on flimsy plastic sheets covering the doors and windows, casting every-thing in a sickly orange glow. Formless shadows danced around me in a rhythmless fashion.

My heart was aching for the comfort of my bed, states away on the outskirts of Savannah. There, the air smelled of Spanish moss. I could almost hear the cicadas' relentless chorus rising into the night, until the shriek of an ambulance shattered the illusion. I flinched against the thin veil of construction fabric as a group of giggling, drunken women staggered past. Their shadows wavered across the partition. I felt as insubstantial as those shapeless silhouettes drifting toward whatever late-night revelry awaited them.

My hand throbbed. I found a slow trail of blood dripping from my clenched fist. Sucking in a breath, I unfurled my fingers. Each joint protested as though I were breaking them open. Glass shards glistened in my palm, the remnants of the wine glass still embedded in my skin.

"Fuck," I muttered under my breath.

Raising my hand closer to my face, I tried to examine the damage in the murky gloom. Bloody grime blurred every line of my skin. Squinting, I caught a faint glow at the mezzanine's edge. It was a first aid kit, half-buried among a pile of discarded tools.

Getting to it demanded three flights of exposed stairs that climbed at a treacherously steep angle. Adrenaline spiked hot through my veins, burning away some of the sorrow that burdened me. If I kept climbing higher, to the top floor, would the rush be strong enough to scorch the rest of my heartbreak? Or would the weight of my failed marriage drag me down, conspiring with gravity to pull me back to earth?

The sharp clack of approaching footsteps cut through the thought, snapping me back into the dark.

A woman emerged from the shadows. She had generous curves hugged by a stained white dress, silky tendrils of auburn hair snaking down her shoulders. My swollen eyes narrowed as a nauseating mixture of recognition and loathing tightened my chest.

hers, her fingers in his hair. They consumed each other. While I... I twisted the ring, watching from the other side of the window.

Then I was inside, a glass full of thick red wine emptied onto the woman who had her face buried into my husband's neck. Her white dress and his suit, a gift that had cost me half a month's pay, were soaked in a ribbon of scarlet. Not my finest moment.

Luke's piercing blue eyes bulged. The blood drained from his face, leaving his normally sunkissed skin a palored gray.

My face, by comparison, was beet red. I could feel it burning with such intense rage that I was sure steam would blow out of my ears any second.

"Ba-babe," Luke stuttered in his stupidly perfect country twang.

"Don't!" I growled so low, so vicious, that I didn't recognize my own voice.

Luke cringed.

This couldn't be me. It didn't feel like me. I was standing in a stranger's shoes. The real me was drifting away, watching the scene unfold below her from a safe distance.

Hurried footsteps scurried behind me. Security? The hostess I'd somehow slipped past? It didn't matter anymore. My gaze snapped to the woman's cruel smirk that exposed extraordinarily white teeth. She must have paid a fortune for them.

"How pathe—"

Her insult was severed mid-breath as the ball of spit that had been brewing in my mouth hit its mark. It splattered across her alabaster skin as her shriek echoed through the room like a crack of thunder. The restaurant collectively inhaled. Then, chaos erupted around me.

Twist, twist, twist.

I was wandering the empty halls of this unfinished industrial building, abandoned for the evening by construction crews. The chilled September air was laden with the scent of dust accompanied by damp concrete. Dim light from street lamps outside bled through

"You know," she approached in her stilettoed feet, "I almost feel sorry about this whole situation."

"What do you want?" I asked in a painfully broken voice.

"Let's see," she hummed, ticking off points on her fingers, "You ruined my supper, you scared off my date. You probably had my name removed from a very exclusive restaurant list. Wine definitely won't come out of this dress. Shall I continue?"

I glared at her, not sorry and with nothing to say. My heart kicked up, fueled by the quiet wrath that built with every word coming out of her mouth.

"Well?" She asked shrilly. "Don't you have anything to say?"

"Not to you," I stood up with no small amount of effort, pressing my hand into my shirt. "Go away."

I could find a first aid kit somewhere else, before I did something stupid. She scoffed, a thin hand gripping my shoulder with surprising force.

My head canted towards her.

"Let go. Now."

My muscles tightened, my senses sharpened. I could feel her standing behind me, smelled the sickly sweet stench of her perfume mingling with something like iron.

"No," a hot breath fluttered against my neck.

Gooseflesh pebbled my flesh as I felt the brush of her lips on my exposed skin. I remembered feeling a sudden stabbing sensation from between her wet, warm lips. Instinct took over as I dropped my weight, pivoted, sending her sprawling with a shoulder throw I'd drilled a thousand times on the mats. She had slammed into the concrete with a satisfying *thwack*.

It was all blurry fragments of memory from there, stitched together by fractured pockets of motion and noises. Her hiss as she bared her too-long canines before launching at me like a hell-cat. My body scraping across the floor toward the mezzanine. The impossible sight of her swinging a sledgehammer one-handed as if it were a baton. The short, savage struggle that followed.

Logic told me that I had fallen back onto years of experience as a Brazilian Jiu-Jitsu instructor at a small MMA gym. Luke must have forgotten to mention that. If he had mentioned me at all.

My bloodied fingernails stung horrendously, torn to the quick. An image surfaced of me kicking her hips over the ledge as I clung to her ankles from my position on the ground. She teetered on those sky-high heels. There was a cool rush of air, then her terrible scream fading as she disappeared over the edge. The silence that followed was as loud as any death cry.

Nausea churned in my gut. I staggered back, bracing against the cold scaffolding, retching until my throat burned. A woman was dead because of me. Wasn't that the definition of murder? Unless it didn't count because she wasn't human. She couldn't have been human.

Only then, what did that make me? A killer? Or just losing my mind?

Questions looped endlessly in my mind until, for the second time that evening, the sound of footsteps dragged me back to the present.

"Well now," a low, gravelly voice sent new panic through my battered body. "This is not what I expected to find."

I spun, limbs trembling, muscles screaming for another fight. Before I could raise a fist, I was caught around the wrists by large hands.

"Easy." The shadowed man held me at arm's length.

I blinked up, his angular features were partially obscured by the weak light. Long, dark waves of hair brushed against me. They fell just past his shoulders. They were soft, as cool as the night breeze. There was something... unnerving about the way he smiled down at me. Like there was not an ounce of feeling behind his shadowed eyes.

My pulse spiked. His grip was iron, so tight my fingers fizzed with pins and needles.

"Get back!" I scrambled away from his grasp.

He stepped back carefully, as though placating a wild animal.

Feeling rushed back into my hands. They shook violently as we stared each other down. He'd melted deeper into the alcove beneath the mezzanine, becoming just a glint of eyes in the dark. A predator waiting for prey to stumble. The trembling spread up my arms, my shoulders wound so tight I thought I might explode from the nervous energy radiating off me.

I wasn't stupid. A soon-to-be divorcée in her thirties, possibly having a mental break, wandering the city at night? I'd practically mailed Netflix the rights to my limited series: *The Disappearance of Scarlet Montgomery.*

"Imagine," His voice drifted from the shadows. "I came to save a little rabbit from a wolf, only to find a wild beast already gnawing off its head."

"Good. You know I have claws," I replied, with only the slightest tremor coloring my words.

"Clearly," he drawled, eyes flicking to the dress that was the only remaining proof that my sanity was indeed intact.

"That isn't what it looks like," I said quickly, taking a half step back.

The specter mirrored my movement, light cleaving his face. Somehow, the way half of his face remained swallowed by severe shadow was even more terrible than before. Heavy, dark brows framed an angular face paired with a proud roman nose. A neatly trimmed mustache curled above his mouth. His one visible eye, an indigo so deep it seemed to drink the light, fixed on me with unnerving intensity.

"Really? It seems quite straightforward," he countered, flashing the ghost of an uninviting smile.

It looked wrong, as though his face was fumbling through the memory of smiling.

My chest hitched in erratic bursts as I forced out, "It was self-defense. She attacked me!"

"Yet here you stand, drenched in her blood."

Fair point. I was, in fact, standing there covered in my husband's mistress's blood, staring down a V-for-Vendetta wannabe like a deer in headlights. I spun on the balls of my feet, bolting at full speed.

I was utterly convinced I had just met the devil himself. The laughter snapping at my heels didn't do much to convince me otherwise. If anything, it felt like hell itself was giving chase.

2

―――――――――――

NOT YOURS TO CARRY

Why hadn't I just stayed home? Why hadn't I drowned myself in a bottle of wine like any normal victim of adultery? Why had I flown all the way to New York City to confront my husband? Most importantly—why the fuck had I worn heeled boots tonight of all nights?

Those were the questions scorching through my brain as I ran for my life on wobbling ankles. The slick soles skated across concrete, I nearly ate pavement twice. Each slip sent me spitting curses, as scattered construction debris turned my escape into the world's most terrifying obstacle course.

"There's no use in running, little beast."

The man's voice came from nowhere and everywhere at once, like a million invisible speakers blaring in surround sound.

"Jesus," I gasped, skidding to a halt in front of the only locked door in the entire building.

The handle rattled uselessly in my hand. I tapped the panel; it was particleboard. Thank God.

"No Jesus here," he crooned, closer now.

Heat pressed against my back, a presence so heavy it felt like it could burn through my skin. I had two options: run toward the source of that slithering voice, or break through the door. The crunch of approaching footsteps made the decision for me.

I sucked in a breath, hopping back to slam a punishing front kick beside the handle. Pain zinged up my shin, thin boot soles doing me no favors. Yet the door cracked. The frame shuddered. It took two more vicious kicks for the thing to give way, collapsing inward.

With a strangled cry of victory, I barreled through shoulder-first. Darkness swallowed me whole. Perfect. If I couldn't see him, he couldn't see me, right?

Clinging to that brilliant logic, I scrambled forward, palms sweeping across concrete until they hit a large rectangular object. A desk. Relief flooded me. I ducked behind it, smacking my forehead on the edge as I dove under. Biting back a curse, I peered out through the wiring hole, eyes locked on the thin slivers of light cutting through the wrecked doorframe.

I counted ten, fifteen, twenty heartbeats before the hinges creaked.

"Is this really necessary?" His voice was maddeningly calm. A hand toyed with the broken door, pushing it back and forth like he was inspecting my handiwork. "You're keeping me from a very long to-do list. Although..." he chuckled softly, "this is quite impressive, I must say."

My nails dug half-moons into my palms. With one wrong move I'd wake up in some dugout well, listening to him croon *"Goodbye Horses"* while reminding me to moisturize.

This was not how I wanted to die. Death was supposed to tiptoe in one night to steal me away in my sleep, preferably while I was eighty and surrounded by grandchildren. Not here, not now, in a half-built hellhole that still smelled like wet drywall.

"You won't come out, will you?" He sighed, like I was the world's most inconvenient errand.

I couldn't see his eyes, but I'd have bet my entire paycheck they were locked right on me.

"Not even if I say *please?*" The absurdly courteous lilt in his voice made my throat seize. Who the hell chased a woman into a dark room while sounding like he was inviting her to tea?

"Fuck off," I blurted from my hidey-hole, then slapped a hand over my mouth.

If there was ever a good time to be impulsive, this was not it. Self control came too late.

He muttered something under his breath about "annoying humans," then strolled over like this was all just mildly tiresome. One hand caught the lip of the desk. With a casual flick, he tossed it aside. The crash against the concrete rattled my teeth.

"Holy hell," I squeaked, jaw flapping uselessly between terror and awe.

"Yes," he said smoothly, lips curling. "Holy hell. Now—" his hand darted toward me "—I think you'd better come along with me."

Resistance was futile. That didn't mean I didn't give it my best shot.

I kicked, bit, scratched, even threw in some tears for good measure. All I received for my efforts was being slung over his shoulder like a sack of discount potatoes while my fists pounded uselessly against his back.

None of it fazed him. Not the elbows, not the heel to his ribs, not even the head-butt I was particularly proud of. I could hit hard, years of training at the gym had seen to that, except he didn't so much as grunt. He just sighed, grumbled, then carried on.

With all the effort of tossing laundry in a hamper, he dumped me into the backseat of a sleek gray Bentley. By the time I sat up, we were already zipping through the city. The streets were mostly empty at this hour. There was no traffic, no witnesses. No chance in hell of me rolling out the door without becoming roadkill.

He ignored every insult I hurled, every curse and creative defamation.

In a last-ditch effort, I snapped, "Let me go, you discount Captain Hook."

"No." He replied flatly, though his fingers drifted over the neatly groomed edges of his facial hair.

"Then at least tell me your name."

"Sorin."

"Sorin," I repeated, rolling it around my tongue. It tasted of rust joined by arrogance. "My name's Scarlet."

"I know."

My scathing retort was cut short by the car slowing to a stop.

We pulled to a stop in front of an all-too-familiar building. My stomach dropped. The ground floor stretched wide, a sprawling restaurant dressed in dark cherry-stained paneling that climbed up into the second story. From the entryway hung a clover-shaped sign glinting under the streetlight: *Crimson & Clover*.

The place where I'd once hurled a glass of wine all over my husband—and his mattress.

Now, in the eerie silence of night, it looked less like a trendy hotspot than a gaping maw of some beast waiting to swallow me whole.

The blood drained from my face.

"What are we doing here?" I whispered, pressing myself as far as I could into the corner of the car.

"Get out," Sorin ordered, stepping from the driver's seat. He tossed the keys to a handsome, light-skinned man whose eyes glittered with gold eyeliner.

I froze. He had a kind face. Maybe he'd help me. I opened my mouth to plead. Before a sound left my throat, my door was yanked open. I spilled backward into waiting arms.

They locked around me, pulling me against the hard wall of a well-muscled chest. Anyone watching might have thought we were locked in a lover's embrace. But my ribs creaked from the pressure, the breath crushed out of me.

"Don't speak. Don't move. Don't even breathe without my permission," Sorin murmured into my ear, his voice like smoke curling through my skull. "Nod if you understand."

The car was already vanishing around the corner. My vision blurred as I nodded furiously, growing frantic for air. At last, his hold slackened, allowing blessed oxygen poured into my lungs. Dizzy, I staggered forward, only to be snatched back by the collar of my sweater. The fabric tore with a sickening rip.

"Get the fuck off me!" I slapped at his arm, twisting to bolt.

His hand clamped around my wrist with bruising force.

"This would be much easier if you'd just comply," he complained, dragging me inch by inch toward a shadowed side door.

"I'm not going to let you murder me!" I seethed, heels scraping against the pavement as I fought him.

"Murder? Is that what you think I'm going to do?" Sorin arched a brow as he punched a code into the keypad.

"Oh my god." I froze, my eyes bulging. Panic ignited a white-hot flame inside me. "Please don't traffic me."

His eyes flew wide. "I'm not going to—"

"I'm way too old to be trafficked!" I cried, yanking back so hard my shoulder screamed in its socket.

"No, listen—"

"You wouldn't get anything for me! I'm thirty-one, I—"

Sorin jerked me inside. A strangled yelp tore from my throat as my back slammed against a felt-lined wall. The thin padding did little to soften the jolt that rattled my spine. I gasped, my scream muffled by his hand clamping over my mouth.

"Scarlet Montgomery," he said firmly, pressing the underside of my nose so I couldn't bite off his fingers. "I do not intend to murder you, traffic you, or cause you *any* harm tonight."

Pinned beneath the weight of his chest and thighs, my breath tore out in ragged bursts against his palm. Frustrated, I wiggled uselessly against him. His body might as well have been carved from stone.

Muscles screaming from overuse, I finally sagged in his grip. Hot, defeated tears pricked my eyes. I bit down on the inside of my lip to keep them from spilling.

"As long as you stay close to me for the rest of the night, you will be safe. Is that clear?" Sorin's voice was low, like we were surrounded by people instead of alone in a cavernous dining room.

"What are you going to do with me?" My question came out far too small.

"Hopefully nothing," he said, loosening his hold. "Besides have you sign a few papers."

"Papers?" I echoed stupidly, certain I'd misheard him.

He didn't bother with a reply, slightly gesturing for me to follow before stalking through the kitchen door.

Feeling dazed, I trailed after him through the kitchen and a maze of offices until he pushed us into a stairwell that stretched higher than I cared to climb.

"Is this your building?" I asked through clenched teeth, trying to distract myself from the way my body protested.

"Yes."

"Not really much of a conversationalist, are you?"

"No."

I scoffed.

Halfway up the first flight, I dropped onto a step to yank off my ruined boots.

Sorin sucked his teeth at the delay.

"This will only take a second," I huffed, rolling my ankles with a groan at the sweet freedom from elevated heels.

"Shall I carry you?" He bit out.

I glanced at him, waiting for a smile to crack the scowl carved into his face. Sure, maybe he could carry me over flat ground, but I wasn't exactly light. I'd earned every muscle that corded my body.

"I'm fine," I grumbled, pushing myself back onto my sore feet and limping upward.

The night was taking its toll. With adrenaline ebbing, the battering was setting in. My right leg protested with every step. The bones in my feet throbbed from kicking in that damn door.

"Could you move faster?" Sorin's voice drifted down, dry as old parchment. "I'd like you to still be young by the time we reach the twelfth floor."

At the top of the landing, he tapped his foot impatiently. I shot him a glare.

"Stop being stubborn. Let me carry you," he pressed.

"I'm too heavy," I snapped back. "And I don't need help climbing a staircase. I'll make it on my own."

Despite my words, my heart sank as pain gnawed at my foot. Soon I'd be hobbling, or worse—dead weight.

Many floors later, we entered an open concept entertainment space. I eyed the multitude of couches longingly, my legs trembling from the arduous climb up the stairs. White washed walls passed me by as we made our way deeper into the floor.

"Do you also own the restaurant downstairs?" I asked in an attempt to break the quiet rhythm of our footsteps.

He nodded, stepping aside to allow me passage through the doorway. The walls and ceiling in this room were painted satin black, framed by intricate crown molding. A commanding table of polished black wood stood proudly in the center of the room. Its surface gleamed under the golden light of wall sconces and a grand chandelier. A small fire flickered on gas logs on the other side of the table, adding some warmth to the room's opulence.

"Must be a successful business."

I swallowed thickly as images of myself being sacrificed a thousand ways on that table flitted through my mind's eye.

"It is," a honeyed voice replied from my peripheral.

I cranked my stiffening neck to the side to see a beautiful woman with deep brown skin as lustrous as the polished wood surrounding us. She looked straight out of a magazine cover with her pouting lips turned up into a radiant smile. Close-cropped hair complemented razor-sharp cheekbones under onyx eyes. They seemed like black holes holding the weight of entire universes, catching the flicker of the flames and bending them to her.

She glided toward me, extending a hand, "I'm Odessa, Sorin's partner."

Partner as in wife? Lover? Either would be good, because my organs were feeling very at risk at the moment.

Her eyes flicked downward until I realized her hand still hovered between us.

"Oh, sorry," I shook her hand hesitantly. "I'm Scarlet."

"What a lovely name," she replied, pulling out a chair for me.

Keeping them both in sight, I sank into the seat.

Odessa smiled brightly, "Poor thing, let me get you a drink."

Sorin rolled his eyes, settling himself on the opposite side of the table.

"Try this," she said, pouring red wine into a crystal glass from a bar cart with a practiced flourish. "This is a 1997 Château Margaux."

I stared at the full glass. "I don't really drink, sorry."

"It's quite good," Sorin remarked, staining his lips red with the glass to his lips.

"Well, it's just that... I don't really know either of you," I admitted, trying not to sound like my heart was trying to pound out of my chest. "And I don't think accepting drinks from strangers is the best idea, given my, uh, circumstances."

"Ah, " Odessa nodded sympathetically before swiftly snatching the goblet off the table before taking a large drink. "See? All good."

Sorin frowned, refusing to break his stare on me.

Getting the message that refusal wasn't an option, I accepted the glass and took a cautious sip. The velvety liquid flowed over my tongue, leaving a warm, lingering trail as it slid smoothly down my throat.

"Oh wow," I said, downing another mouthful. "That really is good."

"Mhm," Odessa chirped, looking pleased. "Are you hungry?"

"No."

My desire to leave was greater than my hunger.

"You're a terrible liar," Sorin sighed, typing away on his phone. "I'll have something brought up from downstairs."

I gripped my hands together tightly.

"Thank you, but I'd really rather leave now." I began to rise from my seat.

"We need to talk about what happened," Odessa interjected, her voice dropping to a deadly serious tone.

I immediately sank back into the chair.

"What about it?" I asked, panicking at how much the ethereal beauty might know.

"Well," she said, taking a measured sip from her glass, "you don't really think you could simply walk away after killing someone, do you?"

"That's not what happened," I shot back defensively, feeling the walls closing in around me. "She attacked me."

"Semantics," Odessa shrugged. "Don't worry. You're not in any trouble with us."

Sorin scoffed softly. My clammy fingers tightened around the stem of the glass. I took another sip of wine. The warmth settled into a gentle buzzing within my head.

"Who are you?" I asked, kicking myself for allowing such a strange man to lure me into an even stranger place.

"Who do you think we are?" Odessa's voice lilted with mock innocence.

My eyes darted between them, lingering too long on their wine-soaked teeth. Except it wasn't wine. It was too thick, too dark, clinging to the glass in sluggish rivulets. My stomach dropped. Sweat prickled at my temple.

"What happened tonight, when Valerie was... impaled?" Odessa asked, clearing her throat delicately.

Was it the shadows, or did sharp points glint against her bottom lip? My breath hitched. Nails dug into the arms of my chair until wood splintered under my grip.

"I wonder, Scarlet," Odessa leaned forward. "Has anything caught your attention about us?"

Fuck me. Those were definitely fangs sliding free of her mouth. Her pupils constricted almost imperceptibly. I had to run, had to get out of here. I shoved back in my chair.

"She won't say it," Sorin muttered, arms crossing. "Probably thinks she's lost her mind."

Odessa shot him a warning glance.

"Who are you?" I demanded, my voice breaking high with terror. The room swam, edges blurring until only their faces stayed in sharp focus.

"Let's see..." Sorin's tone was almost bored. "Sharp fangs. Superior strength. Speed. Prowess beyond human." He tilted his head. "Give it your best guess."

I couldn't say it out loud. I opened my mouth, the word *vampire* sticking like a bitter pill without a coating on my tongue. My throat constricted around a ball of dread.

"This isn't possible," I wheezed, feeling like I was both sucking in too much and too little air at once.

The lump in my throat became unbearable. I took a long drink, hoping the wine would help find my voice.

"Why don't we start with last night?" Odessa suggested. "Just tell us what happened."

The past seemed easier to swallow than the impossible truth before me that I was not ready to admit. What did I really have to lose at this point? My shoulders sagged in defeat as Odessa leaned forward to hear my confession.

"Luke," my voice caught on his name. "My husband. I found him at your restaurant with another woman."

3

SIGN HERE TO SURVIVE

When I finished giving the condensed version of what had happened, my lips were trembling over an empty wine glass. I wasn't exaggerating when I said I didn't drink. Between the torrent of emotions and my empty stomach, the wine hit me like a double shot of hard liquor.

"And how do you think she found you?" Odessa promoted, clearly trying to lead me to some conclusion.

"She must have followed me all the way from the restaurant," I said uncertainly.

"No," Odessa replied. "Sorin had a little chat with her after you left."

Sorin clasped his hands in front of his expressionless face as he listened.

Furrowing my brow, I realized I had no logical answer. I didn't even have my phone on me, so location tracking was out of the question.

"How about that?"

Odessa pointed to my bloodied hands.

Holding them up, I racked my brain for a reply that didn't involve fictional beings that should only exist in cheesy romance novels. The answer eluded me. I turned to Sorin with suspicious eyes. How had *he* found us? He smirked as if he could read the question written on my face. I wanted to slap it right off his smug face.

"After she, erm, fell from the platform," Odessa pressed, "Didn't it strike you as odd that she disintegrated?"

"What are you getting at?" I snapped, unable to keep the heat out of my voice.

This was absolutely ludicrous. If I hadn't gone crazy, then they had.

"Scarlet, you know the answer to that," Odessa replied softly.

"No. Vampires don't exist. Monsters don't exist," I stamped my foot, standing. "It's simply not possible."

"You saw her eyes, her teeth."

I shook my head violently. Distantly, I registered that only a few moments ago, that motion would have been incredibly difficult. My neck pain was gone.

Our eyes locked while I panted in terror.

"She tried to bite your throat, didn't she?"

Wordlessly, my trembling fingers drifted to the spot on my neck where I thought she had tried to kiss me.

"What is happening?" I cried, stumbling away from her.

"Don't be frightened," Odessa said, stalking my movements with cat-like grace. "You know what this is. You know what we are."

Breath sawed through my throat as the room spun around me.

"Shall I intervene?" Sorin interrupted, watching me with a detached curiosity. "You might give her a heart attack."

"Don't you dare," Odessa retorted hotly. "She was your decision. Let her adjust."

Gripping the edge of the table, I lowered myself to the floor before I passed out.

"Breathe," Odessa sat down in front of me.

"Are you—" My hand instinctively covered the scars on my neck. "Am I a... vampire?"

The word shot from my mouth like a bullet, leaving behind a

greasy residue on my tongue. Sorin erupted into a fit of laughter that filled the room.

"You aren't. That wasn't a true bite," Odessa said softly, casting Sorin a withering glare. "Please ignore him. He's long since aged out of good manners."

"Not true!" Sorin objected, attempting to smother his laughter. "Apologies, I'll try to restrain myself."

"Vampires are real," I said each word with measured consideration.

"Yes," she confirmed as she helped me up. "And it takes far more than a tooth scrape, painful as that must have been, to turn into one."

I slumped into the chair, my mind reeling. Vampires. Actual freaking vampires. My eyes jumped to Odessa just in time to catch her smiling. Sharp fangs glinted from beneath those dewy lips.

A strangled yelp escaped me as I scrambled out of the chair. Her smile vanished as abruptly as it had appeared.

"You're safe here!"

She stepped back, her hands slightly raised.

"I just... I think I need a minute," I croaked. My throat was so dry it felt like I hadn't had a drink in centuries. "Can I have some water?"

"Of course," she replied, trotting back to her seat. "You can tell Malik to bring in her dinner now."

Sorin inclined his head, typing something on his phone. A brief moment later the handsome man who had driven the car strode in carrying a tray. He set down a steaming plate of bread, a large bowl of beef stew, and a generous slice of rich chocolate cake in front of me without uttering a word. He placed a large glass of ice water beside the food.

"Thank you, Malik," Sorin dismissed him with a curt nod.

I drank deeply from the glass of cool water, eyeing the food before me. My stomach gurgled painfully.

"How do you feel?" Sorin asked clinically.

I considered his question as I glanced suspiciously at the meal.

"Really good, actually," I admitted.

A warm hum had settled over my body. Physically, I felt better than new. I eyed the food again.

"And really hungry."

Sorin nodded, seemingly satisfied with my response.

"That's to be expected. A side effect of the wine."

He said "wine" with a subtle emphasis, as if it were something more. And didn't it have to be?

"What was in the wine?" I asked, horrified at what I might have just ingested.

"Just a few drops of Sorin's blood."

By the way Odessa said it, you would have thought she was discussing adding vitamins to a drink.

I choked on the water, coughing violently.

"It would've been mine," she added, as though that explanation might somehow make it better, "only his blood is much more potent due to his age."

"Extreme hunger after receiving vampire blood is normal," Sorin informed me. "You should eat now. It will only get worse."

"Anything else I should know?" I asked accusingly, bringing a piece of bread to my lips.

I wanted to enjoy the buttery crust crunched under my teeth. Unfortunately, the taste and pillowy texture were lost to my unease.

"Far more than your short lifespan could comprehend," Sorin murmured as if he were already exhausted by the conversation.

"The blood heals injuries, as you've seen," Odessa cast an unimpressed glance at Sorin. "It can also grant humans extraordinary strength, speed, sometimes agility. But there are significant drawbacks."

The bread fell from my fingers.

"It's highly addictive." Her expression darkened. "And it comes with an intense comedown. Too much can cause a euphoric high, followed quickly by an overdose. When consumed too often, it has been known to drive people mad."

I had already spent most of this night thinking I was going mad. Now they were telling me there was a chance it was really going to happen? Splendid. Bitterness clawed its way through the anxiety holding residency in my chest. It sank into a strangely hollow place that had been reserved for when I finally decided to process Luke's infidelity.

"So, basically, you just roofied me?" I asked accusingly, glaring between them.

"I wouldn't say that," Odessa said placatingly.

"You're sick. This is all sick." I shoved the plate away, bile burning my throat.

"That's a bit harsh," Odessa said, frowning.

"Her opinions don't matter," Sorin cut in.

"They absolutely do," I shot back.

Sorin's eyes narrowed, pinning me in place.

"The only thing that matters, Ms. Montgomery—"

"Mrs.," I corrected, though the title was circling the drain.

"It hardly matters," Sorin said, rolling his eyes as he reached into his jacket to produce a leather-bound folder with a flourish, placing it neatly in front of me. "Here's a contract. Sign it, or die. The choice is yours."

"Sorin!" Odessa's exasperated voice cut across the room. "Must you be so dramatic?"

"What would you prefer, Odessa? That I lie to her? Those are her choices, whether she likes them or not."

"Why are you telling me all this?" I asked warily, gaze fixed on the leather binding that seemed to hold the shape of my fate.

Part of me didn't want to know the answer. Though they wouldn't have fed me if they were just going to kill me, right?

"These devices," Sorin held his smartphone aloft, "are shaping the world faster than even I anticipated. The shadows in this world are shrinking. There are fewer places left for people like us to vanish into."

"So, we've chosen you as our little test case. A step toward the inevitable reckoning. Congratulations!" Odessa chirped like I'd just won a prize.

"But... but I don't want to be a test subject. I want to go home," my voice cracked in disbelief.

They looked at me impassively, faces devoid of empathy. Nausea churned my gut.

"*I killed* that woman. Don't you think that makes for a bad test subject?"

"Her name was Valerie," said Odessa. "And I wouldn't say you killed her. It was more of an unfortunate accident."

I dropped my eyes, letting the name brand itself into my mind.

"Valerie had been a thorn in our side for some time," Sorin said dryly. "The reason I followed you last night wasn't out of idle curiosity. It was to keep your name out of the morning headlines under 'Missing' or 'Murdered.' She was sloppy. Every move she made risked exposing us."

"If it hadn't been you, it would have been something or someone else. These things are inevitable, Scarlet."

Odessa's words only deepened my unease. My breath came in shallow puffs, my fingers twitched at my sides. My legs felt as if they were cemented to the floor. The room tilted slightly. This was all too much at once.

"W-when does it end?"

More importantly, what would happen to me if they didn't get the result they were looking for? A panic attack was simmering inside of me, ready to surge up and drown every coherent thought I was struggling to form.

"Only until the Halloween Summit. There's a High Council we will present our results to," Odessa patted me on the shoulder.

I thought I might faint. That was over a month away.

"Are you going to make me stay here?" I asked tightly.

"Yes," Sorin said courtly.

I clutched the edge of the table as the room tilted again. No way in hell was I staying here until Halloween. I had a life: a museum to run, classes to teach at the gym, and, oh yeah, a husband to divorce.

"I can not," I gritted out between clenched teeth.

"You will," still preoccupied with his phone, Sorin cast me a casual glance. "Or you'll die. Either way, it'll be fascinating to watch."

I stared at the folder, the edges of the papers peeking out like yellowed teeth. My hands refused to move. The air seemed too thick for my lungs to pull in. My pulse thudded loudly in my ears, dulling the sounds of speech around me.

"This is insane," I breathed.

"It's a formality," Odessa's tone softened ever so slightly. "Still, it's one we must insist upon."

Sorin returned his full attention to me, "Take a moment to weigh your options. Just don't take too long. We hate loose ends."

4

REPEAT UNTIL TRUE

Inside the folder were three pages of densely packed text. The words seemed to blur, swimming in confusing patterns as I tried to focus. I found myself re-reading each section multiple times, struggling to make sense of the content while under duress.

"So, in summary..." I set the papers down. "This is an NDA prohibiting me from saying or communicating anything about you—"

"About our kind," Sorin clipped.

"About vampires," I repeated, the word felt absurdly foreign on my tongue. "And... that's it?"

"That's it," Odessa confirmed warmly as she placed a disproportionately heavy golden pen in my hand.

I hesitated, the pen unmoving in my fingers. Sorin exchanged a glance with Odessa. Odessa's lips twitched into an encouraging smile, her composure unbroken.

The signature line loomed before me like a bear trap ready to snap shut. My name would be the final trigger, only what would really change? They already had me by the throat. Without signing, the likelihood of me walking out of this building felt slim to none.

The pen dragged my name across the line in black, runny ink.

"Marvelous," Odessa clapped her hands together with a bright smile. "You must be exhausted. Can I show you to your room?"

Making a vague gesture of consent, I followed her out of the room then down several floors. Thanks to Sorin's blood, the descent was significantly easier than the ascent. On the eighth floor, we turned into a narrow hallway that was so long, the patches of darkness between the sparse wall sconces seemed impenetrable. I could make out dark wood floors and rich red wallpaper, which reflected shimmering gold designs in the pools of light.

Odessa's red-soled Louis Vuitton heels clicked as I trailed behind her, hoping it was too obvious I was hopping through the pockets of darkness. Halfway down the corridor, she stopped in front of a door labeled 823.

The room was claustrophobic. A double bed was jammed against a tall window, smothered by a heavy black curtain. Across the way, a bathroom barely large enough for a single body crammed in a toilet, sink, and shower. The neighboring closet looked too narrow to fit a hanger straight.

Inside the closet hung a varied collection of women's clothes. Mis-matching dresses, blouses, trousers, and shoes were strewn haphazardly around the tiny space. This did nothing to improve my opinion of the room.

Odessa's "tour" was as brisk as the room was small. She delivered a polished smile as she promised that the essentials would be delivered soon. I only nodded, knowing I wouldn't be needing toiletries. I wasn't about to rot up here like some medieval damsel locked in a twenty-first-century tower. So I kept my plans locked behind my teeth, arranging my mouth into a grateful smile to convince Odessa that I was precisely the docile prisoner she wanted me to be.

"Anything else you need before I leave, dear?" Odessa's voice dripped with saccharine sweetness.

"No, thank you. I'm just so tired," I yawned to emphasize that I was totally exhausted and utterly incapable of anything besides going to sleep. "I'll pass out as soon as you're out the door."

"Dawn approaches," She said wearily, tugging the heavy curtain aside to reveal a charcoal sky paling blue with the dawn. "Sleep well. I'll see you this evening."

I couldn't muster a friendly goodbye. Instead, I offered a stiff wave. The click of a lock sliding home sent a spasm of electrifying panic through me. I pressed my hands beneath my thighs until the rhythm of her heels faded down the hall.

Whipping out my phone, I saw the battery was less than 10%. I'd have to be careful about using it. Calling the police briefly crossed my mind, but then how would I explain the blood covering me? Nobody, no crime, right? Wrong.

I could already see the windowless interrogation room, two detectives hounding me until I cracked, babbling about fanged monsters. Best case, I'd end up in court. Worst case, I'd rot in the psych ward, choking down pills while some detached therapist asked how that made me feel.

Luke was probably still in the city. My hand fell limp at the thought of what he might be doing now. I pursed my lips against the tears prickling in my eyes. Lying back on the mattress, I let the terrible reality press in on me. A watery laugh escaped me.

Trust me to cry over my husband's infidelity rather than the fact that I had practically killed someone, was a prisoner in all but name, and had my reality turned on its head.

"Vampires are real," I said to the empty room, letting the words escape then settle over me.

I repeated the words several times until they sounded more like the truth rather than I actually did belong in a psych ward.

"Vampires are real... and my husband cheated on me."

Had been cheating on me for months if I trusted my gut instinct. The worst part was that I wanted to believe that less than believing that monsters existed. I couldn't think about that right now, or I might end up a helpless, weeping mess in the corner of that tiny shower.

"Vampires are real, and I drank vampire blood," I said quickly to distract myself from the panic attack lurking at the edge of my mind.

Standing, I crossed over to the door to give the handle a shake. Locked from the outside. I rapped on the solid wood door, fiddled with the frame. This would require significantly more force than the particle door to bust through. My breath hitched, increasing with the falling odds of my escape.

"Vampires are real, and I drank vampire blood," I muttered, feeling grossed out all over again.

Was that cannibalism? Did it count if I hadn't known what it was?

Forgetting the door, I shoved the curtains aside from the window. Even if it were the type of window that could be opened, it was not; I was eight floors above the city. There was no way I would survive the drop.

My heart skipped a beat, then kicked into overdrive. A cold sweat beaded at my brows.

"Vampires are real, and I drank vampire blood," I whispered as I staggered into the bathroom.

There wasn't even a window in here. Black spots danced in my vision. I had to clutch the edge of the sink to keep from doubling over. There was no way out.

"Vampires are real and—vampires are—God, vampires, vampires —" The word fractured in my mouth, breaking apart as fast as my breath.

My reflection stared back with steel-grey eyes stretched too wide, whites showing all around. There was something off about it. It was as if someone had airbrushed me into a reality. My fingers couldn't stop running over my face, feeling every change in texture.

Nothing was the same anymore. Not my face. Not the world. Not my marriage. Soon, even my home would no longer be mine. That lovely little bungalow with its screened-in porch, where we used to sit together. Where we had spent mornings with steaming mugs of coffee and evenings with chilled glasses of wine, our dog dozing contentedly at our feet. Luke's name was on the deed. Luke, who could afford the kind of lawyer I couldn't dream of.

"God damn it!" I snarled, fingers crushing the porcelain sink until a crack shot through the white glaze.

"Vampires are real. And I *drank* vampire blood."

Vampire blood made humans stronger, according to Odessa. I was already strong. I may have had a chance of breaking down that door after all.

I backed into the room, bracing to ram the door. Then froze. Odessa had only left an hour ago. Sorin might still be awake. Others might be here too. The thought curdled my gut.

So I waited. Waited until the sun pressed early-fall warmth through the curtains, casting the lilac comforter in bruised shades. My nerves boiled into a torrent I could no longer contain.

"Vampires are real and I drank vampire blood," I reminded myself, rolling my neck, stretching my arms.

When the door came down, it would be loud. I'd need speed and precision to sprint down the stairs without being stopped. Heart thundering, I dropped to the floor to rattle off push-ups.

I didn't need Luke to save me. I didn't need the police. All I needed was my own strength and the clarity to use it. At forty push-ups my arms began to burn, so I relented.

In an attempt at stealth, I shoved with both hands pressed against the door. The wood groaned, refusing to give. I stepped back, sizing it up like an opponent. I hadn't kicked in many doors before. Where was the weak point? Over the lock? Or should I just aim to smash a hole big enough to crawl through?

Thinking it would take fewer hits to bust the locks, I reeled back, placing another front kick right over the handle. The door shuddered, still not budging. My leg sang a bit less than it had before.

Encouraged, I twisted my hips, snapping another kick into it. Nothing.

Growling, I spun and delivered a backward kick. A harsh crack split the air. My heart leapt until I looked down. The door hadn't broken. My boot's heel had. It dangled at an ugly angle that brought to mind Valerie's neck after she'd fallen.

A frustrated cry tore from my throat. I launched into the door with everything I had. Elbows. Knees. Fists. Feet. I pummeled it like a heavy bag, each strike fueled by my fury and panic. At first, the surface barely dented. Then a thin fissure spread beside the handle, splintering outward into a jagged crater. Wood chips flew as I battered it down, until at last a ragged hole gaped wide enough for my hand to punch through.

Reaching through the splintered gap, my fingers scrabbled blindly along the other side until they brushed the cold metal of a deadbolt. A sob of relief escaped me as I twisted it, toppling forward as the door gave way. A jagged spike of wood raked across my forearm, I barely registered the sting.

I was free.

I bolted into the hall and flung myself into the stairwell without resistance. No one was here. They'd underestimated me. That was their mistake.

The broken heel dragged at my stride, yet my blood sang with unnatural speed. Even hobbled, I was flying. Down, down, down I plunged, skipping stairs, vaulting handrails, landing hard and pushing off again before my breath could catch.

When the restaurant level came into view, I knew I had done it. I was going to make it out. Grinning manically, my hand shot for the handle just as the door ripped inward. I collided chest-first into Malik.

5

RUNNING ON EMPTY

Malik's eyes bulged as we impacted, the shock sending us both staggering. Smudged gold eyeliner ringed his wide eyes, and the sour scent of liquor clung to him.

For a heartbeat, we only stared. I was gauging if I could dart past him. He was maybe wondering if I was a mirage conjured by his drinking. Our gazes slid in unison to the cracked door.

It didn't take longer than a few heartbeats to decide to try to make it past him while the opportunity still presented itself. I lunged.

He shrank away, covering his face with his hands and crouching into a squatted fetal position. It wasn't the reaction I had anticipated. I had expected him to grab me, to try dragging back up to that horrible purple room.

So, when he called out for me to wait, it made me pause long enough to look back over my shoulder at him.

"Take this," he whispered as he stripped off his jacket, offering it to me. "You're still covered in blood."

I glanced down at the sweater sticking to me in stiff, brown stains. With a shaky hand, I snatched the jacket. Sandalwood intertwined with vanilla enveloped me as I shoved my arms through.

"Thanks," I rasped.

"Don't mention it. Really. Don't." His slur thickened as he added, "And don't tell anyone." Then he slammed the door shut between us.

Not chancing another second in the shadow of that godforsaken building, I ran. The subway was easy enough to find, and I dove onto the first train. My eyes remained locked on my shoes until I scraped together the nerve to figure out which way led to the airport.

One overpriced ticket, two claustrophobic hours in a metal tube hurtling through the sky, then a taxi that bled my account dry later, I was finally standing in front of my own home. Broke, shaken, but alive.

The modest bungalow sat quietly in a secluded clearing, perched on a narrow riverfront lot where the current swirled gently into a broad, open bay beyond. Between the house and the water stretched a lush bed of marsh, its stillness broken only by the delicate serenade of night creatures stirring to life in the late afternoon.

Their harmonious chorus wove through the air, loosening the tight knot in my chest until a soft sob escaped me. No light shone from within the house. Devoid of its typical comforting glow, it felt abandoned to the fading day.

The porch groaned under my weight as I approached the silent house. My hand fumbled for my keys as the insect sounds receded into a distant hum. Holding my breath, I eased the door open. The cool, dim interior welcomed me with a stillness that swallowed me whole.

"Luke?" I called.

No answer. Our dog, Milo, was still at Tucker's. There was no friendly clack of paws scrambling to greet me. Swallowing hard, I flicked the light on, banishing the silence with the buzz of electricity.

A quick sweep of the living room, kitchen, small office, half bathroom, and back deck revealed no signs of Luke's return. Already feeling discouraged, I began my ascent to the second floor.

"Luke, are you here?"

Upstairs, there were two small bedrooms connected by a shared bathroom. The master bedroom was located further down the hall. The pictures of us lining the walls felt like fragments of a shattered kaleidoscope. Each one twisted the knife in my back a little deeper as I silently crept toward our bedroom. I paused at the door. It was as though all those memories were peeling off the walls to press tightly behind me, waiting to burst through as soon as I cracked it open.

Taking a deep, shaky breath, I let the door swing inward. Slowly, I surveyed our neat bedroom. The warm wood, wicker accents, and soft swaths of light greens and blues held their usual tranquil atmosphere. It was empty.

Anger slammed into me as I burst into our whitewashed bathroom, untouched since I left. I pulled my phone from my pocket, speed dialing Luke. It went straight to voicemail.

"Luke, please, I'm really worried. Where are you? Call me back." I ended the call, then sank to the floor, burying my face in my hands.

"Where are you?" My voice broke.

A chaotic hurricane of emotions tore through me. Anger at Luke for, well, everything. A quiet sense of relief that he wasn't home, sparing me from facing him right now. Worry gnawed at me, growing with the unanswered call. Even with the affair, this was unlike him. Above all, I was deeply, deeply hurt that he could just toss me aside like some one-night stand.

I was his wife. He was my husband. Did that mean nothing to him?

My chest ached. Each tremor in my body intensified as my labored breathing shallowed. Shoving my head between my knees, I squeezed my eyes shut so tightly it hurt. A feverish ringing began in my ears before the metallic taste of iron coated my mouth.

Sound faded away, leaving me alone with the vivid, tormenting images flashing in my mind. Over and over again, I was trapped in a strobe of memories that began with Valerie's laugh and ended with the sickening squelch as she fell onto that piece of metal.

When I came back to my senses, it was completely dark. My cheek had gone numb from lying on the cold tile floor. My legs carried me to the shower. I turned the faucet on full blast, twisting the knob to scalding and watching steam waft out.

Stepping into the blistering spray, I let it hammer against my skin. I wanted to burn away the icy chill that had taken root deep in my bones. Crouching, I wrapped my arms tightly around my legs, resting my forehead against my knees.

A terrible chasm yawned open inside my chest. I needed to run, to scream, to drive my fists into something until my knuckles split. I craved the sensation of pain. I wanted to hurt and to be hurt in return. The intensity of that desire unsettled me deeply.

After a while, my knees stiffened. I reluctantly turned off the water, wrapping myself in a fluffy white towel. Dizziness swamped me as I dried off. I scrubbed at my burning eyes. I'd napped on the plane, but I hadn't truly slept in over twenty-four hours.

The night no longer held safety. How could I sleep, knowing there were creatures out there? A dull throb built behind my temples in answer.

I needed a task, something simple and mindless. Milo. I needed to get my dog from my brother's house. Pulling on jeans with a T-shirt, I shoved my feet into tennis shoes and gulped water from the bathroom sink.

Hunger twisted in my stomach. I flung open the fridge, crammed two mozzarella sticks into my mouth, jamming my keys into my pockets.

The world blurred as I unlatched the door, stumbling toward the car. Once I had Milo, everything would be alright. I'd sleep at Tucker's. Tiffany would feed me. I'd curl up with Milo and—

A body slammed into my side, hurling me into the thick, manicured grass Luke was constantly obsessing over. The air punched out of my lungs as I tumbled with my attacker. Though they pinned my wrists, I managed to use the momentum to kick them over my head by wedging a knee between us.

Unfortunately, with no air in my chest, all I could do was collapse onto my hands and knees, wheezing like a cat choking on a hairball. Not exactly intimidating.

A pair of pristine white sneakers entered my field of vision. My lungs refused to inflate fast enough. I tried to push up, to look them in the eye and make it clear I wasn't about to go down without a fight.

Glowing red eyes glared back at me from beneath a wild mane of dark, wavy hair.

"Did you really think you could run?" Sorin demanded, his voice a gravelly rumble as he brushed dirt off his immaculate white linen blouse.

I should have been terrified. The pain singing through my ribs left room for only indignant anger. With what little air I'd managed to claw back, I growled a response.

"What?" he asked, crouching down beside me.

"I said," I panted, my voice still shredded, "that fucking hurt."

I swung a sloppy fist at him. Given that I was still on the ground, in addition to just having the ever-loving piss knocked out of me, he dodged easily.

"You're angry. Good. I'm so bored," he said, lips curling as he spread his arms wide. "Come on. One free hit."

Groaning, I forced myself to my feet. Everything hurt. My body felt like my muscles had been drained then left to shrivel in the sun. Lack of food, lack of sleep—it all crashed into me like a hammer. Regardless, how often did you get the chance to knock a smug bastard on his ass?

He stood there with that little smirk plastered on his too-perfect face, arms open like he wanted a hug. I wanted to knock it clean off. I *would* knock it off. For the papers. For the body slam. For every damn thing.

One step forward. Another. I squared myself in front of him, teeth bared, fist clenched at my side.

"Go on, I dare you," he taunted.

The world swam in and out of focus, colors leaching away. How long had it been since I'd eaten? A day? Two? Didn't matter. All that mattered was the sucker punch I was about to deliver to those full lips.

I drew my fist back, foot sliding into place, and swung.

The punch dragged like molasses, my body too heavy to cooperate. I never even made contact. Mid-swing, the floor tilted out from under me. The strength bled from my arm, darkness crashing over me before I could blink.

The last thing I registered was Sorin's smirk dropping into mild surprise as I crumpled against him.

6

NO GOOD OPTIONS

"I hadn't pegged you for such dramatics," Sorin's voice dripped with mock concern as he flicked through my copy of *Fall Homes and Garden* that had been sitting on the patio coffee table.

After I fainted, he carried me here and set me on the wicker sofa, leaving me to come to.

Now I sat cross-legged across from him, eyeing him over a steaming mug of chamomile tea paired with the sad excuse for a meal I'd zapped in the microwave.

"I'm not dramatic," I groused, taking a long sip.

He made a non-committal sound, flipping a page. I glanced at the cover, an image of a tiny skeleton leaving its carved pumpkin house. I longed for the peace of something as simple as pumpkin carving.

"How did you get here so fast?"

I sawed through a rubbery chicken breast, shoving a bite into my mouth.

"Vampire, remember?" He lowered the magazine as he arched a thick brow.

I leveled him with an unimpressed look.

"That doesn't actually answer my question."

"You drank my blood," he said slowly, as if explaining fractions to a dim child.

My frown deepened.

"I can tell where you are while it still courses through your veins," he added with a sigh, already bored with the conversation.

"Ew." I shuddered. "How long does that last?"

"Wouldn't you like to know."

"Yes, that's why I asked." I rolled my eyes.

"You have bigger fish to fry than the answer to that question."

I narrowed my eyes, gesturing for him to continue. My mouth was too full of sandpaper potatoes to respond.

"Like your husband," he said casually.

I nearly choked, forcing the bite down with a hard swallow.

"What do you know about Luke?"

He traced a finger along the magazine page, then peered over it. "That he hasn't been answering his phone. And that you haven't heard from him since your little tiff."

"If you know any—"

"Why would I be inclined to tell anything," he cut in smoothly, finally setting the magazine aside to grace me with his full attention, "to a woman who's already broken her contract?"

"What did you expect?" I scoffed. "That I sit up in some tower to rot like a good little princess?"

"Would that be so bad?"

"Yes! I have a life. A dog, two jobs, not to mention a *husband*." My voice cracked on the last word. "Now, spill it."

Luke had a way of diving headfirst into disasters. Last year, we nearly lost the house thanks to his gambling debt. It had taken most of our retirement savings to bail us out. My stomach twisted as I braced for whatever catastrophe Sorin was about to drop on me.

He sat as if weighing his options before he produced his phone and unlocked it. He moved *so* slowly, like he knew it would set me off. I screwed my mouth shut tightly to prevent myself from spewing vitriol at him.

"There, you wild animal," he relented.

I snatched the phone from his hand, the fire in my chest spilling over into my actions. The screen showed a grainy, night-vision image, but there was no mistaking Luke's figure. It was his thick, wavy dark hair, the sharp lines of his jaw. My heart leaped, then immediately sank.

"Swipe," Sorin ordered.

I sucked in a breath and obeyed. The following image hit me like a punch to the gut. Luke looked as if he hadn't slept in days. The poor quality of the photo couldn't disguise the exhaustion written all over him.

"Where is he?" I demanded, shoving the phone back toward him.

My mind was already spinning with frantic rescue plans.

Sorin only shrugged.

"Sorin," I warned him.

"Scarlet."

"You tell me where he is, damnit. Or I'll-"

"You'll what? Faint on me again?" Sorin snorted.

"Please, just tell me where he is."

Tears stung my eyes. I blinked rapidly, determined not to let them fall. Leaning in close, he caught the single droplet that escaped on the tip of a finger. For a breath, he held it to his face.

Gaze locked on the teardrop beading on his finger, he said lowly, "I'll tell you where he is, with some conditions."

"I'm listening," I said in a breathless voice to avoid the tremor.

"First, you come back to New York with me."

That was no great sacrifice. A return trip to New York to retrieve Luke was already in my near future anyway.

"Second, you agree to stay in Crimson and Clover until the end of the Summit."

This condition would be trickier to wiggle out of, but I could figure that out later. I opened my mouth to agree. He held up a hand to stop me.

"Lastly, you must help me to achieve my desired outcome for the experiment. These conditions are non-negotiable."

Confused, I curled my knees up to my chest.

"If this is supposed to be an experiment, why do you need my help?"

"It's better that you don't know, and in your best interest to comply. Trust me," he said, smearing the tear between his thumb and forefinger.

"Trust you?" I scoffed.

"Yes."

His face remained impassive. Still, the finger that had stolen my tear tapped restlessly against the arm of his chair.

"That would be difficult, seeing as I don't even know what the experiment is."

He shook his head, "I can't tell you."

"Then I can't trust you!"

Sorin pinched the bridge of his nose. "Do you want to find your husband, or not?"

The question rang in my ear. Did I? Was I going to risk my life and indebt myself to a monster, agreeing to do god knows what in the process, to save a man who had betrayed me?

Pressing my lips together, I tried to squelch the rising panic at the dull-eyed picture Sorin had presented me.

"Fine," I bit out.

"If you break your word again, I'll kill you."

Sorin's dark eyes bore into mine, sending the little hair on my neck to attention from their intensity. This wasn't a threat or a promise. It was a vow of violence. I nodded numbly, not trusting my voice.

"Excellent," he clapped his hands together, breaking the spell of terror he had cast. "Now, before I indulge you with the faithless cur's location, allow me to share why he cowers there. The reason, I assure you, is far more enlightening than the address."

Feeling sick, I clutched the mug of tea in front of me like it could shield me.

He continued, "You should know that Luke has developed, let's call it an appetite. One that makes him rather unpredictable."

"Appetite?" I echoed.

Waiting for me to catch up with him, he thumped the blue line of the vein on his wrist like he was checking a watch. The realization hit me like a thunderclap.

You mean he's addicted to blood?"

Sorin inclined his head.

"Precisely. I would strongly advise against seeking him out."

"Why?" My hands gripped the arm of the sofa. "I can get him help. Addiction isn't untreatable."

Sorin's expression filled with quiet disdain.

"Do you even understand what you're saying?" His voice dropped into a dangerous whisper. "Luke is no longer bound by the rules of your world. If you try to save him, you may not like what you find."

"Speak plainly," I said, sitting back in my seat as the blood drained from my face.

"When a vampire repeatedly gives a human their blood, it creates an intense addiction. Think of it as a unique strain of heroin. Only that vampire's blood will call to the human."

Sorin waited for me to understand.

"And Valerie is dead," I said for him, the pieces clicking together in my mind with devastating clarity. "He doesn't know, does he?"

"In some ways, I think he senses it. But no, he doesn't know for certain."

I buried my face in my hands. My husband was slipping further and further away. He was pulled into a world I couldn't reach, lost to something I didn't understand. I focused on my breathing. In, out. In, out.

"So, Valerie's blood is the only thing that can help him," I said hoarsely. "But she's gone."

"You mean dead," he chuckled darkly.

"Fine, dead. So what do I do? How do I bring him back?"

"There may be ways," he said, "but none of them are safe."

"I don't care. I'm not giving up on him," I met his gaze head-on.

"The simplest way is to have Valerie's blood overcome by a stronger drug. In other words," Sorin's ageless eyes never left mine, "a stronger vampire's blood."

"Another vampire?"

"Of course," Sorin continued, unbothered by my stunned tone, "he would still be addicted. The recovery process would be very long, excruciating even. But it could be done. If you really want to break his bond to Valerie's blood."

"How do I find a stronger vampire?"

Sorin's expression grew thoughtful, "Vampires gain strength in two ways. One, by consuming copious amounts of blood. This grants a temporary surge in power, but it fades quickly, and the thirst it leaves behind is insatiable."

I shuddered, imagining Luke trapped with a vampire barely keeping control of their hunger, constantly needing to feed.

"The second way," Sorin continued, "is through age. Vampires grow stronger over centuries. Valerie, as I recall, was about 150 years old when she met her second death. You'll need a vampire significantly older if you want any hope of overpowering her blood."

I clenched my fists. The idea of finding another vampire, not to mention one much older than Valerie, was daunting. But what was the alternative? I couldn't let Luke stay bound to a ghost.

"So you're telling me there's a chance?"

Sorin gave me the kind of look that said he knew exactly how deep this rabbit hole went and wasn't sure I was ready for it.

"Ancient vampires," he said, "don't come out of hiding easily. They are powerful, secretive, and cautious. To find one willing to help will be no easy task."

I nodded, "But it's possible."

"It's possible," he admitted. "There is still another option."

"What is it?" I asked, hope blooming in my withered chest despite my better judgment.

"You could find him and restrain him somewhere. Force him to quit cold turkey. But the drawbacks can be devastating. It's rare for a human to survive such an ordeal. Especially with a dependency as strong as Luke's."

Frustration surged through me like a tidal wave. Every option I had seemed like a death sentence for Luke. The image of him from Sorin's phone resurfaced in my mind. He was already experiencing the effects of withdrawal. From the look on his face, it wasn't going well.

"There aren't any facilities for something like this?" I could feel Sorin watching me. "No rehab centers, no doctors who could handle this kind of come down?"

"There aren't. It would be a battle of will, mostly. However, as I mentioned, the human body rarely survives a break from its dependency on vampire blood. It alters you fundamentally. Without it..." He trailed off, the silence heavy with meaning.

I closed my eyes, rubbing my temples as the decision pressed down on me. Restraining him felt like a last, desperate resort, one that could cost him his life. Even so, going after a stronger vampire to replace Valerie's blood came with its own risks.

"Even if I found a place to keep him," I said, trying to think it through logically, "he's already so far gone. What if he..."

My voice broke. I didn't want to finish the thought. What if he didn't survive? What if I lost him completely?

"There are no easy answers, unfortunately," Sorin said as he stood up, pacing with his hands clasped behind his back. "Ultimately, it comes down to how far you are willing to go. How much risk can you bear to save him?"

My tongue felt like a brick. The enormity of the decision steadily increased with each passing second. I had no good options, only bad ones.

"I need to find him," I said roughly. "I need to see him before I decide anything."

Sorin nodded, "Once you find him, you must be prepared to act quickly. Whether you choose to restrain him or seek another vampire, the clock is ticking."

"Then what are we waiting for?" I asked, standing to rush upstairs and pack.

"It's already too late to start driving, thanks to your fainting," he gave me an appraising look.

"But it's only 9 p.m.," I argued.

"To make it before dawn, we'd have to leave right at sundown."

Sorin gazed out at the moon shimmering over the bay, releasing a slow breath.

"Pack your bags," he said gruffly. "I'll be here tomorrow, just after sundown, to pick you up. Be ready."

7

HUMAN CONDITIONS

The morning brought an endless ringtone that dragged me back into the purgatory of consciousness. My hand fumbled across the night-stand until I found the phone and lifted it to my face.

I had a voicemail from Victor, my boss at the museum, asking if I was coming in today. I groaned and pressed redial.

"Hello?" Victor's age-worn voice crackled through the speaker.

"Hey, Vic. It's me."

I pressed a hand to my already aching forehead. How long was this blood hangover supposed to last again? My eyes felt as if they were going to melt out of their sockets.

"Scarlet, where are you?" He sounded concerned. "Are you sick? You sound terrible!"

"I'm…" I hesitated. "I'm not fine. Luke and I had a fight."

Victor was like a second father to me. Actually, he was literally my godfather. My parents had met him in college and stayed connected through the years.

"Ah," he replied carefully. "I take it the trip to New York didn't go well?"

My heart stuttered.

"How do you know I went to New York?"

"Scarlet, dear," he sighed patiently. "You left the printed receipt for the airline on your desk."

"Oh."

The paranoia snapping at my stress-fogged brain eased.

"No, it didn't go well. We had a massive fight, and I haven't heard from him since. It's been almost three days now."

"That's terrible," he said in that soothing voice that had comforted me for so many years.

My lip trembled.

"I'm so worried. Have you heard anything? Has he reached out to you?"

"No, I'm afraid not. The last time I spoke to Luke was when we had dinner together last month."

I exhaled, disappointment reclaiming the hollow space in my chest.

"Take the day off," he said, "I'll call you if he reaches out."

"Thanks, Vic. See you tomorrow."

I couldn't tell him I wouldn't be at work anytime soon. He would ask too many questions that I couldn't answer. Or worse, call my parents. If they got involved, it would add another layer of complication that I wasn't capable of handling.

"See you tomorrow."

I looked around our bedroom. The morning light filtered in through the plantation shutters, casting geometric patterns on the walls.

"I feel like shit," I muttered to myself, crankily throwing off the blankets and striding to the closet to dress.

In Forty-five minutes, I was pulling up to Tucker's cheerful little townhouse, more centrally located in Savannah than our home. Tiffany, Tucker's wife, was already waiting by the front door.

Piper, their four-year-old daughter, came bounding out of the house the moment she saw my dark blue Toyota Camry. Her light-blond hair and tutu streamed behind her as she ran with a small wooden sword clutched in her hand. I slammed on the brakes, quickly shifted into park, and jumped out just in time to scoop her up into my arms.

"Princess Piper!" I squeezed her tight. "How fare thee?"

Her reply was cut short by a slobbering bundle of black fur tackled us to the ground.

"Milo!" Piper and I cried out as the massive lab mix showered us with wet dog kisses.

"Okay! Okay, you monster!" I buried my face in his fluffy coat. "I missed you, too, buddy."

"Aunt Scarlet," Piper scrambled up, breathless and bright-eyed. She grabbed my hand, pulling with surprising strength. "Come see my new toys!"

"Piper," Tiffany called in a tired voice, "manners."

Piper stamped her feet and threw her head back in theatrical exasperation.

"Aunt Scarlet, *please* let me show you my new toys."

I let out a laugh.

"She's way too much like her dad."

I let Piper drag me through the doorway, casting a helpless look back at Tiffany, who wore a rueful smile.

"Don't I know it. Tuckers at work," she sighed, following us inside and scraping her blonde hair into a messy bun. "Coffee?"

"Please," I nearly begged.

Tucker was a construction manager. It was hard work, but it allowed Tiffany to stay at home to raise Piper.

After enduring a parade of toy swords and dolls, Tiffany finally sent Piper off to her playroom. We settled onto their large leather sofa with steaming mugs of coffee.

"Do you want to talk about it?" Tiffany asked.

I had assumed Tucker would have already filled her in. Our unspoken rule was that our spouses were privy to whatever we shared with each other.

"We don't have to talk. We can just have coffee," she offered.

I stared ahead, my fingers tangling absently in Milo's fur.

"I found Luke with another woman," I said quietly. "Threw some wine on them."

Tiffany nodded, her silence a small mercy.

"We fought. I don't remember exactly what we said. I left and haven't heard from him since. That's about it."

Or at least as much as I was willing to tell her at the moment.

"Hmmm," she hummed.

We sat there in the quiet that followed, the hum of the house the only sound. I suspected Tiffany knew there was more to the story, but this was all I was willing to divulge—and probably more than I should have for all of our safety.

"Who was she?"

"Some redhead," I gritted out. "A co-worker."

"I see." Tiffany took another sip of her coffee, her face giving nothing away. "Do you want me to try calling him?"

"Sure," I hung my head. "But I don't think he'll answer."

In fact, I knew he wouldn't. I let her dial Luke on speaker, the call going straight to voicemail.

"Scarlet?"

Tiffany bit her thumbnail, a subtle sign of her anxiety.

"What are you thinking?" I asked.

"You might need to call the police."

My heart skipped a beat. That was out of the question. A sheen of sweat gathered at my temple. I was pretty sure my new vampire acquaintances wouldn't be thrilled about the police getting involved. Sorin's death threats had been compelling last night.

"The last place you saw him was the restaurant?" She pressed. "Are you sure?"

"You're right." My words were a little abrupt. "If he doesn't answer his phone by this afternoon, I'll make a report."

We spent the rest of the morning playing out different scenarios of Luke's return. It was completely draining to pretend that my life was as simple as trying to find a place to live after discovering his infidelity.

"Will you stay if he asks?" Tiffany finally questioned when the afternoon sun was reaching its height, slanting through the kitchen windows.

I chose to focus on the sandwiches I was making for the three of us, not the headache. My throat ached from talking so much.

"I don't know yet," I admitted, the uncertainty settling into the pit of my stomach.

Probably not once he found out I had murdered his mistress.

She slipped an arm around my shoulders, "You don't have to decide that now."

I leaned my head against her slender shoulder. "I'm so glad you're my sister."

She planted a soft kiss on my forehead, "Me too."

I pulled away, wondering if she'd still feel the same if she knew just how much danger I had just dragged us all into.

Sorin returned at precisely 7 p.m. in a large white truck with deeply tinted windows.

"You have a dog," he stated flatly.

Milo growled at him, his hackles rising. The skin on my hand twinged slightly as I gripped Milo's harness tightly. Milo came up to my hip and could easily pull free any time he wanted.

"Correction, you have a hellhound," Sorin took a healthy step back.

"That a problem?" I asked, voice tight with the effort of keeping Milo at bay.

"Not for me," Sorin huffed. "Odessa, though. She might have reservations."

Despite his words, Sorin flipped up the back seats. Moving faster than he had any right to, he scooped up Milo's dog bed and tossed it into the vacant space. My suitcase and duffel bag followed.

"There's no time to argue now," Sorin muttered as he loaded himself into the driver's seat. "Get in."

"What's the rush?" I asked, hoisting Milo up into the cab.

Sorin's eyes flashed. "Sunlight. Vampire. Do I need to draw you a picture?"

Milo bared his teeth in a silent snarl. Good boy.

"We won't quite make it before sunrise," he said, slamming the door and revving the engine to life. "Even without stopping."

I frowned.

"What if I have to pee?"

"Hold it."

Rolling my eyes, I checked on Milo, then slammed my seatbelt into place.

"So, what's the plan?"

I wondered if he would catch fire if the sun touched his pale skin. A girl could dream.

"There's a safe house," he replied, his long fingers drumming on the wheel. "We'll stop just outside the city. It's close enough to get us where we need to be. But it's not ideal."

"Not ideal how?" I asked suspiciously.

"It's not meant for civilized company," he answered as he punched the accelerator, "but it'll have to do."

An uneasy silence settled between us as the truck roared down the highway, the city lights shrinking in the rearview mirror. I couldn't shake the feeling that we weren't just racing against the sun. How long could Luke hold out in his condition?

"Why would Odessa have a problem with Milo?"

The question was meant to distract me from thoughts of Luke on the street. I didn't really give a damn if anyone had a problem with Milo. By God's grace or the devil's hand, he was coming with me.

Sorin tossed up his shoulders.

"Who is she anyway? She said she was your partner, but that's too vague. Work partner? Partner in crime? Netflix and chill partner?" I batted my lashes at him the same way I would if I were trying to drive Tucker up the wall.

"Work partner," Sorin growled.

"What sort of work?"

He cut me a withering glance.

"Speaking isn't required for this drive."

I slumped in my seat, dejection weighing heavier than the seatbelt. The truck's roar filled my ears in a steady growl against the silence. I fumbled with the seat warmers. It was too cold for mid-September. Luke was farther north, where the chill bit even deeper. He might be shivering in the dark.

"Please... talk to me," I requested softly.

His eyes flicked from the road.

"Please," I continued, my voice trembling. "I'm scared. I'm stressed. I need a little normal conversation or something. I feel like I'm going insane here."

"Empathy," Sorin paused, "is also a uniquely human condition."

I looked down at my hands, my vision blurry. Milo whined from the back. The dread that I had been battling back surged up, flooding my chest and making it hard to breathe. I wasn't sure how much longer I could keep it together. Luke, New York, the vampires, this entire situation. It all felt like a heavy chain around my neck, dragging me into unknown waters.

"I'm not asking for empathy," I said deftly. "I just—I just want someone to talk to. Someone who won't make me feel like I'm losing my mind."

Sorin shifted in his seat.

"You're not losing your mind," he said, his voice devoid of warmth and any attempt to comfort. "You're simply struggling to adjust to the reality you've chosen to enter."

"Choose?" I let out a bitter laugh. "Did I choose this? You think I *wanted* this?"

"You chose him," Sorin replied, his voice matter-of-fact. "You chose to follow him into this world. And now you must live with the consequences."

My heart clenched.

"What do you mean by that? That because I love Luke, I'm supposed to deal with all of this?"

He nodded, seemingly unimpressed by my outburst.

"That's precisely what I'm saying. If you wish to save him, then you must accept that this world will never again align with your human sensibilities. The sooner you grasp that, the less difficult this will be."

I stared at him, disquiet clogging my throat. He made it sound as if navigating a life entwined with monsters was as simple as choosing what to wear in the morning.

"You're in this world, too. Do you have no loyalties? No connections? No one you'd risk everything for?"

For a brief second, he opened his mouth as if to respond, then reconsidered.

"Loyalties fade," he nearly whispered, almost as though he was speaking to himself. "Connections break. And the longer you live, the more you realize that nothing is permanent, not even love."

The words stung.

"Well, I'm not a vampire," I glared at him. "I believe in love. And loyalty. And I'm not giving up on Luke."

"Love won't be enough to save him. And it won't be enough to save you, either."

The surety in his words hit hard, and something small within me shriveled up. A fragile spark of hope, extinguished by the dark storm closing in. I glanced back at Milo, his warm brown eyes gazing lovingly back, and silently promised myself that no matter how far I had to dive into this world, I wouldn't let Sorin's words become my truth.

"If vampires are real," I changed the subject, "is there more?"

"More?" he echoed, though I could tell by the gleam in his eyes that he understood exactly what I meant.

"You know," I said, trying not to sound like a child, "like other monsters."

"Monsters?" Sorin chuckled, a deep, mocking sound.

"You know what I'm trying to say," I grumbled, my face flushing. "Are there other things? Like you?"

He stroked his chin, an arrogant quirk playing on his lips.

"I don't think there's another thing like *me* on this planet."

Refusing to acknowledge him, I peppered him with another question that had been weighing on my mind.

"How old are you?"

"That's quite rude," he flashed a toothy grin that didn't reach his eyes.

I didn't return it, holding his gaze in silence, waiting for an answer I knew would astound me.

He sighed, his shoulders settling as if resigned to the question.

"I don't know, exactly."

"You don't know how old you are?" I asked disbelievingly.

"When I was human, it was a different time."

"Obviously," I huffed.

"Truly, it was." His eyes searched the road ahead. "Back then, much of the known world, or at least, the world known to my people, was ruled by the Romani. What you'd call the Romans today. It was the height of their power, though I didn't know it at the time. I couldn't have even told you the Emperor's name. My people lived in a remote country. We were poor, uneducated, and humble."

"The height of the Roman Empire..." My voice faltered, and I stole a sideways glance at the creature beside me. "That would make you around two thousand years old."

"You know your history," he nodded approvingly. "Good."

"I work at a museum," I muttered, still feeling dumbstruck. "You've lived all this time?"

"I wouldn't call it living." A few strands of hair fell forward, shadowing his expression. "Do you envy me for my immortality?"

"Yes," I admitted, then after a heartbeat, "and no."

His eyebrows shot up.

"No?"

"I envy you for all the history you've witnessed," I allowed the words to take shape in my bewildered mind before speaking. "But I don't envy you having to watch everything live and die around you. I wouldn't want that."

All amusement faded from his eyes. I saw a glimmer of the endless years he carried, the faces and lives that might have passed him like whispers in the wind. And then it was gone.

"How are you feeling now?"

Surprised at the kindness in his question, I looked out of my own window.

"I think you already know the answer to that."

The answer was that I felt alone. I couldn't shake the terrible suspicion that no one was coming to save me. That every step forward would be mine alone to bear.

And the road ahead was only getting darker.

8

NOT FORSAKEN

Sometime around 1 a.m., as the darkened landscape rolled by, a gentle lull settled over the truck. I felt my eyelids growing heavy. Despite my best efforts to stay awake, my head began to nod, my thoughts blurring into the quiet rhythm of the road and Milo's steady breathing in the back.

"Sleep, Scarlet," Sorin murmured. "I'll wake you when we arrive."

As if I had been waiting for permission, my head drifted against the cool glass.

A lurch of the truck shook me awake. I groaned, my neck stiff and aching. My thoughts lagged, struggling to piece together where I was.

"We're here," Sorin said, his door clicking open.

I heard the crunch of gravel as he came around to my side. The door flew open. Sorin was suddenly there, reaching in to unbuckle me. I blinked up at him, disoriented.

"What...what are you doing?" I slurred, trying to steady myself as I swayed on uneven feet and pushed him off.

His hand slipped supportively under my elbow.

He leaned in close, his voice a whisper. "We need to get inside. Quickly."

"Why?" I asked, turning to reach back for Milo.

"I'll explain once we're inside," Sorin said, urging me forward. "I'll come back for Milo."

His hand tightened around my arm, preventing me from stopping.

"You must cooperate for now." His voice, though quiet, seemed to reverberate through me, commanding in a way that left no room for argument.

My feet began to move forward, almost against my will. Still, I couldn't help glancing back at the truck. Milo was watching us, his head pressed against the window, a plaintive whine muffled by the glass.

Any argument I had faded on my lips, vanishing in a cold puff of breath that hung briefly in the brisk fall air. Before us loomed a massive Victorian pale pink house. It was silhouetted against the brightening skyline. Lights flickered in a few of the windows, casting a red-tinted glow that seemed both welcoming and foreboding.

Sorin's hand pressed gently on my back, urging me forward. We ascended the steps as quickly as my cramped legs could manage, stopping at eye level with a large iron gargoyle. Its toothy jaws were clenched around a ribbed metal knocker, the metal worn smooth from countless hands.

Sorin reached forward and rapped three times. After a brief silence, the doors creaked open. An unbelievably thin young woman stood there. She couldn't have been more than 20. Her short-cropped silver hair framed a pair of crimson albino eyes.

"Two and a dog," Sorin said, irritation lining his voice as he cast a glance over his shoulder.

In her hands rested a golden platter. Upon it lay a wickedly sharpened knife alongside a goblet, each catching the light with an ominous glint.

"Payment before admittance, Master Draconis." Her voice was

the scratchy whisper of someone who'd screamed themselves hoarse one too many times.

Looking closer, I marked dark circles bruising underneath her eyes.

Sorin released his hand from my back, swiftly taking up the knife and goblet. He drew the blade across his wrist without hesitation. It was a precise motion that brought forth a dark, thick stream of blood that poured into the goblet in a steady flow. I gasped, recoiling from the pulses of blood.

When the goblet was half-full, Sorin brought his wrist to his mouth. His lips pressed over the wound as his tongue traced it. The flesh knit together in seconds, leaving only a faint pink line that faded almost immediately.

The woman tilted forward, her gaze fixed intently on the place where his lips had met the wound. Her own mouth twitched with unmet satisfaction. Taking the goblet in her thin, pale hands and stepping aside, she allowed us entry.

Sorin's hand returned to my elbow, guiding me forward with a grip that I didn't entirely approve of. I braced myself, expecting the queasy churn of my stomach at the sight and scent of blood. As my gaze drifted to the goblet, a different scent met me entirely. It smelled like the coming snow on a frigid winter morning and vaguely of frankincense. The strange fragrance made my tongue tingle. I swallowed thickly as my mouth watered unexpectedly.

Sensing the weight of the woman's gaze, I lifted my eyes to meet hers. She watched me intently, baring her teeth in a sneering smile. They were rounded, without a hint of the fangs I expected. Another human?

"Come, Scarlet," Sorin called as he tugged me toward the looming staircase. "The usual room, I take it, Delilah?"

"Second to the right."

She scuttled away, disappearing into a doorway swallowed by shadows.

I parted my lips to speak, but Sorin shook his head, pressing a finger to his lips as he guided me up the stairs. We moved through the dim hallway to the second door on the right. Inside was a large, windowless room.

A king-sized bed dominated the space. A gas-lit fireplace beside it cast restless shadows over a small, plain dresser.

"Scarlet," he said, the tone a command more than a plea as he steered me into a chair. "This house is not meant for humans. The few who reside here do not often leave."

His eyes bored into mine, his voice edged with a warning that made my skin prickle.

"I'll go and fetch Milo, but you must swear to me, do not leave this room."

I drew a sharp breath, "I'm not a child."

He ran a hand through his unruly hair in exasperation.

"You don't understand the depth of danger you're in without me here. Just one minute, that's all. I'll hurry." His gaze flickered toward the door. "The sun is coming."

Resignation washed over me as I sank back into the chair, watching as he slipped from the room. A nervous quiver tugged at my lips as I recalled the tantalizing scent of Sorin's blood. It had sent a strange thrill through me. That wasn't normal. I knew that much.

I couldn't be addicted to his blood after one hit, right? But a nagging doubt whispered that my reaction was far from innocent curiosity.

I thought of Tucker, who'd once told me he'd stand out in a freezing downpour for a cigarette even after quitting several years ago. An addictive pull, he'd called it. I imagined that what I was feeling now must be similar—the tingle on my tongue, the haunting allure of that scent that clung to the back of my throat. Whatever it was, some part of me was already reaching for more.

The door clicked open, swinging wide, and I shot to my feet. Relief washed over me as Milo trotted in, tail wagging happily as he bounded toward me.

"It's just us," Sorin assured me, setting down a dog mat and one of my bags near the door.

A black backpack clung to his shoulder. He unslung it, already rummaging through its contents.

"Um," I began hesitantly, glancing around. "What is that?"

Sorin shot me a dry look, "My bag."

"Well, yeah," I replied, "but why are you opening it in here?"

"Because I'm tired." He paused to fix me with a steely look. "Even vampires need sleep. You know, the whole sun issue."

"But—" I stammered, "there's only one bed in here."

"You noticed," he said dryly, pulling a toothbrush kit and, of all things, a neatly folded set of black pajamas from the bag.

Sorin, an ancient vampire, was holding a travel-sized toothbrush and pajamas. I struggled to wrap my mind around the sight.

"We can't share a bed!" I protested, scandalized. "I'm married!"

I twisted the golden band around my ring finger self-consciously.

"That didn't seem to stop your husband," he said, turning toward the bathroom with a dismissive shrug.

The words sent a slashing dagger of hurt straight to the heart.

"I am not," I said firmly, emphasizing each word, "sleeping in a bed with you."

"The floor's open. I'm sure Milo wouldn't mind sharing," Sorin said through a mouthful of toothpaste. "You could pay for another room. Although I'd guess your blood might buy you an hour or two in the drawing room at best."

He shot me a look over his shoulder, his mouth twitching ever so slightly. He was enjoying this far too much. I pressed my lips into a tight line, refusing to rise to his bait. It only made Sorin chuckle as he began unbuttoning his shirt.

"What are you doing?" I demanded, quickly covering my eyes and stumbling out of the bathroom.

"Perhaps I should get you a pair of glasses?" he said, his glee at my discomfort growing by the second.

Ignoring him, I stomped over to the bed, grabbing the edge of the blankets to storm off to the bathtub.

"I'll sleep in the tu—"

But before I could finish, I heard the unmistakable sound of water rushing into the tub.

"Bastard," I let the blankets slip from my hands and fall back onto the mattress.

"What's the matter?"

His voice was suddenly a whisper that floated directly into my ear. I let out a strangled cry, stumbling backward and landing on the mussed bed in a heap. He loomed over me, a wolfish grin spread across his perfect skin.

"Frightened to sleep beside a monster?"

"No," I lifted my chin.

"I'm not afraid of monsters," I added, though my voice trembled ever so slightly.

Sorin's smile only widened. I swore his canines protruded a millimeter.

"Fine," I snatched my bag and stomped off to the bathroom, tossing one last glare over my shoulder for good measure.

Once inside, I changed into my trusty gym sweats. "Savannah Strikehouse" was printed down the sides and across the chest, a comforting reminder of home. I brushed my teeth with a furious intensity, taking steady breaths to convince myself I was totally fine. *I could do this.* I hadn't shared a bed with anyone other than Luke in over six years, but I'd survived worse situations. Back in college, I'd fallen asleep beside total strangers more times than I cared to remember. Usually, there was a considerable amount of alcohol involved.

Yeah, I could definitely do this.

Staring at my reflection, I gave myself one last pep talk. Then I squared my shoulders and stepped out of the bathroom, bracing myself for whatever smug remark Sorin had waiting.

"Nice sweats."

"Ugh!" I tossed my bag onto the chair.

Milo was already nestled comfortably on the bed beside Sorin, his dog mat abandoned on the floor.

"Traitor," I muttered.

Milo's ears flattened guiltily against his skull.

"Don't blame him," Sorin ran a pale hand over Milo's scruffy back. "We've bonded."

I narrowed my eyes, crossing my arms.

"Clearly."

Standing at the foot of the bed, I nervously toyed with the edge of the duvet, my fingers brushing over the fabric.

"I haven't slept in a bed with another person besides Luke in a long time," I admitted, my throat clenching around the words.

"Seeing as it'll be day soon, I doubt you'll be asleep for long."

With a heavy sigh, I slipped under the sheets, sinking into the cool, welcoming softness. The bed was comfortable, at least, and despite my nerves, fatigue weighed on me. It was a bone-deep exhaustion that had set in after days of endless stress and heartache. Milo scooted closer, curling into the crook of my arm. I closed my eyes, pressing my face into his fur, breathing in his earthy scent.

"What is this place?" I asked, my voice muffled, still refusing to look at Sorin.

Not looking made it all feel less real.

"It's a safe house for my kind."

I heard him settle back against the pillows. I held my breath, caught between curiosity and dread.

"But humans aren't usually welcomed as guests. They're considered more like..." He trailed off, searching for the right word.

"Livestock?" I offered, daring a begrudging glance upward.

Amusement danced in his indigo eyes as he leaned back against a pile of plush, fluffed pillows. His dark hair fanned out like inky tendrils around him.

"Not the words I would have chosen," there was a hint of mischief in his tone.

"But true?"

"True enough," he admitted wryly.

I pulled Milo a little tighter against me. What would Luke think if he saw me in bed with another man? Would he feel the way I had when I watched him with Valerie?

"So," I began, trying to push away the dark thoughts, "when the sun comes up, do you die?"

Sorin threw his head back, laughing freely. His laugh was rich and unexpectedly warm.

"No," he said, still chuckling. "Though I appreciate the dramatics. Sunlight does weaken us significantly, but I assure you, we sleep and dream like you do."

His laughter faded, leaving a soft smile that tugged at the corners of his mouth.

"We were once human," he explained. "And try as we might, we can't leave our humanity completely behind."

"Oh," I murmured, rolling onto my side to face him.

"Consider this a warning, Scarlet. Vampires are vulnerable in their sleep. But I wouldn't recommend trying anything unwise."

"I wasn't planning on it," I was stung by the lack of trust. "I'm feeling pretty vulnerable myself, you know."

My lack of a bra left me feeling extremely exposed, even under the thick covers. There was just no way in hell I was ever going to sleep with the straps digging into me.

"Had I not seen you in action, my wild animal, I might be inclined to believe those claims of innocence."

"I'm not your anything."

Valerie's face flashed across my mind's eye. My hand rubbed absently at my chest as if I could physically soothe the grief and guilt festering there. Lost in thought, I finally dragged my gaze back to Sorin, uncertain of what I hoped to find in his expression.

"Do you pray before you sleep?" He asked, staring blankly at the ceiling.

"Sometimes," I voiced softly. "Are you religious?"

"With all I've seen, these years and eons I have witnessed," he gave a mirthless chuckle, "Faith changes for someone like me. It no longer revolves around the same things."

"What is it about then?" I was intrigued, feeling an inexplicable tug deep inside, as if an invisible rope were drawing me closer to him. As I pulled on that invisible thread, something shifted. It yanked me forward into a cavernous void. The air felt frigid, endless, like a vast, crushing loneliness wrapped in the dust of forgotten time.

His eyes locked onto mine, and I could see it, feel an abyss within him.

In my mind, his voice echoed, *'It's about survival. About enduring the silence of centuries and millennia, standing alone like a statue with breath. It is about being forsaken and forsaking. Forgiveness and faith become irrelevant. After so much time, you no longer ask for such things.'*

Icy tears slid down my cheek, as cold as the void I saw in his eyes. A shiver coursed through me.

"What the hell was that?" I choked out, already half-rising from the bed.

His hand shot out, catching my shoulder. His thumb traced slow, soothing circles, at odds with the panic surging through me.

"It's a bond," He intoned quietly. "Because of the blood. It's how I knew where you were. I let my guard down. I apologize."

The apology tethered me in place. Or maybe it was the warmth radiating from his touch, seeping deeper than it should have.

"I don't like it when you do that," he murmured, eyes skimming over the wetness on my cheeks.

"Cry?"

He nodded, closing his eyes. When he turned away, I caught his wrist. Freezing, he looked back at me with deadened eyes.

"You are not forsaken," I said, my voice thick with an emotion I couldn't quite name.

Blinking, he carefully withdrew his wrist and returned his gaze to the ceiling. When I finally worked up enough nerve to look at him again, his face was softened by the calm stillness of sleep.

It struck me how, at this moment, he looked almost human. A shadow of the person he might have been once. I tried to imagine his face, framed by laugh lines, tanned by the sun. Mortal imperfections that spoke of a well-lived life.

I drew a deep breath, and Milo nestled close beside me. A sense of calm slowly lulled my stiff body into a state of relaxation.

As sleep claimed me, I whispered a prayer that I wasn't making a mistake by lying beside a two-thousand-year-old vampire.

9

THE CARDS WE'RE DEALT

I inhaled on a deep stretch, enjoying the warmth of Milo's weight across my stomach. My fingers trailed lazily down the arm resting over me, only for my eyes to snap open as I registered the lack of fur.

Sorin's long arm was draped across me, muscle cording his arm from shoulder to wrist. His unnaturally slow breaths tickled my cheek. I froze. Had I rolled into him, or had he moved toward me?

And where was Milo? That traitor. No treats for him.

Worse than my would-be barrier's abandonment was the heat blooming low in my belly that I was furiously trying to ignore. Mortification washed over me as my nipples tightened beneath the soft fabric of my sweatshirt.

I scrambled to rationalize it, blaming the goosebumps racing across my skin on Luke's absence these past few months. It was just biology. A perfectly normal response to a prolonged lack of intimacy. Nothing more.

I began lifting Sorin's arm, trying to free myself without waking him.

"Mmm," he stirred, and I held my breath.

But he rolled away with a deep, rumbling sigh. Relief hit me when I realized I hadn't been the one to close the gap. Milo lay curled on his pad, completely oblivious to the situation he had left me to deal with. I slipped out from under the covers and crept to the bathroom.

It was 10 a.m. and I had no text messages. Well, nothing from Luke anyway.

The soaking tub caught my eye. Pristine porcelain called to me like a siren. I'd begged Luke to remodel our bathroom with something like this. Like everything else lately, it had been pushed aside.

Speaking of neglected responsibilities, I pulled open the text with the gym manager. I let him know that I would be needing a sabbatical. He didn't reply right away, but I'd been at that gym for as long as I had been with Luke. If I needed the time off, I would have it.

I turned the faucet, added a splash of honey-scented bubble bath, and watched the foam rise.

A delicious, all-consuming heat licked at my skin as I sank in. It was a soothing burn that eased away the tightness in my muscles and lulled my mind into quiet stillness.

I poured a few drops of the bath oil into my palms. My hands glided over my neck, arms, and shoulders, then down my legs, leaving a soft, dewy glow that seemed to catch the faint light filtering through the stained glass lighting above the mirror. As the last of the oil absorbed, I lay back in the water, feeling a little more like myself.

When I finally drained the tub, the air felt colder than before. I combed through my damp hair and studied my reflection. The bags under my eyes were just visible now, and crow's feet were creeping into the corners of my eyes. I looked human.

From outside, I heard the light jingle of Milo's collar, followed by a slight snuffling at the bathroom door. Smiling, I unlocked it and swung it open. Milo greeted me with a wide, toothy smile and a slight whine that indicated either he was hungry or needed to go outside.

"Alright, let's see what you need, buddy," I said, kneeling down to rub his head.

Sorin was still as stone, half-illuminated by the soft glow from the bathroom. Taking a few tentative steps closer, I stopped, struck by his disquieting stillness. He seemed more still than any living human could be. There was no longer any gentle rise and fall of his chest. No twitch of muscle.

Did vampires even need to breathe?

His skin had turned an eerie ash color. Even his lips had faded pale. The more I looked, the more he seemed like something from another world, trapped in the liminal space between life and death. He was like a dark prince trapped by an inescapable slumber.

Milo whined again, drawing me back. I needed to feed him, but his food was outside.

"Damn," I whispered, looking between Milo, the door, and Sorin's unmoving body on the bed.

I shifted on my feet, debating my next move.

"Sorin," I whispered, testing the waters. When he didn't stir, I cleared my throat and tried again, a little louder. "Sorin?"

No response. Nothing but the firelight moving lazily across his unnervingly perfect face. He wasn't handsome. That wasn't the word. Dangerous was more accurate. His features held a beauty meant to lure prey in. I shook myself and turned away, suddenly aware of how intensely I was staring at him.

Unable to locate a room key, I stuffed a sock into the key latch and clipped Milo's leash to his collar.

"Let's make it quick, buddy," I gave Milo a reassuring pat as we trotted down the stairs and slipped out the doors.

If Sorin was sleeping, it stood to reason that other vampires would be too. Still, I didn't want to think too deeply on the subject, lest I lose my nerve.

The morning sun warmed my shoulders as Milo sniffed around and did his business. I grabbed his food from the truck, scooped it into the collapsible bowl, and watched him devour it like he hadn't eaten in days. Once he finished, I pocketed a spare can and nodded toward the door.

"Come on, let's head back."

Milo followed with a happy sigh.

As I closed the door behind us and stepped into the dim, cool entryway, a figure moved into view. Delilah's starved gaze took me in with a knowing assessment that immediately set me on edge.

"Enjoying your morning, Scarlet?" she croaked.

I straightened, a nervous heat rising in my chest.

"I was just feeding Milo," I forced a casual tone. "Getting some air."

"Air, sure."

"Riiiight..." I trailed off, unsure of where this conversation might lead.

Milo gave a friendly chuff and padded over, nosing at Delilah's hand. She tilted her head, offering it without hesitation.

"Hey there," she rasped, the smallest smile tugging at her chapped lips.

"Sorry—he assumes everyone wants to pet him," I said, tugging at his collar.

"I don't mind." She crouched, letting Milo press his massive head against her bony chest. "You're a good boy, aren't you? Yes, you are."

Milo's tail whirred like a propeller about to lift him into orbit. If he liked her, I could probably trust she wasn't about to cut me up and wear my skin while crooning 'Goodbye Horses'.

"You hungry?" she asked, not quite meeting my eyes. "Vamps don't usually excel at meeting human needs."

Oh yeah, definitely friend material. Not foe.

"Starving, actually." My stomach rumbled right on cue, and I offered a sheepish smile.

"Stay here. I'll be right back."

She disappeared into the house and returned with a couple of power bars and bottles of apple juice.

"I don't have much. I don't really eat many solids these days."

Delilah tilted her head back, letting the sun wash over her bruised, mottled throat. Fresh punctures mingled with fading ones in a gallery of bites and hickeys.

"Hey, this is great. Thanks." I tore into the wrapper and nibbled at the bar.

We sat together, cross-legged on the porch. The sun was a bright buttery ball above us, drenching everything in the golden light of fall.

"Do you like it here?" I asked, careful to keep my eyes off her neck.

She let out a short bark of laughter.

"That's like asking a rat if it enjoys the maze it's trapped in."

"I see."

I didn't, but what else was I supposed to say?

We chewed our bars in silence. The apple juice slid down my throat in a cool, bittersweet rush. Delilah drained her bottle and studied the crumpled plastic as if it might hold the answers to life.

She looked so young, so tired. Bags pooled under her eyes, the upper lids drooping low and threatening to close. Those angular shoulders tilted down, and she leaned into Milo's side as he pressed into her.

"It's not safe. You should go back to your room." Even as she said it, she eased onto her back, short hair framing her worn face against the rough wooden boards.

"I'm stronger than I look." I gave her a wink, then, after a pause, added softly, "Why not leave?"

Her eyes slipped shut as she exhaled. "I can't."

"Why not?"

"The blood."

Her head lulled to the side so I could no longer see her expression. A tightness pulled at my chest when I noticed her dirty clothes, how her skin shone with a greasy sheen of sweat. Bones carved hard lines against her skin. She looked like a husk of a woman, as if something had drained her vitality and left her brittle around the edges. She was a painful reminder of the photos I'd seen of Luke.

Soon her breathing evened out into a slow cadence. I let her rest, doom scrolling until my skin began singing with sun exposure. Guilt pressed in as I ignored every message from family, friends, and work. They were safer not knowing, and I didn't trust myself with the freedom of unfiltered contact.

Delilah stirred, giving a languid stretch and rolling over to stare at me through bleary eyes. I took my thumb off the call button on Luke's contact, smiling at her like I would Piper.

"How long was I out?" She yawned.

"Only about an hour, go back to sleep," I said, despite my numbing butt cheeks against the hard floor.

She tilted her head side to side, "I have chores. But thanks."

Sensing our time on the porch was drawing to its end, I stood as I asked, "Do you have a phone?"

She nodded and handed me a battered device. Spider-webbed cracks veined the screen, the silver case dulled by time and use. I typed my number and name into her contacts before passing it back.

"Call me if you ever change your mind about leaving."

"All that's waiting for you up there is a living corpse," she whispered, lowering her head.

My shoulders sagged, "I'm just doing my best with the cards I've been dealt."

With a small wave, Milo and I slipped inside, jogging up the staircase. Every window was shrouded in thick drapery, allowing only slivers of sunlight to filter into the manor. The air in here felt stale and heavy compared to the breezy porch.

As softly as I could, I slipped back into the room, securing the lock and gently tugging to ensure the watchful shadows wouldn't follow. Milo retreated to his bed, and I kicked off my shoes, sliding beneath the covers. I would pay an ungodly sum of money to be anywhere else but here. Pulling the blankets up to my nose, I stole a glance at Sorin. He lay as still as before, *a living corpse.*

I reached out, brushing his hand with the backs of my fingers. They were so hard and cold. Like what I'd felt through our bond. I thought of my own recent isolation and what it had done to me over just a few months. How terrible must it have been for him to experience that for over two thousand years? I couldn't fathom it.

As I watched, his breathing deepened, the slow rise and fall of his chest becoming just visible. A wash of color returned to his face, softening his ashen pallor. Transfixed, I watched the subtle changes in his expression, wondering what they could mean. I didn't risk further touches, feeling mildly embarrassed that I'd even tried it. Easing away, I pulled out my phone to face the music and check my emails.

Victor had advocated for temporary remote work with the university museum. God, I loved that man. I scrolled through my phone, and my gaze landed on the background photo of Luke, Milo, and me at a spring picnic. Those memories softened the edges of my thoughts until my eyelids grew heavy, and sleep fogged my mind.

The bed shifted as the man beside me rose from the mattress. It took a moment for my mind to catch up, to remember that it wasn't Luke lying next to me. I quickly retracted the hand I'd instinctively reached out to him.

"Good evening," Sorin drawled from where he stood.

"Hi," I said, sitting up awkwardly. "How did you sleep?"

"Like the dead," he replied dryly.

Swinging my legs over the edge of the bed, I tried to stand. My feet tangled in the blanket, and I stumbled forward. Strong arms wrapped around my waist, snatching me centimeters from the ground.

"Careful, you—" he paused mid-sentence, inhaling sharply. "You smell of honey."

"The bathroom had soap," I mumbled, feeling utterly ridiculous as I lay draped over his arm like a wet blanket.

Turning my head to look at him, I felt my breath catch. Had I thought he looked human earlier? I was so wrong. Sorin's pupils were massive, blown out far past any reasonable proportion. His lips were slightly parted, revealing the faintest glint of fangs peeking out beneath soft flesh. Nostrils flared, hunger had etched itself into every feature of his face.

"Sorin?" I squeaked, kicking my legs back beneath me for support.

"Excuse me," he immediately released me and stepped back abruptly. "I'll return shortly—don't leave the room."

In a flash, he was out the door, leaving me standing there, mouth slightly agape.

I glanced at Milo, who was watching me with the same bewildered expression. His head tilted as if to say, *What the hell just happened?*

"I think I was almost dinner... or breakfast," I shuddered, crossing over to where I'd left his can of dog food earlier and preparing his bowl once more.

While Sorin was gone, I changed, tidied, and tried not to think about Luke or Valerie. Which proved to be a difficult task as I roved aimlessly around the room.

"Get a grip," I sank onto the edge of the bed and rubbed my eyes, willing the memories to stay buried.

A soft, irregular rattle started from the opposite side of the room. Confused, I lifted my head to see the door handle jiggling insistently. Someone was testing the strength of the lock.

"Sorin?" I called out hesitantly, taking careful steps toward the door.

There was no answer. Milo slunk closer to me with a rumbling warning growl. The handle shook more aggressively, then suddenly stopped, leaving a ringing silence in its wake. The hairs on the back of my neck stood at attention.

My hand hovered over the door handle, paralyzed with indecision. Sorin had been adamant that I stay put, insisting that I didn't fully grasp the gravity of the situation. It felt like I had already taken too many risks earlier today, sneaking out with Delilah.

Backing away, I motioned for Milo to jump onto the bed with me. My inner child suggested diving under the covers and hiding until

Sorin came back. But I was a grown woman. A mature, capable adult. Who hadn't eaten in hours and was on the verge of chewing the furniture.

He had thirty more minutes, I decided. After thirty minutes, I was leaving to get real food. Creepy door handle or not.

Fortunately for me and Milo's bladder, it only took ten more minutes for Sorin to return. His features appeared fuller, his eyes brighter and more alert.

"Feeling better?" I asked, hoping Delilah hadn't been the source of his revival.

He nodded, "I hadn't realized just how hungry I had become."

Right on cue, my stomach let out a loud growl.

"I know the feeling."

"One moment, and we'll depart," he said, heading for the bathroom. The sound of the rushing shower filled the silence, and he called out, "We'll get you some food as well."

A few minutes later, Sorin and I stood at the door, ready to leave.

"Did you try to come back earlier?" I asked, thinking of the jiggling door handle.

"No," he said, eyebrows rising. "Why?"

"Well," I scuffed my foot against the floor, "someone was jiggling the door handle, and I thought it might've been you."

"You didn't open it, did you?"

"No," I replied quickly. "I remembered what you said."

"Good girl," he said, patting me on the head before swinging the door open to disappear into the hallway.

10

WHEN MICE CORNER CATS

My mouth fell open slightly, irritation flooding through me at the little leap my heart had given at his praise. I scolded myself as I followed him with a scowl. I did not like him calling me that. Not one bit.

"I'm not a pet," I growled at Sorin's back as we approached the steps.

"Shhh," he replied, holding up a finger without breaking his stride.

His dismissiveness only fueled my annoyance, but as I stomped up to him, the murmur of voices drifted up from the entryway.

"They won't be available for another hour," came Delilah's reedy voice.

Did that woman ever sleep?

"Unacceptable," a man replied, voice dripping with barely restrained anger.

"I'm sorry—"

"What about you?" he demanded. "You could suffice, could you not?"

I crept forward quietly. A man loomed over Delilah. His eyes glowed with the same hunger I recognized in Sorin.

"No," she said dully, as if she didn't or couldn't care if the stranger heard her words. "I've already been used today."

The vampire bared his fangs, "You are not off-limits."

My eyes darted to Sorin. He watched silently, unmoved and uncaring.

A deep frown twisted my mouth as I turned back to Delilah. A fresh wound covered the left side of her neck in a dark, angry patch. I could see the exhaustion in the way her shoulders sagged in defeat.

The man grabbed Delilah's wrist, pulling her closer. I exhaled sharply, taking a half step forward. Sorin held out an arm to stop me.

"Stop!" her voice cracked, but the fight was draining out of her.

That was it. I couldn't just watch this happen to the girl who had brought me snacks and napped beside me.

"Let her go," I shoved Sorin's arm aside and surged into view.

The vampire's head snapped toward me, his grip tightening briefly before he released Delilah. She stumbled back, wide-eyed, staring at me as though I'd lost my mind. She shook her head violently, slicing a hand across her throat in warning. I ignored her.

The vampire studied me for a moment, clearly weighing whether I was worth the delay in his meal. He scoffed, looking past me.

"Control your bitch," he spat at Sorin.

My head whipped to Sorin, waiting for him to defend me.

"If you want her tamed, Damian, you're welcome to try," Sorin spared me a frigid glance. "I think you'll find she's a bit feral."

I let out an indignant sound. Was he being serious?

Damian smiled as if he wouldn't mind taking Sorin up on that offer, taking the steps two at a time towards me. Milo snapped his jaws in a hostile warning that froze Damian in his tracks. His eyes narrowed into cold slits.

"I wouldn't recommend trying," I snarled.

His eyes flicked over me again, reassessing the threat I posed. I estimated his weight, his height, taking in the cocky assurance in his posture that spoke of inhuman speed and strength.

"Someone's got to teach the harlots their place."

Harlot? Oh, hell no.

"What the fuck did this fossil just call me?" I asked aloud, to no one in particular.

Sorin leaned back against the wall, crossing his arms like he was settling in for live entertainment. All he needed was popcorn soaked in hemoglobin, hold the butter.

Clenching my jaw, my eyes snapped back to the other vampire just in time to see him surge forward. My eyes bulged with his speed. I'd tangled with my fair share of gym bros hopped up on Red Bull and ego, but this guy was rewriting the laws of gravity. His body blurred toward me, arms outstretched to slam me into the wall.

I had never experienced a miracle, but the Lord handed me a small one today. There must have been enough of Sorin's blood still in my veins, because I managed to sidestep at the last second.

Damian faltered, clearly not expecting me to match his speed. He locked on Milo, leg cocking back for a kick that would've sent my fur baby flying into next year. Years of drilled-in training kicked in; I didn't waste the opening. My right hand clamped around his left wrist, dragging him across so he was between me and the open staircase.

He got out half a curse before I dropped to my knees, arms snapping around both his legs just above his kneecaps. Every muscle in my back and thighs burned as I heaved him upward, aiming to dump him flat on his back at the top of the stairs.

Delilah let out a strangled cry as we hurtled over the landing, suspended in a sickening, stomach-flipping moment of weightlessness when gravity finally remembered it had a job to do.

I curled tight, tucking my chin so my neck wouldn't snap on impact, letting Damian take the brunt of the fall as we crashed down the steps. His extended belly cushioned me just enough to ricochet me sideways. Mind numbing pain exploded into my ribs as I burst straight through the banister.

Thankfully, the floor was only a few feet below. I slammed down hard, rolling involuntarily. It was my second miracle of the evening, as well as the most likely reason that I didn't break every damn bone in my body. Still, it was going to take more time than I had to recover from the landing.

Groaning, I flexed my hand around the broken piece of oak banister that had snapped off when I'd tried to grab hold to stop my fall.

"Get up!" Delilah stammered, crouched near the massive fireplace, its flames throwing frantic shadows across her face. "He's coming!"

My legs weren't cooperating, so my body compromised by flipping itself over to face the threat. Damian advanced, murder burning in his eyes, glowing a dim silver.

Above him, a second pair of eyes glowed crimson from the stairwell. Sorin had Milo tucked securely under his arm like precious cargo. Milo was writhing madly, trying to rush down the stairs to my side.

"Damian. Enough." Sorin's voice rolled out like thunder, heavy and absolute.

"What's the matter, Sorin? Afraid I'll break your new toy before you're done playing with it?"

Damian sneered down at me, continuing his approach.

"This *toy* just put you on your ass," I shot back, crab-walking toward Delilah.

"Be silent, trollop," Damian seethed.

I blinked, then scoffed, "Seriously? Do you have any insults from this century?"

Damian roared and dove for me, reckless as a roided out linebacker on his last brain cell. Distantly, I heard Delilah squeak in terror. I wished I could've told her not to worry—that I had this underhand. Damian had nothing but brute strength coupled with supernatural speed, no fighting strategy whatsoever.

My hand shot up with the broken chunk of banister still clenched in my fist. He practically impaled himself on it, a satisfying *thunk* vibrating down my arm.

We both froze for half a second with matching stares of wide-eyed disbelief.

Sorin uttered a guttural sound, something that might once have been a curse in another tongue. "Oh, wow," I blurted, too stunned to withdraw my hand.

Then his undead weight drove us both backward. I shoved hard, pivoting on muscle memory, and sent him toppling straight into the fireplace. Flames roared as his coat caught, the smell of singed vampire filling the air. He didn't even scream, going up like a Halloween decoration too close to a candle, then burning down to a crumbled pile of ash on Delilah's beat-up Converse.

I pushed myself up, breathless. "Didn't see that coming, did you? You overgrown mosquito."

"You...you killed him," Delilah breathed.

I dusted ash off my sleeve. "He tried to kick my dog."

"You don't understand. This is neutral ground," she whimpered, dragging her hand across her trembling mouth.

"So?" I demanded, feeling the rush of violence thinning into dangerous territory.

Two kills in less than a week. I was doing my best not to think about it. At least this time, there were witnesses to back up my claim of self-defense. Still, the way Delilah was staring at me, you'd think I'd just signed my own death warrant.

"There are consequences," she managed, crouching deeper into the corner, rocking back and forth as she tugged at her short hair.

"What consequences?" I asked, fear finally worming its way into my chest.

"Death," Sorin's voice rumbled from directly beside me. His arm looped firmly around my waist as he pulled me away from the scene.

"We need to leave. Now."

"Yeah, one second, asshole." I ignored the double take Sorin gave me and held Delilah's red-rimmed eyes for just a moment longer.

"If we leave, you do too."

She looked between me and the bite marks that freckled her skin. "I'll die."

I glanced down at her ash-streaked toes and noticed a flash of metal among what was left of Damian. My foot swept through the cinders, sending a set of keys skittering in her direction.

"Sounds like your odds are about the same if you stay," I said.

Doors opened, then shut from somewhere upstairs.

"We must leave, Scarlet," Sorin insisted, his hand returning to my lower back to urge me to the door.

A look of grim determination sank onto Delilah's haggard face. She bent, snatched up the keys, and sprinted out of the door.

"Good luck," I called as we followed her into the brisk fall night.

Milo had given up his struggle, hanging in limp defeat from Sorin's arms. The chill bit through my shirt, and leaves crunched underfoot as I struggled to match Sorin's hurried strides.

"Slow down!" I puffed, stretching my legs so I could at least be halfway in the truck before he took off.

An engine revved to life, and a black coup peeled out of the long driveway into the night. Delilah's white hair practically glowed from the interior as she vanished into the distance.

The second I slid into the passenger seat, Sorin dumped Milo into the back. Moments later, we were tearing down the opposite road. I glanced at Sorin. Then, at the blur of headlights outside. Then back at him. My mouth opened, shut, opened again.

"What is it?"

"What?"

"You keep opening and closing your mouth. You look like a fish."

"I do not," I huffed. "Why didn't you say anything back there?"

"Do you stop a cat every time it corners a mouse?"

My entire being stiffened.

"A human being is not a mouse," I bit out. "Didn't you feed off her?"

"What of it?"

He sounded as if I'd asked him if he'd had an afternoon snack.

"The least you could do is defend her! She was helpless."

"But you weren't," He cut me a sideways glance. "What would you have had me do?"

"I..." His question caught me off guard. "Something... like telling Damian to go away."

Sorin raised a brow.

"And," I drew in a deep breath, "I would've liked it if you'd defended me, too."

His voice dropped to a purr, "With two vampire slayings under your belt, you hardly need defending. Honestly, Scarlet—" he cracked a sardonic smile, "—I know a predator when I see one. And tonight, it wasn't Damian."

"You really know how to sweet-talk a girl, fang boy," I preened, wondering when being called a predator had somehow become a compliment.

Sorin stifled a laugh, slowing as he turned down a side road crowded with foliage.

"I haven't been called a boy since—" His words trailed off, eyes catching in the rearview mirror.

Headlights slid into view, casting his gaze in a flat, wolfish glow. His shoulders went rigid, knuckles whitening against the wheel.

"What is it?" I asked, twisting to look at the vehicle tailing us.

"We're not alone," he growled, grimacing as his foot pressed harder on the accelerator. "They've stayed on us for the last three turns."

My blood turned to ice. Delilah had said there would be consequences, I just didn't think they would arrive so soon.

"Do you think they're from the manor?" I asked, heart hammering in my chest. "It looks like there's more than one."

Multiple silhouettes shifted in jerky, unnatural motions inside the cab of the vehicle as it barreled toward us at a perilous speed and distance.

Sorin nodded once. "Houses like that are usually run by a group of vampires called a murder."

"Like a murder of crows?" I blurted, horror twisting my gut.

"Yes." His voice was flat, his foot slamming harder against the gas pedal. "They likely came after us the second they saw what happened. Put your seatbelt on. And grab Milo."

I flopped into the seat, yanking the belt snug across my chest. Milo lumbered into my lap like the oversized lapdog he thought he was, smothering my face with frantic licks.

"Buckled in?" Sorin asked.

I grunted, tightening my grip around ninety-five pounds of panicked canine crushing me. "I'm basically wearing him as body armor at this point."

"Try to hold on."

That was all the warning I got before my stomach dropped and I realized Sorin's definition of "holding on" meant praying we survived the next five seconds.

11

MURDER ON THE BEND

"Shit, shit, shit, shit," I chanted as the world spun into a blur of headlights and shrieking tires.

My stomach pitched into my throat, the laws of physics hell-bent on launching Milo and me straight through the windshield. Milo howled, claws digging into my thighs as the truck spun a perfect, nauseating circle before snapping back into the road.

A cream-colored sedan rushed past so close I could taste the rush of air it displaced. It was impossible to catch any distinguishing features of its occupants besides the flash of wickedly sharp fangs.

Without so much as a blink, Sorin slammed the gas. The inertia of the truck sent my head slamming into the headrest, driving a wheezing gasp out of me as Milo's thick body followed suit. Milo yelped, crushed against my arm as I held him tight, both of us panting in the wake of death we'd barely dodged.

The sedan screeched to a halt, brake lights bleeding into the interior of the truck and painting Sorin in a malevolent wash of crimson. A devilish gleam lit his eyes, matched by the sadistic smile twisting his lips as he steered back toward the wider road. His long hair was tied loosely at the nape of his neck, wild strands tumbling free around his face. He was completely arresting. Like a demon escaping hell, torn directly from a nocturnal oil painting.

My breath halted somewhere between my lungs and lips. Was he actually enjoying this?

The growl of an engine stole my attention from Sorin. The sedan was already closing the distance, gaining fast.

"They're back! Drive!" I clutched Milo tighter to my chest.

"Pretty sure that's what I'm already doing, sweetheart." A devil-may-care chuckle spilled out of him.

My heart stuttered, a blush flushing my cheeks.

"Don't call me sweetheart," I mumbled, struggling against the swarm of butterflies trying to take flight in my stomach.

Likely, it was nothing more than motion sickness, brought on by Sorin careening the truck back onto the wider road.

The murder must have done some tampering to increase the speed of their car. It was eating up the distance, headlights vanishing beneath the truck's tailgate until the world jolted with a bone-rattling slam.

I sucked in a sharp breath as the impact shoved us forward, my foot braced against the glove box to keep me and Milo cemented in place. Panicking, my hand grasped Sorin's shoulder, fingers digging into the hard muscle there.

"Sorin!" I gasped out.

His head tilted just enough for his profile to catch the ambient light from the sedan's headlights.

"Don't worry," he murmured, steady as iron. "I have you."

That should have been reassuring, but with his eyes still blazing, it did anything but. I searched the sharp planes of his face, wondering who I was entrusting with my life.

Maybe vampires really could read minds, because seconds later his hand found mine, fingers tightening in a brief squeeze. "You're safe with me, Scarlet. All right?"

He glanced from the road back to me, waiting for my affirmation.

"Okay," I breathed, releasing his shoulder and sinking my hand into Milo's thick fur.

"One more big shake," he warned. "Ready?"

My head bobbed, more trembling than nodding, as I readjusted my grip on Milo. "Do it."

The road curved sharply ahead, power lines and trees closing in tight on either side. The sedan fell back, revving for another strike. When it lunged forward, Sorin yanked us into the empty oncoming lane. The sedan overshot us. Relief punched the air from my lungs too soon.

Sorin wasn't finished. His foot pressed harder, and for one insane second, I thought he meant to ram them as well. As the curve reached its sharpest angle, he veered right, clipping the sedan's back left panel.

The car lurched, wobbling across the asphalt, acrid smoke seeping through the vents as their tires screamed for purchase. Sorin struck again, harder this time, the truck's weight slamming into more of its side.

The sedan spun out, the space around it stretching into slow motion. Metal shrieked. Headlights whirled. Then it lost its grip entirely, skidding off the bend. We shot past as it rolled onto its side, cartwheeling end over end before crumpling against a power pole and utility box in a collision of twisted steel.

"Holy shit." My jaw dropped as we slowed to a stop. "Why are we stopping? We should be—oh, I don't know—escaping?"

"Have to make sure we're not followed," Sorin said smoothly, glancing back at his handiwork like he'd just parallel parked.

"I think you killed them," I muttered, groaning as I let Milo go.

He immediately abandoned me for the back seat.

"No." Sorin waved a hand dismissively. "It would take far more than that to kill a murder of vampires."

As soon as the last word fell from his mouth, the utility box sparked. A heartbeat later, the sedan was engulfed in a fireball, a mushroom cloud of flame licking the night. Muffled screams bled from the wreckage.

Sorin froze mid-motion, hands still tangled in his hair tie, dark strands falling forward like a curtain across his astounded face.

"I stand corrected," he said at last, the words rough with disbelief.

"Should we... do something?" I asked, making no move whatsoever to get out of the truck.

His mouth pressed into a grim line. "We should leave. This will draw too much attention."

Spinning around, he slammed the truck into drive and rocketed us away from the flames. We didn't speak for a long, long time. Occasionally, Sorin's mouth would twitch or his eyebrow would furrow.

"Care to share what's going through your mind?" I asked, finger coming my hair into a ponytail.

"I'm thinking..." His lips pressed together, considering. "That maybe I shouldn't have chosen you after all."

"Chosen me for what?"

Doing my best to bat away the little sting of rejection that his statement delivered, I fixed him with my blankest stare.

"The experiment."

"Oh. That." I grumbled, turning toward the blur of trees rushing past the window. "It's not like I asked for this, you know."

"I know," He replied softly.

"So why did you?" I kept my eyes fixed on the scenery. "Choose me, I mean."

Sorin inhaled deeply, held it, then let the breath leak out in a long sigh.

"You seemed strong. And alone. Like you could take care of yourself."

Unsure if that was meant as praise or an insult, I turned to gauge his face. But he'd already pulled the mask back into place, the man with the glowing eyes hidden safely behind it.

I dropped my gaze to my hands, chewing on the truth of what he'd said. I was alone. Without Luke, the only people who bothered to check on me were Tucker and Tiffany. Everyone else did it out of obligation—my parents—or out of the inconvenience my absence would cause—my jobs.

I loved the gym, but when class ended, everyone went back to their real lives. Their families. Their homes. And me? I went back to silence.

Loneliness had always been my constant, and I'd worn it like armor. As a child, my parents poured most of their attention into my overachieving brother. I didn't blame him, but as an adult, I'd drifted away from them. Since Luke started pulling away last year, that armor had grown heavier, sinking in at odd hours and pressing on my ribs. For the first time, I wasn't sure I could keep pretending it didn't matter.

Clearing my throat, I asked roughly, "So, where did you learn to do that kind of driving?"

Sorin cocked his head and threw me a fiendish smirk. "Saw it in a movie."

Every thought fluttered out of my head like confetti in a leaf blower.

"Hold up," I said, raising both hands. "You're telling me you almost turned me and my dog into roadkill, because Vin Diesel told you it was a good idea?"

His smirk split into a wide, satisfied grin. "It was Tokyo Drift, actually."

"Are you touched in the head?" I demanded.

His smile dropped. "Facing a murder wasn't an option."

"And why not?" I shot back. "You're two thousand years old, for crying out loud. Couldn't you just do some ancient vampire hoodoo and blast them?"

"Vampire hoodoo?" He echoed skeptically.

"Well, I don't know what you call it. Magic? I'm new to this," I tossed back.

"No, I can't 'blast them with my vampire hoodoo' as you so eloquently put it," he said in an overly exaggerated southern drawl.

"I do not sound like that," I glowered.

"Yes, you do."

A thought occurred to me. "Why don't you have an accent?"

"Must you always ask questions?" He sighed like my very existence was wearing him thin.

"Shut up and answer," I nudged his arm with my elbow.

He pulled his mouth to the side, delivering a disapproving glare before saying, "It would be rather difficult for an ancient vampire to blend in if he still spoke with an accent."

My eyebrows shot up. Now that he'd pointed it out, his voice really was scrubbed clean. There was no trace of region, no hint of origin. If I were pressed, I couldn't have guessed what part of the country he was from.

"Of course," he added, each syllable caressed in a posh English accent, "I can always speak like this if you promise to be a good girl and keep your mouth shut for the rest of the drive."

I swatted at him, heat crawling up my neck. "Stop calling me a good girl."

"Bad girl then? You like that?" he teased, switching into a flawless, lilting Irish accent.

A laugh burbled out of me. "Stop that!"

"Or perhaps you prefer something with a little more spice." His voice dropped, rolling his r's, vowels heavy and molten. Turkish, maybe. Whatever it was, it poured over me like warm chocolate, leaving goosebumps in its wake. My body tightened, and I squirmed against the seat.

"Definitely likes a little spice," he grinned, holding onto that maddeningly attractive accent.

"Oh my God," I groaned, clapping my hands over my ears. "I liked it better when you were pretending to hate me."

He frowned, "I never hated you."

"Not caring is worse than hating." I dropped my hands, fingers worrying the hem of my heather-grey sweater.

"What do you mean?" he asked, cutting me a sidelong glance from the driver's seat.

"I mean when you conveniently neglected to defend me or that other helpless human earlier." The words scraped out of me.

"What I did wasn't neglect."

"Then what was it?"

"In our world, things aren't as simple as right or wrong, do or don't." His voice dropped, words settling heavy in the cab. "There is only the breathing...and the dead. The true death."

Our world? Had I, without realizing it, made the transition from my world to the metaphysical?

I stared at him, wondering if the irony of immortality was that it pushed evolution into reverse. Did eternity strip away the layers of rationality and empathy that set humanity apart from beasts? In an endless existence, did survival eventually become the only instinct left?

For all the wisdom that immortality had the potential to bestow, did it simply drag you back to a world where the strong preyed on the weak and relationships were formed out of necessity, not trust?

The concept saddened me. I looked back at the blur of the road, thinking about questions I wasn't sure I wanted answers to.

"But, I am sorry that I did not defend you as you thought I should have."

I didn't know what to say, so I stayed silent.

"I will try to consider your sense of mortal justice moving forward," he continued in a mix of amusement and sincerity. "Misguided and uninformed as it may be."

"You really know how to ruin a perfectly decent apology, you know that?" I crossed my arms over my chest, trying to hold onto the remnants of my irritation even as a reluctant smile tugged at my lips.

"I aim to please," he adjusted his position, eyes gleaming with that unruffled confidence that both infuriated and fascinated me. "Though sometimes my aim is a little off."

After an hour, we pulled off at a fast-food drive-thru. Sorin quickly became absorbed in a string of phone calls dealing with the crash, leaving me to order a small feast for myself. As penance for stressing him out, I got Milo his own pack of nuggets. He inhaled them greedily, rubbing against me in appreciation. I laughed, rubbing his ears as I polished off my own food a little too quickly.

A sudden, sharp *hic* broke the quiet. I slapped a hand over my mouth, startled, then waited, hoping it was just one. But a second hiccup followed, just as loud.

"Are you alright?" Sorin asked with a bemused smile as he ducked back into the truck.

Hic. I nodded, pressing my lips together in a futile attempt to stifle the next hiccup.

"Just a hic—" *hic* "—cup," I managed.

Another hiccup escaped, louder than the last.

"Maybe you should slow down. Do you realize you looked like a feral cat gulping down scraps?" His lips pressed into a restrained smile.

"Oh, ha-ha," I grumbled between hiccups. "I'll have you know,—*hic*—some people just happen to eat—" I paused, hiccuping again "—quickly."

"Yes," he sighed. "But do you also have to eat like you're defending your kill?"

"Defending my..." I trailed off, rolling my eyes. "Look, we don't have all—*hic*—night."

He gave me an appraising look, "Perhaps one day you'll discover the art of pacing yourself in eating and, well, other matters."

"I don't—*hic*—know what that means, but I—*hic*—don't think I like it," I glared at him.

"It means," he said lightly, "that there's no halfway with you. It's admirable in its own way."

His mouth softened just slightly.

"You don't know me that well," I replied a touch defensively.

"Perhaps not," he said in a tone that felt less like an admission and more like a promise.

Just as I was about to respond, another accursed hiccup erupted from my throat.

The rest of our journey passed with an unspoken truce settling between us. I stroked Milo's fur absentmindedly as I watched the world blur by until the first lights of the city finally illuminated the skyline.

We navigated deeper into the city, winding through the crowded streets. I couldn't help but search disparagingly for any sign of Luke among the sea of faces we passed. Each man with dark hair that I saw made my heart skip a beat. But there was no sign of him.

We ended up at the restaurant where my journey had begun. The few days I had spent away from here felt like a lifetime. My world had shifted so drastically since then. Anxiety roiled through my stomach as I looked through the glass windows, memories of that night replaying in the back of my mind.

Sorin drove around the back, taking a steep descent into a parking garage. Three levels down, he punched a code into the keypad beside a large metal gate. It swung open to reveal a brightly lit garage with covered vehicles scattered throughout the space.

Odessa stood by the large open doorway leading into the building. She was beaming with what I pegged as her signature, dazzling smile. I couldn't help but smile back, giving her a small wave as we parked and unloaded. Odessa bounded up, wrapping her arms around me in a warm embrace.

Unprepared for the contact, I stiffened as she squeezed me tightly.

"Odessa! I didn't expect—"

"Oh, hush!" she cut me off as she held me at arm's length. "I've been wondering when you'd turn up again. Sorin wasn't exactly generous with the details."

He ignored her, unloading the items from the truck in pensive silence. I curled my lip at Sorin's rudeness. His constant flip between polite and prickly was giving me severe whiplash.

"So grumpy," Odessa tsked, eyeing him with playful exasperation. "Was the company tolerable?"

She looked at me for an answer, but Sorin cut in before I could respond.

"Wasn't the worst company I've kept," he replied curtly.

Odessa let out a good-natured laugh, and I stifled an insult to hurl at him.

"High praise coming from Sorin. I hope—"

She paused mid-sentence, her smile faltering as Milo bounded out of the truck.

"Oh," she took a small step back, her expression a mix of surprise and... was that fear? "You brought a dog."

I placed a reassuring hand on Milo's back as he looked up at Odessa with his usual soft eyes, oblivious to her reaction.

"Yes, he's my partner in crime."

I shot her a small smile.

"He's harmless and potty trained. Promise."

"It's not him, exactly," Odessa looked from Milo to me, her unease turning to faint embarrassment. "I have a bad history."

She studied him, "He's big."

"You'll find Milo's more tolerable than most humans," Sorin said, a hint of approval sneaking into his tone.

Odessa's lips lifted into a strained smile as she met Milo's gaze.

"Well, as long as he doesn't bite, I think we'll manage just fine."

She gave him a stiff pat on the head, and Milo's tail thumped. I let out a sigh of relief as Odessa chuckled softly.

"Come on, then," she said, gesturing toward the doorway. "Let's get everyone inside. It's been an eventful few days, I'm sure."

Odessa led us back to the small room I remembered.

"One moment, Scarlet." Sorin's hand caught my elbow. He leaned in so close I felt the warmth of his breath brush the shell of my ear as he whispered, "For both our sakes, say nothing of what happened tonight. To anyone."

12

SKELETONS IN THE CLOSET

My breath hitched at his proximity. I nodded dumbly as he drew back, his fingers brushing my shoulder like pulling away an invisible thread.

"You just had something there." He gave my shoulder a casual pat, the whisper erased as neatly as if it hadn't happened at all. Then he walked in.

What in the hell was that? I gave myself a mental shake and filed into the room. If I was going to be staying in a building full of vampires, I couldn't get distracted by whisper-soft warnings and possessive hands. Handsome culprits didn't make it less dangerous.

"I had all that clutter removed," Odessa commented, noticing me peeking into the closet with a wary eye.

"Thanks," I was unable to hide the relief in my voice.

The thought of all those abandoned clothes had been haunting me.

"Couldn't leave my guest in a messy space like that, now, could I?"

Her voice was warm, and she cast a glance at Sorin, who looked away uncomfortably.

"Sorin, don't look so stiff," Odessa seemed to sense his discomfort. "You'd think you were hiding skeletons in that closet."

He bristled, "An interesting choice of words."

I had to shake off a shudder at the image of so many women who had never returned for their clothing. What had happened to them?

"I have things to take care of," he said, giving me a meaningful look.

"Of course, Sorin," Odessa replied, a trace of amusement in her voice. "We wouldn't dream of keeping you from your duties."

"If you need anything, call," he gave me a curt nod.

I watched him stride out of the room with a last, wary glance at Odessa.

Once he was gone, Odessa let out a bemused sigh.

"Always so efficient, that one," she shook her head. "You're going to be far more fun to have around."

She winked at me.

"Glad to be of service," I offered her a small smile.

"Trust me," she guided me further into the room, "we'll make sure your stay here is much more appealing this time."

"Seeing as all my bones are intact, I think we're off to a great start," I replied, setting my bags down on the tiny bed and shoving the chair aside to make space for Milo's bed.

Odessa stayed near the far wall, her gaze drifting between me and Milo as he sniffed around.

"What are your plans for this evening?" she asked, keeping a careful distance from Milo as he snuffled underneath the bed.

Every time he moved, she flinched a little. I wondered what kind of past could make her so wary of dogs.

"I don't know what Sorin has told you," I said, yanking my denim jacket from the bag and slipping it on. "But I'm planning to hit the streets for Luke ASAP."

I hoped Sorin would follow through on his promise to help me. The search for my husband needed to end as soon as possible.

"I heard through the grapevine," she crooned. "And what will you do when you find him?"

"When," not "if," I liked that. It sounded as if she believed in my success or maybe even wanted it.

"I don't really know," I said, glancing around as I considered. "I suppose I'll cross that bridge when I get there."

"How bad is he?" she asked, lowering herself to sit on the edge of the bed.

Holding very still, she allowed Milo to sniff her hand. Sensing her reluctance, he approached with his tail tucked submissively between his legs.

"Bad," I admitted. "I don't know exactly what's going on with Luke, but I know it's not good."

My chest tightened. I thought of how terrible Luke had seemed the last time I saw his picture and wondered how things had progressed in the time since.

A slight frown creased her smooth brow, "Addiction is a powerful thing, Scarlet. Certain things in life can consume us entirely if we're not careful."

My heart felt heavy. "I have to try to save him, I don't care how far gone he is. I can't just abandon him."

"Loyalty like that is both admirable and intriguing."

She reached out and gave my shoulder a squeeze.

"Thanks," I blew out a watery breath. "You sound a little like Sorin when you say that, you know."

"We couldn't be more dissimilar," she chuckled. "He's too careful. Sometimes caution is just another form of avoidance."

I grimaced, trying to make sense of her words as I prodded at the sore spot where my ribs had met the banister.

"What do you mean?"

"Sometimes, to truly help someone, you have to get involved. You have to make sacrifices, put yourself on the line. Even if it's messy. Sorin, well..." She paused to think. "Sorin likes to find ways to observe life from a safe distance."

I couldn't deny the truth in her words. Sorin's cold detachment with Delilah had grated on me earlier, and my back carried the price. The bruise pulsed with a deepening ache, the kind that wouldn't fade overnight. Days, maybe weeks, if I had taken the hit wrong. I was almost positive I had.

"*You're* like me, though," she continued in an approving tone, oblivious to my thoughts. "You have fire, passion. The kind of conviction that can change things, maybe even make a difference."

"A difference in what?"

While I was flattered that she thought we were similar, I had no clue what she was talking about.

She studied my reaction. I had the uncomfortable feeling that she could see right through me. I glanced away, suddenly feeling exposed.

And then it hit me, the experiment that she and Sorin were running on me.

"I don't know what this experiment of yours is," I said cautiously, "but if you're implying that it can help Luke, then fine. I'm in."

I would do anything to get him back. Besides, what did I care about some stupid experiment? There was no way that it would directly affect me. I would play both her and Sorin until I got what I needed. Then I would find some way to untangle us from this mess.

Her eyes sparkled with satisfaction, and she lowered her voice conspiratorially, "You could help him, Scarlet. Together, we could help him in ways Sorin never will. But it might require a different approach."

"What are you saying?" I shook my head, unsure of what she was getting at.

Her smile sharpened.

"Let's just say, if you ever need a little extra help, I'd be more than willing to offer my assistance." Her gaze was so laser-focused on me that I thought I felt a strange pull, an allure to her offer that made my heart skip a beat.

"I'll keep that in mind," I managed to get out after mentally slapping myself for staring at her wordlessly for at least thirty seconds.

The woman might think I was falling in love with her. Hell, with a face like that, maybe I was.

It was possible her blood could be powerful enough to overcome Luke's current addiction. I had to take this chance. She could be a viable option, and it would be stupid to turn away any help I was offered.

"Good," she almost purred. "The world changes because of people like you, Scarlet. People who are willing to break the rules, to challenge the boundaries."

I couldn't shake the sense that she wasn't just talking about helping Luke. There was something more hidden beneath her offer, but I wasn't brave enough to dig into it.

Feeling utterly confused and heartsick, I leashed Milo, and we exited the building. Odessa's cryptic words still played in my mind. She had exchanged numbers with me, texting me the security code that would grant me access to the building whenever I needed it. I pocketed my phone, trying to shake off the strange, foreboding feeling her words had left behind.

I pulled out my phone and texted Sorin instead, asking if he had Luke's location yet.

Almost immediately, a set of coordinates pinged to my screen. My heart hammered away as I plugged them into my GPS. The location was only about an hour's walk away. I was so close to finding him. Relief and anticipation swelled in my chest, urging me forward.

Milo and I set off into the night, following the directions that would take us straight to Luke and maybe even a few answers.

13

WHO LIES BETWEEN US

I had hoped for the best but expected the worst. Somehow, life still found a way to limbo under the low bar I had set for my expectations. The GPS directed me to a dimly lit alley between two run-down apartment buildings. I glanced down at Milo. Bringing him with me had served as a reminder to keep my wits. Both for his sake and Luke's, because I sure as hell wasn't going to do it for myself.

A shadow moved at the far end of the alley. My heart leaped as I recognized the familiar frame.

"Luke?" I called softly.

He was slouched against the wall, head bowed and knees drawn to his chest.

"Scarlet?"

His eyes crawled up to meet mine.

"It's me and Milo."

I took a tentative step closer, hoping the sight of us together might draw him back to sanity. Or, at minimum, make him have a conversation with me.

"We've been looking everywhere for you."

Swaying slightly, his gaze flicked to Milo. He pulled toward Luke so hard I had to wrap the leash tighter, letting the burn in my palm chase away my tears.

"Why?" he rasped. "Why bother?"

"Because I care about you," my voice came out so thin and wobbly. "I love you. And you don't have to go through this alone. Come back with me."

Come back to me.

"I can't come back, not anymore," Luke's face twisted in despair. "I'm not worth it, Scarlet."

Milo let out a low whine. Luke moved towards us, approaching the crack of artificial light that had slipped between the buildings.

"Just come with us," I said in a voice barely above a whisper. "We can figure this out together."

"You don't understand, Scarlet," he answered hoarsely, stepping into the light.

I tried to stifle the strangled gasp pressing against my throat. Luke looked even worse than the grainy photos I'd seen. His once-strong frame had wasted away to hollow, bony limbs. His hair hung limply on his scalp, streaked with grime. Bruises mottled his skin, dark stains littering his exposed neck and arms. He looked as though he'd been starving on the streets for months, not days.

"Luke," I sobbed, wrapping my arms around him and willing warmth back into his body. "Please, let me help you."

He stood rigidly in my arms, breath laboring against my cheek.

"You don't understand, Scarlet."

"I do," I only cling tighter to him. "I know everything. About the vampires, about that woman's blood and what she did to you."

"You know about Val?" His head jerked up frantically, "Have you seen her? I need to find her."

Every nerve in my body tensed. In one instant, the grief that had threatened to overwhelm me mutated into ugly betrayal.

"I have to find her, Scarlet. I need her," he broke free from my grasp and sent me stumbling back.

"Luke, I—"

"I'll die without her," he pleaded in a high-pitched whine. "Please, Scarlet, help me."

"Luke, I can't."

"You're being selfish!" he snarled furiously.

"You can't—she's not..." I couldn't finish what I wanted to say. That he couldn't find her because she was never coming back.

His eyes widened, then slit thin, brimming with venom. Hatred warped his features into something cruel and accusing.

"You did something, didn't you?"

My hands flew to my face, shielding the tears I could not hold back.

"What did you do?" He yanked my hands down. "What did you do, Scarlet?"

"She attacked me." I dropped to my knees, my hands raised, palms open.

His face went blank, then shock bent his mouth into a bitter grimace. I knelt there, my whole body trembling as he glared down at me.

"She attacked you?" his voice rose in a tone that implied that he didn't believe me.

His words crushed me. I had been fighting so hard to find him, to understand what had happened. I never imagined he'd speak to me with this kind of loathing.

"I... I thought..." My voice came out in broken fragments as I struggled to find the right words that wouldn't send him over the edge. "I thought you needed me."

He let out a harsh laugh.

"Need you? Scarlet, I needed you to leave this alone. To let me be with Valerie. But you—" His hands clenched into fists, his entire being radiating outrage. "You've ruined everything."

"Luke, please," I reached out to him. "I have a plan."

But he jerked back away, the rejection sent a wave of grief crashing over me.

"You have no idea what you've done. You might as well have killed me," he spat.

I watched helplessly as he retreated from the light.

"Luke!" I cried, but I couldn't move.

All I could do was watch him leave me on my knees against the frigid asphalt. My breath sawed in and out of my lungs. Poor Milo lay curled in a whimpering ball of fur beside me.

"I'm sorry, Milo." My head lolled to the side as I took him in, and regret washed over me. I never should have brought him here tonight.

"I am so worthless."

My voice cracked as the truth settled over me like a weight I could no longer bear.

"I can't help anyone."

I clenched my jaw, fighting back tears. They came anyway, carving hot trails down my cheeks. I pressed my fists to my eyes to drive out the helplessness and the fury. I felt so small, so utterly alone and far away from home.

A soft breeze drifted in from the mouth of the alley, cooling the flushed, overheated skin of my neck. There was no one but me, myself, and Milo here. No one was coming to the rescue, and crying wasn't going to solve anything.

"No one's coming," I spat out in a wobbling voice, swiping at the wetness covering my face. "It's just me."

I had to overcome this. Only I could save us from the disaster we had landed in. With a deep, unsteady breath, I pushed myself upright on shaky legs and guided Milo gently out of the alley.

When we finally reached Crimson & Clover, the restaurant that Sorin and Odessa owned, my legs felt like lead, and Milo trudged beside me wearily.

Together, we climbed the stairs, crept down the quiet hallway, and into the small room. Milo headed straight for his water dish, lapping up every last drop before collapsing onto his dog bed with a soft, canine grunt.

After a long shower, I collapsed into bed, too tired to care that I was still naked. I picked up my phone, its screen casting a pale glow across the dark room.

A message from Sorin waited at the top.

> Sorin- Were you successful?

I stared at the screen, thumb hovering over the keys.

> Scarlet- No.

> Sorin- That bad?

I bit my lip, everything I couldn't say ricocheting inside my head. Setting the phone down, my thoughts drifted to Odessa's offer.

If there was even the slightest chance of saving Luke, I'd take it. Even without any hope for a future together, or if it meant getting myself further into whatever mess I was already in.

I held my breath, staring at the screen, then typed a message to Odessa.

> Scarlet- Are you free? I'd like to talk about your offer.

Odessa was busy, but we arranged a meeting over dinner for the following evening. In truth, I was relieved. My eyes burned with the effort of staying open. That could also be due to all the recent crying I'd done. It didn't matter. I let myself sink into the softness of my pint-sized bed, eyes drifting closed. Just as I was about to fall asleep, my phone buzzed with one last message from Sorin.

> Sorin- Make sure you lock your door.

I groaned, his reminder making me realize that I'd forgotten to do that very sensible action. Throwing off the blankets, I trudged across the room and turned the lock with a metallic click. Milo snored heavily in the corner. I bent and brushed a hand over his floppy ears as I passed him. Climbing back into bed, I closed my eyes, letting the steady rhythm of his snores lull me.

14

____

DOORS I SHOULDN'T OPEN

"Scarlet... Scarlet... Scaaarlet..."

My name rasped through the dark, drawn out in a coarse, grating chant that clawed me awake.

I jolted upright, hand scrabbling for the broken banister I'd left at the manor. Straining my eyes to pierce the pitch-dark room, the late-night silence raged against my ears. It was broken only by the faint sound of my own heart thundering in my chest as my eyes adjusted to the darkness.

There, between the bathroom door and the closet, the shadows bulged, gathering into a shape. My breath caught. My throat clenched around a scream that wouldn't come, the silence crushing it down into nothing. Nails bit deep into my palms until I felt the skin tear.

"Help me," I croaked, voice retreating from my terror. "Help!"

The shadow twitched, then lurched forward. Each dragging step stretched into eternity, as though time itself bent to its advance. I thrashed against invisible chains, forcing my trembling hand toward the light switch.

Click.

White light blasted across the room. I flinched, gasping, as spots blinked in my eyes. When my vision cleared, two indigo eyes stared back into mine.

I choked on a cry. "Sorin!"

At my bedside stood Milo and Sorin, with their heads cocked in uncanny unison. The canine tilt might have been endearing on Milo. On Sorin, it was disquieting.

"Was-" I glanced nervously past him toward the far corner of the room that remained unlit by the lamp, "-was I dreaming?"

Sorin extended a hand toward me, his fingers grazing my shoulder. I flinched back, clutching the blanket to my chest as it slipped precariously low over my bare skin.

"Yes, I think so."

His eyes drifted over the exposed curve of my side to the swell of my hip.

I clutched at the blanket tightly, fingers digging into the fabric as I demanded, "Why are you here?"

"I came to check on you. Your door was open," he glanced back toward the door, which now stood slightly ajar, creaking softly as it moved.

"That's not possible. I locked it right after you texted me."

Sorin's intense expression made my skin prickle with an odd, tingling dread.

"Are you sure?" he asked lowly.

I nodded, knowing I had locked it before I fell asleep. Wrapping myself tightly in the blanket, I stood and padded over to the door. I tried testing the lock a few times. It clicked into place each time, seemingly in perfect working order.

I rested my forehead against the cool wood, letting my eyes close. A faint pounding began behind my eyelids. My gut clenched with the unnerving certainty that someone had been in here while I slept.

"Are you well?" Sorin asked.

"I'm probably just tired." I took a deep breath, trying to shake off the horrific dream.

"I'm sorry I woke you," he said, taking a step toward the door. "I'll arrange for another lock to be installed on your door."

"Stay." My hand darted out, fingers shaking as I caught the cuff of his sleeve. "Just for a bit. Please."

He looked down at my hand. I braced myself for a dismissive remark or for him to pull away. But then he turned his hand, his knuckles tentatively grazing across my fingers. Just as I had done for him back at the safe house. Heart skipping a beat, my eyes met his.

The lamplight threw deep shadows across his face, sinking his eyes into hollows that made him look severe and otherworldly. For a fleeting second, I thought I saw some kindness in him. There and gone in an instant.

"Do you remember me doing that?" I asked breathlessly.

"I had a vague sense of it." There was something about the way he spoke, his voice so uncharacteristically soft. "It was warm."

It would've been a nice moment, if not for the wrongness hovering just outside my door. The awareness brushed over my skin, light as a breath, impossible to ignore.

"It feels like something is waiting out there," I turned to the hallway. "Like there's something just outside of my peripheral vision watching us."

Sorin's expression became guarded. He moved to the door, easing it open just enough to peer out. His broad frame blocked me from the exterior, shielding me from whatever lay beyond. I was struck by how oddly safe that made me feel. I was usually the one protecting others. Even at home, I insisted on sleeping closest to the door. His dark hair caught the dim light as it slid over his shoulder in a glint of movement as he searched the hall.

"I have a few minutes to stay," he said under his breath as he pulled his head back inside, shut the door with a quiet click, and locked it.

"Thank you."

I pulled out a pair of pajamas from the back of the closet and slipped into the bathroom to dress.

When I returned, I smoothed the blanket over the bed, sitting cross-legged with a pillow clutched tightly to my chest.

After a few minutes of awkward silence, Sorin asked, "What went wrong tonight?"

"I don't know," I hugged the pillow closer, unsure if I was ready to unravel the mess in my head. "At first, it seemed okay."

"And then?"

I swallowed, "He thought I didn't know anything."

Sorin's eyes fixed on the chandelier, "Did you tell him otherwise?"

"I tried. He was so angry. He just kept looking at me like I was..." I paused to swallow, my voice trailing off as the hurt settled in all over again.

"Like I was a monster," I finished lamely.

Sorin frowned slightly.

"I thought I had a chance of saving him. I thought maybe, somehow, we could work it out. Or at least part on decent terms. I wanted to help him."

I choked back a humorless laugh.

"Luke is lost," my shoulders slumped. "And I...I can't save him."

The painful truth lodged itself deep in my chest. I couldn't follow him down this path of self-destruction. I wasn't sure I could survive without him, either. If he—

A cool hand cupped my cheek, snapping me from the spiral. I leaned into it, eyes closing. I just needed the world to stop spinning for a moment.

"You're trembling," Sorin rumbled.

He sat beside me, the mattress dipping beneath his weight. My body shook so hard that the bed moved with me. When I opened my eyes, he was still watching. His thumb brushed across my cheek so softly, it almost hurt.

"Sometimes, the hardest thing," he murmured, "is knowing when to let go."

His words resonated in the hollow ache I'd been carrying since I first suspected Luke was seeing another woman. My lip wobbled. I bit down on it, hard, to keep the tears at bay. The sharp tang of iron flooded my mouth, and the momentary sting filled my mind. Gave me something better to focus on than heartache.

Sorin's hand stiffened against my cheek. His eyes darkened.

"You hurt yourself."

His thumb, which had been brushing just below my eye, slid to my lip. Pressing down, he pulled it gently from between my teeth until it slipped free with a soft pop. He leaned in closer, his thumb smearing the faint line of blood over my lip.

"Pain, it makes me forget," I admitted, eyes downcast so I could watch the rise and fall of his chest.

"There are other ways to forget, Scarlet," his voice became a husky whisper.

I watched, transfixed, as his tongue darted out. A flash of warmth against his skin as he cleaned the blood from his finger. A shock of desire rippled through me, sinking low in my belly.

"Allow me to show you."

My head tilted up, wavering between leaning closer and pulling back. Part of me craved the escape he offered, a distraction from the grief and pain. Another part resisted, rooted in the remnants of what felt like a crumbling morality. Besides the fact that I was still married, should I really be turned on by watching someone lap up my blood? My penchant for pain was rising to concerning levels.

"This is wrong," I said weakly.

"It feels right."

He was so close, the space between us barely there. His breath was warm against my skin, edging me closer to a line that couldn't be crossed. The grief and emptiness inside me were slowly being replaced by a dizzying heat. His scent enveloped me, pulling me into a world of pristine white snow. My eyes fluttered shut as I inhaled him. His hair brushed against my cheek, featherlight, and my fingers danced across the unspeakably soft waves.

"I—" My voice faltered as I struggled to reclaim even a sliver of space between us. "I'm sorry. I just can't."

Summoning every ounce of self-control in my possession, I forced myself back against the headboard, letting my head tip back in surrender to the growing distance.

Through the veil of my lashes, I watched his eyes travel down my body. They paused longer than they should on my too-heavy breasts. I quickly sat on my hands to keep them from wandering to the very places his attention lingered.

Sorin leaned forward as if to close the space again, then stopped short, exhaling heavily as he raked a hand through his long hair.

I opened my eyes a little wider, studying him in silence. What was really holding me back? Luke had made it abundantly clear there was no future for us. It was a question with an answer I wasn't ready for yet. My life was already going to hell in a handbasket; I didn't need to grease the wheels by getting freaky with Dracula's moody cousin.

What I definitely didn't need was to be thinking about how full and kissable his lips looked, or how his irises had dilated so wide I could see my own reflection in them. I couldn't focus on the little vein popping at his temple or imagine how that would look with him positioned over me as we—

I gave my brain a mental smack and booked that lewd thought a one-way ticket to horny jail. No visitors.

"Goodnight, Sorin," I whispered, half hoping he would do us both a favor and launch himself at me anyway.

Unspoken words flitted across his face, but he stood, brushing a hand over Milo's ear. Milo grunted, curling into a tighter ball at the foot of the bed.

Sorin paused in the doorway, a barrier against the encroaching shadows. The glow of my lamp caught his eye. The way it glinted sent my pulse skittering.

"Lock this door when I leave," he ordered.

I nodded once.

Once the door clicked shut, I bounded from the bed and slammed the deadbolt into place. A deep chuckle reverberated through the door. Receding footsteps faded into the hallway like the retreat of a stalking beast.

I cursed under my breath, pressing a trembling hand against my chest, trying to steady the frantic rhythm beneath. I let my head thunk against the hard surface. Something was seriously wrong with me.

My fingers ghosted over the spot where his thumb had brushed my lip, the phantom touch still burning on my flesh. I felt empty and overly sensitive at the same time, my skin prickling with an excruciating, unmet ache. When had I last been touched like that?

Months ago, at the very least. Possibly longer.

I squeezed my thighs together and sank to the floor, searching for some kind of friction to ease the throbbing between my legs. My hand traced the path Sorin had made with his eyes earlier. Palming my breast, I sucked in a breath as I rolled the nipple between my fingers and squeezed. My other hand clamped tightly over my mouth as I strained to hear beyond the door, listening for any hint of movement or the subtle creak of a floorboard. After a long stretch of silence, my hands continued their slow descent. Reaching into the waistband of my shorts, I slipped my fingers into my slick heat.

As my fingers circled around the bundle of nerves there, I squeezed my eyes shut. Images of Sorin flooded my mind's eye. I couldn't stop picturing the press of his thumb against my lip, imagining how it might feel to have his mouth on mine. How I might have answered by spreading my legs, pulling him against me. The thought of pressing into him sent a vicious orgasm tearing through my body.

I came hard and fast, my core clenching around empty air. Eventually, I clambered back into bed, feeling completely unsatisfied. A gnawing emptiness lingered deeper than my physical body. Loneliness weighed on my heart, coupled with no small amount of shame. That vacant throb sank deep into my chest.

Yanking the covers over my head like a flimsy shield, I clutched the edges of the blanket as though it could somehow keep the wolf at bay. As if they could protect me from the man with indigo eyes who had looked at me like I was something worth wanting. I couldn't shake the knowledge that this might be a wolf I might like to let in.

15

———————

THE NIGHTINGALE

Sweat dripped off my nose, splattering onto the textured black floor of the nearest gym I could find. After a restless night, I'd left early to walk Milo before the city woke and headed to the gym afterward. Now, I was bent over a weighted barbell. My lats strained as I pulled it up to my upper ribs, then slowly lowered it back down.

"Four," I huffed through gritted teeth. "Five, six—six."

My grip faltered. The sixth rep always felt impossible when I was lifting heavy.

"Six, goddamnit!"

My back and arms trembled with the effort, still tender from my scrap with Damian. Palms burning from gripping the bar, I set it down with a dull thud then straightened. My chest heaved as I sucked in deep breaths. An hour later, my arms hung like dead weight, and a faint twinge ran through my back. But it still didn't feel like enough.

I craved the challenge of grappling. I wanted to face the raw aggression of facing another person. To walk the razor-thin margin between focus and failure that ended in a punishing submission. But every time I thought of stepping back onto the mat, Valerie's face rose up to meet me. The screams of burning bodies tolled like funeral bells in my head, and my hand still remembered the shudder of wood punching through a chest.

Would I ever roll again without those memories dragging me under? Or was I doomed to freeze, stuck in an endless highlight reel of blood and bad decisions?

Using a towel to wipe the sweat from my face, I attempted to banish the worrying thoughts. I headed toward the exit with my bag slung over my shoulder.

The walk back to Crimson & Clover didn't do much for my mental health. The day was gloomy and a bit muggy for September. I dropped my bag on the bed with a thud.

Milo padded over to greet me with gentle sniffs, his tail wagging like I was the highlight of his day. I wished I could borrow some of his fathomless optimism. I wanted to be stronger than this. I wanted to go back to who I was before I was burdened by the unshakable ghosts of the vampires I had killed in self-defense.

Well, I hadn't exactly killed *all* of them. More like inadvertently contributed to their deaths. Damian was the only one I could technically claim as mine. I snorted to myself. Maybe there was a vampire slayer organization out there that would take me and Luke in. Although I wasn't sure how far I'd get with a résumé that read: *Accidentally killed around seven vampires. Will bring snacks.*

Peeling back the thick curtain, I looked out across the sundrenched cityscape unfolding before me. Ant-sized people milled through the streets, embarking on their own morning routines. I found a comforting anonymity in watching so many of them going about their daily lives. We were all just doing our best to make it.

I just needed to get through one more day. Maybe I needed to try, one last time, to salvage the wreckage of my marriage, to save my husband from the path he'd chosen. Shit, maybe I needed a therapist. Or a priest. Or both.

Stripping off my sweat-soaked clothes, I shuffled into the bath-room to shower. I didn't notice the bottles at first, tucked neatly into the corner of the shower shelf. The heavy glass casings were covered in black labels and adorned with a small bee.

Curious, I unscrewed the cap and leaned in, sniffing cautiously. Honey. The same honey scent from the safe house, or hotel, or what-ever that place had been. My lips twitched into a smirk. Sorin must have really liked the smell.

"Don't mind if I do," I rifled through the collection of shampoo, conditioner, body wash, and even the same body oil.

It was ridiculous, really, how a set of premium skincare products could shift my mood. But damn if a twinge of happiness didn't wriggle its way into my weary heart. After my shower, I set up camp on the bed with my laptop to tackle what I could for the museum.

Emails flooded my inbox, most of them answerable with a two-second web search. I slogged through digital catalogs, updated spreadsheets, and ticked off the endless drudgery that came with museum upkeep. It almost felt like a normal day.

Except, of course, for the fact that I was working from an ancient vampire's skyscraper, lusting after said vampire and preparing to spend the evening with his partner. Who I was... double-crossing? Triple-crossing? Whatever—betraying both worked.

Not to mention this all started because I killed my husband's mistress. My husband, who now hated me and wandered New York as a blood-addicted junkie. Right. All that.

Staring blankly at the wall, willed my mind into silence. The endless loop of guilt, grief, and self-doubt was grueling. My eyelids dipped lower as the exhaustion of another sleep-deprived night crept over me.

Milo woke me with a nudge to my hand, followed by an insistent growl. I peeled my eyelids open and squinted. The room was bathed in a streak of sunset orange.

"Sorry, buddy," I wiped the sleep from my eyes, swinging my legs off the bed. "Let's go outside."

After a short walk, he bounded up the stairs next to me. I, on the other hand, was dragging. By the time we reached the bedroom door, I felt like I could collapse straight back into bed. I blamed the blood hangover on my lack of energy.

Pulling out my phone, I confirmed the 9 p.m. meeting with Odessa. I looked at Milo. The goof was already curled up on his bed as if his work for the day was done.

"You're so lucky you don't have to deal with any of this vampire bullshit," I sighed.

I couldn't help but feel a little nervous as I pulled on a clean black blouse and brushed my hair. Odessa had this disarming way about her. But maybe that was just the thing about vampires. They made it impossible to tell if you liked them, hated them, wanted to fuck them, or if they simply made you feel something too powerful to categorize.

I dabbed on a touch of makeup, scrutinizing myself in the mirror. My blue-gray eyes were rimmed with kohl, my chestnut brown hair pulled back into a sleek ponytail, and my lips were tinted a subtle berry-red. I looked fine. But my gaze lacked warmth, like I'd left behind some vital part of me that felt farther away every day.

Forcing a smile, I watched as my lips lifted one corner at a time. I thought I'd read somewhere that even fake smiling could trick your brain into happiness. To me, I just looked like I'd wandered out of a terrible mugshot. I let the smile drop with a sigh.

Milo watched me from his dog bed, his dark eyes wide and patient. I glanced at my phone. Still an hour to kill before Odessa. Milo had been cooped up all day. He deserved more than just the five-minute "do your business" routine.

"Fancy another walk, my love?"

His ears perked up. I couldn't resist bending down and planting a few fat kisses on the top of his massive head before we headed out into the night. The energy of the city seemed to hum a little louder at night. People spilled out of bars, couples strolled hand in hand, and the occasional street vendor hawked late-night snacks. It wasn't entirely unpleasant.

Finishing our walk, we came around the backside of the restaurant, near the double iron doors I'd been using to come and go. A smaller door swung open, a familiar face peeking out. It was the light-skinned man who had given me his coat.

We locked eyes. I struggled to remember his name.

"Hi," he said.

"Uh—hi."

I gripped Milo's leash a little tighter to keep him from wandering over for pets. Milo, of course, was undeterred by my efforts.

"Odessa is looking for you," he said, pushing the door open wider.

A warm wave of garlic and thyme scents wafted out from the hallway behind him. My stomach reminded me that I hadn't eaten all day with a loud growl.

"Oh, it's not quite nine yet," I stammered, feeling a little flustered. "Let me return Milo, and I'll be right there."

"She said you can bring the dog."

He gave a polite smile.

"Thanks... I mean, uh, okay. That works," I smiled back, letting Milo edge forward.

"I'm Malik, by the way," he introduced himself, stepping aside to let me in.

"Scarlet," I replied, following him inside. "And this is Milo."

Malik led me through a maze of sizzling pans, clattering dishes, and the occasional bark of a chef's voice. We entered a small, private dining room tucked away from the restaurant's bustling atmosphere.

I sat at a large polished mahogany table set for two. Soft candlelight cast a golden glow on the walls as I looked around, half expecting Odessa to already be waiting.

"She'll be here shortly. Make yourself comfortable. I'll let her know you've arrived."

"Thanks," I unhooked Milo's leash as he flopped contentedly at my feet. "For everything."

I looked at him meaningfully. He put a finger to his lip, winked, then left me in silence.

Waiting to have dinner with a vampire felt bizarre. It was like I'd wandered into a cheesy Halloween movie, just waiting for the comic relief to show up with a one-liner that would make a paid audience chuckle on cue.

But then again, that had been my reality for a while now. I was living life in the shoes of a strange, lonely woman. On an exhale, I rested my forehead in my hands, elbows braced against the hard table. Milo curled into a tight ball on top of my feet. His warmth spread into my toes, still chilled from the fall air. I allowed the warmth and the faint hum of the restaurant to lull me into a fragile sort of peace.

The doors swung open. I jerked upright as Odessa entered, wearing a crisp chef's coat and a wide smile. Two other chefs followed behind her, wheeling trays of steaming food that immediately filled the room with mouthwatering scents.

Milo leaped up to greet her. His tail wagged furiously as he nudged a friendly nose under her hand. To her credit, Odessa only faltered slightly before patting him.

"Hello, my darling," she said to me.

I managed a weak smile, but the effort felt like dragging a stone uphill. For some reason, the sight of this vibrant, friendly woman made me want to break down into hysterics.

"Hey," I said in a wobbly voice, unsure if I could hold it together much longer.

"I heard last night didn't go well," she said, resting a light hand on my shoulder.

I shook my head quickly, trying to hold back the flood rising in my chest, but it was too late.

My eyes filled with tears, and my throat tightened as I choked out, "Sorry."

"Oh, honey," Odessa shooed the staff out of the room with a flick of her hand before wrapping me in a firm hug.

It was completely disarming, breaking some hard knot loose inside me. I let the tears fall as I sank into her embrace.

"Let it out," her voice was soft in my ear.

Milo pressed his head against my leg as I tearfully re-told my story of what happened with Luke. When I finally pulled myself together, my throat felt raw and scratchy. I hiccuped embarrassingly loud.

"Men are the devil's work," she said, sweeping over to the trays to uncover them with a practiced flourish.

Steam billowed out, carrying the rich scents of roast chicken, savory gravy, shepherd's pie, and French onion soup. Several kinds of bread accompanied the spread, with thick pads of butter that gleamed like golden silk under the soft lighting.

"But if there's one thing I remember from my years as a human, it's that good food can soothe any wound."

Odessa placed each dish in front of me as though she were presenting treasures.

"Thanks, but I'm not really hungry," I stared at the feast.

My hunger from earlier had vanished, leaving behind a queasy, empty feeling.

"I know the look of a woman who hasn't eaten all day," she chided, pushing the plate of roast chicken closer to me.

"And besides, I'm working on a new menu tonight. Could you do me a favor and taste-test these for me? It's not the same if I do it. We have different tastes."

The corners of her mouth quirked slightly.

Reluctantly, I picked up the knife with the idea of cutting the chicken into minuscule cubes. If they were small enough, I could force myself to eat without vomiting.

Odessa settled across from me, pouring a thick, amber liquid into a glass from a sleek black bottle..

"What's that?" I asked, determined not to meet her eyes as I carefully speared a microscopic bite with my fork.

It all but melted on my tongue, and I couldn't help but shut my eyes as I chewed, no longer worried about feeling sick. If I was going to vomit from eating, this meal would be well worth it.

"It's Sorin's little project," Odessa glanced at the bottle, then smiled, swirling the liquid in her glass. "Bottled blood tastes like shit, but it does the trick in a pinch."

I coughed, the mention of Sorin unearthing thoughts of last night I wasn't ready to discuss.

"What was it like?" I asked. "Your human life?"

Odessa stared into her glass as though it might contain an answer. Her lips pressed into a thin line.

"It was not a happy life."

"Was that rude of me to ask?" I put the fork down, regretting the question immediately. "You don't have to tell me—"

"It's alright," she interrupted coolly. "I was born in Louisiana in 1895. It was... well, it was loud."

She refilled her glass and drained it in two gulps, as if swallowing down the memory itself.

"I was a singer," she said, her thin fingers brushing the column of her neck.

I chewed the inside of my cheek, mind racing through what I knew of Louisiana at the turn of the century. My throat tightened.

"Jim Crow?"

Her answering nod was dark enough to silence the room.

"Singing was the closest thing to freedom I could touch. I remember those clubs along the river, choked up with tobacco smoke—you could hardly breathe, let alone sing. They called me the 'nightingale,' dressed me in feathers and sequins. The applause was sweet, but the eyes on me," She pressed her finger along the rim of her goblet until it rang, high and shrill, like a soprano's note about to shatter. "The eyes never let me forget I was entertainment, not equal. Still, when I opened my mouth, for those few minutes, I was untouchable. Music gave me power before I knew what real power was. And when the song ended, the world put me back in my place."

Her mouth curled bitterly.

"I'm so sorry," I said softly, the words feeling inadequate in the face of such suffering.

She waved a hand dismissively, though her expression didn't soften.

"What happened to me wasn't even the worst story from that time. I've lived long enough to know that much. But what they didn't expect," her eyes glinted dangerously, "was that I was a survivor."

The steel in her voice sent a chill rippling through me. I was both entranced and horrified by her story.

"When I got older, I found friends in higher places," Odessa let out a vitriolic laugh, and I jumped. "But even that small taste of power came at a cost."

Lifting her left leg, she rolled up her pants to reveal a jagged scar carving its way across her calf and behind her knee. The skin there was gnarled and discolored, its texture rougher than the rest of her flawless complexion.

"My new connections sent me to steal from an old plantation master," she said flatly, as if reciting the weather. "They set the dogs on me." Her eyes narrowed, voice dropping to a lethal whisper. "And then they left me for dead."

Her eyes flicked to Milo, who snored softly in the corner.. A shadow crossed her face before she readjusted her pant leg and took another sip of her drink.

"That's when I was turned," she said, folding back into that calm, composed woman.

I wanted to say something to make it better. But there was nothing I could offer that wouldn't feel shallow compared to her story.

"Now," she said, setting her glass down with delicate finality and gesturing toward the food. "Try the shepherd's pie before it goes cold. I'd hate for all that effort to be wasted."

I nodded dumbly, lifting my fork, though her story still throbbed in my head. Beneath the charm and beauty, Odessa was carved from steel. A survivor who would claw her way through anything, no matter the cost. I couldn't decide if that made her a woman to admire or to fear.

"Now, about your husband. What's his name again?" Odessa asked.

"Luke," my voice was muffled by the mouthful of mashed potatoes.

"Yes, Luke." She fixed me with a penetrating stare. "Are you ready for my help yet?"

"Yes."

I'd been ready since the moment she first offered. Like her, I thought I was willing to do whatever it took to survive.

"Good!" Odessa chirped, her demeanor shifting instantly as a bright smile curved her lips. "Allow me to call in some assistance."

She picked up her phone, fingers flying across the screen as she murmured, "These things really are a marvelous bit of ingenuity."

The moment the text was sent, the door banged open with explosive force. A tall woman strode in. She had broad shoulders, olive-toned skin, and piercing dark eyes that measured the space in analytical silence. I could tell at once she was a fighter. Everything about her radiated strength. It was in the way she held herself, the unshakable confidence in her stride. She crossed to Odessa, cupped her face with one hand, and kissed her full on the lips.

I choked on my water, caught completely off guard by the passionate display. My hand flew to my chest as I coughed. My eyes watered from the sudden assault on my windpipe.

"Carmen!" Odessa laughed as she pulled back. "I haven't told Scarlet about us yet."

"Are you embarrassed?" Carmen teased, her words colored by a smooth Hispanic accent.

She tipped Odessa's chin upward with two fingers, her thumb brushing lightly over her cheek.

"Of course not," Odessa replied, pecking Carmen's lips again. "I was just waiting for the right moment before you came blasting in."

I couldn't help but smile. There was something oddly heart-warming about Carmen's powerful energy juxtaposed with Odessa's elegance.

Carmen turned to me, "So, you're the one who's stolen the attention of my Odessa."

"Um, I guess?"

I looked at Odessa for a lifeline.

"She's been through a lot," Odessa placed a hand on Carmen's arm. "Be gentle."

"Gentle isn't my specialty," Carmen replied, a sly smile tugging at her lips. "But for you, I'll try."

"It isn't really my thing either," I offered with more of a grimace than a smile.

"Odessa tells me you fight," she said, settling into her chair and draping an arm casually around Odessa, who poured her a matching glass of what I could only assume was blood.

"I mostly teach grappling," I replied, avoiding looking at the red stain around Carmen's lips. "Jiu-jitsu, specifically, at a small gym back in Georgia."

"Scarlet is very strong," Odessa said with a wink, sinking deeper into the crook of Carmen's arm. "She killed Valerie."

For the second time, I inhaled my drink wrong, dissolving into a coughing fit that burned my lungs. I barely managed to keep from choking outright, clutching at the table as I fought to maintain what little dignity I had left.

"Really?" Carmen chuckled, her dark eyes lighting up with intrigue. "Now *that* is interesting."

I frowned as I set down my water.

"Is there anything stronger than water in here?"

Odessa reached behind herself to a sleek drink trolley, producing a crystal decanter of amber liquid. She poured a generous measure into a glass and slid it across the table.

"I believe Valerie was Scarlet's first. First kill that is."

"Valerie was a whore," Carmen sniffed, her lip curling slightly. "I'm glad she's dead."

"Wish I could say the same," I muttered.

I wrapped my fingers around the glass. Lifting it to my lips, I took a deep drag, savoring the burn of fine bourbon as it slid down my throat. When I closed my eyes to relish it, Valerie's jade-green gaze flashed behind my eyelids. My eyes flew open, the taste suddenly pungent.

"How did you do it?" Carmen asked, draining her glass in a single smooth motion. "You are human, are you not?"

"It was more of an accident," I looked away from them to a very interesting spec on the wall.

Carmen motioned for me to continue, so I swallowed hard and went on.

"She underestimated me. There was a ledge, I swept her over it."

Carmen nodded sagely.

"Pushing her off the ledge would have seriously injured Valerie, but not killed her," Odessa tapped her nails across the surface of the table. "So what happened next?"

The bloody memory of Valerie's impaled body hooked itself deep into the gray matter of my skull. I needed a moment, so I blurted, "I saw Sorin."

"Sorin?" Carmen's eyebrows shot up in surprise while Odessa nodded in confirmation.

"Yes," Odessa said quickly. "Sorin had followed her after that incident I told you about at the restaurant."

"Very well," Carmen said impatiently, "but how did you kill her?"

"She—" I cleared my throat. The words tasted of bile. "She fell onto some rebar. It went through her heart, I think."

I fought the urge to gag as the memory overwhelmed me.

My words were brittle and distant, as though I were recounting someone else's story. But the vivid image of her blood, the resistance of metal ripping through wet flesh, and the sound of her gasps were all mine to live with. I stared at my hands, suddenly cold.

"Death can be difficult to process when you've been sheltered from it," Odessa smiled sympathetically at me. "But we are not here to dwell on death tonight. We're here to discuss getting Luke back for you."

16

____

PULSE IN THE DARK

I tried to squelch the little leap of hope that fluttered in my chest at Odessa's words. Hope was a dangerous thing that I didn't need. What I needed were actionable solutions. Draining the last of my bourbon in one determined swallow, I straightened in my seat.

"Carmen has volunteered to help you retrieve Luke," Odessa said as her fingers traced the sharp line of Carmen's jaw.

My hands fisted in my lap as I waited for the catch.

"From your description, Luke has regressed farther than I anticipated," Odessa said.

My mouth flattened into a tight line as Luke's skeletal face crossed my mind.

"He will need medical intervention once we find him again."

"I can get his location from Sorin," I offered. "He gave me Luke's location last night."

"He did?" An unhappy expression crossed her face, but she quickly smoothed it away. "Interesting."

I winced. Smooth, Scarlet. Sneakiness was *obviously* not my thing. At this rate, I wasn't playing both sides. I was basically handing out flyers announcing *Welcome to my double-cross!*

But really, what reason would either of them have to keep secrets from each other? They were supposed to be partners of some kind. But it was clear enough that these two didn't exactly see eye to eye.

"What kind of partnership do you have with Sorin?" I ventured.

Odessa's head tipped back, surprise flashing across her sculpted features.

"Sorin didn't tell you?"

"I tried asking. He wasn't exactly forthcoming with answers."

I waggled my eyebrows like we were discussing a bad landlord or the DMV. This was how I played them against each other for information. Or at least, that was the plan. If by plan I meant clumsy improvisation.

Odessa huffed a knowing laugh.

"I am Sorin's Lieutenant, for now."

"Sounds like there's more to that," I leaned forward, practically wagging my tail like a golden retriever waiting for the ball.

Odessa's smile deepened, but before she could elaborate, Carmen checked the golden watch strapped to her thick wrist.

"Later," she interjected firmly. "We're short on time."

Disappointment slumped my shoulders.

"You're right, of course," Odessa patted Carmen's thigh. "Get Luke's location again. "We'll bring him back here."

"Here? But won't he need a hospital?"

"It's not the same kind of medicine," Odessa replied. "Besides, the policy is to kill blood addicts before they reach that level of dependency or need that amount of care. It's a matter of discretion."

"So why help him at all?" I asked, but I wasn't sure I wanted to hear the answer.

"I like you, Scarlet." Odessa's lips lifted into an unnerving smile as she reached out to squeeze my hand. "You're like us. Strong. A survivor. And survivors deserve allies—friends in higher places. Call it passing the favor along."

I felt as though her eyes were flaying me alive, bearing every secret thought I had onto the table between us. Goosebumps covered me, and I had to fight the urge to shudder and rub my arms.

Over the next hour, we mapped out a bulletproof plan. I'd give Luke one last chance to come willingly. If he refused, Carmen would handle it. While I was capable of dragging him back myself, it would cause too much of a scene. Carmen would get him into a waiting car and down to a basement room Odessa claimed had "the necessities." However, she hadn't elaborated on what that meant. We talked until Milo stirred, stretched, and gave a polite whine by the door.

"A dog!" Carmen exclaimed as her gaze darted nervously between Odessa and Milo.

"It's alright, dear," Odessa soothed with a tight smile. "Milo is a friend of Scarlet's and, therefore, a friend of ours."

Carmen gave her a doubtful look but settled back down, placing herself between Odessa and Milo.

"I was beginning to think our Scarlet had shifter blood," she muttered, tugging Odessa closer. "Glad to know I'm not losing my mind."

Prickling at the jab about my personal scent—and maybe a little protective of Milo—I gathered his leash, giving him an extra scratch behind the ears for good measure. Ignoring the shifter comment was a conscious choice. My brain already had enough reality-bending truths on its plate without adding werewolves to the buffet.

"Go find Sorin. The sooner we have Luke, the better," Odessa ordered.

I nodded automatically, pausing mid-motion when I realized I had no idea where Sorin actually was. My confusion must have been evident because Carmen spoke up.

"There's a club two floors down," Carmen said with an air of disinterest. "He's normally running things down there this time of night."

"Oh," I replied, feeling a little out of my depth.

I hadn't been to a club in years. They weren't really my scene.

"You might consider changing," Odessa said as she slid gracefully into Carmen's lap. "Sorin can be a prickly bastard. And the quickest way to a man's heart is through his pants."

They laughed together. Heat crept up my neck, but I couldn't muster a response. I turned and left, their laughter trailing after me as I tried to get my head on straight for what I was about to do.

I hadn't packed anything remotely suitable for a club. Despite last night's questionable encounter, I had no intention of making good on Odessa's suggestion about getting into Sorin's pants. What I had on would have to do.

Still, I made a small effort by brushing my teeth and reapplying lipstick. Life always felt better with clean teeth and a little color on your lips.

Before leaving, I turned to look longingly at my warm little bed. Milo was curled into a tight ball on his dog bed beside it. It would have been so much easier to crawl under the covers, pull the blankets over my head, and spend the evening pretending like nothing existed outside of my little cocoon of safety.

My foot reached toward the bed. I pulled it back with a heavy sigh. Shoving my phone, the room key, and some cash into my pockets, I straightened. Hiding wouldn't solve anything. No one was coming to save either Luke or me. I had to suck it up and save myself.

Hand on the door handle, I rolled my shoulders back and whispered, "Nobody's coming but yourself."

I locked it behind me and headed for the stairwell. The club was easy enough to find. The deeper I went, the harder the bass thudded through the floor, rattling the walls until I reached a pair of double utility doors. The sound beyond was so loud it made the handles quiver in their frame.

I grimaced, momentarily tempted to plug my ears before stepping inside. I grasped the vibrating handle and pulled the door confidently toward me, willing my heartbeat to steady. Too late to back out now. I stepped into the dark hallway, squinting against strobing red lights as I moved past the bathrooms toward the central room.

Did vampires even need bathrooms? They had to consume something, and I couldn't help but wonder if that led to the obvious biological consequences. The heavy doors clanged shut behind me. I tested the handle. Locked.

"I'm trapped in vampire hell, and my last thought was vampire bowel movements," I grumbled as I stepped forward into a cavernous space bathed in swaths of rich crimson and inky black.

Every decadent inch screamed old money. Plush velvet drapery cascaded from the high ceilings. Glints of gold accents framed the room like veins snaking through the walls.

Above, cages hung suspended from the vaulted ceilings, filled with dancers who moved with a hypnotic sensuality. The ironwork glistened under the moody lights, their occupants just out of reach of the crowd below. Every sway of the cages dared the crowd to reach for their forbidden, gleaming bodies.

Several bars glittered across the space, their obsidian counters manned by bartenders who moved with the precision of performers. Shadowed alcoves lined the walls, promising stolen moments or maybe places you entered and never came out.

The very air throbbed with decadence and lust. It clung to the dancers, a feverish sheen blurring one body into the next. Hands grazed my arms, stroking with uninvited familiarity.

Before I realized it, I was moving too—bobbing to the beat, swaying with the crowd's rhythm. I pinched my arm hard, trying to break the spell. I wasn't here to drown in the music. I was here for Sorin. The sooner I found him, the sooner I could leave.

Scanning the room, I searched for the most likely spot he might be. Sorin was a man who enjoyed observing and studying. Well, he liked staring at me anyway. If I were him, where would I lurk?

My gaze snagged on a shadowy balcony draped in velvet. Bingo. Perfect vulture perch.

I quickened my pace, weaving through the crowd. Even if he

wasn't up there, at least I'd get a decent vantage point and maybe a break from the bass trying to fuse with my ribcage.

Slipping through a doorway beneath the balcony, I climbed a narrow staircase, hand sliding along the cold rail. The sudden hush was jarring after the riot below.

The stairs ended at the balcony, conspicuously lacking one broody, long-haired vampire with a mustache too perfect for its own good.

"Shit," I hissed under my breath.

Pulling out my phone, I fired off a text to Sorin.

Scarlet- Looking for you. We need to talk.

I walked forward to the railing, leaning against its polished edge. Staying close to the velvet curtain, I let its soft, cool fabric brush my cheek as I surveyed the crowd below.

There had to be at least a hundred people down there, each a potential dead end in my search. The flashing lights and pounding music were too disorienting. My chest tightened with frustration. Finding Sorin in this writhing sea of bodies felt like trying to pick one vampire out of a Twilight convention.

With my eyes closed, I tried to reach for Sorin through that strange thread between us. On a slow inhale, I searched for the bridge I'd once felt. Only silence remained there. The buzz of my phone shattered the fragile calm I had created.

Sorin- Where are you?

Scarlet - In the club. I don't see you.

I watched the typing bubbles dance on the screen. The delay stretched my nerves until, finally, his response flashed on the screen.

Sorin- I see you.

My eyes snapped back to the crowd, scanning for that familiar shock of black hair. Creeping forward, I leaned cautiously over the ledge. The room flashed in strobes of red and pitch black. Red and black, light and dark. The colors bled together in a head-spinning rhythm. The crowd pulsed in time with the infectious beat that my breath had begun syncing with.

But still, I didn't see him.

The hairs on the back of my neck prickled, and goosebumps rippled across my arms. As the next pulse of red faded quickly into darkness, a hand wrapped firmly around my waist. I was spun around, my stomach lurching as a scream clawed its way up my throat.

It never escaped. Another hand clamped over my mouth, muffling any sound as I was shoved back into the wall beside the doorway. The velvet curtain cushioned the impact as I struggled to suck in breath around the fingers at my mouth.

Red light bathed the balcony, illuminating Sorin like a portrait of sin itself. His depthless eyes caught the light, gleaming with... arrogance? Amusement? I couldn't tell. My heart stuttered, eyes wandering over the sharp planes of his face, lingering on the line of his jaw and the slight tilt of his head. Those full lips were quirked in a reserved smile. In between the pulses of red, I strained to hold his image in my mind.

"Screaming down here would be unwise."

His hand slipped from my mouth, the loss of its pressure sending a lick of heat through me.

"What are you doing down here?" he asked, resting both hands on my waist.

They were so large that they nearly met at the small of my back.

"I—" My voice caught, and I licked my lips, tasting him. "I need to ask you something."

His smile grew as though he could see every salacious thought I tried to bury.

"You couldn't have texted me?"

"I hate texting," I breathed.

The music thundered on, too loud even for his preternatural hearing. He stepped closer, brushing back his hair with a slow motion to expose one ear. Perhaps the music was meant to drown out voices in a room full of heightened senses. My hands found their way to his chest, hovering lightly over the soft fabric of his white, linen shirt.

I pressed down, using him as a brace to lean in and repeat myself.

My fingers skimmed the edge of his shirt where a few undone buttons teased the dark curl of chest hair beneath. Heat radiated through the thin fabric, sparking along my skin. My breath caught as my gaze followed the shadows carved across his chest, every line an invitation I had no business accepting. Inevitably, my eyes rose to the dangerous curve of his mouth.

"Don't look at me like that," his words vibrated with a feral edge.

He smelled of winter air and dark frankincense.

"Like what?"

Neither of us moved. The world seemed to narrow to the air caught my heartbeats. A delicious pressure coiled between my legs until I pressed my thighs tightly together. His pupils blew wide, irises catching the red light like dying embers.

"Careful," he warned, jaw clenching tightly.

His hands didn't move, but he pressed closer. He had this gravitational pull I couldn't seem to resist. Blinking hard, I forced myself to focus. This wasn't why I was here. But the way his eyes kept landing on my lips before darting back to my eyes robbed me of the ability to think clearly.

"Sorin," I whispered in what might have been a warning of my own.

The world below us carried on, laughter carrying up from the crowd. It pushed me into the reality of everything that couldn't, shouldn't, be acknowledged.

"I need you to find Luke again," I said bluntly.

I shouldn't be feeling this way. I should be happy that I stopped myself from making out with the monster in front of me. I should be thinking about Luke.

"Why?" He asked.

Unguarded disappointment filled his face before he dropped his head slightly, eyes falling from mine.

"I have to try again." I kept my face neutral, unwilling to acknowledge his reaction. "I'm not ready to give up yet."

"Are you sure?"

"I'm sure."

"When do you need it?"

The physical space between us didn't change, but his tone placed him miles away. I had to stop myself from reaching out and trying to pull him back.

"Soon," I said, looking away and biting my lip hard enough to feel the sting of the cut from the night before.

His hand rushed up, grabbing my chin and lifting it upwards. His frown deepened, his eyes flicking down to my mouth. Without warning, he closed the distance between us and swept his tongue across my lips.

Startled, my mouth parted open, allowing him entry. His tongue traced over the stinging sensation caused by my teeth. He withdrew just as quickly, leaving me flushed and breathless.

"Don't bleed here," he said, head nodding toward the crowd.

My hand flew to my lips, meaning to erase the feeling. But I pressed against them, trying to catch the memory of his tongue.

" I-I need to find Luke as soon as possible," I huffed, jerking my head away.

"You don't sound happy about that," Sorin's breath brushed against my cheek.

"Why the fuck would I be?" I snapped, the words spilling in a clash of discontent and confusion.

It wasn't my best moment, but anger was an easy balm to my confusion.

"Then why bother at all?"

"Because I can't quit," I hissed.

My fingers clenched the luxurious fabric of his shirt, pulling him closer as my voice cracked.

"Because I won't let him die while there's still a chance to save him. If he dies before I've done everything—*everything*—I can to save him, then I don't know how to go on. I'm all he has left. No one else cares, and I won't just stand by and let him destroy himself."

If Luke died, a piece of me would go with him. I might as well let myself die, too. I didn't realize I was crying until Sorin's thumb brushed the wetness from my cheek.

"Alright," His voice softened as he placed a large hand on the back of my head, pulling me against him. "Alright, don't cry. I'll help."

My breath steadied as I leaned into his chest, my frantic heartbeat clashing against the unnatural stillness of his.

When he pulled away, his expression slipped back into its usual mask of cool detachment.

"Give me one hour."

He pulled out his phone, scrolling and texting rapidly.

Without looking up, he asked, "What will you do with him this time?"

I felt my shoulders tense at his question.

"Let me worry about that."

He paused mid-motion, searching my face.

I broke our eye contact, "Don't ask questions you don't want the answers to."

His lips twitched, but he returned to his phone without another word, leaving the silence between us to speak for itself.

"As concerning as that statement is, I need you to leave now," Sorin said, shoving his phone into the pocket of his tailored black pants.

"Why?"

"You're distracting." His hand found the small of my back, guiding me toward the stairs. "Don't take it personally."

I could practically hear the smile tugging at his lips.

"Don't worry, Sorin. I'd have to take *you* personally first, and that requires a pulse." I quipped, feeling the sting of his dismissal a little too sharply for comfort.

His smirk vanished, replaced by a glacial stillness.

"There's someone important visiting tonight, and I need to be able to focus."

I shrugged. This was probably for the best, I had more important things to focus on myself. Soon, I'd have Luke's location, and I needed to let Carmen and Odessa know the plan was a go.

"Fine, but small problem." I looked around. "I have no idea where the hell the exit is."

The alcoves all looked the same, and the doors I came through had locked behind me.

"How did you even get in?" he chuckled.

"The utility stairwell. Don't judge me. It locked behind me," I muttered.

"Then back that way." His hand pressed lightly to my back as he steered me through the crowd, who barely spared us a glance. "I'll let you out."

We were nearing the bathrooms when a male voice boomed behind us.

"Sorin? Is that you?"

17

HANDCUFFS AND TRASH BAGS

Sorin's hand stiffened on my back. In an instant, he spun around, positioning his body so my face pressed in between his shoulder blades.

"Paul!" Sorin spread his arms wide in a gesture that further shielded me. "You're early."

Before I could decide whether to step back or stay put, a massive figure loomed over Sorin. He was easily a head taller with broad shoulders that filled the narrow hallway. A thick, red beard framed his brutish face. His hair was the same fiery hue, and his eyes were empty. It was as though every drop of feeling had been siphoned out of them. He looked like a lumberjack turned warlord, dressed in a tailored coat that barely contained his massive frame.

With a hearty laugh that didn't reach those dead eyes, he clapped Sorin on the back hard enough to rock Sorin slightly.

"Well, you know me," Paul said, his voice carrying a slight twang that spoke of a rural life. "Couldn't keep away."

"How was dinner?" Sorin stepped to Paul's side and began to guide him away.

"Filling," Paul replied good-naturedly, though his massive feet remained planted. His eyes were fixed on me. "But you know, I'm always saving room for seconds."

My teeth clenched as I took a half step back. Paul would've been big enough to kill me with a single hit as a mortal man. As a vampire, I figured my best defense was hoping I didn't look like dessert.

"Paul," Sorin's tone took on an edge of authority. "This is Scarlet Montgomery. She is a guest."

The word *guest* came with a subtle emphasis. It was an unmistakable implication of protection, a claim to territory. The meaning wasn't lost on Paul or me.

"A guest," he repeated with a wolfish grin. "Isn't that interesting?"

"I need to be going now," I tried to make myself appear as small and insignificant as possible. "So, Sorin, if you could just let me out, I'll be on my way."

"Indeed," Sorin was already steering me to the door by the elbow.

I barely registered the soft beeps as he punched in a code on a keypad mounted to the wall. My attention was locked on Paul. He remained where he was, his piercing stare fixed on me.

My instincts screamed at me not to look away, as if turning my back might trigger his prey drive. The doors finally swung open. Sorin gave me a firm shove through the doorway, unceremoniously depositing me into the corridor.

"Goodbye—" I started, but Sorin had already turned back to Paul before the doors hissed shut.

Racing back up to the room, I slipped into joggers, a hoodie, and my trusty jean jacket. It wasn't much, but it would have to do for the cold night. There had been a record cold snap; temperatures would plummet to near freezing tonight. The minutes crawled by as I waited, twisting the wedding band on my finger until the skin beneath it burned.

Half an hour later, the coordinates were glowing on the screen.

I left Milo behind and hailed a taxi. City lights streaked by until we pulled up to, what else, another ominous alley. I sighed. Why break tradition? A rustle by the dumpster drew my eye. There was Luke, huddled beneath trash bags like a tragic raccoon.

"Luke!" I called, my voice warping around the walls of the alley.

He looked up, his lips tinged blue, his nose bright red against the almost waxy tone of his skin. Before doing anything else, I fumbled for my phone and sent my location to Odessa. I turned to Luke, slowly approaching as his sour stench hit me.

"Luke," I said softly, breathing through my mouth.

He shuffled back like a frightened animal, his movements jerky and uncoordinated. I slipped off my jacket, holding it out to him as I took another cautious step forward.

"Put this on. You're freezing."

His eyes darted between me and the jacket before snatching it with a sudden, uncanny speed. I flinched back as he wrapped it around his shoulders.

The sight of him in my jacket made my stomach drop. Luke was usually at least two sizes larger than I was. My jacket hung off his frame the same way his clothes used to hang off mine. I crossed my arms over my chest, trying to conserve what little warmth I had left. The sting of the cold did nothing to distract me from the horrifying reality before me.

"Hey," I lowered myself into a squat to meet his eyes. He watched me warily, his gaunt face twitching with mistrust. "I have someone who can help us."

"I don't need any help," he slurred. His lips trembled as his gaze darted away. "I need blood. I need Valerie!"

The last words broke from him in an animalistic whine, slamming into me like a baseball bat to the gut. I swallowed the ache flooding up my chest and pushed past it.

"It's a vampire, Luke," I said, keeping my voice as steady as I could. "Her name is Odessa, and she's going to help you."

"What?" He sat up slightly.

"Come with me," I extended a hand toward him, keeping my voice steady. "I promise this will make things better."

"I-I don't know if I can, Scarlet."

His hand inched toward mine. Icy fingers barely brushed against my own before he recoiled. He scrubbed his face with trembling hands. His breath came in uneven bursts.

"It feels like reality is slipping away from me. I get these moments of clarity, and then it's like—"

His voice cracked, and I clapped a hand over my mouth to stifle the sob that threatened to betray me. I had to hold it together for both of us.

"It's like I'm drowning. It hurts so bad, I can't breathe. And the only thing, the *only* thing I can see to pull me out of it is Valerie's blood." He paused, his voice breaking with desperation. "That's all I think about. I swear to God, Scarlet, I can taste it now."

The taste of Sorin's blood, fresh snow, flooded my mouth. I dug my fingertips into my palms in an attempt to guard myself against the mouthwatering sensation that made my jaw ache. If I felt this way after just a small taste, it was a miracle that Luke was managing to keep it together enough to even speak.

"Just hang on a little bit more. We'll find a way to help you, I promise. I'll protect you."

"I'm so sorry, Scarlet." He peered at me through trembling fingers, his bloodshot eyes glistening with unshed tears. Those eyes used to crinkle when he laughed. The hands that used to hold me so gently were now gnarled and covered in small cuts.

"I'm so fucking sorry," he choked out before he bolted upright, his movements wild and frenzied as he prepared to sprint.

"Please don't run," I begged, lunging forward to grab the belt loop of his too-loose pants.

"You can't save me!" he screamed. "You aren't her!"

I winced as the sound tore through the air, rattling my eardrums.

Her. Valerie. That redheaded viper who had sunk her claws into our lives and ripped them apart for her own amusement. She'd slowly addicted Luke to her blood until he became a shadow of the man I knew. My hatred for her burned in a place jealousy couldn't quite touch. It manifested in an ugly undercurrent roaring beneath my skin.

"She's dead!" I spat as I locked my eyes on his.

I felt my emotions drain away, leaving only cold, simmering rage behind.

"You're obsessed with a dead monster who tried to fucking kill you, you stupid bastard! She's dead, and she's never. Coming. Back."

That stripped him of any fight he had left.

"I can't live without her," he said in a small, broken voice.

His head drooped as if he could no longer bear the weight of his grief.

"Too bad," I took a half-step closer. "You don't have a choice."

Quick as a whip, I spun him around. My arms cinched around his torso. He didn't even have time to struggle before I hooked his heel with my foot and dropped to the ground. A startled grunt escaped his lips as we crashed onto a pile of lumpy trash bags that reeked of rot. Luckily for him, I let myself bear the brunt of the fall.

"Let me go!" He clawed at my face and neck, leaving a stinging trail just below my right ear.

"Hold still!" I gritted out, wrestling his flailing hands and pinning his wrists above his head.

The ease of it, his weakness, only steeled my resolve. Still, I cringed as I pulled the handcuffs from my pocket. Not because of the situation, but because I'd have to admit (to myself, and to absolutely no one else) that these had once belonged in our nightstand drawer back in Georgia.

"Handcuffs? Really, Scarlet?" he spat, jerking against them. "What the fuck?"

"Yes, really. Now shut up—it's not like you were using them anyway."

Not on me, at least. That little fact deserved some extra snugness, so I gave the cuffs another click.

I released his arms and dove for his ankles, flipping him over like a damp quilt. From my other pocket, I yanked out a strip of curtain rope I'd ripped from my room earlier and tied his ankles with a knot that would've made a Boy Scout cry. Panting, I stood over him while he thrashed and yowled like an alley cat losing a trash-can brawl.

"I'm sorry," I crooned, crouching to cover his mouth. "I—OW!"

His teeth sank into my hand. Pain shot up my arm, and I tumbled back on my ass, clutching my throbbing fingers.

"Great plan, Luke. Let's bite the only person dumb enough to help you. Really stellar survival strategy."

As I pushed myself up, a sharp sting shot through the back of my left thigh.

"Dammit," I growled, looking back to find a thick shard of glass embedded in my leg. "Great. *Just great.*"

I grabbed at my leg, grimacing as I tore the glass free with a small, involuntary shriek at the fiery pain.

"Fantastic! Now I'm bleeding," I tossed the shard aside.

Blood soaked through the dark grey of my favorite pair of joggers.

"Luke, you are literally a giant pain in my ass!"

I glared down at him as he thrashed like an overgrown toddler having a tantrum.

"Honestly, you're the gift that just keeps on giving—"

Someone chuckled deeply behind me. I spun on my heel, and for the briefest of seconds, I expected to see Sorin there. The insult I'd been preparing for him died in my throat as my gaze landed on a large, redheaded man.

"I *knew* you would be interesting," Paul said from the entrance of the alley, his broad frame leaning against the wall as if he owned the entire street.

The breath whooshed out of my lungs as he straightened. Even Luke grew still. My eyes flicked downward to him before I shuffled forward, positioning myself between Paul and Luke. Luke was in no shape to fight. He'd be a danger to both of us in his condition.

"This is none of your business," I said, forcing every ounce of courage I could muster into my voice. "Leave us alone."

"Oh, come on," Paul's sharp fangs pressed against his bottom lip in a way that made him look like a badly formed gargoyle. "That wouldn't be any fun now, would it?"

"I'm not looking for fun," I deadpanned. "I'm about as exciting as a textbook on political science."

He stopped, leaving about ten feet between us. His stillness was almost worse, like he was waiting for the perfect moment to strike.

"Anyone involved with Sorin has to have an interesting story."

"Sorin and I aren't involved," I sputtered, cheeks reddening. I glanced down at Luke and added, "This is my husband."

"Your husband?"

He placed his massive hands on his hips and shook his head.

"Bless me, that has to be complicated."

My gaze darted around, searching for something to help myself with. I had no idea how long it would take for Carmen to arrive. And even if she did, could she take Paul? He was a goliath.

There was a metal pole jutting from behind the dumpster. It wasn't sharp enough to impale someone. It would take a considerable amount of force. But if I could manage to maneuver Paul...

A chill gust of wind stirred the hair around my numbing face. There was no way it would be possible. He had me in size, strength, and speed. It would be like a mouse attempting to impale a lion on a toothpick. I abandoned the idea of the pole and fished for a way to distract Paul.

My voice wobbled as I asked, "How do you know Sorin?"

"Sorin and I go back quite a way. With everything going on with the Summit, I thought I'd stop by and see how things are going." He rocked forward on the balls of his feet.

Everything going on? Did everyone know about this experiment but me?

From the corner of my eye, I spotted Luke trying to crawl away. With his hands and feet bound, he slithered awkwardly, like the snake he was. A flash of irritation shot through me, and I pinned him in place by pressing a foot down on his ankle. Not enough to injure, but enough to make him think twice about his little getaway.

The moment cost me. In the blink of an eye, Paul closed the distance between us.

"Don't worry, little bird," he crooned. "I just want to talk."

"It sure doesn't seem like it," I squeaked.

Could I go for another double-leg takedown like I had with Damien? The odds weren't in my favor. I started to shift my weight in preparation for the attempt when the screech of tires filled the alleyway.

A windowless black van careened into view, skidding to a halt just behind Paul. The passenger door slammed open, and out stomped Carmen. She was a storm wrapped in leather. Her dark eyes burned as she locked onto Paul, expression promising death. Paul took a step back, wariness creeping into his stance as he yielded his oppressive position over me.

Without a word, Carmen marched past me, boots clicking against the pavement. She reached down, grabbed Luke like a sack of potatoes, and slung him over her broad shoulder.

Turning back toward me, she threw a muscular arm around my shoulders.

"Off limits," she barked.

"Always a pleasure, Carmen," Paul inclined his head in a mocking bow as we passed.

Carmen's only response was a raised middle finger. She guided me toward the back of the van without breaking stride. The vehicle's interior was cramped with cleaning supplies but blessedly warm. She shoved the door open and tossed Luke onto the hard metal floor with a thud. He groaned, writhing slightly.

I slumped in between a mop and a corded vacuum, adrenaline draining from my body as the relative safety of the van enveloped me. Carmen climbed in after me. The door slammed shut behind us, sealing Paul and the alleyway firmly on the other side.

"Drive," Carmen barked.

I looked to the front just in time to see Malik, features tight with concentration, shifting the van into reverse. Tires screeched as we peeled out of the alley. Paul's inhuman eyes reflected the light of our headlights with a matte glare. Shuddering, I turned away and placed a trembling hand over my racing heart. My body felt distant, a different kind of cold spreading over me.

"Where are you hurt?" Carmen's voice broke through my haze, her expression tightening. "I smell your blood."

"Oh," My hand drifted to the back of my left thigh, where a dull, stinging pain had been simmering beneath the adrenaline. "It's nothing. Just a piece of glass from the trash."

"Forgive me," she covered her mouth and nose with one hand. "I'm not as in control as Odessa."

She made her way to the front of the van, casting a glance back at me.

"Get to the very back," she ordered firmly, and I obeyed without hesitation.

When we finally arrived, Carmen snatched Luke's unconscious form up in her iron grip. He had passed out during the trip. She carried him across the parking garage beneath Crimson & Clover.

"Malik," she called over her shoulder. "Help her with that cut. Meet us in the basement when you're finished."

She disappeared inside with Luke still draped over her shoulder. I tried to follow, but the sting in my leg grew with every step until I was limping awkwardly. Malik, who had been quiet until now, turned to me. His golden eyeliner caught the overhead light, refracting in small, mesmerizing sparkles.

"Are you okay?"

18

STAIRS AND STITCHES

I was unsure how to answer his question. I really wasn't alright. Only, it wasn't because of my leg.

"Um, no," I said, letting the truth out. "But this just stings a little. I need an alcohol swab or something."

Malik offered a reassuring smile and extended an arm to help me up the stairs. I accepted it gratefully. Milo rushed to greet us, his nose immediately zeroing in on the cuts and scrapes covering my body. I had to bat him away as I opened the door to let Malik in. Once inside, I locked the door firmly behind us.

"You'll probably want a shower," Malik crouched, allowing Milo to conduct a thorough scent investigation. "You kind of smell like trash."

He wasn't wrong. The too-sweet stench of decay and rot clung to me. I'd need to toss my entire outfit, not just the ruined joggers.

In the bathroom, I slowly peeled off my blood-soaked pants, grimacing as the fabric tugged against dried blood. A dark stain had seeped down the entire back of my thigh. Turning to the mirror, I tried to get a better view of the damage and immediately cursed under my breath.

A large gash, angry and red, glared back at me. It was about an inch long, inflamed, and pulsing with heat.

"How bad is it?" Malik called from the other side of the door.

"It's definitely going to need stitches," I replied, trying to keep the edge of panic out of my voice. As if it could hear me, the wound throbbed harder.

"I'll grab the medical kit while you shower," Malik said.

I heard the door to my room open and close softly behind him.

As the shower's spray hit my leg, I bit down on my knuckle to keep from screaming. The sting was white-hot, searing through my nerves like a brand. My breath came in ragged gasps as I leaned heavily against the wall.

The pain made the room spin. I punched the tiled wall in frustration, forcing myself to stay under the spray until I could breathe normally again. Slowly, my body adjusted to the pain, or at least ignored it enough for me to rinse off.

By the time I finally hobbled out, my leg felt like a mess of stinging flesh. The cut was so high up that my butt cheek brushed the edge of it with each step. Pulling on pants wasn't even a consideration. Skipping a bra, I slipped into an oversized T-shirt and a soft grey pair of panties. I plopped onto the bed, stomach down, using a towel to cover my lower half. Milo climbed up beside me, resting his head on his paws as I absently stroked his soft fur. I controlled my breathing, exhaling slowly until I finally heard the sound of the door opening. Malik stepped in, a large medical kit in his hands. I raised onto my elbows to greet him.

"Don't get up," he instructed, kneeling on the floor and opening the kit.

He pulled out a pair of gloves, a bottle of iodine, gauze, and several other items.

"Sorry," I shifted on the bed uncomfortably. "I couldn't put on pants. It hurts too much."

"Don't worry about that," Malik looked up briefly. "Trust me when I say I've seen much worse here."

"And, uh... you're not really my type," he added.

Oh. *Oh.* That would put things in a different perspective.

"Right. Okay. Cool," I blinked. "Good to know."

"Not that you asked or anything," Malik shook his head as he snapped on the gloves. "But yeah, women aren't really my thing. Figured I'd clear that up before the awkward silence got too unbearable."

"I guess that's one way to avoid awkwardness," I laughed, glancing back at him.

The corners of his mouth twitched as he dabbed my wound with an alcohol swab. I tried not to flinch. It stung, but having another human nearby was oddly comforting. I rested my head on my folded arms while he worked.

"Looks like there are still some small shards in here. I'm gonna have to pull them out," Malik rummaged through the medical kit. The metallic sheen of the medical tweezers he produced made my stomach twist.

"Do it quick," I bit down on the blanket, bracing myself once again.

Nodding, he planted one hand around the cut and went in for the kill.

"Agh!" I cried out, tears pricking my eyes as the first tug sent a bolt of pain shooting through me.

"Almost done..." he leaned closer for a final probe.

The tweezers dug in again, and another sharp cry escaped me.

"Aaaand—got it. You did great," he said, holding up a bloody sliver of glass between the tips of the tweezers like a trophy.

I tried to catch my breath as the searing pain eased into a dull throb.

"What about the stitches?"

I clenched and unclenched the blanket, trying to bleed off some of the tension buzzing through me.

Malik picked up a small bottle of clear liquid, tapping it lightly before meeting my gaze with a reassuring smile.

"Do you trust me?"

"Fuck. I guess so."

Let's be real, he was digging around in my leg while my butt was in the air. If I didn't trust him now, I couldn't trust anyone. There wasn't much of a choice either way. It didn't seem like Sorin or Odessa would be very willing to let me make a trip to the hospital.

"Hold still," He pressed the torn edges of the wound together and applied the liquid.

A burning pain blossomed across my skin, but it was bearable compared to what I had experienced earlier. I felt the liquid set quickly. Malik finished by dressing the wound with a thick white patch of bandages.

"All done," he said, pulling off his gloves.

"Thanks for that," I said quietly.

My body was still trembling, but the pain had dulled.

Malik looked up at me as he packed away the tools. "It's nice to have another human around for a change."

"Yeah," I said softly. "It is."

Still limping slightly, I crossed over to the closet and pulled out my baggiest, most comfortable pair of sweats. The fabric was soft and forgiving against my leg.

"So," I ground out as I slid the pants on, "how did you end up here?"

"Odessa is my aunt."

I stared at him, pants halfway up, "I'm sorry, what?"

"She's not my direct aunt," he explained, clearly amused. "She had a sister, a younger sister, back in the day. Her sister never turned. She didn't make it."

He paused to consider.

"I'm something like her great-great-great-great-great-great nephew."

I blinked, counting the six "greats" on my fingers. When I looked back at him, I saw the resemblance was there if you knew where to look: the tilt of his eyes, the set of his mouth, even the dimples that popped into his cheeks when he smiled.

"How did you find each other?" I asked, astonished.

"She keeps track of us," he shrugged, eyes dark and heavy. "Family's important to Odessa. But I'm the last, you know. I was an only child. My mother died when I was young."

"Odessa's been there for me in her own way. She raised me."

"Family," I turned the word over in my mind, leaning against the wall. "Guess she's full of surprises."

"You've got no idea."

"Shall we go to see Luke now?" I asked as he snapped the kit closed.

Milo had returned to his bed, having lost interest after deciding that I was not, in fact, dying.

"Let's," Malik opened the door and waved me through.

I cursed the architect of this elevator-less hellscape as we descended into the bowels of Crimson & Clover. Each step sent a fresh jolt of pain through my injured leg. I counted at least seven flights of stairs before we finally reached the bottom. My leg was trembling, my breath uneven, but I managed to keep up until Malik came to a halt in front of a featureless white door.

He pressed his thumb to a pad beside the door, and it slid open with a mechanical hiss.

Filtered air rushed out, carrying the sterile scent of disinfectant. Harsh white ceiling lights reflected off pristine floors and walls. It looked like a windowless hospital unit with an endless corridor of identical doorways. At the far end of the corridor, a door hung ajar, and I caught a glimpse of Carmen's unmistakable broad shoulders. She leaned over a table, speaking to someone I couldn't see.

Malik gestured for me to follow, "Over there."

I limped after him, my trepidation growing as we approached.

Would Luke already be recovered? Would one drink of Odessa's blood heal him like Sorin's did for me?

At last, we rounded the corner. Odessa and Carmen stood imperiously over a bed where a freshly bathed Luke lay, eyes closed and deathly still. The sight of him hooked up to machines, his pale hand resting limply on the sterile white blanket, made my heart lurch. An IV dripped steadily beside his bed in time with the soft beeping of monitors.

I rushed to his side, clutching his frail hand in between mine. It was cold to the touch. A tremor ran through my fingers as I tried to convince myself he was still there, still alive. Across the room, a young red-haired man with a mop of frizzy curls stood scribbling notes into a yellow pad. His pale skin was a canvas of pocked acne scars, a detail that immediately marked him as human.

"Are you his doctor?" I asked, swiping at the tears brimming in my eyes.

The man glanced up, his red-rimmed eyes darting nervously between Odessa and me.

"He is a nurse practitioner," she explained curtly.

Her gaze never left Luke as she frowned down at him.

"Luke's condition was very poor. He's been placed into a medical coma."

"A coma?" I looked at Luke's unnaturally still face, my grip on his hand tightening. "Why?"

"His body required serious rest and stabilization. Most likely, he's been ingesting blood for longer than we anticipated. Or his bond with Valerie was powerful. Severing that must have had adverse effects on him."

"But your blood—" My voice caught as I recalled what Sorin had said to me about the consequences of something happening to him while we were bonded.

The blood drained from my face.

"It's not quite as powerful as Sorin's. Yet," Odessa exchanged a meaningful look with Carmen. "Have some patience. These things take time. I hear things didn't go as smoothly as we hoped?"

Odessa rounded the bed with a graceful step and placed a delicate arm around my waist.

I sighed heavily and leaned slightly into her embrace.

"Some vampire named Paul followed me from the club, I think."

"That brute," Odessa scowled. "It was fortunate that we sent Carmen."

She turned me so my injured leg was facing her.

"I also hear you got a little sliced up yourself?"

"It's just a cut," I stepped away. "Malik already fixed me up."

"Well done," she said, delivering a pleased smile to Malik.

"It was nothing," he said with a shrug, though a flush warmed his cheeks.

I watched Luke, wondering how long it would be before he woke.

"Do not worry," Carmen stepped beside me and patted my shoulder. "He will likely be awake before the sun sets tomorrow."

It was, at least, twice as long before Luke woke up. Four days spent walking Milo, punishing my body with relentless workouts, and avoiding Sorin like the plague. Yet, no matter how far I ran or how many push-ups I ground out, I couldn't get him out of my head. He had pressed himself into my mind like a thumbprint in soft clay.

Every quiet moment was haunted by the memory of his skin brushing mine, the heat of his breath against my neck, the weight of his hand on my hips. It was a maddening tug-of-war between the guilt gnawing at me over Luke and an inescapable pull toward Sorin.

Sitting outside a café with Milo stretched at my feet, I finally gave myself permission to release the thoughts I'd clenched into the corners of my mind. What I felt for Sorin wasn't romantic. It was reckless lust that had been forged in absence, loneliness, and pain. I had been trying to patch the broken parts of myself, and he just happened to be there. He was a convenient patch, but it wasn't fair. Not to me, and not to him. I couldn't play a game I wasn't willing to finish. I dug my fingers into my eyes and rubbed, wiggling to avoid the pull of the liquid stitches in my leg.

Since Malik patched me up, we'd been sharing breakfasts in the private dining room of Crimson & Clover. A tentative friendship had started to form between us. When my phone pinged, I glanced at the screen to see a text from my new friend informing me that Luke was finally away.

I moved as quickly as I could with Milo at my side, careful not to let excitement or dread get the better of me. To talk to Luke, I needed to be calm—calm enough to listen, to hear his side of the story.

Back at the building, I ushered Milo into my room and forced myself down the stairs, each step tugging at my stitches. Slow. Careful. Down, down, down until I stood before the white door. His pale, gaunt face from the other night flashed in my mind. It had been a lot to process then, and I wasn't sure I was ready to face it again.

I raised a hand and knocked lightly, the sound barely louder than my own unsteady breathing. After a moment, the door whooshed open.

Malik stood on the other side, waiting for me.

"Are you ready?" He stepped aside as we approached the door that separated me from Luke.

I forced a smile and shrugged, "I don't think it matters either way."

Malik nodded, then knocked, waiting for my approval with his hand on the door handle. I took a deep breath, grimaced, and dipped my head at him. He swung the door open and stepped back, offering me the opportunity to enter alone.

19

RUNNING OUT OF LIGHT

The room was filled with the steady hum of medical equipment. Luke reclined in the hospital bed, various tubes running into him like veins from a mechanical heart. Color had returned to his face, and his freshly cleaned hair gleamed in thick waves across his temples. The gauntness was still there, but his cheeks had regained a touch of fullness. Some of the despair that had darkened his eyes had retreated.

"Luke," I said softly. "You look—"

"Better," he finished.

His voice was fuller, too, though not quite whole.

"Yeah," I choked out, tears burning at the corners of my eyes. "Can I get you anything?"

In the past, I wouldn't have hesitated to take his hand, smooth the hair from his forehead, and kiss his temple. But there was some intangible separation between us. We were like two sides of a magnet refusing to connect.

"No," he shook his head. "Sit. Let's talk. We need to."

I dragged a chair from the corner and sat beside him.

This conversation had been coming for a long time. That didn't mean that I wanted to have it. I shut my eyes, willing reality to warp back to the comfortable life we had once shared. But that life had died a long time ago, and we had to start somewhere.

So I opened my eyes, dragged in a clarifying breath, and asked him, "When did you wake up?"

"A few hours ago," he observed his hands. "It's been slow. I still feel a little fuzzy."

"I see."

I noticed the fresh, pink skin around his fingers and knuckles where his wounds had healed. We listened to the rhythmic beeping of the heart monitor.

"I'm so sorry, Scarlet," Luke breathed. "I never meant to pull you into all of this."

"Then why did you do it?"

I covered my mouth with one hand to stifle the hurt words that wanted to pour out of me in a bitter torrent. I wasn't just asking about the addiction. It went deeper than that. His betrayal was still a hot knife twisting into my back that I couldn't quite reach to pull out.

"I-I don't know," he averted his eyes, staring intently at a spec on his blanket.

Such a bullshit answer. But what did I expect from a man who had been avoiding his wife for the better part of a year? I fought for control over my temper.

"I thought we were happy."

My voice shrank, the words barely made it past my lips.

"We were."

"Then tell me why."

I needed him to tell me what I did that was so wrong that it drove him to another woman.

"It wasn't you," he winced. "I was working so much, pushing so hard, and then she was just... there."

His lips twisted into a grimace.

"I hate myself for how easy it was."

It felt like my chest was collapsing inward. On my next shuddering breath, I might crumble and scatter across the floor in a pile of ash.

"I kept telling myself I would end it, but she was so beautiful," he continued, oblivious that his every word shredded whatever fragile scaffolding I'd built around my heart these past weeks.

Though maybe I hadn't healed at all. Maybe this was the reckoning I'd been bracing for since the moment Luke started slipping away. My soul recoiled as his confession gutted me.

"Before I knew it, it had gone so far, and I couldn't go back."

My mouth opened, but no words came. I turned away, my ribs tightening as if my heart had shriveled to nothing but broken glass and air.

"Oh."

It was all I could muster.

"Then three months ago," his voice grew distant, a strange light filling his eyes, "she let me drink. She was going to turn me, Scarlet. We were going to stay together."

Hurt and betrayal spiraled through me, ripping apart everything I thought I knew. He looked at me then, anger roiling in those ice-blue eyes. Ah. There it was, finally. His accusation was my permission to let loose on him.

"And what about me?" I demanded, slapping a palm on my leg. "Did you conveniently forget about, oh, I don't know—your wife?"

"What about you!?" He screamed, the veins on his neck popping out with the effort.

"Did you kill her?" He panted, fixing a hard stare on me.

We stared at each other, both locked in a battle of guilt and rage, neither of us willing to back down.

"Yes," I whispered, the word leaving an acrid taste on my tongue.

He collapsed backward, his posture crumbling as a sob tore from his chest. His hands covered his face, muffling the sound but not the pain behind it.

"She was going to kill me," I said flatly, done dancing around the ugly truth. "I didn't have a choice."

Guilt smothered my anger, leaving behind a bone-deep weariness. My hand rested on the edge of the bed as tears began to blur my vision. God, I didn't want to be here. I wanted to climb into bed, close my eyes, and never wake up to reality ever again.

"I... I still love you," I murmured.

It was another tender, heart-wrenching truth that I could no longer avoid.

"I know," he replied after a pause, then said no more.

That hurt worse than his screaming. It knocked the damn air out of my lungs, and the world swayed beneath me. It was as though the entire axis of my life had shifted with that one, short sentence.

"I guess that's all that needs to be said, then," I stood, trying to hold myself together. My nails dug into the flesh of my arm. "I'll have someone draw up the papers when I'm back home."

"Scarlet—" Luke started, but I didn't let him finish.

"You need your rest," my voice caught as I turned away, unable to meet his eyes. "I'll let you rest."

At the doorway, I slid the simple gold wedding band from my finger, placing it on top of a haphazard stack of papers. The gold stood out starkly against the black and white text. Then, the door clicked shut behind me. I left him and whatever love I still clung to behind me.

Thankfully, the hallway was empty. I pressed a trembling hand to my chest, feeling the frantic crashing of my heart. I wished I could reach inside myself, rip it out, and hurl it into the gutter. I wanted to leave it behind that door with all the pain, all the emotions threatening to bury me under a mountain of grief.

"Damn you," I cursed myself under my breath.

The hallway blurred as I wiped furiously at my face, tears spilling faster than I could catch them. "Stop crying, goddamn it."

I shoved through the stairwell door and bounded up the steps two at a time. Each one sent a spike of pain up my leg as the stitches pulled. I welcomed it, letting the ache drown out the mess my life had become. Red-streaked light from the setting sun filtered through the narrow windows in the stairwell as I left the subterranean part of the building.

A door swung open on the restaurant level, and Malik's head appeared, concern etched across his face.

"Scarlet?" he called.

"I can't—" was all I managed before barreling past him on my frantic ascent.

All at once, I knew where I was going. My room wasn't far enough. I needed distance—real, physical distance from what had just happened. I'd never been to the top of a skyscraper before. Today, I would. My breath came in ragged pulls as I rushed past my floor, climbing into the building's quiet, hollowed-out upper levels. The stairs felt endless, each flight stretching further into the dark.

A soft, rhythmic, dripping sound made its way into my consciousness. I spared a glance down to see bright red blood leaking from the open wound on the back of my leg. It trailed up the stairs behind me. I stared, then kept moving.

Maybe some monster would find me. Maybe not. What did it matter? It felt like I'd just died in a quiet, secret way only I could feel. Luke had reached inside me and delivered the fatal blow. Some part of me was still sitting beside his bed and would never leave that room. If this wasn't death, then death had nothing left to take. I tried to outrun my emotions, didn't want to stop and feel them. There was only movement. Movement, and the creaking sound of a door opening below.

"Scarlet?" Sorin's deep voice reverberated up the stairwell.

Panic shot through me. This breakdown had been building for a long time, and I needed to have it out alone. I couldn't tell how far he was. Whether he was close or still far below. I sprinted upward, my heart hammering in my chest like a wild drum. Exhilaration coursed through me like fire. The growing shadows seemed to stretch and pulse with each floor I passed. They swathed the walls like opaque curtains, whispering secrets I couldn't understand.

My feet pounded the steps in a blur of motion, driven by the low growl rolling up the stairwell. I had to be faster, to climb higher. My body moved with a speed I didn't know I possessed. Every thought that crossed my mind was a useless burden. I cast them away, becoming a ghost chasing freedom. It was so close, just steps away. But I could feel him closing in. Not in sound but in pressure that pressed at the edges of my mind.

My fingers gripped the cold steel of the door that would release me to the roof. With all my strength, I ripped it open. The howling wind sank its freezing fingers into my hair, sending loose strands whipping around my face.

Behind me lay a beckoning void that nipped at my heels. Ahead, the world sprawled in the chaotic melody of city life, preparing for twilight. The skyline was stretched with a sea of glittering light as if the stars themselves had descended to earth for this moment.

"Scarlet."

My name slithered around me like an invisible caress that sent gooseflesh skittering across my arms. I watched the shadows from the corner of my eye, my heart thundering as the wind roared around me.

"Do not make me chase you," he warned.

The rigidity in his words told me he was fighting his own battle for control. I swore I could feel his failing restraint. It pulled me towards a boundary that I couldn't escape crossing. I didn't want to resist anymore. Perhaps this was a game I was willing to play after all.

I stepped forward, one foot reaching into a golden stream of light that spilled across the rooftop.

"Don't," he bit out.

I moved fully into the light, the last saturated rays of day wrapping me in a glowing halo. But its warmth faded fast as the sun abandoned me to the hush of the coming night.

Sorin's silhouette loomed in the doorway, pulsing a shade darker than the gathering dusk. Two eyes glinted through the gloom, glowering at me from across my shield of dying light.

My chest heaved in shallow breaths. Instinct screamed at me to keep running, but there was nowhere to go except off the edge of the building. My eyes flicked to the ledge, the intrusive thought flashing briefly through my mind.

A feral snarl erupted from the shadows, sending fresh apprehension surging through me. I stumbled backward. A creeping dread seeped from the inky stairwell and quickly overwhelmed me.

"Sorin," I exhaled, my eyes widening with alarm.

But it was too late. The last dregs of light fell into darkness, and then he was upon me.

20

KILL ME WITH KINDNESS

Our collision sent me skidding backward, arms flying up to shield my face as we crashed across the rough surface of the rooftop. The world tilted as our limbs tangled together and landed with his weight pinning me down.

"You torment me." His face hovered inches from mine, eyes burning with an unhinged intensity that chased away the memory of breath.

We were partitioned from the world by the dark curtain of his hair. It filled my senses with his bewitching scent.

"Let go," I demanded, not convincing anyone. I made no effort to separate myself from him.

His pupils were so endless that I couldn't tell where the iris began or ended. They were black holes sucking me in, pulling me apart, and reordering every atom until I revolved around him. With terrifying clarity, I realized I wasn't ready to stop resisting. I already had.

"You should really not be looking at me like that," he said, slowly releasing a breath.

His lips peeled back, exposing teeth that lengthened into impossibly sharp points. The thin mask of humanity slipped away, leaving only a predator made of hunger and carnal ferocity. Heat flushed through me, my breath breaking into shallow, needy gasps. My jacket hung open, the thin tank beneath straining over my chest as though it, too, wanted to give way to the creature looming over me.

His weight pressed down, deliciously suffocating, every inch of him driving me deeper into the ground until the air left my lungs in a rush. Even my organs had conspired against me to let him closer, to deliver me into his hunger.

His unblinking gaze dragged over me in a ravenous sweep. I felt like his quarry. But I was braced for the catch, not to run.

"Like what?" I whispered, allowing my head to sink back against the hard floor.

"As if you want to be devoured," the last word was a deep, bestial rumble.

"Maybe I do," I opened my thighs wider in invitation, staring through heavily lidded eyes as his body melded into mine.

His nostrils flared, and that little vein popped out above his left temple. I met his eyes with a subtle lift of my chin in a defiant challenge to push further. Sorin went utterly still above me, dark eyes roaming over my face as if he were committing me to memory. Lithe fingers trailed down my injured leg, stopping at the damp warmth of blood seeping through the thin fabric.

I sucked in a guttural breath as he tore my leggings apart at the wound, fabric ripping like a gasp between us. Frigid air licked at my newly bared skin where the fabric had just clung. Never looking away from me, he brought his bloodied fingers to his mouth to lap up the deep red coating them.

My tongue darted out, coating my lip with a dewy sheen of saliva before I caught the tender flesh between my teeth. The bite stung sweetly, but it wasn't enough. Need was building inside me, swelling into a gnawing need that begged for more than the tease of pain.

His hand clamped down on my thigh, rough and claiming. My battle for control was lost. Fisting the deep blue cotton of his shirt, I yanked him to me until our mouths crashed together in a blistering kiss. The scrape of his fangs against my lips set lust surging through me like fire in my veins.

So long, ex-husband. Rest in pieces, marriage. I had a fanged upgrade right in front of me, and he deserved my full attention. Priorities, right?

Still, even with that tidy little farewell, the image of my wedding band against the stark white of the medical papers was burned into my retinas. The final nail in the coffin of us. Deep regret tried to pull me under, so I leaned in, deepening the kiss, chasing the memory away with the silk of Sorin's hair in my hand, how he moved against me. His arousal strained hotter, harder, with every shuddering sigh that fled from my lips.

In response, his bloodied fingers squeezed around my throat, driving my head back to the ground. Following me down, his mouth dominated mine. His tongue plunged inside, searching, teasing, and dancing with my own. A velvet-soft groan slipped from me, trembling into the heat that burned between us.

I arched, grinding against the rigid evidence of his desire in a silent plea for more. He inhaled deeply as his mouth traced a burning path down my neck.

He lingered at the hollow of my throat, lips grazing, teasing, before descending lower. His unsteady breath wrapped around me. Each exhale sent shivers skimming over my fevered skin.

His hands roamed upward, fingers gliding over the curve of each breast before he hooked the edge of my top and tugged. The fabric slipped down, baring the delicate bralette beneath. The sheer lace did little to hide the flushed peaks of my aching nipples. His eyes glazed over, dark with hunger. Dipping his head, his mouth closed around me through the whisper-thin fabric.

"Oh god," I gasped, hips bucking against him.

Teeth replaced his lips around the lace, tugging with a wicked hum that stole the breath from my lungs. The vibration rippled all the way up to my skull, scattering all thought into a thousand sparks. His tongue followed in a languid sweep over the dampening fabric, each stroke fanning the ache coiled low in my belly. Pleasure crested in torturous waves until every nerve was screaming for more of his touch.

The contrast of his soft, wet mouth against the rough lace sent my hips grinding harder, the friction compounding into a feral need my body refused to be denied. Just as my pleasure peaked, something inside me twisted. My attention drifted past him to the rooftop's edge, the city skyline shimmering like a mirage. A distant engine revved, and suddenly Luke's voice rose back to the surface.

Sorin's hand stroked through my hair, sliding down to cradle my head against the asphalt. It was a kind gesture meant to shield, to comfort. But I didn't want comfort. I wanted to burn. I craved the kind of pain that stripped you raw, that left blessed silence in its wake. Only agony could drown out the demons that hounded my subconscious with Valerie's death rattle, with the screams of bodies burning in that car. And Sorin wasn't giving me enough of it.

"Bite me," I murmured, too soft for human ears.

He went rigid, "What?"

"Do it," I ordered, arching my neck a little more.

Sorin stilled further. He pushed himself up onto his elbows, retracting from me.

"Please, Sorin," the words broke free like a hapless plea for release. "I need it."

He cupped my face, fingers gentle as they brushed against my jaw.

"This won't help you," He dragged at a fat tear rolling down my face with his thumb.

"I don't want help."

"You're hurting."

"So what?" Unchecked tears blurred my vision.

My heart clenched as the immense burden of my wrecked marriage crashed down on me. It hurt so much worse than anything physical that I could inflict upon myself. Sorin sat up fully, pulling me with him. Air rushed between us. I shivered violently, unable to tell whether it was from the cold or pure emotion.

Warmth returned as arms wrapped around me, turning me so my back rested against his chest as we overlooked the city together. I didn't resist as he pulled me a bit closer, his chin resting on the top of my head. His deep, steady breaths synced with my own.

"Don't be kind," I said quietly.

I could handle the infuriatingly cruel version of Sorin. I could rage at him, fight back, sharpen my edges against his. Kindness, though. Kindness would peel back every layer of my armor. It was more intimate than any kiss could ever be.

Ignoring me, he murmured into my hair, "Why were you running up here?"

Wind swept around us, weaving together our strands of chestnut brown and deep black hair in a fleeting tapestry that blurred the boundaries between our bodies. When I didn't answer immediately, his fingers tilted my chin so I was looking at him. His eyes were quiet, patient.

"Luke and I ended things..." I trailed off, turning my face away to stare into the night. "I just needed some air. To be alone."

"Were you going to jump?"

His hand smoothed over the tangled mess of my hair.

"I..." My voice faltered. I gave a hapless shake of my head. "I don't know. It all feels so dramatic now."

I cleared my throat, "Listen, I know this experiment matters to you. But you don't have to pretend."

He didn't answer immediately.

"Pretend what?"

"This." My hand fluttered between us. "That you like me. It's confusing."

Grasping his forearms, I tried to wrench myself free. He only pulled me tighter to him.

"Who said I was pretending?" he asked when I had ceased struggling against him.

"Please, Sorin. I'm depressed, not delusional," I grumbled into the night.

Sorin gave a low chuckle, "I'm too old to waste time pretending, it's exhausting."

"Likely story."

Against my better judgment, a bit of the tension bunching between my shoulder blades uncoiled.

"More importantly, you secured Luke?" He steered the conversation back to the source of my misery.

That was my cue to leave, I made to stand. There was no way I was going to let him know that Odessa was helping me. That would make things infinitely more complicated. But his arms snatched me back, holding me in place once again. His fingers petted the exposed skin of my neck and chest, sending another shiver through me.

"Yes," I said a bit distractedly, the soft touches returning a flush of heat to my cheeks. "He's—he's somewhere safe."

Another half-truth, another lie to add to the web. How would I ever remember them all?

"And he was in such good condition that you had a logical discussion about your relationship?" He asked wryly.

"Mhm," I hummed, avoiding his gaze.

Everything was becoming so complicated. I had saved Luke, if not our marriage. And in doing so, I'd tied myself to Odessa. At the moment, I was quite literally tangling myself up with Sorin. Who was really pulling the strings here? Because the more I thought about it, the more it felt like the only one being played was me.

They both wanted something. This experiment mattered to them desperately. But what was it? And why me? It couldn't just be because Sorin thought I was strong. Nothing was that simple here.

The questions scraped at my skull until the only thing I could do was release a heavy sigh.

"Is there more?" he asked, his thumb tracing slow circles along my jawline. "What about your leg?"

"It's a small cut from falling in an alley. But..." unable to help myself, I turned my cheek into his hand. "Can you tell me what the experiment is? It's driving me insane."

He turned to the horizon, pointing to the twinkling city lights.

"This world is changing, Scarlet. Faster than it ever has."

His hand returned, fingers tracing the edge of my shirt now, ghosting over my skin.

"Creatures like us, who remain unchanged, must find a way to adapt to this world. It goes against our very nature to become something we were designed never to be. Yet it is the price of an immortal existence."

"What are you saying?"

I frowned as I tried to piece his meaning together.

"Vampires and our other metaphysical constituents must evolve," he said meaningfully, "or adapt the landscape to suit us."

I sat with his words as they settled over me like a thick fog.

"What does that even mean?" I asked, tugging at a strand of hair.

How did I play into this? Either Sorin had vastly overestimated my competency, or he was speaking fluent Vampire Nonsense. Likely both. I shoved "other metaphysical constituents" into the same mental junk drawer as Carmen's casual shifter comment—already overflowing with things I had no business dealing with: unpaid parking tickets, IKEA instructions, and now, supernatural politics.

"That's all I can say for now," he said, mischief curling back into his voice. "You just need to stop murdering my kind long enough for me to fix the situation at hand."

"Murder is a strong word. It was self-defense," I sniffed.

"All seven?"

"All seven," I confirmed, gripping his arms to banish the phantom shudder of the banister splitting through Damian.

If he wasn't willing to tell me the whole truth, then I wouldn't feel so bad about hiding my dealings with Odessa from him. The omission settled heavily into my gut.

Sorin's fingers drew idle circles across my stomach, drifting to toy with the frayed waistband of my ruined leggings. Concentration slipped through my grasp like water, that heavy pit in my belly melting into something far more dangerous... and far more tempting.

21

GREEDY LITTLE BEAST

"So," he purred, "what is it you need now?"

"Why do you..." My breath hitched as I arched slightly under his arms, his touch too distracting. "Why do you care?"

I resented the pitiful edge to my words. But less than an hour ago, I ended my marriage. My heart was already bruised and fragile. The last thing I needed now was to throw myself into the next pair of open arms, no matter how tempting they might be. I had to guard what was left of my heart to protect it from splintering completely.

"You make me feel," his voice was a low, molten rumble.

His left hand roamed upward. Long fingers splayed across my chest before ghosting along the column of my neck. His grip tightened slightly as his palm cupped the right side of my face, tilting my head back. The motion bared my throat fully to the searing warmth of his breath that was fluttering over my pulse.

"Feel what?" I rasped, my vocal cords thrumming against his hand as his index and middle fingers pressed firmly against my right jugular.

"Alive," he confessed in a hushed tone.

His lips hovered near my ear as his whispered words brushed against my skin.

"For the first time in centuries, I feel warmth, Scarlet. I have been so cold for so very long."

His mouth grazed the tender spot above his fingers, pressing the softest of kisses there.

"You are too cruel."

"Cruel?" I gasped as his tongue traced the same path his lips had just claimed.

My mind went hazy, every thought scattering in the presence of his wandering hands.

"Hope," he breathed, voice quivering with unguarded emotion, "is a cruelty I thought I could no longer endure."

"I make you hope?"

"You make me want to keep going. To stay. To see how things might turn out."

The confession would have dragged tears from me if not for his right hand gliding over the curve of my hip, lingering just long enough to make me ache for more.

"Do you still wish for me to bite you?" he asked, his fangs grazing the delicate swell of my vein. Tiny pricks of anticipation burned through me, and I pressed my neck further into his grasp.

"What—" I stuttered as his hand slipped beneath the barrier of my waistband, "what will happen to me if I do?"

My head buzzed, light and untethered, and I realized that his thumb was pressing against the opposite side of my neck, where my other jugular vein pulsed under his thumb. The static pressure thrummed down my spine, pooling like liquid fire between my legs. A strangled groan escaped me as I constricted against the sensation.

"If I bite you," his index finger snapped sharply against my skin, releasing a sting that pulled a small cry from my lips.

The pain was fleeting, replaced by a wave of heat that rushed through me. I inhaled deeply, the dizzying oxygen twisting my senses into a heady whirl.

"You would crave me. My bite. My venom. It isn't permanent, unless you want it to be."

His fingers slipped lower, seeking a barrier that wasn't there. The realization that I wasn't wearing panties hit us both simultaneously, and his breath caught sharply. Truthfully, I'd just been avoiding laundry. Though with his hand already there, modesty was a ship that had sailed, sunk, and been eaten by sharks.

A thunderous rumble began deep in his chest as his hand slid lower, gripping the inside of my thigh with enough force that I knew I'd feel the imprint of his hold for the rest of the night.

"No," I whimpered.

I'd been upset earlier—hell, I still was—but I'd regained just enough sense to know that I wanted my free will to remain my own. If I made bad decisions, at least they'd be *mine*.

His hand began to withdraw. My own shot up, catching him by the wrist.

"But that doesn't mean I don't want this," I admitted quietly, a blush staining my face.

It had been nearly a decade since I'd been touched like this by another man. Luke's absence had left me starved for so long that I had almost forgotten what it felt like to want and be wanted. I couldn't help but cling to the intoxicating pull of the moment.

"Greedy little beast."

A grin tugged at his lips as his hand resumed its purpose.

"You're the beast," I shot back breathlessly as his nails raked across the tender skin of my neck and the inside of my thigh in one searing pull of both hands.

His smile deepened dangerously as his head dipped closer. And then his lips were on mine once again, crushing me with a brutality that sent my heart racing. His kiss was as much a claim as it was a dare to match him. His hand released my thigh, finding its way to the wetness pooling between my legs.

A long finger glided over my throbbing clit, orbiting my opening.

Every fiber of my being was begging to convey the unrelenting need for more of him everywhere and all at once. Thighs tightening with anticipation of his touch, my hips rose into his palm in a wordless request. With an excruciating slowness, he sank a finger into me. An anguished moan spilling from my parted lips as he filled me with another finger.

"Scarlet, Scarlet," he breathed as he buried his face into the curve of my neck just behind my ear. "You're so soft," and he worked a third finger.

I sighed his name, fingers threading through the hair near the nape of his neck. His hand slipped from my throat, trailing down to free my breasts completely from the confines of the lace. Rolling a nipple in rhythm with the rock of his hand, he pressed scraping kisses along the back of my flushed neck. With each touch, I spasmed around his hand. The muscles of his forearm flexed while he worked us into a rhythm.

It was so unlike Luke, who had always been all quick touches and hurried motions. Sorin rushed nothing. He acted with an intoxicating savagery that made me feel as though the world had narrowed to just this moment, just us.

"More," I pleaded, my hips chasing his hand frantically. "I need more."

"Manners maketh man," he hummed, withdrawing his hand.

He was utterly, maddeningly evil.

"Sadist," I hissed.

He began to pull completely free of me.

"Please... please, Sorin," I begged, my pride disintegrating into nothing.

"That wasn't so hard, was it?" he crooned, working a fourth finger inside.

"Fuck," I croaked, my head snapping back as he plunged into me, tearing another ragged sound from my throat.

His fingers splayed wide, drawing out that delicious, overwhelming feeling of being filled.

"Say my name," he grunted, each word punctuated by the pace of his movements as he worked me faster and faster.

His mouth parted slightly as he watched my body tighten against him, every motion bringing me closer to release. My thighs shook, muscles seizing as my cunt clamped down around his fingers. It was unbearable, winding around him until I felt ready to split open and detonate on his hand.

"I think I'm going to—oh, god!"

"I want my name on your lips when you cum," he growled, ruthlessly pounding into me at a brutal pace that stole every shred of breath I had left.

My exposed breast bounced with the motion of his efforts. His mouth captured one, teeth and fangs scraping over the swollen flesh as he sucked hard enough to bruise. A scream ripped out of me, muffled only by my own hand clamping over my mouth, as I shattered. My body convulsed, writhing uncontrollably while a hot gush spilled over his fingers, streaming down my trembling thighs.

"Say it!" he barked, releasing my breast and tearing my hand from my lips.

"Sorin!" The name spilled from my lips like a prayer, over and over again. "Sorin, Sorin, Sorin..." Eyes rolling back, my vision sparked with black at the edges as the tremors of release wracked through me. My hands clutched at the corded muscles of his shoulders, dragging nails over skin as my orgasm raged on.

Between pants, he nuzzled along the length of my neck, his motions slowing in time with the gradual ebb of my climax. I turned to him with an unfocused stare. He offered a satisfied smile, eyes half-lidded in lazy contentment. My heart skipped at the sight of his unfettered expression.

Truthfully, I'd always thought Sorin was handsome—in the way of a classic Roman statue. He was all sharp angles and perfect symmetry. But now, seeing him like this, he was... beautiful. A small dimple appeared on his cheek, and a faint flush lent warmth to his otherwise pale complexion.

I had to look away, begging myself not to cry at the sudden rush of sadness crashing over me. Insidious guilt began crawling across my exposed skin. The lump in my throat was burning as if I had swallowed a hot coal.

That mental breakdown was going to happen one way or another. Might as well ruin a perfectly good orgasm with it.

Scooping me into his arms, letting me lean into him.

"Sorry," I sniffled, hiding my tears in the crook of his shoulder.

"It's alright," he murmured, smoothing my hair back from my forehead with a gentleness that only made the tears harder to hold back. "You just need to rest."

There, pressed against the silence of him, I let myself grieve. Not just for Luke and the marriage I had chosen to leave behind, but for the pieces of myself I'd lost along the way.

Cold wind gusted over us, stealing my body heat from the thin jacket hanging off my shoulders. A full body shiver racked from the top of my head to the tip of my toes.

"Let's get you inside," Sorin said, kissing the tip of my shoulder before sliding my jacket into place.

His arm snaked around my waist, bearing most of my weight as I hobbled down the stairs.

Leaning on him was shockingly easy. He didn't complain once as he matched his stride to mine on our way down.

"I'll ask Malik to take another look at your leg," he said as we reached the last flight.

"Don't bother, I'll text him," I replied, keeping my tone light.

Still, I didn't pull away. My shoulder stayed tucked against his chest, my steps falling into rhythm with his until we reached my floor.

"I didn't realize you–" Sorin stopped abruptly, nearly knocking me off my feet.

Eyes glinting crimson, he glared into the black hallway that stretched to my door. There was no flicker of faux candlelight. It was a perfect, swallowing black.

"What is it?" I asked, stepping free and squinting into the dark.

The air felt charged, static prickling along my skin and raising every nerve to attention.

"I smell blood," Sorin growled.

"Milo's down there!" I cried, launching myself into the corridor.

"Scarlet, wait!"

Sorin's warning was lost on me as I hurdled down the hall. If Milo was hurt, I'd be a one-woman apocalypse for the undead. John Wick would call me for tips, and Buffy would take notes while the smoke cleared.

My foot struck something massive, and I pitched forward. Pain jolted through me as I slammed into the wall and crashed to my knees.

Before I could even curse, Sorin had me upright in a firm grip.

"Must you always rush headfirst into dangerous situations?" he muttered from the impenetrable dark, his hands skimming over me in search of injuries.

I shoved him away, teeth clenched. "Stop fussing and turn on the damn lights."

A beat later, the cold blue beam of his phone flashlight cut through the black. The glow swept across a sprawling shape in front of my door. Sorin drew in a sharp breath as recognition struck him.

It took me a second longer to process Paul's limp body, collapsed across the threshold in a puddle of blackened blood.

22

DARWIN AWARDS

If you'd asked me a few weeks ago if my first reaction to finding a man facedown in a pool of his own blood would be, "I didn't do it," I would've laughed. Yet, those were precisely the words that slipped out as I sidestepped the corpse and shoved the door open.

A shaky breath of relief flew from me when Milo appeared, tongue lolling, tail thumping against the wood floor.

"Thank God," I whispered. "Don't look, buddy."

Milo's face dropped as I slammed the door, cutting off the carnage. His innocence deserved shielding, even if mine was long gone, gutted and left to rot.

Sorin nudged the edge of Paul's boot with his toe, studying the scene with detached intrigue.

"Is he dead?" I squeaked. "Shouldn't he be—" I made a whooshing sound with my mouth "—burning up or something?"

"Yes," Sorin rumbled. "He really should."

Paul lay sprawled on his stomach, face mashed into the dark wood. I crouched beside him, bracing a hand on his shoulder to push him over. When had I gotten so casual about corpses that I was shoving them around barehanded?

Then again, I'd been hooking up with a vampire a few minutes ago, but that was beside the point.

Sorin stooped next to me, his hand pulling mine away.

"Let me," he said, positioning himself between me and Paul. "He could still be alive."

My hand tingled where Sorin had pulled it from Paul's shoulder. I shook it out, trying to rid myself of the pins and needles.

Peering over Sorin's shoulder, I nearly gagged. Paul's face had been mangled. The triangle where his nose should have been was little more than shredded flesh. A foamy bubble erupted from the wound, followed by a wet gurgle rattling up his throat.

"Oh, shit." I stumbled back a step. "He's not dead!"

Sorin made a noncommittal sound in the back of his throat, then let Paul's head drop unceremoniously to the floor with a dull thud.

"It appears so." He rose smoothly, wiping his fingers against the dark gray of his tailored pants.

The lights blazed back to life, electricity humming through the walls. The sudden brightness stabbed at my eyes, leaving me blinking against white spots. Footsteps thundered from the stairwell. When my vision cleared, Carmen, Odessa, and Malik stood before us, their expressions fixed on Paul's mangled body.

"He's alive," Sorin said flatly.

Malik dropped to his knees without hesitation, hands flying over Paul's ruined frame.

"Obviously," Carmen tutted, pacing around Paul.

Sorin rolled his eyes, already pulling out his phone, thumbs moving with practiced disinterest.

I edged a step toward my door, calculating whether slipping inside would look conspicuous. With Sorin and Odessa in the same space, every breath felt like handling nitroglycerin. One wrong move, one poorly thought-out sentence, and I'd be blasted to pieces between them.

"What she means," Odessa purred, flashing me a too-polished

smile, "is that we heard a noise and came running. Scarlet, dear, are you quite alright? What happened?"

"He needs blood," Malik informed us, fingers pressing down on Paul's thigh. "A lot of blood."

Odessa's lips curled as her nephew worked over the broken vampire at her feet. The disgust was gone in an instant, vanishing beneath a closed-lipped grin.

"Did he hurt you?" she asked, voice dipping in concern that didn't quite reach her eyes. "If this was self-defense, then—"

"I didn't do it," I blurted before she could plant the idea. "Sorin was walking me back to my room. He was already like this."

Odessa's gaze flicked between us, lingering on me before sliding to Sorin, who was absorbed in his phone.

"And what exactly were you two doing together?" Carmen cut in.

Damn. I *knew* this would happen.

"We, uh—" My tongue tripped over itself, my brain suddenly blank.

Sorin finally lowered his phone, his expression wiped clean of the flicker of warmth he'd shown me earlier. What stared back was nothing but cool, guarded stone. Odessa arched one sleek brow.

"Look, the lights were out, it was creepy, and he's tall. That's it," I said with a brittle shrug. "We just crossed paths on the stairwell."

Carmen barked a laugh. "What a good hall monitor you make, Sorin."

Sorin shoved his phone back into his pocket.

"Someone has to be around to clean up the messes," he said, voice dull as iron.

Shame curdled in my gut, sour as old milk. My eyes dropped to the blood oozing into the toes of my cheap tennis shoes. Sorin deserved better than that.

"Clearly it isn't safe," Odessa said, extending a hand toward me over Paul's body. "Why don't you spend the night with us?"

Sorin watched her hand as if it were a venomous snake poised to strike.

It wasn't like I wanted to snuggle up in a room still buzzing with attempted homicide. But accepting Odessa's invitation was the express lane to Darwin Award winner, 2025 edition. If I said yes, Sorin would smell something was up a mile away.

"No thanks," I scuffed a foot, flinching as it squeaked through Paul's blood. "Milo's in there, and I'd rather sleep in my own room with him."

"Even with that?" Odessa's hand flicked toward my door.

Shoulders hiked up to my chin, I turned toward the door in jerky motions. It had been easy to miss in the dark. An inverted triangle was slashed with a line through it. Carved deep into the wood, its grooves were filled with fresh crimson. Blood snaked downward in slow rivulets, dripping onto the floor.

"What the fuck," I breathed, pulse slamming in my ears.

The cut wasn't clean. Its depth and width wobbled like it had been done with an unsteady hand. Horror and nausea pulled me forward at the same time, a sick curiosity forcing me to look for meaning in the blood-filled grooves.

Sorin's hand landed on my shoulder. "Maybe you should consider sleeping elsewhere."

I shook him off before anyone could clock the tenderness in it. He recoiled like I'd zapped him with a live wire.

"I'll be fine," I snapped. "Goodnight, everyone."

Yanking the door open, I ducked inside and shoved the lock home. Every piece of furniture, except the bed, got scraped against the door in a barricade. The results weren't impressive: a mostly empty dresser and the small chair. My fortress of crap, defending a piece of crap and her dog. Milo was the only one in this room worth protecting.

Not trusting the lock or my sad excuse for fortifications, I dragged the bedding into the bathroom and made a nest on the tile. It was cramped in her to begin with. With Milo wedged against me, there was just enough room for us to curl into a fur-and-person burrito, clinging to the illusion of safety. Luxury accommodations courtesy of Scarlet's Bed & Breakdown.

The next morning, I sat in my tiny shower, letting the water rinse the suds from my hair and body. I watched them swirl lazily around my crossed legs and spiral down the drain. This morning, Paul was gone, and the blood had disappeared when I had taken Milo out for an early morning walk.

It was the first of October, typically my favorite month of the year. The old southern mansions lining the streets of Savannah would already be adorned with pumpkins on porches wrapped in festive wreaths of orange and gold with matching mums. Luke and I used to spend those autumn days running between coffee shops, admiring the vibrant decorations.

I scrubbed my face with my hands. A well of uncertainty and frustration bubbled within my chest. What was I supposed to do now? There was no one I could talk this out with. I had been deliberately avoiding contact with my family and friends back home. Every time I picked up the phone, my mind would go blank, my fingers frozen on the keyboard.

An endless barrage of questions loomed on the other end of these texts: *What happened? Where is Luke now?* How was I supposed to explain any of it? Just the thought of reliving the details and concocting enough lies to cover the truth left me utterly exhausted. It was only a matter of time before Tucker got worried enough to come to New York himself. I couldn't let that happen.

Counting down from twenty, I forced myself to stand, shutting off the stream of water and stepping into the chilly air of the bathroom. A shiver ran through me as I toweled off as quickly as I could. My clothing options were dwindling. Two of my favorite pairs of pants had been shredded.

I pulled on my dark jeans and a grey sweater, running a brush through my damp hair. Putting off the inevitable, I took my time blow-drying my hair then applying a light coat of makeup.

Eventually, there was no more delaying. I clipped Milo to his leash and stepped out into the streets of the city that had become my strange, chaotic refuge. I was just one of many here. When I thought of it that way, my problems seemed less significant.

Bracing myself, I unlocked my phone and dialed Tucker. He picked up on the second ring.

"Scarlet, where the hell have you been?"

"Hey, Tuck," I bit my lip as guilt twisted in my chest.

"Don't 'Hey, Tuck' me," he snapped, imitating my voice. "You haven't answered your phone in *days*, Scarlet!"

"I've been replying to emails," I grimaced at the weak excuse.

"Yeah," he huffed, "Nothing says 'I'm fine' like getting updates about my sister through Victor."

I winced.

"You'd better tell me what's going on right now, or I swear I'll come up there myself. Tiffany and I are worried sick about you, and she does *not* need that stress right now."

"What's wrong with Tiffany?"

"You first," Tucker demanded in a way that told me arguing would get me nowhere.

"I had to come back to New York because of Luke," I started, my voice wavering with unease.

"What about him?" Tucker demanded.

"Luke, he—" I struggled for the right words. "Luke got into drugs while he was up here. When I found out he was cheating on me, he went on a bender. We fought. A lot. I've been busy trying to get him some help."

It was close enough to the truth. Believable.

"And you couldn't have called me? Not once?" Tucker's anger softened just enough to let the hurt bleed through.

"I'm sorry, Tuck. It's been tough for me. And we—" I paused, choking on the words. "We're getting a divorce."

The words were foul in my mouth, and I spat them out like poison. Milo glanced back at me, his big, questioning eyes full of quiet concern. I reached down to scratch behind his ears.

"Jesus, Scarlet," Tucker sighed heavily on the other end of the line. "Can't you just come home now? Let's deal with this back here. We'll clear out the guest room for you."

"I can't," I scrambled for an excuse. "At least, not right now. I... I still need to stay with Luke until he's recovered enough to come home."

The line went quiet.

"Think it's time to tell Mom and Dad yet?"

"Please don't," I begged, my voice tight with emotion. "I can't bear the thought of the look Mom's going to give me. And Dad—you know how he is."

Dad wouldn't accept the divorce. He was deeply religious and always preaching about forgiveness, about turning the other cheek.

"Okay," Tucker relented. "But you know they're going to find out one way or another."

"I know," I gripped Milo's leash tightly. "I just need space right now. Tell me what's wrong with Tiffany."

"Now's not the right time," Tucker said.

"If you don't tell me now, I'll just ask her myself."

"Don't!"

Tucker sounded like when we were kids, and he had done something that might get him in trouble. "I promised her I wouldn't say anything yet."

"What's going on?" I pressed.

"She's pregnant again," his voice teetered between excitement and apology. "But it's still early. We just found out."

"Oh... wow," I said, forcing enthusiasm into my voice. "That's amazing!"

"Thanks, little sis," Tucker sounded relieved. "I'm hoping for a boy this time."

"The last thing this world needs is a Tucker Jr."

"Screw off," he laughed, then sobered. "But seriously, Scarlet, come home soon. There's nothing for you up there."

"I know," I replied softly. "Love you, Tuck."

"Love you too," Tucker said gently before the line went silent.

Numbly, I slipped the phone into my back pocket. Life carried on around me. Shaking my head, I decided that was enough of a pity party for one day and turned my focus back to Crimson & Clover.

Malik was already waiting for me there. I realized I'd missed the breakfast we'd been sharing lately.

"Hey, sorry I missed breakfast," I said with an apologetic smile.

He shrugged a little too casually.

"What's on the agenda for today?"

"I think I've got a little work to do," I replied, brushing a strand of hair behind my ear, "and then I was planning to go shopping for some new clothes."

"Can I come?" he asked.

I raised an eyebrow at him, noting his stylish outfit. He wore a corded knit sweater tucked into slim-fitted pants that managed to look both chic and comfortable.

"Sure," I said, smiling more fully now. "But only if you promise to help me figure out what to wear. My taste is terrible."

"Deal," he grinned back. "But don't blame me when you've got men crawling on their knees just to get your attention."

"I was thinking more like athleisure wear," I laughed.

"Oh no," Malik gave me an appraising once-over. "You need a night out. I'm not going to let you waste away in that creepy room any longer."

I chewed the inside of my cheek. The idea of a night of mindless dancing didn't sound so bad.

"Yeah," I drew out the word. "Okay. Give me two hours, and then meet me back here."

Malik's grin widened. "It's a date."

Two hours later, I slid into a taxi beside Malik.

"Upper East Side," he instructed the driver.

I shot him a grimace.

"That might be a little out of my budget."

"Don't worry about it," he said, flashing me a pitch-black American Express card. "Company perks."

"Are you sure we can do that?"

The idea of spending someone else's money didn't sit quite right with me.

"Think of it like this," Malik slid the card back into his wallet and turned to me. "With the type of company we keep, our life spans aren't exactly expected to be long. It's the least they can do for dragging us into this mess."

"If you put it that way..." I trailed off, trying to shake the disturbing truth from his words.

"Let's go spend other people's money," he said, a wicked gleam lighting up his dark eyes.

23

BORROWED WARMTH

I watched him for a moment, wondering if he hated this life as much as I did. Maybe, like me, he was just another casualty of someone else's choices. I wondered if he ever let himself imagine what normal might feel like.

Hours later, we were tucked into the corner of a cozy little Italian restaurant and slurping up the most delicious spaghetti I'd ever tasted. Malik sat across from me with a glass of red wine in hand, a half-eaten plate of Alfredo cooling in front of him. A litany of shopping bags was piled haphazardly at our feet.

From the pocket of his bomber jacket, Malik retrieved a tiny glass vial no larger than his thumb. I watched as he uncorked it and tipped it over his wine, letting a single droplet fall into the deep crimson liquid. He stirred the glass, watching the drop vanish into the wine like it had never existed. Then he took a sip.

"Is that blood?"

I stared, my fork frozen midway to my mouth.

"It's just a microdose," he said as if he were talking about adding sugar to coffee.

"Aren't you worried?" I asked, astonished. "About becoming like Luke?"

"This little amount won't do anything too intense. It makes a few subtle improvements, like better skin and a jaw that could cut glass. And," he paused, drawing out the next word with a wink, "it feels *amazing*."

He held the glass out toward me.

I raised a hand quickly.

"No, thank you."

Sorin's blood still made my skin crawl whenever I thought about it. I wasn't about to go down that road again.

"Suit yourself," Malik shrugged, taking another sip.

"What's your story?" I asked, pushing my glass of water aside and diving back into the spaghetti. "How'd you get involved in their, um —business?"

"Odessa adopted me," Malik set his glass down, leaned back in his chair, and crossed his arms. For a while, he just stared blankly past me. "She told me my mom was a junkie. She died when I was a baby. There was no one else, no place for me to go. So Odessa took me in."

"She raised you?"

"Yeah." Malik nodded wistfully. "She raised me like I was her own. And when I got older, I just stayed. It's not like I had anywhere else to go. She never made me feel like I should leave."

He stared at his hands for a while. I reached forward, resting my hand lightly on his.

"I'm glad you're here now. You've made staying here much more bearable."

He returned a little squeeze before letting go and turning back to his wine.

"What's the plan for tonight?" I asked as I scooped the last bit of spaghetti from my plate.

"We go home, cry into our pillows for twenty minutes, call it a nap, then party like we haven't been trauma-bonded into oblivion."

I snorted involuntarily.

Later, standing in front of the mirror, I tugged nervously at the hem of my skirt. Behind me, Milo watched from the bathroom doorway.

"How do I look, Milo?" I asked, turning to him with a self-conscious smile.

His tail gave a subtle wag as he padded over, pressing his broad head into my stomach in an affectionate nudge.

Thanks to Malik's impeccable sense of style, I looked fantastic. The outfit was a form-fitting, sleeveless black dress paired with a burgundy leather coat, matching knee-high boots, and dotted sheer tights. A simple silver chain with a matching bracelet hung from my neck and wrist. It cost more than I'd ever dreamed of spending on clothes, but Malik had swiped his card like it was nothing.

I'd taken my time getting ready, blowing out my hair until it fell in soft, voluminous curls that brushed my shoulders. My lipstick was a shade lighter than the burgundy jacket I was wearing. I gave my reflection a final check and felt a tiny spark of confidence in myself. A half-smile tugged at the corner of my lips.

After making sure Milo was set for the night, I slipped the key into the inner pocket of my jacket and locked the door. I triple-checked my pockets—key, cards, phone. I could do this. I *needed* to do this. It was time to move on, and I wouldn't let myself wallow in self-pity for another second.

Malik was waiting outside, leaning against the wall like a runway model on break. That thin gold liner framed his eyes, catching the light like always. The metallic geometric pattern on his shirt appeared to have been painted onto him.

"Wow," I said, genuinely impressed. "You look amazing!"

He turned to me, his expression as dazzling as his outfit.

"So do you! That dress? Those boots? It's giving sexy Dana Skully. Now spin for me," he demanded, twirling his finger in the air.

"You nerd," I laughed, obeying his command.

"May neither of us pay for a single drink tonight," he said, making a cross motion over his chest.

"Amen!"

Another taxi ride later, we were standing on a crowded rooftop bar, drinks in hand. The wind sliced through my thin layers of clothing. I was cold and acutely aware of how out of place I felt. Malik was immersed in a lively conversation with a group of Japanese businessmen that reminded me a little too much of Luke.

Another gust of wind made me shudder violently.

"Cold?" One of the men asked, stepping closer to me.

His body radiated warmth, and I didn't back away. It was a good baby step.

"Yeah," I replied with a tight smile. "It's warmer where I'm from."

"Scarlet's from the South," Malik cut in. "Don't you love her accent?"

The man's eyes crinkled with a smile, "Her voice is lovely."

"Thank you," I said, feeling heat climb up my neck.

Malik's phone buzzed, and he excused himself from us. I clutched my drink, tearing at my napkin with the other hand as I wandered what in the hell I was doing there.

The band shifted to a jazzy tune.

Without thinking, I blurted, "Oh, I love this song!"

Then immediately wanted to crawl into my own grave. Maybe the band could play something peppier for my funeral.

"Would you like to dance?"

One of the men offered a hand to me. My first instinct was to decline, to laugh nervously and wave him off. Dancing was something I used to do with Luke. Doing it with a stranger whose name I couldn't remember felt like a test I was doomed to fail. However, failing was something I'd been doing a lot lately. Fuck it.

"Sure." I downed the rest of my drink.

His hands slid across my lower back as we swayed back and forth. It felt familiar but not quite right. The conversation drifted toward the safe, predictable topics you could recycle with anyone in a suit. I even found myself asking him the same kind of questions I might have asked Luke about his corporate job.

I closed my eyes for a second and let the buzz of the drink dull the edges of the world. If I leaned into it, I could almost pretend I was having fun. When he dipped me at the end of the song, I went along with it. But I stepped away the second my feet were back on solid ground.

I said a polite goodbye before making my way back to Malik.

Last night with Sorin had been different. Messier, sure. But it was real. This felt like a performance I was staging for myself. I could look in the mirror and say, *'See? 'You're fine. It's not as bad as you're making it out to be. So stop being dramatic and get on with your life.*

"Ready to go?" Malik asked, greeting me with an outstretched arm.

I nodded, relieved to have an out. "But maybe not home quite yet."

"Trust me, I've got one or two more places in mind before we're done for the night."

Ushering me away from the bar with his usual charm, he waved goodbye to the men over his shoulder.

"Odessa and Carmen are going to meet us at the next spot," he said somewhat excitedly.

The couple waited for us by a sleek marble counter at an upscale bar in Greenwich Village. A red-lipped woman crooned in a throaty voice from a tiny stage in the corner. They greeted us warmly, each pressing a cool kiss to my cheek as they balanced goblets filled to the brim with dark liquid that shook in tiny viscous waves.

"How has your night been?" Carmen asked, reclining against the counter.

The blue sweater stretched over her muscular frame made her look like she could pick up the bar itself if she wanted to.

"Too many men and not enough drink," I joked, earning a laugh from her.

"Let's fix that right away," Odessa signaled the bartender with a flick of her wrist.

He practically floated over, eyes glued to her as if she'd cast a spell. She didn't bother returning his dreamy smile.

"A dirty martini for Malik," she gestured to my companion, then turned to me with an arched brow. "And Scarlet, dear, what will you have? Another bourbon?"

"That sounds great," I flashed a polite smile at the bartender as he turned to prepare the drinks.

Odessa and Carmen exchanged a glance. I couldn't help but wonder what silent conversation had just passed between them. It was easy to see why they were a pair. It was the way they moved through the world. Two lionesses who knew their place at the top of the food chain.

"Luke is improving," Odessa remarked coolly, surveying the room as if she were only half-invested in the conversation.

"I know. I saw him yesterday," I said, taking a measured sip of bourbon.

If I didn't pace myself, I was going to end up on my ass. But with where this conversation seemed to be heading, I wasn't sure I wanted to remember it anyway.

"Brave girl," Carmen said, giving my shoulder a firm pat.

I smiled weakly in return, feeling much more like a wilted houseplant than a 'brave girl.'

"How did it go?" Odessa leaned forward on her elbows, her attention now entirely on me.

"We're getting a divorce," I said flatly.

There was no reason to sugarcoat it. Honestly, it felt good to say it out loud.

"Ah," Odessa said. "Good riddance then."

I barked a short laugh, taking a longer pull of bourbon. The liquid burned its way down, but the knot in my chest refused to loosen as it usually did with the exquisite small lick of pain. My shoulders slumped forward, and I tried to sink back into the uncomfortable chair.

"I think I need some water," I grumbled, looking for an easy way to escape.

I pushed back my chair and turned toward the bar.

"We could stop his treatment," Odessa's voice followed me.

I turned back slowly, meeting her unflinching gaze.

"I don't want that."

Odessa's expression remained as measured as always. One finger tapped her goblet, a long nail gently scraping the geometric pattern of the glass. My eyes tracked the condensation gathering and dripped off the pad of that perfect, dark finger.

"What's the point if you are just going to split?" Carmen asked, draping an arm over Odessa

"I don't know," My eyes flicked around the room, landing on anything but the goblet of blood. Because that's what it was, blood.

I wasn't sure how they were preserving it to drink later, and I didn't want to think too hard about it.

"Our relationship is over, but I still love him. And I want him to live. Please don't stop."

I didn't want Luke to die. No matter how much pain lingered between us, there would always be a part of me that loved him. I couldn't stop that, even if I wanted to.

"You are so sweet," Malik said, his voice light and teasing as he pulled me into a one-armed hug. "You're gonna make me cry."

His attempt to diffuse the moment worked. I let out a shaky laugh, leaning into him briefly.

"There's nothing worse than heartbreak," Odessa sighed theatrically, leaning against Carmen. "It's a wound both of us suffered as humans."

"I wouldn't know," Malik side-eyed the handsome bartender, who was polishing the spotless countertop. "No one ever sticks around long enough for me to find out."

"Your time will come!" Odessa affectionately gripped his chin and tilted his face up to hers. "Scarlet's free now. What do you say, Scarlet?"

She turned her playful grin on me, her eyes sparkling with mischief.

"I'm sorry, but isn't Malik... doesn't he, umm..." I choked on the last of my bourbon, coughing as the burn hit my throat. "I'm not really his type?"

"You know I'm gayer than a pride float in June," Malik said, swatting Odessa's hand away.

"But you would make such adorable little babies," she pouted as she motioned between the two of us.

"Don't listen to her, Red," Malik said dryly.

The nickname caught me off guard, and I found myself smiling.

"She's obsessed with the idea of me procreating. Thinks I'd make some kind of genetically perfect child or whatever," he said.

"I stand by it," Odessa was utterly unrepentant. "It would be a crime against humanity if you didn't contribute to the gene pool."

"Too bad for humanity, then," Malik shot back. "Besides, I need someone who could actually keep up with me. Trust that there aren't many of those."

It was hard not to feel a little lighter in the presence of their easy banter. The music picked up, and my foot tapped to the reverberating rhythm of a bass guitar.

"Your cups are empty," Odessa pointed out. "Malik, would you be a darling and fetch the next round?"

With an exaggerated bow, he headed toward the bar, weaving through the growing crowd.

The moment he was out of earshot, Odessa leaned in slightly, her eyes alight with curiosity. "Scarlet, what are your plans for the future?"

"I'm not sure," I blinked. "Probably go home, move out of our house, and get back to life as usual. Whatever *usual* even means now. After this experiment—whatever it is—is over, of course."

"Hmmm." Odessa tapped a manicured finger against her chin.

"You could stay, you know," Carmen offered, withdrawing her arm from Odessa.

"And do what?" I looked between them, searching for some hint of a joke. "My entire life is in Savannah."

"*Was* in Savannah," Odessa replied. The correction stung. "Do you really want to go back to all of that? What will your family think?"

Her words landed like tiny daggers, each one chipping away at my injured heart.

I could already see the disapproval etched into my mother's face, the way her smile never quite reached her eyes. Her quiet judgment would hum beneath every polite word like it always did when something didn't meet her approval. Like how I worked at the gym when she thought I should aim higher. Or my most recent offense, failing to provide her with grandchildren. This would be no different.

"We could make it all go away," Odessa invited in a pillow-soft voice.

My eyes snapped to hers.

"How?"

She gestured between herself and Carmen, "We could make you like us."

"Like you," I repeated. A chill wormed its way up my spine as I grasped her meaning.

Her tone grew conspiratorial, "I know a good investment when I see one. Think about it, Scarlet. No man could ever hurt you again."

24

LIPSTICK AND TEETH

Reality went a degree off. My instinct shouted to run, my body wanted to laugh to keep from crying. The idea was monstrous, but it was a clean fix. My humanity in exchange for the power to walk through any threat untouched. For one dizzy heartbeat, it nearly sounded reasonable.

A large-bellied glass full of ice and amber liquid slammed down in front of me with enough force to rattle the table. I nearly jumped out of my skin.

"This," Malik announced overly loud, "is called a Zombie. And it is *precisely* what the doctor ordered after a long week."

His grin was plastered on, stretching too wide.

"Cheers," I raised my glass.

The others followed suit, our glasses clinking softly at the gentle collision. A ribbon of blood sloshed into my Zombie, curling and eddying like a loose vein that I watched through the frosted glass.

"What's a drop of blood between friends?" Odessa said a little too innocently.

Malik's smile faltered. He didn't say anything, but a subtle crease formed between his brows. Iron coated my tongue as I choked down the swallow.

Carmen steadied me as we loaded into the back of a cherry-red Hellcat, her strong hands firm against my shoulders as she buckled me in.

"You need some water," she said, pressing a damp bottle into my hand.

I cracked it open, enjoying the chill seeping into my fingers as I raised it to my lips.

"You weren't kidding when you said you were a lightweight earlier," Malik clicked his seatbelt into place beside me.

"Sorry," my cheek thudded lightly against the window.

"I think you're done for the night," Malik shook his head in disappointment.

"Booo," I whined, dragging it out like a petulant child. "But I wanna dance!"

"Maybe another time," he said with a placating pat on my head.

"Nonsense," Odessa interjected. "The girl said she wants to dance."

"Dess," Carmen said, shooting her a doubtful look.

"We're just going downstairs at Crimson & Clover," Odessa snapped. "She'll be fine."

Carmen sighed, settling back in her chair in resignation.

When we unloaded back at Crimson & Clover, I was able to walk on my own as we descended the narrow staircase. We passed through the restaurant above, entering a small antechamber that stood before an intricately designed iron door. The faint bass of the music thumped through it, teasing me with the promise of physical escape just beyond.

"I am *not* letting you walk into the lion's den looking like a sheep for slaughter," Malik smoothed out the smudges in my makeup and straightened my dress. He tilted my chin up gently, reapplying a fresh coat of lipstick.

"I'll be fine," I reassured him, flipping my hair back.

In truth, I was officially at the point of drunkenness where I was trying to *act* sober. Head buzzing, I could feel my balance wavering. The excitement thrumming in my chest overshadowed it all as the beat on the other side of the door vibrated through the walls and into my bones. I wanted in. I wanted to lose myself in the crowd, to let the music drown out every lingering thought and worry.

"I just need to move," I slurred.

"Then by all means, stagger majestically," Malik stepped aside. "But maybe let me hold onto your stuff."

I thought about it, then nodded. I wasn't nearly sober enough to be trusted with important things like a phone or remembering where my pockets were. Sluggishly, I handed him my belongings.

"Don't get lost in there," he laughed, giving my ass a slap.

The doors hissed, swinging open, and we stepped into the pulsating crowd. Just like before, cage dancers gyrated above us in fluid movements. Strobes of red and pitch-black streaked through the room. Music wrapped around me like a rip-tide current, sweeping me into a riot of motion. Time dissolved away like sand in an hourglass.

There was no telling how long I'd been moving, or how many hands had grazed my skin, or when my jacket had slipped from my shoulders. All I knew was sound and movement, flashes of light, then deep shadows. My thoughts were drowned beneath the beat that possessed me.

A man stepped into my space, moving in easy rhythm with me. He swayed closer, aligning his movements with mine until we were dancing together. He was willowy, tall enough that I had to crane my neck to meet his gaze. Shining brown hair framed a freckled face and sparkling green eyes.

"Wow," I breathed.

He gave me a heart-stopping smile with noticeably unsharpened canines. Not a vampire. A strong start.

"How did you get in here?" He asked, leaning in to speak in my ear.

No fangs, no problem. Tonight was about fun, and I was going to wring some out of it if it killed me. I gave him my best come-hither smile, which I was 60% sure looked more like a challenge to a bar fight. Which, frankly, I was far more qualified for than flirting. Either way, I'd call it a win.

As I parted my lips to speak, he angled his head to listen. His hair slipped aside with the motion, revealing the pointed tip of an ear.

My eyes bulged, hands reaching out to brush my fingertips lightly against the pointed lobe. His hand snapped up instantly, catching mine mid-air.

"Touchy, aren't we?" He didn't let go of my hand, pulling it down to stroke a distracting finger up the blue veins of my wrist.

I staggered slightly to the side, thrown off balance by the way he began to stroke me. He caught me, a slim arm latching around my waist.

"Want to come with me?" he asked in a hypnotic cadence, pulling me away.

He didn't grip my arm tightly, but the way he herded me through the crowd was difficult to resist. And really, why resist? Handsome—no, beautiful—man, mysterious dark corner... What could possibly go wrong?

I followed blindly, my thoughts drifting to Luke. Who was Luke again? The name felt distant, unimportant. It was easier to let that part of me fade away. I needed to focus on the thumb tracing lines up and down the tendons of my wrists as they flexed.

We stopped in front of one of the shadowed alcoves that lined the massive room. The light cast flickering shadows across his face. What was his name? Had he said Eyrin?

In the shifting light, his features were more gaunt. The flashes of red made his eyes appear inhumanly large. I stumbled and pulled back, my breath quickening.

He said something, but the pounding music drowned out his words.

"What?" I asked, stepping sideways before we stepped fully into the dark.

He leaned down, his lips brushing against the shell of my ear as he spoke, "It's just through here."

Eyrin's other hand flew up, and a shimmering powder exploded into my face.

I flinched back, coughing as the strange substance burned my nose and throat. My vision blurred as the world spun out of control. The music warped until it became a faint, distorted echo. It was like I had been stunned.

My feet moved of their own accord as we passed through a thickly curtained partition into a small, circular room bordered by a deep-set couch. Sounds reached me slowly, fragmented and distant, like echoes of conversations rather than coherent sentences.

There were others in the room, shadowy figures. Their faces were blurred and indistinct, making it impossible to focus on them.

"Sit here." The command blasted through my eardrums.

My body obeyed as though it no longer belonged to me. I tried to speak, to stand, to move. It was like being trapped in a nightmare. My mouth wouldn't form the words, and my limbs refused to respond.

Tears pricked at my eyes as many sets of hands began to brush over my arms, sliding down toward my legs. Panic flared like a live wire as they tore at my tights, and a strangled cry finally escaped my parted lips.

"Shhh, shhh," someone soothed.

A face nuzzled against mine. It was too close. Skin against skin. I recoiled inwardly, my body still unresponsive. A tongue flicked out and lapped at the tears streaking my face. I begged myself to wake up. This was a nightmare, not real. I had to wake up.

Needling teeth sank haltingly into my cheek. Like it was sampling before fully committing to the bite. Another bit into my thigh. Then, the soft, defenseless inside of my arm. The bites weren't clean. They tore. Ripped. Burned. Each one lit up my nerves like fireworks under my skin.

Screams refused to form in my throat. I howled inwardly, frantically beating at the cages of my mind. But my limbs continued to deny my movement. A whimper might have made it past my lips, but it choked on itself. The only sound I made was a wet gasp. The thick, metallic smell of iron poured into my nose and down my throat. My own blood. I was tasting my own blood.

The creatures snarled, slurped, and tore. Their teeth cut like broken glass. Time stretched into an endless spool of pain. Darkness crept at the edges of my vision. It wasn't sleep, nor peace. This blackness was the final void, the thin lip of whatever came after.

"Stop," I mouthed, but the sound dissolved in my throat.

I didn't want to die like this; I needed to find some way to save myself.

But it didn't stop. I fought and fought, teeth gritted, but my body wouldn't listen.

Collapsing forward, I pitched into the waiting arms of oblivion. Oblivion ended up being a shoulder pressed solidly against my forehead. I was being held like a lover, my limp frame rocking gently in cadence with their gulps. The music still pounded around me, indifferent to my demise. The wet slap of tearing flesh mixed with the rhythmic soundtrack to my death.

Adrenaline drained away, taking with it my panic and pain. Warm numbness bloomed in my toes, creeping upward like a wave eager to claim the rest of me.

Then, a jerk—a sudden wrenching sensation—and the creatures' teeth were gone. My body convulsed, and I realized I was free-falling as I thunked onto the floor in a crumpled heap.

Piercing screams erupted around me, disjointed in my lagging consciousness. Strobes seared behind my eyelids and, all at once, the world snapped into brutal clarity.

He stood above me, eyes coals of rage. His sculpted face was terrifying in its stillness. Sorin looked like a fallen angel, a preternatural embodiment of rapture's wrath.

In his hand dangled the lifeless body of someone nearly identical to Eyrin. A woman whose neck was snapped brutally to the side. Her glassy eyes stared blankly past me, mouth frozen in a grotesque O of surprise. Where her teeth should've been, hundreds of infinitesimal spikes jutted out like shards of bone.

I tried to call his name, but my voice withered after the first syllable. Tongue turned traitor, my mouth was slack and useless as the strange paralysis seized me again. His eyes found me. The feral fury burning in them would've stopped my heart if it hadn't already been stuttering from blood loss.

His lips curled back into a savage sneer. The gums withdrew and his teeth elongated into an expression that was judgment incarnate.

"Sorin," Eyrin pushed himself upright from the tangle of groaning limbs strewn across the ground. "I—"

"I warned you last time, Eyrin," Sorin growled, his face mutating.

A tremor ran across him, a subtle suggestion that turned into a mutiny of bone and muscle. His nose pulled forward into a blunt muzzle while his cheekbones knifed into harder planes. The whites of his eyes slid back as the irises flooded with crimson light and the pupils thinned into hungry slits.

"This is neutral ground," he continued in an inhuman snarl. "No hunting. No killing."

"Forgive me," Eyrin bowed deeply. "I did not mean to offend. If this one belongs to you, then I—"

"It's too late for apologies." Sorin's voice became deadly calm, a still lake on a freezing night.

The temperature plummeted. My skin prickled with cold, and I began to shake.

Around us, the others began to stir. Bodies that bore an unsettling resemblance to Eyrin. Siblings to the lifeless woman tossed on the floor like garbage that shared those dead eyes, bulging from their sockets. They rose in unison as if roused by a signal, like limbs of a single body.

They moved toward Sorin in loose formation, a hive with Eyrin pulling the strings.

"Don't be rash," Eyrin said shrilly, adjusting his posture. "We wouldn't want things to get messy. Not with the current state of your Province. Would we?"

Sorin chuckled, the sound a promise of violence and pain. The laugh of a killer savoring the hunt. Every step he took forward was like the ticking of a clock counting down to carnage. He tilted his head, a lupine habit that was magnified by the monstrous distortion of his face.

"I kept the peace. Held the line. Gave warnings."

Another step.

The group froze, their confidence faltering. One by one, they took wary steps backward.

"And all it did was teach people like you that I wouldn't bite. So, let's get messy. Maybe it should've been messy a long time ago."

With a sudden *pop*, the chandelier's light vanished, plunging the room into darkness.

25

____

TETHERED

Only Sorin's glowing eyes remained, twin embers scorching through the black. Faint crimson light seeped through a crack in the curtain, offering brief glimpses of a clawed hand raking downward, tearing across a throat. A wet, gurgling wheeze followed.

Another quick strobe of crimson. A lifeless figure fell as Sorin turned. Then darkness. A sickening thud and the unmistakable squelch of flesh yielding to force. In the next brief flash, Sorin had both hands buried deep in the chests of two victims. Their feet kicked feebly before falling still.

"Unseelie blood makes my skin crawl." Sorin's voice resonated through the suffocating darkness, like the growl of a beast that had been woken against its will.

I couldn't see his eyes anymore. The absence of that fiery glow made the space feel even more ominous. I held my breath, straining to catch any sound of movement. My heart hammered in my ears as I waited for the next strobe of light. When I relented to the burn for oxygen in my lungs, my own breath returned in wet gargles.

"However," Sorin's voice rang through the space like a death toll, "I think it's time to make an example."

The next red flash split the darkness, and I saw Eyrin pinned to the floor just a foot away from me. He was trapped beneath Sorin's clawed grip, arms thrashing uselessly.

Sorin's jaw unhinged itself, cracking open with a harsh click. It stretched far too wide, shadows sinking into the unnatural gape of his mouth.

From my crumpled position, I saw it all upside down. The nightmarish scene was further distorted by my waning vision and the white-hot cramps racking my body. A second set of fangs slid into place, thick canines jutting from the bottom of his jaw. They gleamed like forged blades in the hellish light, framing a grin that belonged to no living thing.

My stomach lurched, heaving against itself. I gagged on sour whiskey rising in my throat, the burn mixing with bile until my eyes watered.

Eyrin's mouth opened, but nothing came out. Only a voiceless cry swallowed by panic. The flash vanished. Darkness swallowed us again. But Sorin's monstrous form was seared into my memory, glowing behind my eyes like a brand.

There came an obscene squelching. When the light flickered again, Sorin's teeth were embedded deep into Eyrin's neck. His lips puckered against a skirt of black blood. A choked gasp escaped my lips at the macabre sight.

I urged my body to move, to flee, but my limbs refused to obey. All I could manage was to scratch weakly at the ground beneath my fingertips in a useless bid to pull myself away from the horror unfolding before me.

The slight motion caught Sorin's attention. His head snapped up with inhuman speed. As his fangs tore free, they pulled Eyrin's neck upward. The skin stretched before releasing with a slick, popping sound. Blood spurted from the twin pairs of puncture wounds. I squeezed my eyes shut just as the scolding droplets splattered across my face.

"Open your eyes, Scarlet," Sorin thundered. "Look at what you have caused."

What the—what I had done? The only thing I was guilty of was falling into a literal thirst trap.

His command cracked at me like a whip. Something buried deep inside me, older than fear, lurched to obey. My eyes flew open to hell.

Eyrin hung limply from Sorin's grasp, neck leaking unnaturally dark blood. Sorin had moved to tower over me, no longer a man. He was a beast. A perfect apex predator of this world, humanity discarded like a skin he'd outgrown. A stifled sob escaped me as our eyes met. His stare was a furnace of disdain that blistered my skin and incinerated my insides.

A figure rose unsteadily from the floor behind him. My eyes flared in warning, but it was too late. One of the creatures lunged onto Sorin's back with a snarl. The light vanished again. Sorin's enraged bellow tore through the darkness. Footsteps thundered past my ears, close enough to touch.

Eyrin was alive, bloodied but moving. He slipped behind the curtain and vanished into the crowd, who danced on, oblivious to the massacre a breath away. The music continued to pound against my eardrums.

Was Sorin dead? Was I? I couldn't be far from it. Warmth spread beneath me in a growing puddle. It pooled, sticky and thick. I was bleeding out. The chandelier above flared, then gradually brightened. Full light spilled over the room, revealing the wreckage in all its splendor. Six motionless bodies lay scattered across the floor.

In the center of it all was Sorin, crouched low. Blood clung to his hands, dripping against the floor. His eyes lifted to the curtain where Eyrin had vanished, then swung back to me. His mouth twitched.

I didn't understand the conflict running rampant across his face. His jaw worked like he was chewing on the weight of a decision. Vengeance or mercy. Retribution or... whatever it was he saw in me that was holding him back.

A low groan escaped me as I opened a palm to him, every movement dragging knives through my nerves. My trembling fingers clumsily tugged at the hem of his pants. As close as I could get to speaking.

Please. Please, I wanted to live.

For a heartbeat, he was that ancient statue untouched by time or feeling. With a full-body shudder, he rubbed at his face. The monstrous sharpness of his features rearranged themselves into something close to human. He stared down at me, but lower than my face. I followed his line of sight to the circular bite mark on my wrist. Its surface was riddled with jagged punctures, a gory constellation embedded in my skin.

It hurt. God, every inch of me was screaming. I wanted that numbness to return. My eyes roamed back to him. Five long, vicious scratches ran from beneath his chin into his hairline. He didn't even seem to feel them. I was beginning to wonder if he felt anything at all.

"Stupid human," he muttered as he knelt beside me.

His dark hair had come untethered. It fell around his face in wild waves as he leaned over me.

"You'll die like this," he said as if pointing out a mild inconvenience.

My reply was a garbled noise. He slid an arm beneath my shoulders and another under my legs. Carefully, he cradled me gently against his chest. It still hurt like a bitch. I let out a low, broken moan as my head dropped against him. Unconsciousness rippled the edges of my vision.

"Stay with me," he said gruffly.

I tried. I really did. But the world was beginning to slip away like sand through my fingers.

Sorin stepped to the wall, balancing me on an upraised leg as he tugged a cushion from the couch. His hand moved behind the backrest, and a hiss echoed in the room. I watched, dazed, as the entire section of the sofa swung inward.

Replacing his arm around me, he stepped into the passage. We passed into the shadows, and I whimpered. Was my vision failing? My hand weakly clawed the front of his shirt, clutching at the only solid thing I could latch on to.

"I've got you," he rumbled.

The walk felt endless. I gritted my teeth against the agony, too weak to do much else.

We stopped at the top of what could have been a hundred flights of stairs for all I knew. A small dial pad glowed to life, casting swaths of cold blue light over us. Sorin quickly entered a code, the light changing to bright green. My breaths came in shallow gasps, my chest rising rapidly and not deep enough. My eyes fluttered, rolling upward. Everything narrowed into dark smudges.

"Stay awake." Sorin's grip tightened around me. It hurt, but my sight cleared slightly.

A door hissed open, light spilling out. Brighter here. Warmer. We moved again. I couldn't tell if I was walking or if he was still carrying me. The only thing I could make out was the wobbly outline of Sorin. He lowered me onto something soft and warm, and I sighed in relief. My eyes drifted open, watching the ceiling above me swim.

"Scarlet," Sorin's voice floated to me, strained and distant, "open your mouth."

I didn't want to move anymore. Even that slight adjustment felt like a monumental effort, like lifting a mountain with my jaw. I ignored him, fixated on the soft edges of the world around me. The pain was gone at last. I didn't need to do anything more.

Pressure surrounded my lips, forcing them to part. I tried to pull away, mildly irritated. But I was too far gone to really care. Fingers worked their way into my mouth, guiding it open.

Something warm and metallic trickled onto my tongue. It filled my mouth until a rivulet trickled out of the corner of my mouth and down my chin. I wanted to spit it out, but Sorin's grip only tightened.

"You must swallow." Fingers moved to my throat, massaging gently. "Please."

My throat bobbed with the motion of his hand. Viscous liquid slid down into my stomach.

"That's my girl." There was a tremor of relief in his voice.

With each swallow, the taste evolved. The metal dulled, replaced by a crisp coolness, like breathing in winter air. An earthy warmth unfurled across my tongue and spread down my throat. It *pulled* me. Dragged me from the soft quiet I'd been slipping into.

My feeble hands latched onto his arm. His wrist hovered near my face, the open vein weeping crimson life. My lips met the wound; all at once, I was starving for him. I couldn't get enough of the blood he offered. I needed it to fill me until I couldn't take another swallow. My eyes fluttered closed as I drank greedily, drawing another deep pull.

A guttural rumble emanated from deep in his chest. His hand curled up behind my head. Fingers tangled in my hair, tethering me to the blood. To the pain. To life. To *him*.

He allowed me one final swallow before his hand clamped around the base of my skull. With a jerk, he pulled me back. I strained against him, leaning with my full weight toward his arm. The last of that precious red slipped from my lips, spilling onto the black velvet beneath us in shimmering droplets. I could have sworn I heard the fabric soak up each drop.

Sorin lifted his arm to his own mouth, running his tongue along the open wound. The jagged tear sealed beneath his touch, flesh knitting together as though it had never been touched.

It felt wrong to see it healed. A soft whine escaped me. He let me guide his arm back to my lips, where I kissed the flawless skin. I inhaled his intoxicating, electric scent. Snow and frankincense. It would make a perfect candle.

My overstimulated lips glided along the curve of his arm, savoring the faint give of muscle beneath the skin. I nipped at him with a playful, pleading bite. A brat's request for more.

His hand lashed out, catching my jaw in an iron grip.

"Do not tempt me, woman," he growled in a midnight whisper that brushed past my ear.

His words barely reached me. Inside, his blood was a wildfire that burned up every soft and mortal thing I'd once been. Shockwaves of heat crashed through my body. My skin vibrated. My blood *sang*. I was lightning in flesh. Every vein surged with power, alive beneath the surface, thrumming and unstoppable.

I wasn't just healing. I was becoming. If I wanted to, I could flip a car. Outrun sound. Break the world in half. I relinquished his arm to raise my hands to his chest. His hands covered mine. We stayed there, every inch of air between us quivering with the danger of uncrossed boundaries that threatened to change everything.

"Or what?" I whispered.

Then I shoved—*hard*.

26

———————————

DEVIL'S FOREPLAY

Sorin's eyes widened as he was thrown back onto the mattress. My vision had returned, and I could see *everything*. Could count every thread in the Egyptian cotton sheets beneath him if I cared to. The air itself felt alive, brushing against my skin like silk.

I inhaled deeply, intoxicated by this new awareness. By him. By me. By the blood that had transformed me. Nothing had ever felt this good, this powerful. Swiftly straddling him, I trapped his arms beneath my knees.

"Scarlet," he cautioned.

The exquisite, minute details I'd never noticed before captivated me. His deep blue eyes were speckled with shards of black that I had somehow mistaken for shadows before. Now I could see them clearly. Endless oceans of the deepest blue were framed by lashes so impossibly long and thick they seemed almost unreal.

With that hair and those carved-from-sin features, he was a walking Sephora ad. Or maybe the devil's idea of foreplay explicitly designed to torment me.

"Ever think about doing drag?" I asked, half-teasing, half-serious.

I leaned in, letting my fingertip trace the edge of his lashes. They were absurdly soft, a whisper against my skin. The touch sent a tingle racing down my arm. I was so caught up marveling at his unfair genetics that I didn't notice the shift in his body until it was too late.

In one fluid motion, he caught my shins, flipping me sideways with a graceless little *oof*.

"I don't need makeup with a face like this," he smirked as he pinned my wrist above my head.

"I just wanted to see your eyes." I pouted up at him. "If I can't touch you, then I want to leave."

It felt unfair to have so much new detail about him, and he wasn't allowing me near any of it.

"Let me go," I wiggled underneath him. "You can't keep me here."

He released an exasperated breath, passing both my wrists to one hand. The other raked down his face and lingered over his mouth as though physically restraining whatever he wanted to say next.

"You're drunk on alcohol and blood," He shot me a sidelong glare. "You're not going anywhere."

I scoffed. Feet planted, I attempted to buck my hips and throw him off me. All I managed to do was bring our faces so close that I could feel the brush of his breath against my skin.

"Okay, fine," I said, my eyes wandering shamelessly over his face.

I took in the slight furrow of his brows, the way his full lips parted just enough to let a single irritated exhale slip through. The faint shimmer of light catching the nearly imperceptible black flecks in his irises was mesmerizing.

His jaw tightened.

"You smell like cheap whiskey," he grumbled.

I blinked at him.

"That's so rude. At least call it *mid-shelf* whiskey."

I surged up against him, managing an inch off the bed before he slammed me back down like swatting a fly.

"You'd know all about rudeness," he grunted, straining to hold me in place.

I stilled. He meant last night, with Odessa. My head lolled to the side, peeking at the room through the curtain of his dark hair.

"I'm sorry," I whispered, sheepishly.

He shifted, pinning me more securely, his nose wrinkling.

"I don't need your apologies. I just need you to bathe."

My mouth dropped open.

"What's that supposed to mean?"

He kicked his leg free and ground me down with his hips.

"It means if you weren't so recklessly determined to throw your-self at every dangerous situation that crosses your path, maybe I could actually enjoy this moment."

I raised a brow, a teasing smirk tugging at the corners of my lips. "Oh, so you're enjoying this?"

His icy silence was answer enough, though the subtle flare of his nostrils didn't escape me.

I blew at one of his long tendrils of hair. "I can never get a read on you."

"Just go bathe," he said flatly, sitting back slightly but still keeping my wrists firmly pinned.

"Why?" I demanded, slightly offended.

I liked how he smelled. A sharp sting of snow and the earthy warmth of frankincense. I wanted him to like how I smelled, too.

Trying to be as discreet as my current state allowed, I tilted my head to the side and took a subtle sniff. Oh. Oh no. A wince snuck onto my face. Okay, fine. Maybe I smelled a little ripe. Eau de Super-natural Bar Fight with top notes of fae blood and regret.

He released my wrists, shifted back entirely, and rose from the bed with me over his shoulder like I weighed nothing.

"Hey!" I yelped, squirming against his hold. "Put me down!"

"Be silent," his hand came down with an abrupt slap on the sensi-tive skin of the back of my upper thigh.

Thanks to the torn tights and a skirt that had hitched up far more than was decent, my skin was bare underneath his hand. I squeaked, the sting shooting straight to my core. Heat bloomed across my cheeks as I pressed my thighs together tightly, mortified at my own reaction.

"Behave," he uttered darkly.

It only made me wriggle more.

"Or what?" I challenged myself.

A little thrill of excitement zinged in my chest and caught in my throat. His low chuckle wrapped around me as he carried me out of the room and into a hallway. We passed a worn marble statue of a woman draped in a gauzy toga. The craftsmanship was so exquisite it almost seemed alive.

"Holy shit," I gasped, reaching out. "Is that authentic? We would die to get a piece like this back at the museum."

The answer came not in words but in another firm slap to my behind. I gasped, the flesh feeling raw and swollen beneath the sudden bite of his palm. As I inhaled to protest, his hand moved in soothing circles over the aching spot. Words died on the tip of my tongue. A pleasant buzz radiated from the touch, leaving me momentarily speechless.

"I said be silent," he said, with a wry edge to his tone. "Or do you require another reminder?"

I bit down on the response that begged to escape. My hands fumbled for purchase on the smooth fabric of his shirt, sliding over the rugged ridges of his bulging lats. I realized what I was gripping and swallowed dryly.

He paused in a doorway. "Say the word, Scarlet, and I'll put you down. I'll wait."

Each second of silence turned my face hotter and redder, but I didn't make a sound.

"Thought so," every syllable was saturated with smug satisfaction. "You do like it, don't you?"

A tiny, mortified sound of affirmation escaped me. The response earned me another brisk smack. My teeth sank into my lip as tears pricked in my eyes. Tears of pain. Or was it pleasure? My toes and fingers curled involuntarily.

"You've been very naughty this evening," he reached out and flicked a switch.

A soft, golden glow spread through the room as low lights illuminated a stunning black-and-white marble bathroom. At the far end of the room sat a massive, detached, oval bathtub. A large glass-walled shower stood behind it, and a sleek double vanity stretched along one side of the room.

The floors and walls blended seamlessly, as if the entire room had been carved from one perfect slab of marble. Its swirling patterns snaked around the room under the gentle light. Golden candle sconces lined the walls. I watched them curiously as we approached the tub.

"Sit here." He set me down on the edge of the tub. "Don't move."

"Who died and made you boss?" I scowled.

He withdrew a box of matches from his pocket, "Quite a lot of people, actually."

I watched him, thrown off by the apathetic delivery of such a grim statement.

"Care to explain?"

He moved around the room, methodically lighting each candle. I watched the undulating light ripple around the room.

"I'll tell you when you're sober," he replied, not even glancing back.

"I'm fine now," I insisted, then immediately noticed the way my body swayed, teetering precariously on the edge of the tub.

Self-preservation kicked in, and I slid down to the marble floor. The cool stone made me shiver slightly, but it felt steadier down here. With the candles now lit, the marble veining appeared in starker contrast. I reached out, tracing the flowing patterns with my fingers.

"This is gorgeous," I sighed distantly.

"It has its charm," he replied, pacing toward me and stopping just in front of where I sat.

My attention dropped to his shoes, polished leather dulled by grime. My eyes tracked upward, taking in his tailored dark blue pants and matching shirt. Both were torn in places, the fabric stained and matted with viscera. I frowned slightly at the ruined outfit.

"Sorry," I muttered gloomily, resting my chin on my knees.

"For what?" he crouched down so he was nearly at eye level with me.

"For tonight. For losing control like that. And last night. Hell, for the rest of it." I exhaled, defeated. "For all the bodies that keep piling up around me. I'm starting to look less like your damsel and more like your accomplice."

I was one chalk outline away from being my own crime scene. My eyes remained fixed on my shoes, unable to meet his penetrating gaze.

His hand cupped my face. Through my lashes, I caught a fiendish glint in his eyes.

"You're no damsel."

My world tilted as he pulled me upright. He steadied me on my feet before kneeling before me.

"Now," he commanded, "don't move a muscle."

I froze in place as he began to work. One by one, he unzipped and removed each boot. Then he prowled behind me. The hiss of my zipper filled the room as he dragged it down my spine. Cool air kissed the skin of my back as the dress slithered down my torso. Candlelight flickered across me, gilding the swell of my breasts. I trembled faintly, trying and failing to keep myself still.

I couldn't sense his movements behind me. He made me completely vulnerable. Turned me into prey standing before its predator. Every muscle in my body screamed with the instinct to flee from the ludicrous danger I had willingly subjected myself to. The monstrous vision of Sorin looming over Eyrin played in my mind.

"You reek of other men," he said in a voice that vibrated against my skin.

Hands pushed under my arms, nails dragging at the waistband of my tights. Arms locked around my torso, binding me against an immovable wall of darkness rising behind me. A deep, animalistic sound thrummed against my back. I arched into him, the action as involuntary as breathing.

"Never," he rasped. "Never come to me smelling of other men again."

I sucked in a sharp breath as his nails elongated into razor-sharp talons. They bit into the mesh of my tights, puckering the delicate fabric and grazing the supple skin beneath.

My chest rose and fell in ragged breaths, lungs working overtime to fight against the panic trying to rise inside me. I wanted to run. I wanted to scream. I wanted to bend over and let him ravage me. To rip open his belt, fall to my knees before this exquisite nightmare, and drown my fears in want.

"Nod, if you understand." There was a choice hidden within his words.

Some small voice in the back of my mind shrieked that this wasn't healthy, wasn't normal. My toes hovered over the threshold of a line I knew, deep down, should not be crossed. If I stepped over, my world would shift again, the axis tilting beneath my feet.

Could I survive it?

Luke crept into my thoughts, an unwelcome phantom at the edge of my consciousness. It dragged with it the bruised feeling of an unhealed heart. Poisoning my resolve with a soft, insidious whisper:

What if. What if. What if.

What if I get hurt again?

I closed my eyes, willing thoughts of Luke to dissipate and leave me alone with the choice at hand. I nodded once, my cheek brushing against the silken strands of his long hair.

"Say it," he said thickly. "I want to hear you out loud."

A hushed rip announced the delicate cloth of my tights succumbing to the pressure of his claws.

"I won't."

My words trembled as I stumbled closer to the precipice of that treacherous threshold.

"Won't what?"

Another rip stole a precious millimeter of fabric.

"I won't come to you smelling of another man ever again," I vowed with a shuddering breath.

I didn't want another man. I wanted the monster looming behind me. I wanted Sorin. God help me, I was going to get him.

27

HONEY, BEHAVE

"So obedient," he purred, sweeping the hair away from my neck.

Need clawed at me as I thrust my hips back. In answer, he spun me around. My arms flailed, latching onto the broad expanse of his shoulders for balance. Nausea clenched my stomach with the motion. Spit flooded my mouth as I choked back a gag.

His claws hooked the delicate fabric of my tights and shredded what was left of them. The mangled remnants fell away. His eyes darkened as they roamed over me, claws dragging in a feather-light graze across the curves of my breasts and hips.

As I watched his hands move, the shapes around them began to blur at the edges like watercolors bleeding on paper. I locked my knees against the tilting room and had to clench my fists to keep from toppling over. Sorin grasped the underside of my elbows to steady me.

"Shower," he said, nodding toward the glass doors.

"W-what?"

"You need to shower."

"I don't feel well," I whispered, shaking my head to clear it.

I wanted him, but the discomfort rising in my body was getting difficult to ignore. I had to lean heavily on him for support as I took a wobbly step toward the shower.

"Why do I feel like this?" I pressed a hand to my forehead. "I thought your blood was supposed to make me feel better."

"You lost too much of your own blood, but you didn't drink enough of mine to turn. So, your body is rejecting it, fighting it off like a virus. Add that to the alcohol in your system... How much did you drink?"

"A lot," I confessed, glancing at him.

He was still covered in dried blood splatters and smudges of grime.

"You're dirty too," I said. "Take your clothes off."

He studied me closely, then leaned me gently against the cool marble wall. His fingers undid the buttons of his shirt, one by one, before shrugging it off his broad shoulders. His pants followed, sliding to the floor with a soft whisper before he kicked them out of the shower.

My eyes traced the inviting trail of hair that dusted his chest, following it downward until it disappeared into the waistband of his boxers. His thumbs snagged the elastic. With a tug, he stepped out of them. He didn't try to hide anything as he stooped to collect me again.

My mouth went dry as I tried to grasp him, but he gently pushed my hands away. Reaching around me, he turned the nozzle, and warm water cascaded over us in a soothing rush. I looked up at him, disappointment twisting inside me.

"You're drunk," he said.

Adjusting the switch, he redirected the flow to a movable nozzle, then turned me so my back was once again pressed against his solid chest.

He pulled me closer, wrapping an arm around my waist as the warm spray cascaded over my hair. Soon, his fingers were kneading my scalp, working a thick lather into my hair.

"We'll revisit this when you're sober," he breathed against my shoulder.

A pout tugged at my lips, but I couldn't hold onto it. His touch melted away my resistance until I was pliant. I would have purred if I could have.

"It smells like honey," I said, inhaling the sweet fragrance.

My thoughts wandered to the honeyed oil I had smoothed into my skin the night we spent at the safe house.

"My favorite," he hummed in response as his hands moved to spread the suds down my arms and hands.

I nearly groaned at the way his thumbs dug into the tight knots along my spine. When his soapy hands glided over my breasts and down between them, his touch was fleeting. Then his fingers slipped lower, lathering my folds with a stroke that sent a needy whine tumbling from my lips. My hips pressed back against him, seeking more.

"Brat," he tsked.

His hands shifted from my belly to my pebbled nipple. Holding my breath, I was sure he was about to squeeze.

He flicked it hard. I yelped, jumping at the sharp sting.

"No moving," he chuckled.

"Don't tease me," I clenched my jaw.

When I reached to rub the tender spot, he batted my hand away. I reached out, snatching the bottle of soap from his grasp. Pouring a generous dollop into my hands, I worked it into a lather and began rubbing the blood from his body. The dark streaks ran down his skin in rivulets that were too thick, too dark, to be human.

Stiffening, his head turned to meet my gaze.

"Just returning the favor," I murmured, softly waggling the bottle at him.

I worked the soap into his palms, between his fingers, then up the firm length of his forearms. Standing on my tiptoes, I rubbed over the contours of his throat. His adam's apple bobbed beneath my touch. From this angle, I was perfectly eye-level with his achingly kissable mouth. My attention snagged on a dark smudge of blood at the corner of his lips. I reached up, wiping it away with my thumb.

He sucked in a breath as my thumb tugged gently at his lower lip. My eyes climbed to meet his, stomach tightening at the sound. Those deep blue eyes locked onto mine before flicking down to my mouth, then back again. A bead of water slipped from the corner of his lips, bridging the scant space between us before splashing softly onto my own.

"Lean down," I requested.

His mouth opened to protest, but I cut him off before he could speak.

"Just going to wash your hair," I assured him. "You're too tall for me. Now, come here."

Sorin leaned down to let my fingers sink into his scalp, reluctance still evident in his stiff posture. As my fingers traced down to the nape of his neck, I felt the unexpected weight of his forehead resting against my shoulder.

I counted the rise and fall of his chest. Once... then four... then five, followed by the soft give of his shoulder sinking into me. It occurred to me that he might have finally, truly relaxed for the first time since I'd met him. Readjusting my stance to accommodate his weight, I took the ends of his hair and gently worked the shampoo through it.

I had conditioned his hair twice by the time he rested fully against me. If not for the growing quake of my legs, I might have asked for a brush to comb through it.

"Sorin," I whispered, "I'm done. Do you want to get out?"

I hated breaking the moment. He didn't seem like someone who allowed himself this kind of peace often. But my strength was slipping away as quickly as the water down the drain.

Rumbling his agreement, Sorin pulled himself away from me. Without his weight to brace against, my fatigued legs overcompensated, and I stumbled forward. He caught me then turned off the water.

"Why do I feel so tired?" I slurred. "Something isn't right."

"The sun is about to rise." Sorin's arm remained around me as we stepped out of the shower. "My blood is affecting you like it does me."

"How are you moving, then?"

My mouth felt like it was packed with cotton. I stood there, dazed and useless, as he wrapped a thick black towel around me.

"It gets easier with age," he muttered, scooping me into his arms.

"This is familiar," I hummed, my head lulling against his chest.

He gave a crooked smile, a dimple gracing his left cheek, "It seems you like to find your way into my arms."

I huffed, unable to say more.

I silently observed the apartment as he carried me back to the bedroom. Deep emerald green walls were adorned with what I could only assume were priceless paintings and other artworks. Some looked older than others, likely worth more than entire homes.

We entered his sprawling room, the floors swathed in unspeakably expensive rugs. A four-poster bed awaited us on the far side of the room, flanked by two massive armoires. More art cluttered the space, but the most impressive pieces were the enormous wall tapestries hanging from floor to ceiling. Any windows would have been entirely obscured by the fabric.

I was too tired to make sense of the dark figures stitched into the tapestries.

Sorin peeled back the thick black velvet duvet and deposited me onto the dark gray sheets. As I sank into the pile of fluffed pillows, he swapped my damp towel for the duvet, letting it fall to the floor.

Then, his own towel followed.

I shouldn't have looked. I *definitely* shouldn't have looked. But it was impossible to ignore the perfectly sculpted globes of his ass as he stalked to the other side of the bed. He slid under the covers, his presence taking up the majority of the room.

"Lights?" My voice was thin as I glanced around at the dim room.

A myriad of lamps and wall sconces added to the artificial

twilight that seemed to haunt the entire building. Sorin smiled then, his teeth too white and perfect. It didn't reach his eyes.

SNAP. The sound cracked through the air like a gunshot.

I flinched, my heart trying to accelerate as the room plunged into impenetrable darkness. The absence of light was sudden and complete. I blinked, once, twice. Nothing. No shapes, no outlines that I could see. Suddenly, the sheets around me felt too tight. My ears strained for sound, to catch the subtle whooshing of Sorin's breath. If he was breathing at all by now. I thought of the night we had spent together, when he was as still as a cooling corpse beside me.

I was alone. Weak as a kitten. Flat on my back in an unfamiliar bed. And somewhere in all that black, still space lay a monster. A monster that had killed for me, yes. But a monster that I knew could just as easily decide I'd look better as an entrée than a bedmate.

Reason and logic had a funny way of finding their way back to a girl when she wasn't drowning in the pheromones of a morally questionable vampire.

Curved, merciless claws flashed through my mind. Blood. Carnage. I pictured my skin tearing under those claws just as easily as my tights had. Felt the phantom sting of the teeth that had pierced my skin, returning to finish the job. My pulse thundered in my ears.

The dizziness returned in full force, and the room slipped sideways. Had I taken too much of his blood? How extremely was my body rejecting it?

Maybe I was dying alone in the dark. Cut off from the world.

"Sorin?" My whimper slipped past my lips with the last scrap of strength I had left.

A pause.

"Here, Scarlet," his voice was hushed, close. "It's alright. I'm with you."

His thumb brushed over my palm before his hand engulfed mine. But I was already slipping. My mind was fracturing, the edges going dark. As I sank, one final thought coiled around my mind.

What if I never woke up?

28

—————————————

UPPER EAST THRONE

I groaned, pressing a hand to my pounding head. A sick roiling churned in my stomach, and sweat clung to my skin. Everything was too hot. My throat felt like I had swallowed a fistful of sand. Eyes still closed, I kicked off the heavy blankets.

"Good evening, Scarlet," Sorin's smoky voice crooned from beside me.

Evening? Gasping, I shot upright, only for a wave of dizziness to slam into me. Black spots danced across my vision. I had slept through the entire day.

"Oh my god. Milo!" I scrambled from the bed. "He's been stuck in that little room all night and day!"

"He's with Malik." Sorin's hand caught my arm, keeping me from toppling over. "And has been since early this morning."

Breathing hard, I collapsed back against the pillows, pressing a hand to my chest. My very naked chest. I sucked in a sharp breath, yanking the sheets over me with a mortified gasp.

"What happened last night?"

The memories surged back as I asked. My body against his, the shower, the press of his hands.

"Oh my god." I hid my flushed face behind my knees. "Don't answer that."

"Your shyness is a little late," he mused.

He sat up, shifting the blankets dangerously low on his hips. I made the grave mistake of looking, though I needed no reminder of his very generous package from the night before.

I was never going to make it through this. I had to at least attempt to salvage what little dignity I had left.

"I'm so sorry," I said without looking at him, and I swung my legs over the edge of the bed. "I should probably go—ah!"

I was suddenly flat on my back, my arm held in place.

"Oh no, you don't," Sorin loomed over me, his body caging mine as he brought us nose to nose.

"Sorin," I narrowed my eyes, self-preservation taking over embarrassment. "Let me go. Now."

"Not until we've talked about things," he countered.

I rolled my eyes.

"What things?"

"Don't play coy."

His fingers brushed wayward strands of hair from my face. Our eyes locked, and my pulse went wild. The flecks of black in his deep blue gaze looked like swirling twin galaxies.

" I-I don't know what you mean."

"Oh," he breathed. "I think you do. I think you remember perfectly well, Scarlet."

"No," I denied, definitely not hyper-fixating on the warm fan of his breath against my throat.

"You do. And it frightens you."

"I am not frightened of you."

"Liar."

His eyes searched mine.

"You don't know anything about me," I bit out. "Get out of my head."

Drinking his blood didn't mean he could tell me my own damn feelings.

"I would happily not be in it if you had been able to keep yourself together last night," he shot back, his own anger rising to meet mine.

"You think you have me all figured out, don't you?" I spat. "That I'm some lost, weak thing who can't handle this world? Newsflash, Sorin, I didn't ask for any of this."

"And yet here you are, running like a scared little kitten," he said with a haughty expression.

"I'm not running!"

"Aren't you?"

I sucked in a long breath through my teeth. He wasn't entirely wrong. But if I said it out loud, everything would finally crash down on me in one colossal emotional mudslide.

My broken marriage.

Being shoved into a suddenly unfamiliar world full of lethal monsters.

This inescapable pull toward a devil who ran hot and cold. Who got under my skin in ways I hated and craved in equal measure.

I stopped myself. I couldn't think about this now.

"I'm handling things just fine," I gritted out.

His gaze flicked to my trembling mouth.

"Your lies taste like soot," he grimaced.

"Shut up," I seethed.

His fingers twitched against my wrist, and a vein in his temple throbbed.

"This feeling isn't easy for me to process, either," he finally ground out roughly.

"I'm shocked you feel anything at all."

The words were out before I could stop them. The moment they registered, I sucked in a breath, opening my mouth to soften the blow. But nothing came out.

Sorin pushed off the bed, hands flexing at his sides as if to cast off the memory of my touch. Maybe touching me was dangerous for him. Maybe everything about this was.

"Right," I sat up too fast, dizziness making my vision blur. "Who's running now?"

His shoulders tensed, but he didn't turn back.

"Did my words on the roof mean nothing to you?"

The softness in his voice made my stomach clench with an emotion heavier than anger.

Deciding to throw it all out into the open, I admitted, "I just don't understand you. Sometimes you're so thoughtful, but then I see the way you act towards me or towards Odessa—"

At her name, he craned his neck, watching me from the corner of his eye.

"Odessa? What does she have to do with this?"

"What does she—? You're partners." I shot him an incredulous look. "And I get that emotionless cruelty is like... a vampiric thing. I do." *I didn't, actually.* "But the way you tear into her—do you have to? The way you talk to her is awful."

Maybe it wasn't my business, but I couldn't shake those cold, dismissive exchanges. The way he regarded her like she was nothing.

"You don't know what you're talking about."

"Of course I don't! Because no one will tell me anything! I was just ripped from a world where the biggest issue I had was my husband's affair and tossed into this insane reality of fantasy creatures!"

I sucked in a shaky breath, my heart hammering against my ribs.

"I feel like I'm still walking around in the dark. I almost got fucking eaten last night, Sorin! By fairies! You get that?"

Sorin finally turned to face me fully with a piercing glare.

"And there's clearly more going on here." I gestured wildly at the space between us. "This. Whatever the *hell* kind of twisted experiment you're running on me. The Summit you refuse to talk about. So yeah, forgive me for wanting to run when every step I take feels like I'm walking straight into a bear trap."

I turned away from him. Darker thoughts of Luke and my home life unspooled into a horrible fissure within me. Footsteps sounded, and I felt a hand brush my own in a silent request.

"What else?" He asked lowly.

I swallowed hard, wanting to slap his hand away and shove the truths into the farthest corners of my mind. But I was too exhausted to pretend apathy. The unspoken agreement between Odessa and me would have to remain buried. But there was something else. Something far more pressing.

I sank back onto the bed, "I can't go on pretending there's not something between us."

Sorin stilled, the lines of his face tightening.

"And what kind of woman does that make me?" I let out a bitter laugh. "My divorce isn't even finalized."

He threaded his fingers through mine, "A beautiful woman."

I shook my head, "A weak one. A woman who should have more control".

"If you think that, then you are blind," he said, sitting beside me.

I exhaled heavily through my nose.

"I'm serious, Sorin. My life is falling apart, and the last thing I should be doing is..." I gestured vaguely between us, the heat of my own shame creeping up my throat.

He gave a cheeky little smile, "Falling into my very tempting arms?"

I scoffed.

"I'm not even sure I can trust you. For all I know, you're just manipulating me to get whatever result you're looking for out of this experiment."

His smile faded, and we sat in silence for a long, long time.

"You're right," he sighed. "You don't even know my last name."

He leaned back slightly, his hand falling away as he studied me.

"Draconis."

"What?" I asked.

"My last name. It's Draconis."

I arched a brow, digesting that. *Sorin Draconis.*

"And I do feel." He let out a measured breath. "More than I'd like to, thanks to a certain human."

I looked down at our legs, just a breath apart. The depression of his weight on the bed tilted me subtly toward him as if gravity itself conspired against my better judgment.

"Then this certain human needs some details." My voice was less edged, "Or you'll probably end up with a certain corpse."

"I won't let that happen."

Clutching a pillow against my chest, I lay back down to face him. A sense of defeat washed over me.

"I don't see how you could stop it unless you plan on escorting me 24/7."

"If I say you aren't to be harmed, then you won't be."

The absolute finality in his tone made my stomach flip. He said it as if it were law.

"And why, exactly, would your word make a difference?" I barely restrained my eye roll.

Sorin exhaled through his nose, his lips twitching.

"You haven't been paying very close attention, have you?"

I raised an eyebrow at him.

"I think I might have been right. You are blind," he said flatly.

I swatted at his hip, and for a second his lips quirked before his expression evened out again.

"The reason for all of this—the estate, Odessa's contract with me, the club and restaurant—is because *we* run it."

"Be specific, please," I requested, doing my best not to sound too annoyed at his continued vagueness.

Sorin lay back against the pillows, propping his head against his knuckles as he looked at me.

"New York. The upper East Coast, if you want specifics."

My mouth popped open.

"I'm sorry. You run *what* now?"

His expression didn't change.

"We are the sovereign entity here. For all metaphysical beings."

I stared at him, unblinking. "You're in charge of everything... metaphysical?"

He nodded in confirmation.

"So there really is more? More than just fae and vampires?" I let out a slow breath, my blood roaring through my ears. "All those stories, the myths and legends, you're telling me they're true?"

"Where there's smoke, there's fire."

Cryptic as ever. I had the sinking suspicion I'd only just scratched the surface.

"I think I need a minute to process," I said, scrubbing at my face.

The fae's words from last night replayed in my mind.

We wouldn't want things to get messy—not with the current state of your Province.

My fingers slid down, parting just enough for me to peer at Sorin.

"What's wrong with your Province?"

"That is complicated." He turned his gaze toward the ceiling, jaw tightening. "And none of your business."

Ouch.

"Fine."

Rolling away from him, I slid out of the bed, not bothering to cover myself.

Behind me, Sorin called, "Where are you going?"

"Shower," I said without looking back, forcing myself not to be self-conscious about my nude strutting.

After all, he'd seen everything last night. I padded down the hall-way, feeling his stare searing into my skin. At the doorway, I paused. Without raising my voice, knowing *damn well* he would hear, I glanced over my shoulder, lips curling.

"And then maybe to find another man who's capable of filling me in..."

I let it hang. Then added, sweetly, "With information, of course."

I stormed over to the sink, twisting the faucet with more force than necessary. Drinking deeply, I didn't come up for air until my lungs screamed. I straightened and met my own reflection. My eyes caught sight of a darkened figure looming behind me.

I whirled on Sorin. We really needed to talk about him sneaking up on me like that.

"There is unrest," he said tightly. "Odessa and I have vastly different views on rulership."

He took a step forward. I shuffled back, only to hit the unforgiving corner of the sink. My breath hitched as he cornered me.

"We are at odds," he rumbled softly. "And thus, so is our Province."

"What kind of differences?"

Sorin's jaw ticked.

"Ask her if you wish to know. I do not care to speak of her now."

He took another step.

Hunger and dominance warred in his eyes. It was the same wolfish gaze I remembered from the first few days I had known him. When I had truly feared him. I tracked his every movement, every twitch. My palms, slick with sweat and water, fumbled behind me only to find the smooth surface of the sink.

Sorin bracketed me against the counter. The world shrank to where he had my body trapped between him and cold marble.

"There will be no other man who can 'fill you in'," His voice dropped with each word as his fingers encircled either side of my arms.

A pulse of desire flared to life in my stomach. I thought of the way his fingers had plunged inside me on the roof. His head dipped so our mouths were just a breath apart.

"Only me," he rasped against my lips. "Not that pathetic excuse for a man. Not anyone else. Me."

Pathetic excuse for a man? Ah. Luke.

My chin tilted up slightly, giving him better access to my parted lips, "Sorin—"

His name barely passed my lips before he surged forward, silencing me with a whisper-soft kiss.

29

ORBIT

Comparing Luke to Sorin was like comparing a coffee stain to the night sky. Like a watered-down ink blot to the deepest, richest black paint. I once watched an art student at the university create a pigment so dark it swallowed light, turning the canvas into a void. A black hole against stark white.

Luke was the white paint. And I, I had been led here, to this moment. I was teetering on the edge of a bottomless abyss that was Sorin, with no way to claw myself back.

His knuckles grazed the underside of my breasts, then dipped lower. A palm skated just above the apex of my thighs, heat pulsing in its wake. His lips brushed the shell of my ear, and I trembled.

"Listen to me," his fingers curled into my hip. "I want you to be mine, Scarlet. *Mine.*"

I should've stopped him. Should've reminded him I wasn't an object to own, that I answered to no one but myself.

But I didn't. His proximity rewired my thoughts, flattening the clean lines I'd drawn around myself until they blew away in smoke. I didn't want what was right. I wanted the danger he represented, to satiate the hunger in his grip. The unyielding fire of his fury could consume my body, mind, and soul.

Breath fled from my lungs. My world wavered, balanced on a blade's edge. His fingers traced my jaw, tilting my face up to his, his lips a whisper away from mine.

I wanted to be his. Entirely. That terrified me more than his fangs or claws ever could.

Headfirst into the void I went, a black-haired demon poised to catch me. All I could do was pray that I wouldn't end up on the same doomed path that Luke had taken.

We fought for dominance in a battle of teeth and tongues. My fingers tangled in his hair, fisting the lush strands. I yanked, forcing his head back to expose the long column of his throat. A prize. A weakness. I licked up the length of his ivory neck, savoring the taste of winter air and whispered nightmares.

His hand encircled my throat in a ruthless squeeze that stole my breath. I hoisted a leg around his hips, clit begging for the same attention my throat was receiving.

My spine collided with the unforgiving marble wall as he drove me back. My gasp was swallowed instantly by his mouth. Both legs wrapped tightly around his waist, attempting leverage when the only thing holding me up was him. Back straining, I pressed against the ridged length of his cock.

"You want me to lose control, don't you?" A husky exhale left him as he watched himself slide between my slick folds. "To fuck you so hard you forget your own name?"

Pinned beneath his hand, I forced out on a broken rasp, "I want you to choke me like you mean it."

A sharp hiss escaped between his teeth as he obeyed. Heat flared where his fingers cinched around the fragile column of my throat. The rush in my ears grew thunderous, blood pounding above and below the point where Sorin held me, my face flushing pink beneath the press of his grip.

My nails sank into the bulging muscle of his biceps. I needed the satisfaction of flesh yielding to pressure like I needed my next breath of air. His shaft prodded my entrance. A strangled cry slipped past his grip.

"Speak," he ordered as he drenched himself in the sopping heat of my core.

My lungs seized, vision tunneling, the world narrowing to nothing but the points where we connected. His grip eased just enough to slip a thread of air into my chest—just enough to let me beg.

"P-please, Sorin," My voice broke on a ragged inhale.

Air tore into my lungs, fueling the fire building inside me. Need tangled with dizzy euphoria, a head-spinning rush that vibrated through my skull before plunging straight to my center.

"I should leave you like this. Let you beg until you're nothing but a desperate, ruined mess for me."

But his own carnal hunger betrayed him. Each time he drew back, he notched himself closer to entering me. The hand supporting my ass flexed, claws scoring the arc of my hip. Delightful pricks of pain fizzled up, melting into the rising tide of my pleasure.

Half-starved for air, I panted, "Don't think so."

I refused to be the only one being subjugated tonight. I could still feel the power of his blood simmering within me. It wasn't the uncontrollable fire hydrant it had been last night. It had trickled down to a subdued current that sang beneath my skin. I was strong. Fast. Fast enough to catch him off guard.

His arrogance would be his downfall.

I detached a leg from his waist, bracing the sole of my foot against the wall. With a brutal shove, I launched us away from the cold marble and dropped my weight. Snarling, he was forced to a knee. His grip on my throat snapped open as he caught himself.

He growled a guttural, venomous word I couldn't understand.

A victorious laugh bubbled from my throat as I hooked my arm around his extended limb, collapsed it inward, and drove him further off-balance. At the same time, I threw my opposite arm over his back, twisting into the motion to flip him beneath me. By the time the world settled, my thighs bracketed his hips, and his body was pinned beneath mine.

"You'll pay for that," Sorin rasped, chest heaving.

"Sorin," I admonished, squeezing my thighs around him with a wild grin. "You underestimate me. I'm disappointed."

His lips quirked into a sinister half-smile. "What makes you think I don't have you exactly where I want you?"

My smile faltered as his hand locked around my ankle. Reaching down, I tried to pry his fingers away. Too late. His other leg shot out, hauling me towards my trapped leg. I crashed forward, my ankle the fulcrum as I spilled toward him.

I threw my arms out to avoid a face-first collision with porcelain and caught my weight at the last second, palms striking the ledge of the tub. My body jerked to a halt, ass totally exposed, legs spread to regain some kind of balance.

Sorin shifted behind me, one broad hand settling at the back of my head. He applied just enough pressure to let me know that I was at his mercy. His thighs locked mine in place so there was no room to move. My toes curled against the slick floor as I fought the urge to plead for him to drive the heavy length nudging at my backside deep inside me.

A hollow ache thrummed within me, longing to be filled, to be conquered into silence. I inhaled, doing my best to breathe past the impossible lust pounding through me. If we didn't end this soon, I was going to start screaming.

"Take me," I demanded hoarsely.

His fingers clenched my hair, yanking my head back. He stretched my throat in an exquisite mirror of what I had done to him moments before.

"Did you say something?"

Oh, he heard me. He just wanted to listen to me say it louder.

"Sorin," I gasped, my voice thickening against the pull of my neck. "I swear, if you don't start fucking me right now, I'll die."

His dark chuckle rumbled against me.

"Say please again."

I clenched my jaw, refusing. Until his shaft nudged at my entrance, just barely pushing inside of me. A moan ripped from me. My hips rolled back, desperate to take him in.

The slap came without warning. A hard, stinging crack against my left butt cheek. White hot heat bloomed over my skin.

He pulled back, and a breathless cry caught in my throat. Tears pricked at the corners of my eyes as my body cried out for him.

His palm glided over the tender mark, soothing the sensitive skin. Then he jutted forward just enough for the head of him to breach me. I keened, legs trembling with the effort of keeping myself locked into position.

"Use your words, Scarlet."

"Oh, god—please."

Whatever boundary had once existed, I'd surpassed it, obliterated it. My pride, vaporized.

"I'm not God," he drawled.

He had that right.

"Damnit. Sorin, I need—"

"You need what?" He pressed a fraction deeper.

"You." The word fled from my mouth like a prayer, a sob, a curse. "Inside me."

My face burned, and I submitted with nothing left to give but my very soul.

"You beg so sweetly." Then he drove himself inside me, sinking to the hilt. "Do it again."

"Fuck," I moaned, inner walls stretching to accommodate the thickness of him. Biting my lip, I waited as the brief pain ripened into throbbing pleasure. The moment I rocked back against him, he pulled out completely. I nearly sobbed at the emptiness he left.

"You will break for me," he whispered roughly, breath tangling in my hair. "And you will thank me for it."

And oh, I would. This wasn't just about the way he felt inside me. This need was soul-deep. I was an asteroid burning through the cosmos, and Sorin was a planet with a gravity I could never resist. I would either incinerate in his atmosphere, or we would destroy each other on impact.

He thrust in harder this time, burying himself deeper than seemed possible. A choked sound escaped me, half-moan, half-grunt. I was consumed, body and mind eclipsed by the pounding fullness of him.

"Scarlet," he rasped.

His hand readjusted in my hair, pulling me up and backward. My spine arched, body forced into a perfect, helpless bow. He moved at a punishing tempo. Each thrust forced my hands to white knuckle the edge of the tub to stay upright.

"Harder," I pleaded as I clenched around him.

An animalistic sound vibrated deep in his chest. He tore out of me and ripped a towel from the wall. Spreading it on the floor, he lay me down with a surprising gentleness. I bit my lip, watching him as he knelt between my thighs. He spread them apart with a nudge of his knee, his dark gaze consuming mine.

"Why do you insist on looking at me that way?" he frowned.

His lips were parted just enough to flash the sharp tips of his fangs as they pressed into the fullness of his bottom lip. I arched a questioning brow and curled my leg around him, dragging him closer. His hands clamped down on my thighs.

"I am not a good man," he insisted, fingers biting into the fullness of my inner legs.

It wasn't an apology, or even a warning. It was simple truth.

"It doesn't matter." I sat up on my elbows, inhaling deeply, letting the heat between us rise until my blood was nearly boiling.

"Some would call me a monster." His grip tightened as if to prove the point, eyes flaring red.

In a thick voice, I whispered, "Prove it."

There was nothing gentle about the way he descended on me. Tossing my legs over his shoulders, he thrust into me without mercy. There was no escape. No room for resistance. There was only one choice left. Complete surrender. So I yielded. Clung to what little remained of myself until even that slipped through my fingers in a flurry of shuddering breaths, moans, and the sound of our bodies colliding.

Folding me beneath him, he slammed into me so hard I swore I could feel him in my chest. He filled me completely. Drove out every thought, every second guess. I was being split apart, reshaped, and reforged into something new that belonged to him.

His hand flattened against my belly. Pressing down, he amplified the tight fit of his cock until it bordered on agony. His thumb found my clit and circled it with lethal precision. My breasts bounced with every snap of his hips. The wet slap of skin and my broken cries ricocheted off the tiled walls.

A shockwave of blinding pleasure detonated inside me. His fingers were their own savage creatures. One moment, working me into a frenzy. The next, forcing me still, so I felt every brutal inch as he carved himself into me.

My legs quivered, spots bursting behind my eyelids as I clung to him. My nails dug into the hard muscles of his hips as my mouth opened in a silent scream. There was no air to voice it. Only pure, shattering sensation.

"That's it. Give me everything." His grip tightened into the soft flesh of my curves. "You don't cum without me. You don't breathe without me. You will break because I say so."

His speed turned inhuman, becoming a bone-deep, vibrating sensation that shook me apart one molecule at a time.

"Again," he rasped. "Cum for me until there's nothing left of you but my name on your tongue."

And I did. Screaming in earnest, I convulsed. My world splintered again and again. I wasn't burning up or shattering on impact. I had become locked in an inescapable gravitational. A moon in orbit that was irrevocably his.

At last, he released my legs. They fell bonelessly to his sides. But he wasn't done with me. His arms tightened around my waist, lifting me so I sat upright on his lap. He held me against him, his cock still buried deep inside my ravaged body.

My breath came in uneven gasps as I pressed my forehead to his. I peppered featherlight kisses across his jaw, his cheeks, his temple. Worshipped him in the aftermath of my destruction.

He gripped my chin, forcing me back. My breath hitched.

"Look at me."

Those flecks of deepest blue glimmered like shards of ice in the dark. He dragged his thumb over my swollen lips, eyes narrowing.

"We're not finished."

A fresh wave of wet, aching heat flooded my core. I rolled my hips, squeezing him with my inner walls as his hand found my breasts and squeezed viciously. The slight pain mingled with the immense pleasure. A tortured groan slipped from my lips as I rocked him deeper inside of me. His hips pistoned upward, forcing me to take him further. I gasped his name, fluttering around him.

He crushed his mouth against mine. Hands slid down to my ass, parting my cheeks as he lifted me up then slammed me back down. Over and over, he made me take him exactly how he wanted.

"You take me so fucking well," he growled into my parted lips.

I dug my nails into his shoulders, legs shaking as he pounded up into me. My body was his to use, his to wreck. My head lolled back, eyes rolling as he ripped me apart.

"Sorin," I whimpered between ragged breaths. "I'm so close—"

His fingers tangled in my hair, his starved eyes pinning me in place.

"Look at me when you cum."

I felt him everywhere. Elation zinged from the tips of my toes, swirled through my belly, lit up my nipples, and buzzed behind my eyes like lightning trapped in my skull. I was all blazing sensation.

He groaned my name through clenched teeth, his hips jerking up violently as he emptied himself inside me. He held me down on him, cock throbbing with the last remnants of his release. His fingers bit into my flesh, claws dragging just enough to sting.

For a long moment, neither of us moved. My body was limp, my skin slick with sweat. He was still buried inside me, his hand trailing up and down my spine slowly.

Then his lips trailed over my ear, "Good. Fucking. Girl."

30

FRIES BEFORE LIES

I hummed in satisfaction, slumping against him and tucking my head into the crook of his shoulder. His scent wrapped around me like a second skin. The world shifted as he stood, cradling me against his chest as he strode toward the shower.

I couldn't help the exasperated chuckle that slipped past my lips.

"Most men would find it insulting to be laughed at after sex," Sorin said gruffly, flipping on the shower and letting a spray of ice-cold water crash against us.

"I wasn't laughing at you!" I shrieked as the icy water hit me. "I was just thinking about how you always end up carrying me."

He paused for half a second before he grinned.

"I'd say it's instinct." He spun so the freezing water hit his back instead of me. "Can't blame your knees for knowing who to fall for."

The water warmed, but a dull, uncomfortable weight sank in my chest. I pressed a hand against him, pushing lightly in a silent request for release. After a beat, he let me go.

Turning away, I watched the steam fog the glass around us, wondering what in the hell I had just done. The divorce papers weren't even signed yet, and I was fucking a man who was probably using me. Didn't that make Sorin just as bad as Luke? How could I know if he had an ulterior motive to make me his personal blood bag with benefits?

Yeah, I was probably being used. For mind-blowing, toe-curling, body-wrecking sex, sure, but still used. And wasn't this supposed to be the other way around? I was supposed to be the one doing the using.

I shook my head. This was already too complicated. Pressing my fingers to the slick shower door, I shoved it open. Time to get out before I drowned in my own angst.

"I think not."

Sorin's arms locked around me, pulling me back against the hard wall of his chest.

"Sorin..."

My fingers laced over his forearm where it crossed my stomach, but I didn't fight him.

"I need space to think," I said unsteadily. "This was a lot for me."

He said nothing at first. Just held me, letting the water spill over us in sprays of rolling heat.

"It's difficult for me to understand. I do not feel as I once did." A pause as though the words sat strangely on his tongue. "Some things escape me. My humanity is not as it was when I was turned."

Sighing, I leaned my head into the hollow of his throat.

His lips brushed against my damp hair, "But I see how hard you fight, how much of the world you try to carry alone. I feel you here."

His fingers tapped once, twice, against my bare chest, right over my heart.

Another pause, then a breath that trembled through both of us. "And for that," he whispered, "I am sorry."

I couldn't decide if I wanted to run out the doors, maybe all the way home. Or if I wanted to turn and kiss him until I forgot how to breathe. My chest clenched against the icy discomfort lingering inside.

My mouth parted, words hovering on the edge of escape. Maybe I would tell him he was the first man I'd let touch me since Luke in almost ten years. Maybe I would admit how much I wanted something real with him, something warm enough to burn back the cold numbing me from the inside out. But the truth tasted like cinders on my tongue. What good would it do to bare myself to another man I couldn't be sure wasn't just waiting for his turn to break me?

I turned slightly, "Will you wash my hair again?"

His lips turned up. Pouring a dollop of honey-scented shampoo into his palm, he worked through my hair so tenderly.

"I almost envy you," I tilted into his touch as his fingers massaged the base of my skull, easing the tension knotted there.

"In what way?"

"To not feel," I sighed, my throat tight and heart heavy. "To not hurt like this."

His hands froze.

"To not feel," he echoed distantly. "To slip from humanity. It is a stagnant hell I would not wish upon anyone. It is like slowly freezing without the release of death."

I swallowed hard, his words reverberating through me and colliding with the memory of what he'd said on the roof.

You make me feel.

Was it true? Did I actually make him feel something other than cold emptiness? I could almost feel that depthless chasm inside him stretching endlessly like a void that had never known light. My skin pebbled.

And if I did, what did that mean for him? More importantly, what did I mean to him?

I thought about Odessa's offer to become like her and be rid of the persistent pain in my chest. A relentless, aching grief that squatted like an unwelcome guest. Wouldn't it be easier to let it go? Could feeling nothing really be worse than feeling too much?

"So you wouldn't change anyone?" I asked, keeping my voice as casual as possible. "To be like you, I mean."

"Never, " He stepped in front of me, brushing my soaked hair away from my face. "I have done so in the past, and it was a mistake. Each time."

A cold shiver rolled through me. He cradled my face in both hands, thumbs stroking the water from my lashes until nothing existed but the intensity of his gaze.

"Why do you ask?"

"No reason." My too-high laugh betrayed me like a blaring alarm that screamed out my guilt.

His brows furrowed, a little crease forming between them.

"Scarlet," he said, and just like that, my name on his lips was suddenly the most intriguing sound I had ever heard.

He took a slow step closer.

"Why do you ask?"

For some stupid, reckless reason, the truth bolted out of my mouth like a drunk streaker at a football game.

"Someone—someone offered to... you know. Turn me."

Why had I just said that? It was way too close to the truth for safety. If he guessed how deep I was with Odessa, I'd lose whatever flimsy leverage I had in the twisted little game we were all playing.

His entire body went still. The space between us shifted.

"Scarlet."

My name circled around me and burrowed under my skin. His eyes eddied into bottomless pits, and I was stranded in their depths.

"Promise me that you won't."

My pulse stuttered. His words settled over me like I was being wrapped in invisible ropes that I didn't fully understand.

"Swear it."

A fog drifted over my mind, creeping in like mist over water. I blinked slowly, struggling to keep hold of my thoughts.

Why had I even considered it? It was reckless. Foolish. Danger-ous. He was right.

I parted my lips, the words already forming, "I swear."

But a piece of me fought back. My fingers dug into his forearm, nails pressing hard enough to leave half-moon imprints. I wrenched my gaze away, stumbling back like I had broken free of a chain I hadn't even known was wrapped around my throat.

"You're—" My breath came ragged, uneven. "What the fuck was that? Were you *hypnotizing* me?"

Sorin's aversion to eye contact was as good as a confession. Revulsion clawed its way up my throat and curdled on my tongue. I shuffled back in disbelief.

"You don't understand what you're playing with, Scarlet," he said carefully.

"I'm not stupid," I said indignantly. "If there's something I'm not getting, then make me understand."

He exhaled hard, raking a hand through his soaked, unruly hair.

My mind churned through our every interaction, every choice I thought had been my own. The morning when I'd left Milo behind in the truck, even though I wanted to take him with us. The times he had told me to sleep, and I had immediately drifted off.

I'd convinced myself it was all exhaustion. My mind had been so spent trying to process how fast life was coming at me. Now, I wasn't so sure. Now, I suspected Sorin. My lips pressed into a thin line. Anger surged in, conveniently filling all the soft places I had started to open to him.

"It was for your own good," he reached out to me, and I sidestepped.

"My own good?!" I nearly shrieked with rage as I tried to step around him.

"Don't go."

"You can't tell me what to do," I bit out, reaching out and slamming off the water.

"Actually, I can." He closed the space between us, looming over me. His voice dropped to a gravelly murmur, "One word from me, and there won't be anywhere for you to hide or go where you aren't under some kind of surveillance."

"Yeah?" I jabbed a finger into his frustratingly sculpted chest. "You're the big fucking boss, aren't you? I bet demons send you fruit baskets and fairies write you thank-you notes. It must be exhausting, carrying around that ego all the time."

The vein in his temple throbbed. "This is coming out all wrong. Scarlet, I am trying to help you."

"No. God, you are unbelievable," I stomped my feet. "You're trying to control me. Without my consent."

I turned on my heel, stepping out of the shower. The air was chilly against my damp skin, but it couldn't compare to the violation crawling over me.

"Wait."

I barely blinked before he was lunging for my hand.

"Don't," I warned, seriously debating whether I should go for a wrist break or not.

"Just... feel." He took my hand and pressed it to his chest. "What do you feel?"

"Feel?" I glared up at him, holding his stare as water dripped down my face. I let out a long sigh. "I feel your stupid sculpted chest and your offensively perfect chest hair. Honestly, it's rude."

That damn smile. It crinkled the corners of his eyes and bull-dozed half my anger in one go. Fuck me, I had it bad. No. Focus. Angry. I was angry, goddammit.

"No," he shook his head, "Feel. Feel with your other senses. Like you did before."

I grumbled but closed my eyes and focused. Reaching inward, I searched for that invisible tether that I had grasped before in Savannah. I found it quickly this time. Blackness pressed against me like a living thing, whispering in a voice I couldn't quite hear. A chill slithered over my skin, sinking into my bones.

Eons of time stretched before me like an endless obsidian night. Infinite, devouring, eternity crushed down on my shoulders, crushing the air from my lungs. The void inhaled. All at once, it swallowed me whole. I was nothing, and it was everything. The world buzzed around me in a droning roar that blasted through my skull.

I had never been so cold. Felt so forsaken. The chasm widened, ripping open my chest so I bled openly into the void. There was no ground, no sky. Just emptiness drinking me dry. The blood drained from my body in winding rivulets, curling like serpents as they vanished into the ether. Ice rushed in to take its place. My skin stiffened and hardened, and my flesh turned to stone. I could feel it rupturing. Sickening fractures cracked through me, piece by piece.

Trapped in my own mind, I watched as time twisted and unraveled. Years. Decades. Centuries. People became ash in my wake. Their faces blurred, their voices drowned beneath the nothingness. Those close to me that I didn't kill grew, aged, and withered like flowers in a single season. One by one, they died as I remained a silent observer. A statue frozen in time. It was beautiful. And it was terrible.

I searched for my voice, but it had been stolen.

Stop.

Stop. Stop. Stop.

I wanted to scream, but my lips wouldn't move. I slammed my eyes shut, frantic to wake up, desperate to hear the sound of my own breath. But there was nothing. Not even me.

From the toes up, my porcelain body crackled and then shattered. A gasp tore from my lips as my eyes snapped open, and I collapsed to my knees. I was back in the bathroom with Sorin, supporting me.

I looked up at him, but my body was still locked in the aftershocks of that void. My teeth chattered violently. Without a word, he wrapped a large towel around me and led me back to the bedroom. A heavy black bathrobe materialized in his hands, and he guided me into it. Afterward, he pulled on a dark blue set of lounging clothes.

We didn't speak. I didn't think I could if I wanted to.

I followed him silently down the hall, drained and shivering. He sat me down in a small kitchen and brushed my hair out, then his own. As he squeezed a towel through my damp strands, he finally spoke.

"Do you understand now?"

My voice was hoarse, "Was that real?"

"You went too deep. I underestimated how well you'd be able to access our bond without experience." Sorin nodded solemnly. "But yes. "

"Typical man," I grunted half-heartedly.

He shrugged.

I licked my lips, my thoughts drifting elsewhere.

"What time is it?"

I needed Milo. I needed to sink my fingers into his velvety coat and feel his warmth pressed against me.

"Around three in the morning. Are you hungry?" He stepped away, returning the towel to the bathroom.

My stomach had been flipping uncomfortably for a while now.

"Yeah, I should go."

The kitchen was empty of cooking utensils or food. Unnecessary items for a vampire, but a very convenient excuse for me to leave. I moved to stand, but his hand pushed me back down.

"We need to talk."

"But Milo—" I objected, exhaustion dragging at my limbs. "And I'm tired. Very tired."

"I'll have Malik bring him up with food." Sorin was already tapping his phone.

Within twenty minutes, I heard the familiar sound of paws skidding across the hardwood floor, barreling straight toward me.

"Milo!" I barely got the name out before a warm, wriggling body crashed into me.

I dropped to my knees, burying my face into his fur as I murmured, "Hi, sweet boy."

Inhaling his earthy scent, I rubbed his giant floppy ears in between my fingers. Malik followed close behind, an impish glint in his dark eyes.

"What the fuck?" He mouthed silently to me, keeping Sorin at his back.

I shook my head, mouthing back, "Later."

He set a large bag on the counter, handing me a smaller one, then passed me a steaming mug of what I hoped was coffee.

"How did you carry all of this with Milo?" I asked, taking the cup gingerly.

"I am a man of many talents." He grinned, and then his phone buzzed. He glanced down, sighing. "And apparently, with many things to do tonight."

He stepped closer, wrapping an arm around me in a quick embrace.

"I heard what happened with Eyrin. What an ass."

I leaned into his shoulder, comforted by his kindness, "We can talk about it later."

He nodded, "See ya later, Red."

My heart gave a little squeeze at the nickname. I waved as he walked out, and the door clicked shut behind him. Sorin stood there, unmoving, eyes narrowed to slits.

Milo trudged into the living room, sniffed once, then collapsed onto the couch with a heavy sigh. It was way past his bedtime. I glanced up at Sorin, something about his posture setting off a whisper of unease.

I unzipped the smaller bag, pulling out a cream-colored sweater dress. It was soft, probably cashmere. Beneath it, a pair of matching booties nestled neatly in tissue paper.

I frowned, fingertips grazing the fuzzy fabric. I wasn't one to look a gift horse in the mouth. But should I really be accepting gifts from someone who had tried to... what? Steal my mind? Distort my thoughts and feelings? Definitely someone I was still angry with.

It didn't matter how noble his intentions were. That was some top-shelf Sith Lord bullshit. And he'd probably been doing it since the day we met. The thought made me sick.

"These for me?"

"Do you like it?" Sorin stalked toward me.

Not waiting for my answer, he plucked the bag from my hand and set it aside.

"I'm not really sure what I like anymore," I trailed off as his fingers caught the tie of my robe, tugging it loose.

He traced a line along my shoulder, peeling the fabric away exactly where Malik had touched me.

Oh. Maybe he was jealous.

...Was I into that?

A slow, sinful heat unfurled inside me. The robe slid off my shoulders and puddled at my feet. Sorin's eyes darkened, and that little vein popped on his forehead like it was clocking in for overtime.

Oh, yes. I was *definitely* into that. Somewhere deep in my brain, the tiny responsible part whimpered, waving a clipboard. I'd already gotten one warning for inappropriate thoughts. This was a repeat offense. At this point, I was probably due for a permanent cell in horny jail.

"I'm not sure I like that answer," he murmured against my neck.

The scrape of his teeth sent a shudder rippling through me. Every thought of anger flickered out like a snuffed candle.

"That's too damn bad," I rasped, molten heat pooling low as I arched my ass into him.

He hummed his disagreement against my throat.

I should have recoiled. Should have clutched my pearls like a good Southern woman, grabbed Milo, and stormed right back to my room with my dignity intact. But I didn't. If Sorin was a flame, I was a moth with a death wish. Gulping, I tried to regain some semblance of control even as I pressed closer.

My imagination was not compliant with my efforts to remain angry. It supplied me with x-rated imagery of Sorin bending me over the kitchen island and sent my brain into a downward spiral of reckless, needy thoughts.

"Didn't," I started, voice shaky, "didn't you say we needed to talk?"

"Yes, we do," Sorin said, pulling away languidly.

"Put this on," he handed me the dress, "You're far too distracting like this."

Lifting my arms, I allowed him to slip the fabric over me. His hands skated over the warm material, teasing over the curve of my hips. I hadn't even realized how cold I still was until the fur-lined booties swallowed my feet and cocooned my own body heat around my toes.

"This is really nice," I ran my hand up and down the dress, feeling the delicate fabric between my fingers.

"Yes, it is."

Sorin's palm slid over my breast. His fingers pinched my peaked nipple, rolling it between them.

I sucked in a sharp breath, thighs clenching against the throbbing between them. Biting my lip, I gazed up at him through my lashes. His mouth was slightly parted, his other hand sliding down to squeeze my ass.

"How many times do I have to tell you to not look at me like that?" he growled. "It's maddening."

"As many times as I have to tell you not to tell me what to do," I countered, spinning in his grip, pressing my ass against the unmistakable hardness there. Disappointingly, strong hands rested on my shoulders and guided me toward the small table. He pushed me down into one of the sleek, pale wooden chairs. I slumped, frustration momentarily forgotten when he shoved a bag of food in my direction.

Inside was a mouthwatering burger and thick-cut, seasoned fries. My stomach growled, and I dug in, suddenly ravenous. Halfway through, I looked up, catching Sorin watching me with a stupidly handsome smile plastered on his face.

I swallowed thickly, "Do you want to try it?"

"No," he said, crossing a foot over his knee. "Food lost its appeal long ago. Although it's nice to watch humans enjoy it. Especially when you insist on eating like a starved animal."

I rolled my eyes and gave his leg a light kick that was more for my own satisfaction than anything else.

"When I was human," he added, batting my foot away with a lazy flick of his hand, "food was scarce. So it entertains me endlessly to watch you eat now."

I tilted my head, trying to conjure that fleeting glimpse into his past. It was only his second mention of his time as a human. I pictured Sorin as a man diminished by hunger, with sunken eyes and hollowed cheeks. But the image didn't belong. It felt like forcing the wrong piece into a puzzle.

I could not imagine anything else than the well-muscled man sitting across from me with his dark hair falling in waves around broad shoulders and his carefully groomed facial hair. He always seemed to hold this composed regality about him. I couldn't reconcile that commanding presence with the idea of a starving peasant scraping by on the outskirts of the Roman Empire.

"We could try the bond," I suggested curiously, wiping my greased-up fingers on a napkin. "If you can feel what I'm feeling, maybe you could taste what I taste?"

I couldn't imagine not eating food. It was one of life's greatest pleasures, right up there with great sex and everything else beautiful about the world.

Sorin shook his head, "I don't want to crave something I can never keep."

"Oh," I murmured, wondering if there was a deeper meaning behind his words.

And if there wasn't, maybe there should be. My human lifespan was only a bat of an eye to him. Would I be able to see him remain ageless while I withered into a croaky old crone?

"Scarlet," he said, more seriously. "If we are to be involved, there are things you need to understand."

31

BURGERS, BOUNDARIES, AND BARE FEET

"Gee, it's a little late for that, don't you think?" I snorted.

"Better late than never," he shrugged. "As I've mentioned, and as I assume you've discerned, I am more than just an ordinary vampire."

"Right." I straightened slightly, setting my burger down. You didn't have important conversations whilst scarfing down burgers. "Is this where you finally tell me what this stupid experiment is all about?"

"No," he gave a secretive smile.

I groaned, throwing my hands up in resignation before reaching for more fries. He didn't deserve the honor of interrupting my meal. A girl has priorities, and hot fries beat cryptic vampire nonsense any day.

"I am like a governor," he continued slowly, choosing each word carefully. "A patriarch of the First Province in the United States."

"And Odessa?" I asked, voice muffled around my food.

"She is my... lieutenant governor, if you will. Though we hold similar political power."

I looked away, trying to weave this new information into the already tangled web of events unfolding around me. Eyrin had mentioned something about Sorin's Province being unstable.

"What is a Province?" I asked simply.

Simple questions. Simple answers. I would take this one step at a time and puzzle it all together.

Sorin leaned back slightly, "There are four Provinces in the United States. Geographically speaking, we have divided the country into four parts and assigned them to the most powerful to govern. This is not the case in every country. Some still rule as a kingdom, others by council, and more. But as the United States grew and evolved, this is what we chose."

"We?" I echoed, rubbing at my eyes.

"We, as in the supernatural elite," he clarified. "Odessa and I govern the Upper East territory, the First Province."

He continued, rattling off facts, but my brain struggled to keep up with the sheer magnitude of the new information.

"Wait, wait," I held up both hands. "So not only do other creatures exist besides vampires and the fae, but there are enough of you that you need an entire governing body?"

"A rudimentary understanding, but yes."

I scowled at him.

"And you and Odessa rule the First Province."

My brain churned through this new reality. Where did I fit into all of this?

"What's really wrong with your Province? What was Eyrin talking about?" I asked, point-blank. "I need more details than you and Odessa not agreeing with each other."

"Eyrin," Sorin all but spat the name, "thinks he's strong enough to take over the First Province. There's nothing inherently wrong with it. Aside from Odessa and I having our differences. Severe as those differences may be."

He paused, shoulders curling in so slightly that I almost missed it.

"There's unrest among us. Some believe we're standing at the crux of our existence."

The way he said that, the grimace pulling at the corners of his mouth, told me the *crux* had everything to do with his rift with Odessa.

"And what do you think?"

He leaned forward, elbows braced on the table, chin resting on interlocked fingers.

"Many things," he said quietly. "But I must confess, age has brought with it a kind of apathy I find difficult to escape. These politics have grown exhaustive."

A look of sheer weariness crumbled his features, and he turned to stare listlessly out of the kitchen window. Empathy swelled in my chest. Reaching out, I gave his arm a gentle squeeze. He eyed the contact, then slowly opened his hand between us, palm up. I slipped my fingers into his. He closed his around mine with a quiet sigh.

"Has anyone ever told you," he murmured, "that you have rough hands for a woman?"

"Yes, actually. Asshole, " I scoffed, laughter bubbling up. "But I've also been told there's a certain appeal to them."

I waggled my eyebrows suggestively. His gaze heated, but I held up a hand.

"I feel like there's more."

"There is."

I motioned for him to go on.

"It doesn't matter that Odessa and I disagree on things. We can't make the choice by ourselves. These issues will be addressed at the Summit, as well as the outcome of our experiment."

He met my gaze, voice softening, "Your torment is nearly at an end."

"Nearly at an end?!" I squawked.

The Summit wasn't until Halloween. I still had to survive the rest of October without spontaneously combusting from all the secrets I was shoving under metaphorical lock and key. But secrets turned out to be lonely company to keep.

He gave me a hard look for a long moment before continuing. I cleared my throat and took a sip of water.

"It will only be a few more weeks. We're hosting the Summit in the city, and it will be dangerous. These people, beings, don't all coexist well with humanity. That's why I want you to stay close to Crimson & Clover."

"Are you grounding me?"

I pulled my hand from his and leaned back, fingers brushing against the cool table surface.

"I'm trying to keep you safe."

"If it's so dangerous, why do it at all? Won't it draw too much attention and risk blowing your cover?"

If he thought I was going to sit and stay like some obedient lapdog, he had another thing coming. Fantastic sex be damned.

"That's exactly why we do it on Halloween," he said. "We throw elaborate festivals at each meeting. Humans expect monsters on Halloween. They even celebrate them. And that's how we stay hidden."

My eyes widened.

"Please, Scarlet," he said, capturing my hand again. "Just for the next couple of weeks—stay here at night. Do whatever you want during the day, but after sunset... stay in your room. Or mine."

A roguish smile lit his expression, and warmth crept up my neck.

"I'll think about it," I grumbled.

Not that there was much for Sorin to worry about. After last night, I was definitely leaning toward becoming a homebody. Still, there was more pressing on my mind that needed to be discussed.

"Sorin," I leveled him with my most serious glare. "I need *you* to understand a few things."

He let go of my hand, and I gripped the ledge of the table.

"First of all, I don't know how far I'm willing to let this go. My marriage just ended. I'm still dealing with that. And let's not forget my lifespan is like a blink compared to yours."

I grimaced at the thought of being a frail old woman sitting next to Sorin, who would remain as he was for the rest of my lifetime and beyond.

"I can be patient," he said. "As long as I'm the only one in line."

"Why?" I asked.

We hadn't known each other that long. His interest in me didn't make sense, and that made me bite the inside of my cheek. But I needed to know if this was going to last even one more minute. I had to prepare myself in case he was only in this to influence the experiment's outcome.

"Your life *is* short," he smiled softly, kindly. "I'd be a fool to waste it second-guessing how I feel. I don't want to waste your precious time."

Shit. His words planted some tiny, warm feeling in my chest. I felt a smile tug at the corner of my lips, but there was more I needed to say.

"Also," I said, brushing off the tenderness trying to take root, "don't ever try to mind control me again."

"Mind control?" He asked, amused.

"You know what I mean," I waved my hand. "Whatever that was in the shower, I know you've done it before. I don't appreciate it."

Sorin exhaled slowly through his nose, gaze sliding away like a kid caught with his hand in the cookie jar.

"It's not mind control," he said carefully. "It's more like a powerful suggestion."

"Oh, *powerful suggestion*," I echoed, grabbing his chin and forcing him to look at me. "That's cute. However you want to spin it, I'm not buying."

I held his gaze firmly. "Whatever it is, knock it off. I need you to really hear me on this. If you do it again—I'm gone."

He sat a little straighter, nostrils flaring.

"I mean it," I said, letting a little heat creep into my voice. "No more Jedi mind tricks without my permission, or that's the last time you'll ever see me."

He opened his mouth to fire off some smug retort, but I squeezed it shut between my fingers. His tantalizingly full lips puckered, making him look somewhere between a fanged goldfish and an exceptionally offended piranha.

"Yeah, yeah," I waved him off. "I'm sure you were about to say something weird and alpha-y like, *'You're mine now. No one will touch you within 500 miles.'*" I gave a terrible impression of his voice.

"You're thinking of werewolves," he groused through pinched lips.

I rolled my eyes.

"The point is, I'll make it very hard for you to find me."

We sized each other up for a tense few minutes.

"Nod, if you understand," I said, throwing his own words back at him.

He bit back a chuckle and gave a barely perceptible nod.

"Good." I relinquished my hold and called Milo to me, scratching his big head as I dug the key to my room and the rest of my abandoned belongings out of the paper bag that had held the clothes.

"Stay here," Sorin offered, rising with me.

"I can't," I shook my head. I needed space to think alone. "I have to be up today. I probably missed a ton of work yesterday, and I have other things to deal with."

Like finding a divorce lawyer who wouldn't require me to sell a kidney on the black market.

"I don't like you being on that floor," he said, trailing me to the door.

"Then why did you put me there?"

"That was before someone carved a symbol into your door." His voice hardened, but he still opened the door for me with a flourish. "Things are different now."

"See you around, Sorin," I said breezily, brushing past him. My brain was already halfway to my pillow as I stepped into the hallway.

Before I could take another step, his arm curled around my waist, spinning me back into the hard wall of his chest.

"No kiss?"

"I'm tired," I placed a hand on his chest.

All I wanted was to dive back into that deep oblivion where my dreams separated me from reality. Wanted to be on a plane of existence that wasn't so damn complicated.

He didn't say anything. Dipping his head, he pressed a chaste kiss to the top of my forehead. Only when my rigid body relaxed, molding against him, did he let go.

"Be safe," he rumbled. "Text me if anything unusual happens."

"So, basically every five minutes," I muttered with a humorless laugh, already walking toward the steel stairwell doors.

Milo padded beside me as I pushed the door open and descended to my small, borrowed room.

Once inside, I locked the door behind us and peeled off my dress, dropping it to the floor. I climbed into bed and lifted the covers for Milo to join me. He flopped beside me, tucking his warm body into my side.

I clicked off the light. Darkness swallowed the room.

Closing my eyes, I tried to imagine we were back in Savannah. Just Milo and me, in our house with the plantation shutters and the sounds of the water outside. In my mind, morning sunlight streamed in thick ribbons across our bedroom, catching the dust like glitter. I'd stretch, slip into slippers, and head downstairs. Milo would follow, tail wagging. I'd make his breakfast and wait for the percolator to bubble and hiss, the smell of coffee wrapping around me like a welcome blanket.

"*Scarlet.*"

I bolted upright, heart jumping. Everything was pitch black. Milo's soft body was a weight against my side. I listened hard but heard nothing but our breathing. I placed a hand on my chest and focused on slowing my breathing. Inhale. Exhale. Deep and exaggerated. I squeezed my eyes shut and tried to return to the kitchen in my mind. Tried to summon the clink of a spoon against porcelain. The warmth of a mug in my hand.

"*Scaaaaarlet,*" The voice hissed my name louder.

My eyes flew open. I sat up, jostling Milo. He groaned in protest and scooted closer.

"Who's there?" I called out as I fumbled for my phone.

My fingers skated over the smooth glass. I grabbed it and double-tapped the side. Nothing but the blinking red battery icon.

"Little piggy," it sang in an overtly feminine tone.

That voice. No, it couldn't be.

"You're dead," I whispered, frozen in place. "I killed you. This isn't real."

I was dreaming. This was another terrible nightmare.

A throaty laugh grated against my ear. I yelped and slammed backward, crashing into the thick curtain beside the window. Milo threw his weight over my legs as if to shield me, baring his teeth into the darkness.

"Such sad little noises," the voice cooed, now coming from the closet.

Then in a deeper, more guttural voice, "Do you see me when you close your eyes, Scarlet? Because I see you."

My blood iced over. My pulse flatlined, then thundered back in a nauseating rush. No. No. No. There was no way Valerie could have been here. She was dead. I killed her.

This had to be a dream. I pinched the inside of my arm until I gasped. Definitely not asleep.

I had locked the door. I was sure of it. But I hadn't checked the closet. Or the bathroom. As if summoned by my thoughts, the sounds of rushing water surged from behind the bathroom door.

"Who the fuck is there?" I screamed, lurching forward and slamming the lamp switch.

The bulb flickered, then lit with a harsh snap. The water stopped, and there was silence.

The bathroom door creaked open an inch. Jerked. It banged all the way open against the wall. Nothing was there but empty air. And then a soft, wet slap.

The unmistakable sound of a bare foot against the floor.

I whimpered, dragging myself backward across the bed. Milo released a feral growl. Whipping my head to the floor in front of the bathroom door, I found a footprint. It was wet, fresh. Right there on the wood.

No.

Another slapping sound. Another slick print appeared, closer now.

"Stay back!" I shrieked.

My hands flew up, but you couldn't hit a ghost. I had no idea what to do. No weapon. No plan. No clue how to fight something that shouldn't exist.

One step.

Two.

The frantic slap of bare feet tore across the floor towards me.

I screamed, bracing for the inevitable. But nothing came. No phantom hands. No icy breath. No claws ripping into skin. I was still untouched.

Milo trembled next to me as silence pressed in from all sides. The metallic taste of fear flooded my mouth. My breath came in shallow gasps as I slowly lowered my arms.

Above me, the crystal chandelier swayed in slow, tight circles.

Thinking I'd finally lost it, that the monster-fucking was the tipping point after all, I let out a hysteric laugh. Perhaps all the vampire blood was doing its job and pulling apart my mind one thread at a time.

I scrambled for the nightstand, snatching my charger and jamming it into the wall with clumsy fingers. Milo and I were crammed into the far corner of the bed like cornered animals as we waited for the thing in the dark to finish the job. Or for my mind to finally break all the way.

But the footprints were still there. They were clear as day, reflecting the soft beams of my lamp. And Milo wouldn't be able to share in my hallucinations, right? He was right there next to me, ears pinned to his skull and eyes wide.

A sharp ping exploded from the nightstand, and I gasped. Just my phone rebooting. Lunging for it, I fumbled through the lock screen. My thumb slid through apps until I hit Contacts.

Who the hell was I going to call?

Not Luke. Never again.

Tucker?

No. He'd know something was wrong the second he heard my voice. He'd either beg me to come home or, worse, come here himself. Given the current state of affairs, that could put one or both of us in danger of being killed.

Sorin was out. I didn't want to let him see me like this again. And the sun was nearly up. I could feel it building behind my eye sockets, sensing it like the change in air pressure before a winter storm. It now held some sort of barely distinguishable presence that tickled the back of my mind. It didn't feel safe or right to call him now. So I hit Malik's name.

"Red? What's up?" he answered on the fourth ring, voice slurred with sleep.

"Malik," I rasped, my voice thin and wrong. " I-I uh... what are you doing right now?"

"Sleeping." I heard the rustle of sheets. "What's going on?"

I almost said nothing. But then I looked down at the footprints again.

"C-can you come to my room? Please?" My voice cracked. "Something happened."

"Sit tight," he replied, all grogginess gone.

Less than five minutes passed, but time seemed to drag on like hours. Milo didn't move. Neither did I until a polite knock sounded at the door.

Sucking in a shaky breath, I unwound myself from Milo's side and bolted from the bed. I didn't dare look underneath it. Ripping the thin throw blanket off the comforter, I wrapped it tightly around myself and pulled the door open.

Malik stood there, looking only slightly disheveled. Dark shadows pooled under his eyes, and he leaned against the doorframe.

"Thanks for coming."

My lip quivered, and tears welled in my eyes until he became nothing more than a smudge.

He stepped forward, placing a warm hand on my shoulder, "What happened?"

I just shook my head and pointed behind me toward the room.

"What do you see?"

I had to know if he saw them, too. If the prints were real, maybe I wasn't insane. Though I wasn't sure which would be worse. Malik's eyes widened as he stepped inside. His gaze swept the room until it caught on the floor. He moved straight to the footprints, squatting low.

Relief hit me like a tidal wave. I nearly sobbed as I shut the door behind him and collapsed into the sitting chair, clutching the blanket tighter.

"Did you forget to towel off?"

He spoke to me in that cautious way you do when dealing with someone who might have gone off the deep end. Like you're afraid of setting them off, but you need to confirm they're as bad off as you thought.

"No," I said, voice rough with emotion. "No, Malik. They're not mine."

He stayed crouched, studying me now.

"Look at my hair. My feet." I thrust them out from under the blanket. "I'm bone dry. Look at Milo, for God's sake."

Malik turned. Milo was still perched in the far corner of the bed, ears pinned back, tail tucked between his legs. Malik crossed to him and stroked the spot between his eyes until Milo finally began to breathe normally again.

"Tell me what happened," Malik said, his back still to me.

I stared at the ceiling for a moment, letting my head rest against the chair's frame.

"I was lying in bed, almost asleep, when I heard my name." My voice shook. "At first, I thought I was dreaming, but then it happened again."

I told him everything. With every word, I watched his shoulders tighten, his posture growing stiffer.

"I thought I was going insane. I got hurt bad the other night. Sorin gave me blood. Too much, I think. I was worried I overdosed on it or something."

I exhaled shakily.

"But you saw them. The prints."

We both turned to look at them. They were fading, dark outlines shrinking and drying into the wood.

"Do you know about Valerie?" I asked quietly.

He nodded, finally turning to face me and settling on the edge of the bed.

"The voice," I whispered tightly, "It said things. Things she said that night. Things no one else could've known."

Malik hunched forward, resting his elbows on his knees. His teeth worried at his thumbnail restlessly.

"Malik," I said shrilly. "Do ghosts exist?"

He gave a sharp nod.

"Fuck." I buried my hands in my hair, curling forward. Panic cinched my throat shut. "How the fuck does this shit keep happening to me?"

Malik made a contemplative sound in the back of his throat.

"I have a few theories."

32

SHOW AND TELL

"Please share," I breathed. "Because I'm at the end of my rope here."

Malik cast a glance around the room and stood, gathering Milo's leash from the corner.

"Let's talk in my room. This place is making my skin crawl," he said, continuing to gnaw on the tip of his finger.

I dressed and packed an overnight bag before hustling after Malik to a one-bedroom corner apartment, a floor above me. He sat me down on a comfortable gold suede couch and pressed a steaming mug of coffee into my hands.

We watched the sun emerge, filling the sky with soft shades of dusky blue.

"Scarlet," Malik started, as the first rays of light beamed through the skyline, "are we friends?"

Surprised, I turned to him and considered the question.

"Yes... yes, I think so. I consider you my friend."

Malik smiled softly, "I don't have many of those."

I wanted to ask where this was going, but held myself back, taking a sip of the coffee instead.

"What I'm about to tell you- I haven't told anyone. No one at all."

Malik's teeth worked the edge of an already short nail, his gaze darting around the room. "And it could get both of us killed."

I wasn't sure if I wanted to know. How many more secrets could I carry before bursting at the seams? It felt like I wouldn't be able to open my mouth without letting something slip. Still, I needed more information.

It was a minute before I realized he was waiting for me. He was giving me the chance to walk away.

I heaved a deep sigh.

"Malik, you're honestly the only person I know right now who might even remotely understand me. And I think it's possible that you could say the same of me."

He nodded, staring into the steam rising from his own mug.

"Just a few more minutes," he said, glancing at the sunrise. "It's better to wait for the sun to be fully up for this."

I watched him closely. The dark bags had worsened under his eyes, and his shoulders were hunched over his mug. He looked so tired, maybe even a little afraid. His fingers tapped rhythmically against his mug.

When I looked closer, I saw his nails were all chewed down to the quick. The skin was pink and ragged around the cuticles. It was a bad habit Tucker also had when we were kids. We ended up painting his nails with clear nail polish just to keep him from tearing them up too badly. Dad had hated it.

"There." His lips twitched up as light flooded the room. "It's safer this way."

He pointed around the space, and my jaw dropped. I hadn't noticed the mirrors before. They were everywhere, strategically placed to bounce the sunlight into every corner. Every shadow within the apartment had been entirely obliterated by the light.

"I got the idea while I was watching The Mummy," he said, pride filling his voice. "Vampires, they thrive in the shadows. They won't touch the light in any way. Physical or otherwise."

"Otherwise?" I squinted against the sheer brightness filling the apartment.

"How much do you know about them now? I'm not sure where to start, with you and Sorin being a thing. Which I would very much like to know about," Malik finished with a half-hearted wink.

"Not much," I huffed grumpily. Sorin wasn't exactly an open book. "If you have something to tell me, it's best to just share it all. Start at the beginning. I'll fill you in on Sorin after you're done."

"Well, vampires exist—"

"Okay, smartass," I chuckled. "Not that beginning."

"Sorry," Malik winced. "Just trying to break the tension."

He sobered.

"Anyway, Sorin and Odessa aren't normal vampires. They're special."

"Like governors, right? They lead the First Province?"

"More than that. Only the most powerful vampires have abilities. They keep them secret, like a trump card."

I mulled this over, wishing I had a notepad to scribble it all down.

"I don't know Sorin's," Malik looked around the room before coming to sit beside me. When he spoke again, it was in a whisper. "But there's something you need to know."

I sat a little straighter, completely entranced by what he was saying.

"Tell me."

"It's not just vampires you have to worry about," Malik ran his thumb over the rim of his mug. "Odessa can call back the dead. And she can use them."

"Use... them?" I squeaked, the blood draining from my face.

"It's why she's in such a high position of power. Most vampires don't reach that level until they're at least a thousand years old."

"That can't be true."

I curled in on myself, drawing my legs to my chest. Malik had no reason to lie, but my mind recoiled from the horror of it.

"I've seen it," Malik said, tapping his fingers nervously against his mug. His voice dropped even lower. "You think death is the worst thing that can happen here? It's not."

I stood, dread launching me off the couch. I had to move and shake off the nervous energy growing within me.

"How?"

"She summons them. Curses them. Sometimes uses them to curse others. It's easier if they already had a vendetta before they died."

Vivid green eyes burning with hate flashed across my mind. Echoes of a dying scream, a sickening squelch. I groaned, rubbing furiously at my eyes.

"Why would she do that?"

To me. To anyone. It was so terrible, so malevolent, I could barely comprehend it.

Odessa had been kind to me. I thought of her warm smiles and the words of support she had offered so easily. My stomach lurched at the thought of pouring my heart out to someone who must have seen every word as a weakness to exploit.

"Because you have something she wants," Malik said, coming to stand beside me. "Or rather, you *are* something she wants. She's chipping away at you. You're easiest to manipulate at your lowest."

"Why are you telling me this?" I asked breathlessly. "Isn't she your aunt?"

I leaned against the window, letting the well-worn ache of disappointment settle deep into my battered heart. Same pain, different face.

"My aunt," he spat bitterly, "is a liar. A dishonest person who will do whatever it takes to get what she wants."

"What could she possibly want from me?"

I wasn't the chosen one. No secret prophecy, no shiny hidden powers. The only thing remotely "special" about me was my Olympic-level stubbornness, which typically made my life harder. I was aggressively ordinary and barely keeping my shit together.

"She wants you to break so she can control the outcome of the experiment. That mark on your door was a calling card, marking you as a target."

"Tell me about the experiment." I stood very still, holding together the last fragile pieces of my composure.

I needed to hear the answer the way a drowning man required air.

"At the Summit this Halloween, the Council is going to make a decision. And that decision depends on you."

I stared at him, already piecing it together, though the way he said it made my gut tighten like I was about to be sucker-punched by a plot twist from hell.

"They're testing how you react to discovering the existence of non-humans. Each Province is running its own experiment. You're ours. How you respond—fear, acceptance, violence—it all matters."

He turned away, his hand drifting toward his mouth before he jerked it away. With visible effort, he lowered it and shoved it into his pocket.

"You've already killed one," Malik blurted in a nervous rush.

More like fifteen or twenty, if we were counting the fae from last night. But hey, who was keeping score? The world lurched sideways.

"I didn't know," I said faintly.

"Still, it's not looking good," he said quietly.

"So if I respond negatively, what happens?" My voice sounded flat, like it already knew the answer.

"They'll shove humanity into a tidy little class system," Malik said, pacing the room. "Feeders. Workers. Enforcers. All with meta-physical creatures pulling the strings at the top."

Lungs working double time, every millimeter of my skin sparked to life under the surge of adrenaline.

"If most of the experiments take it well, they'll try to assimilate us instead," he continued. "Odessa wants you to fight. Sorin wants to assimilate."

"But, why?" I demanded shrilly.

"Technology's outpacing them," he said, fingers digging into his hair. "They know they can't keep up. They want to control the situation before it controls them."

I pulled my hair off the nape of my neck, letting the cool air kiss my overheated skin. A bitter, broken laugh erupted from me. All this time, I thought I'd been holding the upper hand. Turns out, I was playing checkers while they were playing 4D quantum chess in a parallel universe with cheat codes. Odessa. Sorin. They'd been maneuvering me like a pawn from the start. Every soft word from Sorin, every piece of pillow talk, suddenly felt staged and empty.

"They're all trying to manipulate me," I exhaled, the words wet and shaky. "Sorin. Odessa. Every single one of them."

"Yes," Malik's eyes were heavy with sorrow.

Ringing filled my ears. The room spun. I stumbled backward, arms flailing to steady myself. Somewhere in the distance, I heard Malik call my name just as the back of my legs slammed against the coffee table.

I landed hard on my back, the ceiling swimming above me. Something cool pressed against my forehead, and Milo's wet nose nudged insistently at my ear.

"Are you okay?" Malik asked as he dabbed a damp cloth against my brow. "You fainted."

My hand fluttered up, catching his wrist. "I need to get out of here."

I tried to sit up, but a sharp pain stabbed behind my eyes. Wetness dribbled over my lip, and I reached up, dabbing at the thick clot of blood oozing from my nose.

"You can't leave," Malik said apologetically as he slid an arm around my shoulders.

"Watch me." I shoved him away. "I can't do this. I can't be the reason humanity gets enslaved or whatever else could happen."

I would run. I didn't care how. I'd vanish into the woods and live like a hermit if I had to. Never mind that my last camping trip was when I was twelve and spent half the night crying over burnt s'mores.

My brain, ever helpful in a crisis, immediately started making a mental checklist of survival gear.

"You can't leave," Malik insisted, sweat glistening on his temple, panic cracking through his calm facade. "They'll find you, kill you, and then kill me for telling you."

He helped me stagger to the couch.

"And if they don't find you," he continued lowly, "they'll kill your family. Your friends. Anyone they can sink their claws into."

We'd blown straight past worst-case scenario and crash-landed somewhere in hell's waiting room.

"I'm trapped." I pinched my nose and tilted my head back, trying to slow the steady drip of blood.

"You're not alone," Malik said, pressing a wad of paper towels into my hand.

"I don't believe you. I can't trust anyone here."

I couldn't trust anyone ever again. The iron taste of blood and salty tears coated my teeth.

"You're right," he said quietly. "But if you can't trust me, maybe you can trust my reason for helping you."

"You hate your aunt," I pointed out the obvious.

There was no hiding the disdain he'd let slip in the last few minutes.

"I-I do," he admitted, a rueful smile tugging at his mouth. "I've never said that out loud before. Feels good."

"What did she do to you?" I asked.

Nobody hated their family like that without a reason.

"Not just to me. To my mother, and to hers. To our whole family." His voice darkened. "Eventually, to me, too. But not yet. Not ever, if I can help it."

My nose had finally stopped bleeding. I pulled away the paper towel and stared at the crumpled material smeared with red.

"She takes us one by one," Malik clenched his hands. "Raises us. Then tries to turn us. She's been doing it since the night she was turned. Her own sister was the first."

I shook my head in disbelief. No one could be that cruel to their own family.

"Yes. She does." Malik pulled out his phone and tapped at the screen. "She waits for us to grow up and have children. Then she tries to turn us. Changing isn't easy, Scarlet. Most people don't survive it. Odessa is the only one in our bloodline who ever has."

He turned his phone toward me, and a video began to play. A woman with Malik's striking features smiled into a mirror, a toddler perched on her hip. She pointed a hand-held camcorder at the mirror. The room behind them was too familiar. It was this apartment with '90s decor scattered around.

"Malik, look at the camera, baby," she cooed. "Happy birthday, honey!"

The scene changed. Malik, a chubby-cheeked toddler, smashed cake into his face. Laughter. Sunlight in a park. Malik and his mother dancing to Barney. Odessa appeared in some clips, holding him in this very living room.

"My mother," Malik said roughly. "Odessa told me she was a junkie, living on the streets. She said Child Services took me away. That she had to pull all kinds of strings to get me back. According to her, my mom died of an overdose when I was four."

He swallowed hard.

"But that's not what happened?" I supplied.

"There are no records with child services. I checked a year ago." He shook his head. "So, I decided to dig deeper."

Malik pulled a laptop from under the couch and set it on the coffee table between us. The screen glowed to life. He opened a scan of an old police report. I leaned in, heart hammering. It was a missing persons file.

"She didn't die of an overdose," Malik hissed through clenched teeth. "She disappeared when I was nearly six."

I covered my mouth with my hand, stunned into silence.

"Odessa hates technology. Still writes everything down with pen and paper. I snuck into her office and made some scans."

He clicked through a few folders, opening one labeled *Family Records*.

Row after row of scanned pages filled the screen. It wasn't a family tree. It was a ledger containing names and birthdates. Cryptic notes were scribbled beside each one: *Attempted. Failed. Deceased.*

Before me was a cold-blooded inventory of the generations Odessa had created, raised, and destroyed. Malik scrolled down, pausing on a page marked in red ink. There, circled twice, was his name.

A status report, dated four months ago, was scrawled beneath it: *Maturity reached. Pair with viable mate.*

My mouth went dry. Malik glanced at me, guilt flashing across his face. Then he scrolled lower. There, under a short list of candidates with a more recent date, my name appeared.

Scarlet Montgomery. Beside it, a clinical notation. *High survivability, tough. Likely to produce viable heir.*

"She wrote this?" I rasped, barely recognizing my own voice.

Malik's hands shook as he closed the laptop with a quiet click.

"You must have made a good impression," he said hoarsely. "She likes you. And when Odessa likes someone, it never ends well."

33

REGICIDE À LA MODE

Malik and I sat side by side on the small outdoor patio of a tiny café. We had decided to put some distance between us and Crimson & Clover, landing on breakfast as a reasonable excuse. Strangers drifted by as Milo sniffed around our feet, searching for crumbs. Little gourd-shaped lanterns lined the patio, their faux candles dancing merrily inside like tiny souls.

"We can't kill her," I mused quietly, cutting into a pumpkin-flavored pastry.

"You couldn't even if you wanted to," Malik agreed dryly. "Trust me, I've thought about it. She's too strong."

I huffed. "With my luck, she'll take herself out."

Malik squinted at me. "Do you... have a history of people dropping dead around you?"

"Define history."

After I recited my running list of metaphysical casualties, he leaned back, shielding his mouth behind his mug.

"Red, that's like twenty supernatural deaths in a month. This can't be a coincidence. It's statistically impossible."

"It's not like I'm doing it on purpose!" I defended.

"That's not what I think." Malik tapped a finger against his chin. "What if you're cursed? Odessa specializes in that kind of thing. She could be trying to force the experiment to fail."

"Shit," I hissed.

Add that to the growing list of cosmic *screw-you's* my life had been serving up lately. At this point, I was running out of room on my "reasons to drink" list.

I pulled Milo a little closer to me to avoid a group of costumed children passing by on their way to school. Halloween was getting close. It seemed like every window had a pumpkin or witch smiling out of it.

"I'll be honest, Scarlet. I don't know what to do," Malik said, picking at the rim of his cup.

"That makes two of us."

I couldn't retaliate, and I didn't want to see Sorin. The thought of facing him made my stomach churn. Hope slowly fizzled away, one second at a time.

"Is there anything we can do to stop the Summit?" I asked.

"I don't think so," Malik said. "They'd just hold it somewhere else. The decision's going to be made whether it's here or not."

"Could we... I don't know. Get a lawyer or something? Plead our case? Maybe we could petition for assimilation."

Malik snorted.

"Sure. But that won't change the other Province's votes. They each have their own agendas and their own experiments."

Feeling foolish and hopelessly out of my depth, I turned away, watching the wind whisk red and orange leaves down the street.

"You'll just have to hang on," Malik said after a moment. "Keep the body count down until the Summit. It's a miracle the NYPD hasn't put you on some kind of watchlist."

He pulled a small vial from his pocket and tipped a few drops of blood into his water, swirling it absently. Anybody passing by could have mistaken it for a glass of watered-down juice or pink lemonade.

"That doesn't change the fact that I'm cursed. Or that she wants us to have a baby," I grimaced as I pulled apart bits of my pastry to feed Milo.

A young woman with flaxen blonde hair passed us, her arm clinging to that of an older man. She laughed sweetly as she batted her lashes up at him. I caught Malik following them down the street with his eyes.

"Odessa's playing a long game," he said contemplatively. "Setting the board in advance. Choosing pieces without them even knowing."

He leaned back in his chair, tapping the side of his glass thoughtfully.

"Maybe it's time we play a few moves of our own."

"What are you saying?"

"I'm saying maybe we can't stop the Summit, but we might be able to beat Odessa at her own game.

"Which is?" I asked.

"She keeps secrets. Manipulates situations until they best suit her. When the moment's right, she makes her move."

"She and Sorin don't exactly get along," I added thoughtfully. "We could use that to our advantage."

"Right," Malik nodded. "And Sorin's already protective of you."

"So we turn them against each other," I said, slowly piecing it together. "Agitate the tension until Sorin kills Odessa."

Malik paused.

"What about Carmen?" he asked. "She won't let Odessa go down as long as she's around."

I rubbed my forehead. Carmen had saved me from Paul in the alley and always had something supportive to say. She had even tried to advocate for me before Odessa set me loose in Crimson & Clover.

Malik caught my silence.

"She has to go, Scarlet," he said quietly. "She'd be a loose end."

I hummed in reluctant agreement, wishing that I hadn't eaten such a large breakfast. Talk of regicide wasn't exactly sitting well with my Mediterranean omelet. So far, I hadn't killed or caused anyone's death intentionally. This would be my first deliberate action that might result in the death of another.

"I'm not a murderer," I let my palms fall open between us.

"Neither am I."

He rested his hand on top of mine, his warmth seeping into my frigid skin. I shivered in my light jean jacket. It was one of those deceptively bright days where the sky was unbelievably blue, but all the warmth had been siphoned from the air. It could have also been the blood comedown. I knew I had ingested too much, and the chill felt like it was coming from the inside out.

"Let's think of it as fast-forwarding the inevitable," he said somberly. "I don't really see it ending any other way for Odessa. She'll get what she wants or die trying."

I stared at our hands, his smooth, dark skin layered over mine.

"Being seen together is a good start," I said, looking up without pulling away.

"Go on," he leaned in, intrigued.

"Sorin is jealous. Protective, like you said," I said, glancing pointedly down at our joined hands. "Odessa wants us to have a baby. We could use that to stir things up."

"It's not exactly a secret that I like men," he said, pulling back slightly. "No offense."

"None taken. It doesn't have to be romantic. We frame it as a transactional arrangement."

I cringed inwardly at the thought. Malik considered it, sipping his drink.

"That could work."

My mouth went dry watching his throat bob with his swallow. The lingering taste of Sorin's blood surged over my tongue, triggering a wave of saliva. I clenched my fists and turned away. This was not a good sign.

"A few nights ago, Eyrin tried to kill me," I said a little roughly, clearing my throat. "That's how I ended up with Sorin."

"The truth finally comes out," Malik exclaimed. "I've heard of him before, but never seen him. What does he look like?"

"Tall, long, silky hair," I motioned with my hands for further details. "Well—hot until he went full-out dark fae on me."

"Oh, him?!" Malik recoiled. "I've seen him lingering around the bar before. He's so... so..."

I arched a brow at him.

"He's just so damn hot," he admitted with a sheepish wince.

"He tried to eat me, Malik." I leveled him with a look. "His eyes bugged out, and his mouth was full of rows and rows of needle teeth."

I jabbed my fingers out from my mouth for emphasis.

"Yick," he sneered.

"Agreed." I nodded. "But it sounded like he wanted to challenge Sorin for his position."

It was a gamble. The guy had already tried to literally eat me. But honestly, at this point, my life felt like it was already forfeit anyway. My odds of survival shrank with every passing day. It was likely even less than I currently knew. What was one more risk?

"Eyrin," Malik hummed. "Still hot, though."

"He tried to kill me!"

I couldn't help but laugh.

"So we proposition him?" Malik waggled his eyebrows suggestively.

"Ugh." I dropped my forehead into my hands, shoulders shaking as I tried to stifle another laugh.

There was a hysterical edge to it. But it was laugh or cry, and I didn't want to cry today.

"Sorry, sorry," Malik said, reeling in his own fit of snickers. "I swear I'm taking this seriously. Humor's just how I deal."

"It's alright. I probably needed that," I exhaled, dragging a hand through Milo's thick coat.

"Yes. We proposition him," I said dryly, shaking my head as Malik barely choked down another laugh. "If we can't get Sorin and

Odessa to do the dirty work, I bet Eyrin would be thrilled to step in."

We spent the next hour circling the city, spitballing ways to get in touch with Eyrin. Odds were slim he'd show up at the club again. Between the two of us, it turned out we knew very little about the fae at all.

"If he's really serious about taking Sorin down," Malik said later, back in his apartment, "we might not have to find him. He might find us."

"You think he's tracking Sorin?" I asked, sipping from a cold can of soda and swinging my legs gently from the high stool at Malik's island.

"It's possible," he replied, handing me a sandwich piled high with turkey, cheese, and enough mustard and mayo to drown it.

I took it gratefully. The steady stream of food he kept pushing on me told me he'd noticed that gnawing, bottomless hunger I couldn't seem to shake. Or at least he knew what I was going through from his own experience.

If I could help it, I'd never take another sip of vampire blood again. The thought made my stomach twist in protest. I shuddered and pushed it down. No more vampire blood. That was final.

"I think you should go out on a date with Sorin. Be seen with him," Malik said casually.

"Absolutely not."

I ignored the little flip in my chest at the word *date*. Omissions of truth were only another form of lying. Sorin had lied to me, and I was done with liars. I'd learned my lesson the hard way with Luke.

And Luke, oh god, Luke. My dealings with Odessa couldn't stand. There was no way this could end any other way than the death of at least one of us. My eyes burned, likely due to skipping an entire night of sleep. Definitely not from threatening tears.

"Why not?" Malik questioned.

"Because I'm not interested in dating him," I wiped a glob of mustard from the corner of my mouth and lifted my chin.

"Girl, I don't know who you think you're fooling," Malik snorted. "It's written all over your face."

My jaw dropped.

"Pardon me?"

"Don't get all googly-eyed at me. When you two get within ten feet of each other, the rest of us might as well be dust in the wind. Your cheeks are even pink right now."

I reached up, brushing my fingers against my burning face.

"I—I..." I floundered for a defense before grumbling, "He lied to me."

Just like Luke. But I didn't say that part out loud. The soul wound was still too fresh to touch.

"True," Malik said through a mouthful of his sandwich. "But it's for the greater good. And he clearly cares about you."

I stuffed a massive bite into my mouth so I wouldn't have to answer that. It took me three full minutes to chew through it.

"Odessa doesn't really allow me to date," Malik complained.

My eyebrows shot up.

"I know, I know," he held up both hands. "I date casually. But she makes sure no one sticks around longer than three months."

"How?"

I was afraid of the answer.

He shrugged, fixing himself another sandwich.

"Sometimes it's money. Sometimes, a threat. Sometimes worse than that."

I swallowed hard.

"Malik, I'm so sorry. That must be incredibly lonely."

His eyes shimmered a little, and he rubbed the back of his neck.

"So, I go on a date with Sorin. While also making him jealous? How exactly is that supposed to work?" I asked, changing the subject.

"Easy," Malik said, perking up. "We spent the whole day together. He'll smell me on you. Plus, you'll tell him you're moving in with me."

"Am I?"

I wouldn't mind sharing space with Malik, but this was a little fast, even for trauma-bonded friends.

"Do you really want to keep sleeping in that room alone while you're being haunted?"

"Good point," I replied immediately.

I started mentally calculating how fast I could get my stuff to Malik's apartment.

"On that note," he added, "you should tell Sorin about your hauntings. I assume this isn't the first time something's happened?"

I shook my head, thinking of the night Sorin had shown up uninvited in my tiny room. Then, about the door handle jerking in the safe house.

"Perfect. But don't tell him you know what's causing it," Malik wagged a finger. "That'll make him suspicious. Just show up all wide-eyed and teary. He'll go crazy for that."

My lips twisted.

"You want me to play damsel in distress?"

"I want you to weaponize his protectiveness," Malik said unapologetically. "If he cares as much as I think he does, he won't be able to help himself. His instincts will go berserk."

I reminded myself to not get on Malik's shit list.

"He knows it's Odessa's ability, then?" I asked, studying him carefully.

"Duh. They're partners. It's part of the pact they made to share power."

The rest of the day passed in a blur of movement. We cleared out the tiny office nook in Malik's apartment and made two hurried trips to haul my stuff from the cramped purple room.

Thankfully, I didn't have much with me. Malik dug out an old air mattress from the top shelf in the laundry closet, and we took turns pumping it up.

When I finally flopped onto it, a thick cloud of debris puffed into the room, making us sputter and cough. But I supposed anything was better than bathroom visitors from the undead. I made a mental note to buy a mattress topper and pulled out my laptop. It was Sunday, but I was drowning in overdue work.

I was determined to not let Victor down. I could, at minimum, do this much. Emails. Catalog entries. Scheduling. I let the familiar click-clack of my keys lull me into a false sense of normalcy.

"Hey, Red," Malik poked his head into the nook. "I've gotta run. Good luck tonight. Text me if you go out. I'll try to tail you, see if I can't catch Eyrin while I'm at it."

"I'm still not sure if I'm ok with this," I growled.

"Red, he likes you. You like him. He used you, yes, but for the greater good of humanity." Malik pressed his palms together, as if in prayer. "At least try."

I rolled my eyes and waved him off.

Alone again, I let the rhythm of tasks dull my nerves. Between updates and inventory logs, I kept a close eye on the window. As the sun neared the horizon, I felt an invisible part of me shaking awake.

It was such a subtle feeling. A shiver from somewhere deeper than my bones. Like a phantom limb twitching back to life. Or the slow, tingling sensation returning to an arm that had fallen asleep. A soft buzz of static filled a part of me I hadn't known was missing. It was an itch that I longed to scratch but had no means of doing so.

Was this my connection to Sorin? Were my body and soul responding to the tether we'd created when I'd had too much of his blood?

The moment I thought about it, I knew it was true. I could feel it like a rope pulled taut into the distance. I closed my eyes and gave it a mental tug, unsure what I was even doing or why. Nothing.

I turned to the glowing horizon, saturated in soft pinks and burning orange. I let the warmth of the colors wash over me. The sun's final rays passed through the glass and kissed my skin. I gathered that warmth, wrapped it around what little joy I could muster, and sent it down the bond.

Soft as a breath, cold as snow on the wind, the bond answered. It reached out towards me, gobbling up the bright offerings I had sent its way. Frankincense and frost filled my lungs.

"Holy fuck," I whispered, sitting up straighter on the mattress.

Milo perked up, ears twitching, nose to the air.

"You smell it too, buddy?" I asked incredulously. He huffed and padded over to sit beside his food bowl.

"Ok. Obviously, food is more important to you than unraveling the mysteries of the metaphysical world."

I dragged myself to my feet to fix his dinner. My stomach growled in solidarity as I watched him devour it. I pressed a hand to my belly, frustration at myself collecting in my chest. With how much I'd been eating lately, I could probably feed a small army.

"Guess I'm no better," I sighed, eyes drifting to Milo's leash.

There was a pizza place right outside of the building that I'd been smelling since I got here. I pulled out my phone, thumbing through notifications and unanswered texts from Tucker and my mom.

Nope. Not ready for that right now.

"A date, huh?" I said aloud, opening my conversation with Sorin.

Biting my lip, I began to text.

34

GARLIC BREATH AND OTHER WEAPONS

I had to admit it. There was a vindictive part of me relishing the idea of Sorin sitting across from me, forced to watch me feast on a slice of pizza bigger than my head. Bonus points for the extra garlic I'd requested. Extra *extra* points for the fact that if we ended up kissing, he'd have to taste it on my breath.

It didn't matter that he had no interest in human food. Or that the garlic thing was probably a myth. It was the thought that counted.

Smiling gleefully, I dumped a mountain of red chili flakes onto the gooey pepperoni slice in front of me. This probably wasn't the date Malik had in mind, but it suited me just fine.

I preferred this over the stiff pageantry of a fancy restaurant. Though I'd put a little extra effort into my makeup and blow-dried my hair, that was the extent of it. I'd also made a point to use Malik's soap in the shower, knowing Sorin would pick up on it immediately.

He sat across from me in silence, jaw tight, a vein twitching at his temple like it wanted to leap out and strangle me on his behalf. His nostrils flared once, twice, like a bull waiting for the red cape. I bit the inside of my cheek to keep from grinning. Vengeance was sweet. Or, in this case, extra-cheesy and baked with marinara sauce.

"Something the matter?" I asked sweetly, dunking the end of my slice into a container of garlic dipping sauce.

"Why do you smell like that?" Sorin asked in a restrained tone.

"Like what?" I fluttered my lashes at him with mock innocence.

"I think you mean who."

"Oh," I took a massive bite of my pizza and let out a satisfied moan.

The salty, cheesy slice melted over my tongue in a sinful blend of flavor and heat.

"Scarlet," Sorin grated, rubbing his temples.

"Right, sorry." I cleared my throat. "I moved in with Malik."

"What?!" He nearly shouted, gripping the edge of the table.

"Shhhh," I hushed, glancing around at the now-silent restaurant. People were glaring.

"Sorry, everyone. He has a—er—dairy intolerance."

Someone muttered, "Asshole," from a nearby table.

I couldn't have agreed more. The restaurant gradually resumed its hum. I didn't know the extent of what I could do to Sorin, but I was going to make him pay for thinking he could use me. Good intentions be damned.

"Why are you moving in with Malik?" he ground out quietly.

"I have my reasons," I said, sipping my lemon water with a coy smile.

"Which are?"

He clenched his fists, claws extending to lightly puncture the particleboard of the table. I was really testing his limits now.

That was my mark, the cue to start the theatrics. If I were an actress, I'd have summoned a tear or two, maybe added a wobble to my voice for flair. Unfortunately, I was neither an actress nor a convincing liar. I'd have to work with the real exhaustion dragging at me. Even vampire blood couldn't keep that at bay forever. My lack of sleep was starting to make my eyes burn like hell.

"I haven't been sleeping well lately," I murmured, eyes dropping to the table.

I hoped he'd take my reddening ears for shyness and not guilt.

"There have been… things happening. In my room."

"What sort of things?" His hands slowly unclenched, the corners of his mouth turning down in concern.

I restrained mine from turning up.

"Shadows. Voices." I inhaled deeply, rubbing my face. No need to fake the stress. This shit was eating me alive. "They say my name. Sometimes, they move things. Last night, it got worse."

I lifted my gaze, letting my honest fear peek through.

"Why didn't you call me?"

I forced myself not to flinch at the hurt in his voice. A small stab of remorse nicked at my conscience, but I plowed onward.

Vengeance, I reminded myself. We are here for vengeance.

"It was nearly sunrise. You were already asleep. I could feel it."

Truth.

Still, I wasn't sure I was selling it hard enough. He didn't look nearly as distressed as I'd hoped. Though the vein in his temple was mildly concerning. If he were human, I might worry about an impending stroke with how much that vein liked to pop out. Being that he was immortal, it was disturbingly hot.

No. Not hot. I mentally slapped myself. He is not hot. He is an asshole, a massive asshole. I was there to get the revenge I deserved. I pinched my nose, praying that it wouldn't start bleeding again.

"It was awful," I rasped, partly from the memory, partly from how unfairly attractive he was. "My bathroom door opened on its own. Something walked out dripping water. It ran at me."

I gripped Milo's leash tighter.

"It sounded like Valerie," I swallowed, voice dropping to a whisper. "I know it was her. I just don't know how."

Also the truth. I bit down hard on my lip to distract myself from the unwanted tremors coursing up and down my body.

"Can we walk?" I asked, my voice a little too high.

"Of course."

Sorin guided us out of the restaurant. We strolled down an

uneven brick street bathed in the warm glow of jack-o'-lanterns and Halloween lights strung along storefronts and stoops. Giant cotton spiderwebs ensnared iron railings every other house or so. I was studying a massive fuzzy spider that loomed above one particularly well-decorated doorway when Sorin spoke again.

"Move in with me."

Fuck. This was not the reaction I was looking for. Why did he have to be so damn calm about everything?

"I can't."

"Why not?"

"It's too soon." Sweat beaded at the nape of my neck despite the cool breeze. I scooped my hair up with one hand. "We barely know each other."

"And you know Malik so much better?" he asked coolly.

Double fuck. I opened my mouth to speak, but nothing came out.

"It's fine," he said, mercifully putting an end to my floundering.

He placed a cool hand against the back of my neck and gave it a gentle squeeze.

God, why did that feel so good?

"Just consider it. Please."

I exhaled, relieved.

"And stop using his soap. I'll have more of the honey scent sent to you."

"That's very considerate," I managed.

I'd expected him to argue more, to throw a possessive bitch-fit. He nodded and let his hand trail down my shoulders. My skin tingled in his wake.

Wait. Why was I mad at him again?

Oh right. Because he lied. Because he manipulated me. This was all an act. He was buttering me up, and I was a ditzy, love-sick piece of Wonder bread about to crumble in his hands.

"You really like that soap, don't you?" I asked, annoyance filtering into my tone.

"The scent suits you," He gave me a sideways glance from the corner of his eye. "Is something bothering you?"

"No," I kicked a rock out of my path.

Sorin came to a stop.

"You're acting strangely."

"Yeah, well, my world's upside down, I'm getting a divorce, and—"

I stopped myself before I could say more. I could practically hear Malik chewing his nails in the background of my mind. Was he watching us now? Or worse, was Eyrin watching me make an absolute ass of myself?

"And what?" he asked, stepping closer, tension pulling at the corners of his glittering eyes.

Eyes that I—damn it. I had to focus. I spun away, trying to snuff out every indecent thought that Sorin ignited in me.

"I just don't understand you," I snapped, stomping ahead.

But his hand caught my wrist and yanked me back against his chest.

"Tell me what's really going on," He slipped a finger under my chin, trying to tilt it up.

"Don't you dare try that suggestion crap on me again." My palm smacked into his chest, flesh stinging from the force of my blow.

"I'm not, Scarlet, I—" He wrapped an arm around me, pinning my arms to my sides. "Would you stop that? You hit uncommonly hard for a mortal woman."

Years of MMA. Also, a little bit of pent-up rage at lying, manipulative, gorgeous vampires.

"Let me go!"

"We're not moving from this spot until you tell me what's going on," he said, voice ironclad.

Of course. The immortal drama king wanted to hold me hostage until my feelings came out to play. My body betrayed me with a stupid little shiver. Even when I wanted to strangle him, part of me wanted to kiss him too.

I cursed, kicking my legs in the air like a tantruming toddler as he held me aloft with infuriating ease. It was hard to think past the mind-numbing fatigue that fogged up my brain. It was getting worse with every passing second.

"I'll scream!"

Reckless panic began to tear apart my control. I needed to get out of his arms and get some air that didn't smell like snow or frankincense. It occurred to me that maybe some of what he did to me didn't have anything to do with his 'suggestions' but more to do with my biological reaction to him. I struggled harder, gritting my teeth.

In the blink of an eye, the world blurred. A blanket of darkness covered us before we landed in a dim alley. I gagged, stumbling at the sudden shift. Before I could regain my balance, Sorin turned back to me and pressed me against the brick wall, pinning my arms above my head.

"What the fuck was that?" I choked out.

"My gift. Keep your mouth closed about it," Sorin said against my neck.

He pressed his pelvis firmly against mine, preventing me from getting enough leverage to carry out the assault on his legs I was attempting. I opened my mouth, preparing to make good on my promise to scream. A large hand clamped over my mouth. Any sound I might have made was immediately muffled.

Scream if you want," his lips curled into a smile that didn't reach his eyes. "It's late. The moon is waxing. And it's nearly All Hallows' Eve."

"It's Halloween, you old bastard," I said, turning my head to the side so I could speak freely. "And someone would still come if they heard a woman screaming."

"No one will come. You'll only sound like another drunk who is partying too hard."

Fuck you," I snarled against his palm.

"Already did," he laughed venomously.

Something fragile inside me snapped. I slammed my knee

upward. He dodged it, barely, and I used the distraction to yank my arm free. I shoved him hard in the chest, searching for an opening to reel back and hit him.

"You think this is funny?" I whisper–yelled at him, my voice breaking with the effort. "You think you can lie to me, use me, trap me like this—and I'll just fall into your arms like some sappy moron?"

He didn't answer. That unreadable expression had returned. He wore a blank look of stone-cold detachment that made my blood roil inside my veins.

"I hate you," I spat, throwing a right hook that he dodged easily.

But it was so much worse than that because every part of me knew that I didn't mean it.

"Liar," he growled, stalking closer. "You don't hate me. You're furious with me, though I can't imagine why. But you want me anyway, and you can't stand it."

"Go to hell!"

My hair had been knocked wild by our struggle. I swiped my wayward strands out of my face with a trembling hand.

"I already live there," he responded with an empty look in his eyes.

"You're a monster!"

That stopped him dead in his tracks. He watched me with eyes like shards of ice.

"You haven't seen me be a monster yet," he breathed.

The words seemed to displace the air around him. They swept over me, promising that if I wanted to see him become a monster, then I would. The thinly veiled threat enraged me.

"Boo-hoo. Poor Sorin, trapped in his cold, lonely world," I taunted. "You won't lay a finger on me. And I'm not the liar here. You are. You want me to play the pathetic human who falls in love with the vampire. I was only ever another pawn you placed in your sick, twisted fucking experiment."

His expression fractured. Wrath bled through the widening cracks in his carefully constructed mask.

"I'll tell you something else, Sorin Draconis," I jabbed a finger into his chest. "I'm done playing. I will not carry the weight of whatever comes next for humanity after the Summit. That burden is yours."

I panted, watching his eyes cloud and bloom into a searing, unnatural red. My blood turned to ice.

"Who told you?" he growled, voice dropping an octave so low it rumbled through my bones. "Who told you about the experiment?"

"No one," I gasped. "I—I figured it out on my own. It was obvious, really."

Ice raced down my spine. *Idiot. Idiot. Idiot.*

"You truly are a terrible liar, Scarlet." Sorin's voice was scorching as he stepped towards me.

I let him back me into the wall, heart hammering, mind racing for anything I could say to throw him off the scent and protect Malik. I opened my mouth, dragging in a breath, ready to blame Odessa—

"Hope I'm not interrupting," came a low voice from the mouth of the alley.

It had an uncanny lilt to it. Sweet and off-kilter in the most unnerving way. Eyrin offered a sadistic, too-wide smile as he stepped into view. Pointed teeth caught the purple glow from the fake spider porch across the street. It cast shadows from its giant webbed legs, making it look monstrous and inhuman.

His neck, which had been a mangled ruin only two nights ago, was now covered in new skin. Not the seamless regeneration Sorin could produce, but pink, tight, and clean. Completely healed. My eyes shifted to a flash of movement behind him. Malik was there.

He stood behind Eyrin, arms lifted in mute panic, mouthing, "What. The. Actual. Fuck."

35

PERCEPTION, DECEPTION

"Hey, fucker!" Malik tried to yell, but it came out more like an aggressive squeak. "Get away from my baby mama!"

The air left my lungs in a whoosh.

Sorin tensed, slowly turning his head past Eyrin and to Malik. Eyrin, to his credit, only looked vaguely entertained. Like he'd just spotted a feral chihuahua trying to start a bar fight with a German shepherd.

"You are a very busy woman, Scarlet Montgomery," he sounded almost impressed.

There was the scraping sound of a shuffle. Sorin was taking one step forward. His face twisted, muscles coiled and twitching with barely contained violence.

"Wait, Sorin," I grabbed a fistful of his jacket, trying to summon whatever strength I had left from the blood he'd given me. "That's not what he meant. We—"

He cut his eyes to me, red irises bleeding through the dull. I shut up immediately. Then he turned back to Malik. His brows lowered. Double fangs slid out like knives.

Malik gave the tiniest shriek, spun on his heel, and bolted out of the alley.

Good for him. Terrible for me. But honestly? Probably the best-case scenario for Malik. That was at least one death I wouldn't have to add to my steadily growing list.

"Scarlet, what is happening?" Sorin turned halfway toward me.

Eyrin took another step forward, and Sorin shifted, positioning himself between us.

"Okay, that was *not* what it looked like," I said quickly, pointing a finger in the direction of Malik's fading footsteps.

Eyrin prowled closer, malice written all over his face.

"That, " I whispered tightly, "maybe is a tiny bit what it looks like."

I felt those teeth again and remembered the sting as they sank into my skin. This was all wrong. It wasn't how this night was supposed to go.

"Sorin," I began, but he held a hand out in front of me.

"Stay there. We'll talk about this later."

There wasn't anger in his voice. Only a coolness that promised a very unpleasant conversation to follow.

"Nice to finally see you off neutral territory, Sorin," Eyrin stopped about five feet away, hovering right outside of Sorin's reach.

With Sorin's speed, I thought he might have been pressing his luck.

"The only reason you're still alive," Sorin hissed, "is because we're in a public place."

Though I couldn't see his face, I knew it must be shifting. I could hear his ragged breathing as his bone and flesh distorted into those animalistic characteristics in response to the threat before us.

"Leave now, and I shall forget this encounter."

"You know I can't do that." Eyrin's hand disappeared into his pocket, and Sorin moved.

He wasn't fast enough. A cloud of sparkling dust plumed into the air around Sorin. He ducked, but it still caught him at its edges.

I gasped and stumbled back. It didn't take hold immediately, likely because he hadn't received the full-face treatment. Sorin still managed to knock Eyrin off his feet with a savage blow, pinning him to the ground. From where I stood, I saw Sorin straddle him. One clawed hand rose with long, gleaming talons catching the multi-colored streetlight. He was going to punch clean through Eyrin's chest.

"Stop!" Eyrin barked.

Sorin halted, a guttural snarl tearing from his throat.

"Get off me," Eyrin choked out, struggling into a sitting position.

Sorin rose in mechanical spasms. He moved as if marionette strings were pulling him against his will. I knew all too well how it felt. He stopped halfway up, hand recoiling like a cobra aiming to strike. Eyrin's eyes widened in fear as he scuttled away in a backward crab crawl.

"Turn around," Eyrin pointed in my direction. "Walk to her."

My heart seized in my chest as Sorin obeyed. He fought each step as he lumbered towards me.

"Sorin?" I stepped away, colliding with some trash cans.

The smell of rot and decay wafted around me. I gagged, unable to hold back my fear and combat the rancid stench. Sorin's mouth moved, his lips barely forming words.

"What?" I asked, voice trembling.

His throat worked, tendons straining as if he were fighting his own body just to speak. Finally, I heard him.

"*Run.*"

His voice was dry and strained as if he hadn't tasted water for years.

I should have run. Every instinct inside of me screamed for me to dart past him and follow Malik into the safety of city lights. There was not a damned thing I could have done if Sorin lost this battle for control over himself. But I couldn't leave him like this. He didn't deserve to be abandoned to whatever terrible end that Eyrin had in store for him.

Shaking my head, I took a shaky step forward. "No."

"Scarlet, please," the word broke in his throat. He staggered sideways, one hand catching the brick wall beside him, claws scraping stone. "I don't want to hurt you."

In a brutal sweep, he dragged his claws across his own forearms. Dark blood welled up in slow rivers from the deep gashes.

And suddenly, I wasn't so sure Sorin was just using me anymore. The air felt too thick to swallow. That wasn't a strategy or manipulation. That was pure, unvarnished fear. Not for himself, but for what he'd do to me. He was fighting to keep me safe.

"What a fascinating night," Eyrin brushed debris from his trousers and rose to his feet. "When Odessa's charming little pet came sniffing around with promises and propositions, I didn't expect I'd walk away with dinner and a show. You two spoil me."

"Eyrin," My lips trembled. I took another half-step towards Sorin. "This isn't what Malik and I wanted."

"That's not what he said," Eyrin said dryly, leaning against the wall.

Sorin trudged closer. Inhaling deeply, I reached out and took his hands. I noticed that his fingers had elongated with an extra joint, allowing his claws to wrap entirely around my wrists. Sorin froze, achieving his command of walking to me.

I ran a soothing thumb over the back of his hand, doing my best not to flinch at how powerful his hold was. His entire body quivered with the effort it took him to look over his shoulder at Eyrin.

"I didn't take her for your type," Eyrin drawled. "Didn't even know you had a type anymore. Thought you'd aged out of those kinds of things."

Sorin didn't speak, just bared his teeth in a silent snarl. The expression alone was enough to make Eyrin blanch and wipe at the sweat starting to bead along his brow. Holding Sorin wasn't effortless for him. I could see it in the tense line of his shoulders and the tight, focused pinch of his mouth.

"Listen to me. Even if you kill Sorin now," I reasoned with Eyrin, "You wouldn't be able to handle Odessa. You'd achieve nothing."

"Killing you would still be entertaining." Eyrin smirked, "I'm curious to see how he reacts to spilling your blood all over himself. I'd say it's not personal, but it is. Do you know how many of my people died the other night?"

I tried not to think about that too much. Did my absolute best to try to not imagine Sorin lumbering over my body with my throat torn open and his head buried into my neck.

"Besides, I know something you don't know," Eyrin sing-songed at us.

I gasped for breath. I was getting too much and not enough at the same time. My lungs burned like they were filled with smoke, even though the air was clean.

All the fantasy romance novels I read had described the fae as inhumanly fast and strong. I didn't think now was the right time to test that theory. Fighting past Sorin was definitely out of the question. I had to find a way to resolve this without things getting violent or wait until Eyrin lost his hold on Sorin.

Eyrin cocked his head, his gaze dragging down my body in disinterest.

"Be grateful, girl," he said. "I'm going to put you out of your misery. That's more than you'll get from the vampire witch."

He meant Odessa. And the way he said it, like he was doing me a favor, set my teeth on edge. My eyes raked across Eyrin, searching for a crack. Just one slip. His fists were clenched so tightly his knuckles had gone pale, and his breath was coming in heavy gulps now. As if he couldn't quite catch it. I noticed Sorin had turned only slightly. He was pushing back.

Eyrin didn't see it. He was fighting an outmatched battle of wills and was too obsessed with his control to see that his window of opportunity was rapidly closing.

"Why are you fighting so hard?" I asked. "Is power really worth all this? You could die!"

"This isn't about a title," he sneered.

The delay was all Sorin needed.

There was a popping sensation, like a joint dislocating, followed by a ripple in the air that raised the hairs on my arms. A blur of shadow surged in front of me.

Sorin slammed into Eyrin with such force that the Unseelie fae buckled over his fist like a wet blanket. There was a grunt, followed by a sickening smack as Sorin hurled him over his head and drove him down into the pavement.

A second later, Sorin was back on top of him. He straddled his chest, both clawed hands raised, and aimed straight for the kill. I threw my hands over my eyes, not wanting to see what came next. I couldn't take another gory image burned into me.

"Wait!" Eyrin cried. "I know things about Odessa. You kill me, you lose that."

"Why should I believe any of the filth that falls from an unseelie fae's mouth?"

But Sorin withheld his fatal blow.

"Being unseelie doesn't make us inherently evil," Eyrin let his head thunk against the pavement, eyes drifting up to the night sky.

It felt like those were meant to be his last words. The defeat, the utter surrender in them, tugged at my heart. Careful to stay out of Eyrin's reach, I crouched beside them and gently took Sorin's wrists in my hands.

"Please, don't kill him." I guided his hands down, letting the tips of his talons prick my skin as I pressed his palms to my chest. "I don't want another death on my conscience. Or another spirit to haunt me."

I also didn't think a brutal murder in the middle of the city would go unnoticed by the neighbors, no matter how determined they were to mind their own business. That and the whole 'enslave humanity' thing I was trying to avoid.

Sorin glared down at Eyrin for a long, long time.

"Scarlet," he said, "pull out your phone."

The red bled from his eyes. I felt the claws retract; long, slender fingertips replaced them.

"What?"

"No questions, woman." He cut me a sharp glance.

I released him and fumbled my phone from my pocket.

"You have three minutes," Sorin growled, returning his gaze to the fae. "Three minutes to tell me what you know. And I swear to any god listening—if it's not good, you'll end up on someone's porch as a Halloween decoration."

He leaned closer, fangs scraping Eyrin's neck.

"No one will recognize you until you're a leathery husk. And even then," an icy smile curved Sorin's lips, "I might fashion you into a scarecrow."

The gruesome image of Eyrin's dried corpse impaled on a stake sent a shiver skating down my spine. My fingers trembled slightly as I unlocked my phone, pulling up the timer, already guessing what Sorin wanted next.

"Start the timer, Scarlet."

I quickly set the countdown. Eyrin's mouth worked silently, lips trembling. He cleared his throat twice before managing to rasp, "O-Odessa's a necromancer."

"You could've led with something stronger," Sorin growled, grabbing Eyrin roughly by his sweater collar and lifting him off the ground.

Eyrin flung his hands up, shielding his face as he blurted, "The magic has a price!"

Sorin paused, fangs poised inches from the unscarred side of Eyrin's neck.

"And just how did you come by this knowledge?"

"Necromancy originated from fae magic!" Eyrin gasped desperately. "I can smell it all over her."

His wide, fearful eyes darted toward me. Sorin gave him another rough shake.

"And what makes you so sure it's Odessa's?"

Eyrin cried out in pain, wincing. I might have felt some sympathy for him until I remembered the piercing agony of his fangs sinking into my skin.

"I—I can't speak if you keep—agh—shaking me," Eyrin protested, voice strangled.

"How do you know?" Sorin demanded again, punctuating his question by driving a knee into Eyrin's solar plexus.

I grimaced out of familiarity with the breath-stealing agony of that blow.

Eyrin's breath wheezed out, chest desperately trying and failing to expand.

"She—she had to learn it somewhere," his face contorted in pain.

"You taught her?" Sorin eased up just enough to let him gasp in a desperate breath.

"No! No, I swear," Eyrin panted urgently. "But I know who might have. It's a small community. I'd wager you have a strong guess yourself."

Awareness tingled down my back like icy fingertips brushing against my neck. I reached back and rubbed the spot, goosebumps prickling along my arms.

"I might have a few. What, exactly, is this price?" Sorin asked, his voice growing impatient as he lost interest.

"It's complicated." Eyrin hurried through his explanation when Sorin snarled. "Each time she does it, it drains a part of her. It demands enormous amounts of energy. Haven't you noticed she's been drinking more blood than usual?"

Sorin's face didn't betray anything, but his grip loosened. Eyrin collapsed onto the pavement with a dull thud.

"*Scarlet.*"

I whipped around at the whisper, the sudden movement throwing off my balance. I landed hard, pain jolting up through my butt.

Both sets of eyes turned towards me.

"Sorry," I muttered, brushing strands of hair from my eyes. "Thought I heard something."

Sorin turned back to his interrogation. I tried focusing again, but a breeze wafted through the alley, carrying with it a mocking laughter.

Heart pounding, I stood cautiously, facing the darkened end of the alley. Suddenly, searing pain stabbed my right eye, like someone had reached in and was fisting the taut cords buried behind it. I hissed through clenched teeth, pressing my fingers to the pain and scanning the shadows, but nothing moved.

I realized the conversation behind me had ceased. Turning back quickly, I met their stares.

"What?"

They watched me silently, with varying looks of curiosity and poorly masked concern. The timer erupted from my phone in a chorus of ear splitting rings.

"That one's been cursed," Eyrin groaned, rising onto his elbows.

"I'm not cursed." I scoffed, striding back toward them. "I'm exhausted. It's just a cluster headache."

As I spoke, a warm trickle slipped down from my nostril. My fingers rose, coming away slick and crimson. Crap.

"Definitely cursed," Eyrin confirmed grimly. "That's necromantic magic if I ever saw it."

"Don't. Move." Sorin threatened him, already striding swiftly to my side and turning off the alarm still ringing from my phone.

He gently took my chin, turning my face back and forth, scrutinizing me. I didn't miss the dilation of his pupils, how they lingered hungrily over the blood. His fangs extended ever so slightly.

My pulse thudded sluggishly as extreme fatigue overtook my fading adrenaline. My eyelids felt impossibly heavy, gritty heat burning behind them.

"I'm fine."

Blinking rapidly, I forced myself to remain alert. How long had it been since I last slept again?

"You're not."

Sorin slid an arm around me, pulling me securely to his side. From his pocket, he produced a cloth napkin, offering it for my bleeding nose.

I squinted at it. "Tell me that's clean and not from, like, the Civil War."

He gave me a look. I snatched it anyway. Germs were the least of my worries.

Guilt panged in my chest as I held the cloth beneath my nostrils. These weren't the actions of someone who didn't care for me. His thumb traced comforting circles into my shoulder, and the tenderness of the gesture made my stomach knot painfully. My shoulders slumped lower. I let weariness become a cover for my shame.

"I can help with that," Eyrin interjected, rising warily to his knees as his eyes shifted between us. "For a price."

36
____

R.I.P., PANTIES

"In all of my many, many years," Sorin glowered at me from across the table in his penthouse, his arms crossed over his chest, "I have never been so... so—"

"Speechless?" I offered, lifting my mug of tea like a shield between us. "Rendered mute in the presence of my beauty?"

Neither of us laughed at the sorry excuse of a joke. I was too tired to care. I'd been forced to tell Sorin everything on the way home, after we'd agreed on an uneasy truce with Eyrin. He was going to help us deal with Odessa, allegedly. But I still didn't trust him.

Sorin sighed, rubbing his temple, "Why didn't you come to me the moment you found out?"

I dropped my gaze to my hands, fingers tightening around the mug.

"It's not like you've been all that forthcoming yourself. And I was hurt."

Saying it out loud felt like tearing off a scab too soon. I didn't want him to know how he had hurt me. It felt better to just keep it to myself.

Unwilling to say more, I stood and crossed to the narrow kitchen window, prodding lightly at the edge of my nose to distract myself.

"When we met," Sorin's voice rolled across the room, "when I followed you into that building, I never intended for us to become so attached."

My fingers curled around the sink's edge, squeezing until one of my knuckles gave a soft pop. This was sounding a lot like a break-up speech. Hours ago, I would have been elated. Now, my throat constricted, and my heart felt like it was sinking to the floor.

I looked back over my shoulder and gave the slightest nod of acknowledgment.

"You were so much more than I expected. You *became* so much more to me, more than I know how to explain."

From the corner of my eye, I saw him shift in his seat, gaze turning away.

"I haven't felt remotely close to this way in centuries. I didn't think I could anymore."

"You still hurt me," I breathed.

Whatever he felt, whatever his reasons were, it didn't change a damned thing about what I was feeling. I hated myself for trusting another man with my heart so easily. There was learning the hard way, and then there was just plain old stupid. In this situation, I fell into the second category. I bit my lip to keep it from trembling.

"I'm sorry," he stood, moving to stand behind me. "Truly, I am."

His hand slid up my shoulder, cool fingers cupping my chin to tilt my head back until it rested against his chest. I felt strands of my hair shift as he pressed the lightest kiss to the crown of my head.

"By the time I realized where we were headed, it was too late to choose someone else."

His thumb traced the line of my jaw with such aching tenderness I had to squeeze my eyes shut against the sting behind them. I tried to pull away, to get even a sliver of space between us. But his other arm curled around my shoulders, anchoring me in place.

I twisted, trying to break free, but it was no use. His arms were as good as chains. He pinned me to the cabinets, holding nearly all my weight so my toes barely scraped the floor. Every inch of him that was in contact with me seemed to burn.

He nuzzled into the crook of my neck, and I gasped. Fury? What fury? My body tossed that out the window and hung up a neon "WELCOME BACK" sign for my favorite bad decision. Heat roared through me, my blood humming in anticipation of the kind of orgasm that deserved its own Yelp review.

"You matter to me, Scarlet," he whispered. "Never doubt that."

My lips parted to respond, to call him a liar and demand that he let me go. All that escaped was a strangled sob. I hadn't realized I was crying until now.

"How can I trust you?"

How could I trust anyone in this viper's den? Hell, I couldn't even trust my own body. It fiended for him, rocking back to savor the heat that burned through the small of my back.

An approving sound rumbled from his chest. Shifting closer, the thick press of him slid into the hollow between my thighs. I bit back the moan rising in my throat, searching for control I no longer had. My fingers bit into the muscle banding his forearms.

"You can't," his voice wrapped around my mind just as his hand slipped down my front.

He unfastened my jeans, deftly slipping past the barrier of fabric to cup the aching heat between my legs. A single finger slid through the slickness there.

"God," I whimpered, rocking into his touch.

"No." His lips brushed my ear. "Not God."

Three fingers sank into me at once. My knees buckled. I caught myself against the counter, chest heaving. With a fluid motion, he spun me to face him. I was confronted by indigo eyes, eternity smoldering in their depths.

Going back to Savannah was the story I kept trying to sell myself. But my body had already picked a side, and it wasn't home. It was here, with Sorin's fingers buried deep inside me. His free hand tugged my jeans and panties down in one pull, letting them fall uselessly around my ankles. His eyes devoured me.

He was going to claim me again. And I had no intention of stopping him. I clenched around him, chasing the rolling surge of pleasure his fingers were creating inside of me.

"I swear by whatever unholy thing that made me what I am," he vowed as he pumped his fingers in and out of me. "You are safe with me. Your heart, your mind, your soul. Your body."

With each word, he pushed a little deeper. He nipped at my jaw. His other hand found my face, sweeping my hair off my neck.

"I should've never chosen you to be a part of this chaos. I see that now. You would be right to hate me."

He leaned in, lips brushing against the column of my throat, "But we don't have time for pride. If you walk away now, they'll win. And it makes us both monsters if we allow that to happen."

His fingers slowed, deepening their plunges inside of me and coaxing out a tormented whimper.

"Stay. Not just for me. Stay for the world you still care about. For your friends and family at home. For the free existence you've always known. And let me protect you the way I should've from the start."

Panting, I searched his face, hunting for any sign of deceit. I found unguarded yearning. Not just for my body but for my agreement. My surrender. It wasn't only desire. It was a lethal cocktail of desperation, purpose, and obsession. He *needed* me to say yes. I wasn't sure he'd even let me say no. A thrill of fear zinged through me, adding to the insistent pressure building between my thighs.

What if this was just another carefully spun lie? Come Halloween, he could discard me as Luke did. Or worse. He could keep me and twist my mind until I mistook possession for love. A pretty puppet to fuck and feed on.

But he was the one who wanted humanity to remain free. He had been doing all this, and god knows what else, to ensure that exact thing didn't happen.

His full lips sucked softly over my jugular. The press of fangs followed, and I couldn't hold back anymore. A ragged moan escaped my lips. How could a woman make a decision like this?

"Forgive me, Scarlet," his tongue circled that tender spot just below my ear. "Stay, please. Work with me. Be mine."

My fingers tangled in the velvety weight of his hair as he kissed a path down my throat, over the curve of my breast, pausing at the sliver of exposed skin where my shirt had ridden up just above my navel.

Fuck it.

"You'll have to make it up to me," I exhaled.

He looked at me through heavy-lidded eyes, hope sparking behind them like the flashpoint of an atom bomb.

"I don't know how you'll do it," I said in my coldest voice. "You'll have to figure that out yourself."

"Oh," he purred, continuing his descent lower, lower. "I have an excellent idea of where to start."

Kneeling before me, he slid a hand beneath my leg, lifting it until it rested on his shoulder. Warm breath feathered over me as he landed a lingering kiss on the inside of my thigh. Inhaling me greedily, he dragged his mouth closer to my center. Teeth and fangs brushed against me, leaving delicate crescent marks that stung just enough to make my brain short-circuit in that sweet no-man's-land between pain and pleasure.

I bit the inside of my cheek, clinging to the last threads of sanity as I teetered on the maddening edge of euphoria. I didn't want to go yet. I wanted to see how far he'd push—to what depths he'd sink to make me give in.

"Divine," he growled into my center, "You taste like heaven."

Holding my breath, I watched as his tongue lashed out, enveloping my clit in wet heat. A breathy moan escaped as I bucked against him. Whatever else Sorin had spent his two thousand years on—wars, politics, brooding—he'd clearly set aside a century or two for advanced tongue techniques.

He swirled that devilish tongue around my clit, curling his fingers inside me. My entire body convulsed from the steadily mounting pressure building in my core. It was too much. I would have to give in to him sooner than I wanted. Desire flooded down my thighs, his hand drenched with it. Clamping my leg tighter around his head, I denied myself the release he was pulling me to. Unmet need roared through me, savage in its demands that I give in.

"Cruel little beast," he rumbled against me. "I know what you're doing."

His pace increased, fingers pumping with inhuman speed. Crying out, I latched onto his shoulders, my body begging for surrender. But I still wasn't ready.

"Try. Harder," I panted, lifting one hand to cup my breast and tweak the nipple peeking through my unlined bra.

God, I thought I saw a star blink into existence. My vision blurred, spots danced, and a thick haze of lust settled behind my eyes.

With a dark, crooning laugh, his grip tightened. He locked me in place as his tongue doubled down. My legs began trembling violently. This was it. My final stand. I was seconds from yielding to the orgasm I knew was going to tear me apart.

Trapping my clit between his lips, he sucked hard as his tongue worked furiously across the bundle of nerves. My nails dragged down his back, drawing blood as my voice rang out, mindlessly screaming his name. I collapsed over him, clutching at anything I could reach. He slid a fourth finger inside me, stretching me past reason.

My body clamped down, shuddering through wave after wave as my climax consumed me. It devoured every word, every coherent thought, until all that remained was feral longing. I needed this. Needed him to bring me here.

My hips jerked one final time, and only then did he lift his head. His eyes gleamed with smug satisfaction. He gave me a crooked grin and made no move to retreat from between my thighs.

"Scarlet, may I bite you?"

"W-what?" I gasped, blinking down at him in post-orgasmic shock.

"It wouldn't hurt," he said gently, tracing a fingertip over the artery that pulsed high in my thigh. "In fact, I've been told it's quite pleasurable."

My breath caught.

"Would it... turn me??"

I sat up slightly, concern spiking through the last of my haze. It chased off the heat still clinging to my skin. I didn't think I wanted that. My soul, my humanity, felt like too much to gamble.

"I can control the venom," he replied calmly as his fingers brushed patterns over my skin.

My heart thundered, caught in a brutal tug-of-war between anxiety and animal want. Was it wrong of me to like this? The Southern belle in me was utterly scandalized. An even louder, more primal part of me screamed, 'Yes.' Yes, let him bite. Let him sink those ancient fangs into the tender flesh of my milk-white thigh. Let me throw my head back in bliss as that dark crimson offering pulsed beneath his mouth.

My cheeks blazed at the sheer carnality of those erotic images. I imagined him—mouth slick with blood, looming over me, his eyes burning with unholy desire. He drew me in like oxygen, like rain to a parched earth. I could feel his hunger for me in every nerve, every hollow place in my body that longed to be filled with him.

I imagined myself straddling his lap, bouncing wildly as thick cock thrust in and out of me—

The scent of snow hit me. I looked down, fixating on the ragged tear I'd made in his shirt. Tiny beads of blood welled along the scratch marks I'd carved into his back. My jaw clenched, mouth watering and aching. I felt myself inching forward, preparing to lap up every shimmering ruby drop.

Ripping myself away, I shuddered violently. I tried to pretend, for both of us, that it was just the aftershocks of my orgasm. Sorin's fathomless eyes narrowed on me. His thoughts were concealed by the mask that had started to fall back into place.

"Do it," I blurted, thrusting my thigh toward him to keep his unguarded self present with me.

He opened his mouth to speak, but I silenced him by pressing the meat of my upper thigh against his lips. I wasn't a small woman. He could either suffocate or bite, his choice. I needed that pain to drown out the sinking realization that I was growing addicted to his blood.

For a moment, he only stared, brows furrowed in silent conflict. Then, he parted his lips and drew me in, sucking gently on the swell of my thigh. His tongue traced over a small area. First came tingling, then a spreading, subtle numbness. Those deadly, beautiful upper fangs slid free of their confines.

I welcomed the wild spike of fear, the electric surge of adrenaline that coursed through my veins as his mouth closed around my leg. The bite was a whisper of penetration, two exquisitely sharp points slipping beneath my skin without resistance. Heat blossomed instantly, trailing down to my toes and up through my body like molten silk. It wrapped around my torso, cradling me like the arms of a lover.

Together, we sighed as tension drained from our bodies. I felt our breaths merge into perfect synchronization. We breathed as one as my eyes fluttered shut. A dreamy warmth crept up my neck, relaxing each muscle in my face one by one. A small, contented smile graced my lips.

It wasn't the erotic pleasure I'd expected. It felt soothing and peaceful. I became pliable, unresisting, and willing to do anything to maintain this state of serenity. In that moment, anything Sorin wanted—anything at all—I would have given him.

We groaned in unison as he swallowed a generous mouthful of my blood. He adjusted with me as we sank to the floor, cradling my body as I lay fully on my back. Leaning into me, he kept my leg bent over his shoulder so he hovered over me. One hand cupped the side of my thigh, locking it in place. The other glided up my belly, slipped beneath my shirt, and curved around my back. The clasp of my bra gave way with a soft *snap*, and cool air rushed in to tease my freed nipples.

On his next swallow, his palms grazed the swell of my breasts before giving each one a searching squeeze. He rolled my nipples between his thumb and forefinger, eliciting soft gasps from my lips. Every item of our clothing seemed to vanish. Some he peeled away so gently I barely noticed. Other items, like my last pair of reliable underwear, he annihilated with a flick of his claw.

R.I.P. panties. You died a noble death in service to vampire sex.

Just like that, desire overtook my serenity. I became hyper-aware of his firm cock prodding against the back of my thigh. My hips lifted to him. I needed to feel him inside me, moving with me, taking everything from me.

Ignoring my request, his throat continued to work rhythmically. The sounds of his gulps filled my ears with a squelching obscenity of its own. One hand slipped to his shaft, fingers closing around it and stroking. I watched, mesmerized and aching, jealousy blooming low in my gut as he pleasured himself. Our breaths quickened with each pass of his hand.

A creeping dizziness threaded its way into my awareness. I tried to refocus my eyes by blinking a few times. Sorin's outline was off-kilter, like my vision was underwater. My head lolled back with a graceless thud against the floor.

Sorin's eyes snapped open. He released my leg, and the loss of contact made me want to cry. I grasped weakly at his arms, trying to guide him back to me. I needed him to keep drinking. Just a little more.

"Are you feeling alright?" He asked, catching my wrists in his hands.

I nodded dismissively. I could barely speak, my body floating on a cloud of blitzed-out oblivion. But the ache between my thighs screamed for attention. My legs wrapped around his waist, beckoning him closer.

"Need you... inside me... now," I panted, looking at him through my lashes.

"Your wish is my command."

He gathered me into his arms, whisking me into the living room. He laid me out like an offering across the sleek, black couch.

We didn't waste time. My legs parted in invitation for him as he knelt between them and aligned himself with my core. A gush of wetness welcomed him inside me as he filled me in one soul-rending thrust.

"Sorin," I moaned his name, hips rising to meet his.

He drew back, only to surge forward again, stretching me more than he ever had. Our last encounter had been a frenzied taking of possession. This was a tender act of worship. His hands and mouth became instruments of devotion, teasing, sucking, and pinching in time with the slow build inside me.

The unrestrained affection, the raw emotion he poured into every motion, every breath, cracked something open in my bruised heart. He caught my next moan with his mouth, tongue tangling with mine as his pace began to increase. My blood smeared between our lips like a fine oil.

"Scarlet," he breathed, voice strained with need.

Hearing my name dragged from his throat made my pussy spasm around him, begging to be split wider, filled deeper.

"More. Please—more. I need you."

Trapping my wrists above my head, he pounded into me harder. Tiny droplets of blood rolled down my wrists from where his claws dug into me. He threw his head back so that all I could see was the long column of his neck, a single rivulet of red cascading down the length of it.

I was ready to shatter. I wanted to take him with me so we could go over the edge together.

His movements grew frantic, tempo stuttering as he neared the peak of his own pleasure. We came together, our cries tangled in an eruption of strength, surrender, and soul-deep release.

Sorin lay beside me, breathing heavily, one arm draped over my waist like he could bind me to him. I stared at the ceiling, lips parted, but no breath came easily. My body felt spent and satisfied. My heart felt confused.

People were dead because of me. I'd betrayed my vows, although I wasn't sure if it really counted since Luke had beaten me to it. And now I was entangled with a man I was supposed to fear, who had lied to me on multiple occasions. I thought I was more sensible than this.

He shifted beside me, murmuring my name. I flinched because it felt too much like something a man would do with a woman who he saw a future with. It was something people in relationships did. I didn't know if I could survive another one of those ending.

What happens if this burns out? When I wake up and realize I gave myself to a monster? Or he wakes up, and I'm an old woman, while he remains the handsome dark-haired man stretched out beside me for eternity.

What happens if I have to choose between him and my life at home?

Sorin kissed my shoulder, and god help the little flip my heart gave. I was falling in love with him. I wasn't sure if that made me weak or damned.

37

PORTENTS

Five days. There were only five days left until Halloween.

I stared blankly at my laptop screen, ignoring the emails piling up in my inbox. My eyes glazed over, drifting toward the window above Sorin's kitchen sink. I would have given anything to be home, really home, sitting on the porch with Milo with a cup of coffee in my hands while the cicadas screamed their little bug lungs out.

Sorin had insisted that I move in with him. With Malik away most days running errands for Odessa and the hauntings growing more assertive, I'd relented. Less weird shit happened when I wasn't alone. *Usually.*

My days were split between work, punishing workouts until my body collapsed, and whatever eldritch nonsense Eyrin prescribed to keep Odessa's curse from full manifestation. Salt baths had become an admittedly enjoyable daily ritual. Wearing my clothes inside out "confused spirits," which Sorin found endlessly hilarious. But then there were the truly deranged actions like licking the ashes of burned rosemary and salt from my palm while saying my name backwards. Burying an egg filled with my spit under the roots of a hawthorn tree.

Sleeping with a frog in a glass jar on the nightstand so it could "swallow the bad dreams."

Once, he'd even had me hum a hymn into a bowl of cream, leave it on a windowsill, and wait to see if a stray cat would drink it. The cat did. I still heard the screaming of the dying in my sleep.

"Perfectly normal for your incompetent mortal brain," as Eyrin so helpfully put it.

Odessa had been relatively easy to avoid with the looming Summit and the Halloween festival chewing up most of her time. I'd conveniently come down with a bad case of the flu. It was an ironclad excuse to hole up in-quarters while Malik played doting nurse. No sneaking around required.

The sun had set three hours ago. Sorin was off handling last-minute preparations for the Summit, leaving me to fend for myself in his apartment. Milo grunted beside me, nudging his cold nose into my thigh. A polite, insistent request.

"Potty break," I murmured, closing my laptop with a soft snap.

I crossed into the living room to grab his leash. Pulling on my jean jacket and a black beanie, I regretted not packing a scarf. The October wind was brutal today. Fat, angry clouds that looked ready to burst filled the sky.

Despite Sorin making it clear he didn't want me going out alone, I was a grown woman. I could walk my dog by myself and face the consequences later. Consequences that I hoped would involve my fair share of spankings.

A silly grin pulled at my lips as we trotted through the too-dark hallway and down the stairs. Outside, the line to get into Crimson & Clover stretched down the block. I watched them as we passed, wondering who was there to eat and who was lined up to be eaten. Shuddering, I turned away.

"Out for an evening stroll?" Eyrin asked, materializing out of the throng of people around me.

"Holy hell." I stumbled back a step. "Why are you here?"

"I was hoping to run into the cute one," Eyrin grumbled, flipping up the collar of his trench coat with the solemnity of a man auditioning for *Casablanca*.

He looked like a parody of a detective from a 1950s B-movie. He and Malik had been dancing around each other since our incident. Malik was dodging Eyrin harder than I dodged my father's phone calls.

A frigid gust sliced through my jacket, making me shiver. If I stayed in New York much longer, I'd have to cave and buy a real coat.

"You cold?" I asked, sneaking a glance at him.

He just hiked up a shoulder and fell into step beside me. Guess I had a plus one after all.

"Do fae even get cold?"

"We get cold," he said flatly, not even sparing me a glance.

So rude. I twisted my lips. "Not much for small talk, huh?"

Milo growled before Eyrin could answer, a line of fur bristling along his spine.

"Scarlet?"

That sultry voice was smooth as melted butter, sweet as poison. I'd know it anywhere. I forced my lips into a smile, muscles stiffening beneath my skin.

"Odessa. Hi."

I wrapped Milo's leash tighter around my hand, focusing on the rope's bite against my palm. "What are you doing here?"

She smiled a bit too wide.

"Out for a little stroll. It's *such* a lovely night."

A few raindrops plinked against the back of my neck. I reached up to wipe them away, never breaking eye contact with the uncharacteristically disheveled woman in front of us.

Dark circles sagged beneath her wide, unblinking eyes. The whites showed all around her irises, making her look as if she were in a constant state of startled. Her burnt-orange knit sweater, though stunning, hung crookedly on her thin frame. A size too big. The collar drooped just enough to reveal a collarbone that jutted out of her skin painfully.

The changes were subtle unless you knew what to look for. And now that I did, I questioned what else I had missed about her over the last month. She stepped towards us, and I resisted the urge to back away.

"I see you've made a friend." Her gaze slid past me to Eyrin, who stood like a shadow at my back. "You must be feeling better."

I scrambled mentally for any plausible excuse to explain why Eyrin and I were out walking Milo together. A thin hand clapped onto my shoulder, rocking my frame.

"You know me," Eyrin grinned, every syllable dipped in mischief. "Always making new friends. And I just *love* dogs."

Odessa's eye twitched as he reached down to pet Milo. Milo growled, stepping out of reach. Damn it.

"Milo, be *nice* to your new friend," I muttered through clenched teeth.

The little bastard side-eyed me with a huff as if to say *you're on your own.*

Odessa watched the whole interaction with a flat expression. Her eyes, still held open far too wide, never blinked. Never wavered. She didn't believe a word of it. Just as I didn't believe she just happened to be out for a stroll. Not on the exact block I decided to walk Milo. Not five days before the Summit and in the rain.

Mist began to fall in a steady sheen, coating my skin and dampening the strands of hair curling out from beneath my beanie. I shivered.

"You're freezing," Odessa gasped, already turning toward Crimson & Clover. "Come back to the kitchen—let's get something warm inside you."

"No thanks," I shifted on my feet. "I actually have dinner plans with Malik."

Her head tilted.

"Really?" Her tone was casual, but her smile didn't reach her eyes. "That's strange. Because he's waiting for *me* as we speak."

Shit. Double shit.

"What a coincidence," I recovered quickly, forcing a grin. "Sounds like Malik's better at making plans than keeping them. Lead the way."

Behind her back, Eyrin shot me an incredulous look. I gave him a helpless shrug and grimaced. What the hell was I supposed to do?

The stakes were too high for me to fly off the handle and accuse her of trying to rope me into murdering another vampire. This called for caution, compliance, and pretending I didn't want to run screaming in the other direction.

Eyrin sighed loudly but followed as I trailed after Odessa. The moment we crossed the threshold of Crimson & Clover, a creeping ache engulfed the backs of my eyes. I rubbed at them with the backs of my hands as we entered the private dining area. Malik sat at the table, pale and jittery. He jumped when the door swung open.

"Malik," I said, locking eyes with him. "Why didn't you tell me you already made plans with Odessa tonight? We could've rescheduled dinner."

He blanched, confused.

"What?"

"Our dinner plans?" I pressed. "We were supposed to eat together tonight. I ran into Odessa outside. She said you were here instead."

Understanding dawned across his face.

"Oh! Oh—dinner, right." He nodded quickly. "Sorry, Red. Totally slipped my mind. Odessa wanted to meet, and I... forgot."

Odessa took her seat, looking mildly pleased.

"You two have been spending an awful lot of time together," she purred, reaching for one of the bottles of blood chilling on the table.

She poured a generous glass of thick, dark blood and downed it in three long gulps. Without missing a beat, she poured another and gestured toward Eyrin.

"Eyrin, may I interest you in one of our finest blends?"

"No, thank you," he said politely. "You know I prefer it fresh. The bottled stuff never sits well with me."

"Yes," Odessa sighed, swirling the crimson liquid in her glass. "It does lack a certain kind of punch."

She looked up, a gleam in her eye, "I'll have something fresh brought in."

"That's really not necessary," Eyrin cut in quickly, eyes darting to Malik.

Malik refused to even look in his direction.

"Nonsense," she said, waving him off with a cold smile. "It would be poor manners to invite guests in without offering refreshments."

Eyrin fidgeted with his shirt as Odessa pulled out her phone.

"It's Odessa," she said. "Bring me two of the specials for tonight and two fresh Merlos."

Every drop of blood drained from Malik's face leaving him a shade of gray I didn't know was possible.

Her request had sounded harmless. But when the door opened, and two beautiful women with salt and pepper hair entered the room, I understood.

They moved silently, placing plates of food in front of Malik and me. Then, without a word, each crossed the room and knelt on both knees in front of Eyrin and Odessa. They weren't there to serve us. They were willing offerings.

My stomach twisted, bile rising in my throat. I didn't want to see this.

Pushing up from my chair, I tried to steady my voice, "I'm not feeling so well. I should probably go."

"*Sit.*" Odessa's voice cracked like a whip.

I slowly sank back into my seat.

Across from me, Malik raised a trembling hand to his mouth and bit at the ragged skin around his fingernails.

"Malik," Odessa snapped, her fangs extruding from her too-perfect lips. "Stop that immediately."

"Nasty little habit he's had since childhood," she added with a condescending glance toward Eyrin and me like we should be amused.

Malik's hands dropped instantly, disappearing under his thighs. He looked down at his feet. Heat flared beneath my skin. I hated the way she spoke to him as if he were a child.

"It doesn't bother me," I blurted.

"Oh?" Odessa's brow arched with exaggerated curiosity. "You aren't bothered by much, are you?"

What the fuck was that supposed to mean? My inner demons stirred, clawing their way to the surface, and my cheeks flushed hot with anger and shame.

Swallowing hard, I asked, "Is there something you think I should be worried about?"

She tapped her chin, thoughtful.

"Hmm. I suppose there is if you assume your sick husband is still in this building. A man you've seen, what... twice, since dragging him here?"

Every vertebra in my spine straightened at the mention of Luke.

"That's none of your business."

"Isn't it, though?" she asked sweetly, draining the last of her second glass.

She turned to the kneeling woman beside her, reached out with lithe fingers, and tucked a stray strand of silver hair behind the woman's ear. Across the table, Eyrin silently gestured for his companion to sit beside him. She did so without hesitation, eyes remaining downcast.

"Do you even know where he is?" Odessa asked.

My entire body went still. Malik bit his lip. Eyrin's grip on the woman's wrist slackened.

"He's here," I said slowly, cautiously. "Isn't he? In your facility?"

"You wouldn't know," Odessa tilted the woman's head to the side, her mouth hovering a breath away from the soft skin of her neck. "You could find out, but I know you've been rather preoccupied with your conquests as of late."

My lips parted, rage boiling up, an insult halfway to my tongue. Malik's hand closed around my wrist. He shook his head just once. Breathing hard, I slammed my mouth shut.

"Auntie," Malik said gently. "Red and I... we *have* been spending a lot of time together."

Her expectant gaze flicked to him. He gulped and continued.

"We've been thinking about what you want. You know, for us to have a baby together."

He fumbled the words, but the damage was already done. Disgust carved heinous lines across Eyrin's face.

"And we think—we think you're right." He forced a shaky smile. "We want to do it."

I felt Eyrin's stare boring into the side of my face, and my ears heated with a fresh blush. I would have to explain this later.

Odessa stared at Malik. Those too-wide eyes shimmered with something I couldn't quite place. Joy? Madness? Hunger? It was impossible to tell.

"A baby," she tasted the word like it was wine. "Excellent."

Her smile twitched at the corners. For a moment, I thought she might start laughing or maybe screaming. She rose gracefully from her chair, trailing a single finger along the back of the kneeling woman's neck.

"I hope you're not just saying what I want to hear, Malik," she lilted. "You know how I hate to be disappointed."

Her gaze cut to me, "And you, Scarlet, please remember that loyalty is like blood. Once spilled, it's so hard to put back."

Without warning, she leaned in and sank her fangs deep into the woman's neck.

The woman gasped softly as Odessa drank deeply, her eyes shuttering in ecstasy. I watched in horror and perhaps a touch of yearning as the blood ran in rivulets down Odessa's chin, staining the perfect collar of her burnt-orange sweater.

The wet, intimate suck of it made my fingers fly to my inner thigh where Sorin had bitten me before. My body ached for that numbing bliss I knew was burning through this strange woman. When Odessa finally lifted her head, lips gleaming with red, she looked right at me.

"Eyrin, you were right," she sang. "Warm is always better."

38

A KNOCK, A WHISPER, A PROMISE

"She knows," Malik paced tight circles in Sorin's living room. "I don't know what she knows or how much. But she can tell something's off. I am so fucked."

"You are not fucked." I reached out and grabbed his hand, tugging him down beside me onto the couch. "We're going to figure this out."

Despite my words of comfort, I wasn't doing much better myself. I'd called and texted Luke at least thirty times since we left and discovered for ourselves that he wasn't in the medical room. My apprehension grew with each unanswered ring. Here I was again, still worrying over the man who wouldn't even spare me a second glance.

This was a brutal cycle that I needed to break, and I needed to do it soon. I clenched my phone, offering a silent prayer that he was okay until I could figure out how to find him.

"Sorin will be here soon," Eyrin said from his post near the door, glaring at where my fingers encircled Malik's. "We'll sort it out when he gets back."

As he spoke, the lights flickered once, then again, leaving us blinking through brief jolts of light and shadow. I cursed under my breath, holding Malik and Milo as they pressed in close on either side of me.

"What is that succubus up to now?" Eyrin growled, stepping closer to us.

God, I hoped she wouldn't send another haunting into the bathroom. Ever since then, I'd been forced to conduct my business with the door cracked, a flashlight in hand, and the reflexes of a cornered raccoon. I shot a wary glance down the hall toward the bathroom.

Casting an assessing glance over Malik and me as we quivered on the couch, Eyrin reassured us—let's be real, mostly Malik—with a solemn, "Don't worry. It can't hurt us. Probably."

"Probably?" I squeaked.

Malik slung an arm around my shoulders, and I hugged Milo tighter. His little heartbeat thudded against my ribs. The lights gave one last shiver before snapping back to normal, as if to say *just kidding*. We all exhaled at once.

BANG. BANG. BANG.

The sound cracked through the apartment like a gunshot against glass. Every muscle in my body locked.

Malik and I jolted. Eyrin stepped forward, his hand hovering above the handle.

"It's not Sorin," Eyrin tilted a pointed ear to the door.

"How do you know?" Malik whimpered.

"Because he wouldn't knock," Eyrin hissed.

We stared at the door.

BANG.

Just once this time, but louder. The kind of knock that makes your bones rattle. Something was demanding to be let inside. Eyrin backed away. The doorknob began to turn slowly; whoever was on the other side was testing the strength of the lock.

Milo whined in my arms, and my breath misted in the air. Malik's arm tightened around me, preventing the shivers that threatened to tremble down my body.

"Don't open it," I said. "Please, don't do it."

"You don't have to tell me," Eyrin inched back.

CLICK.

The door creaked inward a fraction, revealing nothing but the long, dark hallway on the other side. The corridor seemed to stretch, to warp and twist. Air whooshed into the apartment, sending my hair flying backward. And then every light in the apartment exploded. They shattered in a confetti of glittering glass shards that tinkled onto the marble floor.

Then came the low whisper inches from my ear.

"Scarlet..."

Malik screamed. It was one of those full-throated, terrified screams that vibrated your eardrums and left a ringing in its wake. I couldn't move. I couldn't breathe. All I could do was cling to Milo and try to make out any hint of movement in the residual light from the city leaking through the window.

Eyrin roared, "Don't answer! Don't let her into your mind!"

Cold fingers wrapped around my throat, squeezing just enough to cause discomfort. I let out a gargled choke. Something slammed into the door so hard it burst inward off its hinges. It looked like a thick, wet mist had poured into the room.

It reminded me of the shifting, nearly sentient steam that dances above you after a scalding shower. When you looked from the corner of your eye, you could see it breaking apart into fine, shimmering strands. But the second you looked straight at it, the strands fused together, twisting into a single, writhing shape.

"Enough," Sorin's voice erupted from within the mist.

Darkness recoiled, sucked back through the broken threshold like a retreating tide. The door hung askew on its frame. The lights were dead. And there stood Sorin at the splintered threshold, eyes iridescent and red. A stove light in the kitchen flickered on, bathing the room in a weak, yellow glow.

"This is absurd," he growled, striding into the room.

Sweeping me into his arms, he held me tightly against him. His fingers brushed the throbbing spot on my neck where I had been strangled.

"You're bruised," he said gently.

I exhaled a shaky breath, letting him take my weight while I fought to slow my racing heart.

"I'm calling an emergency council. We can't wait for the Summit."

Sorin turned to Malik, "I'm not sure you're safe here anymore. Is there someone you can stay with? Someplace away from Crimson & Clover?"

Malik gave a defeated shake of his head. My heart twinged for him.

"He can stay with me," Eyrin offered with a sly twitch of his lips.

"Not a chance," I shot daggers at him with my eyes.

"He'll be safe with me. Scout's honor," Eyrin said, holding up a hand in a mock salute.

I rolled my eyes. Eyrin had been looking at Malik as if he were a five-course meal for weeks. "Yeah, no way in hell you were ever a scout."

"Semantics," Eyrin said.

"Can you swear he'll be safe with you?" Sorin asked, voice like flint.

My mouth dropped open. I stared at him, stunned. Did he seriously forget that Eyrin had, *very recently*, tried to eat me?

Sorin leaned in, his voice dropping to a whisper only I could hear, "It's for the best. I've never seen Odessa this unhinged before. I don't know what she's capable of."

"I don't trust him," I said loudly, glaring daggers in his direction.

"You trusted me enough to try to bargain with me," Eyrin tossed back.

"Yeah, and then you tried to kill me. Again."

He shrugged and turned to Malik, "What do you say, handsome?"

Malik gaped at him.

"Give us one good reason he should go with you," I said, coming to stand beside Malik.

The smirk fell from Eyrin's face. He lifted a hand, then drew a razor-sharp nail across the palm of it. A thin line of blood welled up and dribbled to the floor.

"I, Eyrin Morwen Valean, vow to protect Malik by my blood, my name, and my life."

The droplets sizzled as they hit the floor, sending tendrils of smoke snaking into the air.

"There, you have my blood oath," Eyrin said, withdrawing his hand.

"Why should we believe you?" I asked.

"You don't really have another option, do you?" Eyrin sneered.

Sorin growled low in his throat, a sound that made the walls seem to hum with the promise of violence.

"Fine," Eyrin said begrudgingly. "There's more in this for me than personal gain. It's for my people. I want us to be seen as more than monsters. We're a multifaceted people. Flawed, yes, but not inherently evil. We deserve a voice in the world's future. And Sorin is my way in."

Oh. That was surprisingly heartfelt, and I had no comeback to it.

"And, he's pretty cute," Eyrin added with a roguish smile.

Malik's eyes widened, "Wait. *Me* or Sorin?"

Eyrin didn't answer. Just grinned at him with too many teeth.

"Great," Malik rubbed the back of his neck, clearly flustered but trying to play it cool. "Politics, blood pacts, and now *I'm* the damsel in distress."

He glanced at Eyrin again, then quickly looked away.

"Cool. Not weird at all."

I almost laughed.

"You're okay with this?" I searched Malik's face.

He gave a half-hearted shrug. "I don't think I really have much of a choice, Red." His gaze swept across the broken light bulbs and scorched floor before landing on Eyrin. "She's going to be pissed, though. Are you ready for that?"

"I can handle a lot more than I look like," Eyrin said with a wink.

Even I blushed at the forwardness of his advances. Malik's lips parted slightly, eyes flying back to Eyrin with something dangerously close to intrigue.

"Well... erm. I think I'll be okay, then."

I just bet he would be. Malik was a grown man. He could make his own decisions. If Eyrin is what he chose, then far be it from me to intervene.

"Leave immediately," Sorin instructed, utterly unfazed by the flirtation that had just taken place. "Don't even stop to pack. It gives her too much time."

"What about planning for the Summit?" I protested.

"There's no time." His gaze drifted past me, landing on Milo.

The poor baby was still crouched beside Malik, tense and panting.

"Milo needs to go home. It's too dangerous for him here."

He was right. I knew he was. But the thought of sending Milo away wrenched at my heart. My dog looked up at me, those big brown eyes filled with nothing but love and confusion. His tongue lolled as he struggled to calm down.

"He needs to go to my brother's house. Tucker's," I said, turning to Sorin. "I just don't know how to get him there."

"I'll take care of it." Sorin was already tapping into his phone.

"Sorin," I hesitated. "Milo is—he's very... he's my heart. I love him."

I didn't know how to explain to someone like Sorin, who was struggling to come to terms with attachment and romantic feelings, how much a pet could mean. Milo wasn't just an animal. He was as important to me as any member of my family. If anything were to happen to him, it would send me off the deep end.

"Do you trust me, Scarlet?" He asked, the red bleeding out of his eyes until all I could see was indigo flicked with black.

I breathed in, "Yes."

"Then let me handle this for you." He reached out and smoothed my hair into place. "Call your brother. Let him know Milo will be there soon."

"It's two in the morning," I huffed. "I'll call first thing."

Trying to ignore Malik's stare, I pushed up onto my toes and pressed a kiss to Sorin's cheek. His fingers brushed the spot where my lips had been, and a small, surprised smile curled at the edge of his mouth.

Later, as I watched Milo disappear, his nose pressed to the back window of a truck, I wiped a tear from the corner of my eye. I told myself I'd see him again soon when we were both back home in Savannah. This was the right thing to do. He'd be safe. We'd sit on the porch again, and I'd spoil him so rotten with treats that the vet would probably put him on a special diet.

In the meantime, he was with Tucker and Tiffany. He was loved and protected. I would make sure they *all* stayed safe. No matter what happened. Whatever came next, I'd face it head-on.

Sorin slid an arm around my waist, pulling me close and kissing the top of my head. My chest tightened.

It was time to face the music. Time to stop running from the truth that I was falling in love with Sorin. Time to confront Odessa. Time to resolve this without bloodshed, if I could. Time to finally allow myself to hope.

39

BURNING BRIDGES

"I'm already packing a bag. If you don't tell me the truth, I swear to God I'll book the first flight out and hunt you down myself," Tucker raged from the other end of the line.

"Tucker, I can't."

"Drop the bullshit," he fumed. "You're going through something, and this—*none* of anything that's been happening lately—is like you. This is your last chance. There's a flight that leaves in three hours."

I stayed silent. There was nothing I could say that would make this better. Nothing that would sound sane or be safe enough to tell him.

"Right," he bit out. "I'll be there soon."

"Wait. Just wait a minute, Tuck." I ran a hand through my hair. "Look. Luke is in trouble. Or he got into trouble. It's about the addiction stuff, and I had to pull him out. But now he's gone again, and I don't know where he is. And I'm involved now, okay?"

"Now I'm definitely coming up there," he said. I could hear the metallic zip of a suitcase.

"No!" I nearly shouted, jolting to my feet from the dining room table in Sorin's apartment.

He was asleep in the other room. The sun had been up for over an hour, but I wasn't brave enough to leave the apartment alone.

"This will all be over soon," I said, trying to sound composed. "I should be home after Halloween."

Hopefully not in a body bag. But I didn't say that part out loud.

"Why wait? Come home now, today. Let the police handle things," Tucker pleaded.

"Tuck, please trust me on this," I begged. "I'll be home in less than a week. I'll leave on the first flight the next morning."

"Scarlet," he groaned, and I heard the creak of his mattress.

I could picture him sitting on the edge of the bed, hand tangled in that thick mess of dirty blond hair. "Fuck. Fine. But you'd better book that flight now and send me a screenshot."

There was a pause, followed by a shaky exhale. "I'm worried about you, sis."

"I know." Hell, I was worried for myself. "I had Milo shipped back to you. I'll be out a lot over the next few days, and he'll be happier with you guys. Is that okay?"

"Sure. What time's he getting here?"

I opened Milo's tracking app and checked his collar.

"Probably around six."

Tucker grunted in acknowledgment.

"Tucker?" I asked lowly.

"What?"

"I love you."

"Aw, shit. I love you too, you big idiot," he grumbled. "Just come home in one piece, okay? And fuck Luke. Let him lie in his own bed."

"Okay. I'll try," I sniffed back some tears. "Bye."

"Send me your flight confirmation. Bye."

I sank back into the chair, resting my head on folded arms. I was too tired to think anymore. With slow fingers, I booked the flight and sent the screenshot to Tucker. I was ready to go home. If I survived this, and that was a big if, Sorin could figure out how to make it work if he wanted to. That's what I told myself, anyway.

My eyelids drooped again, and I forced myself upright, dragging my body into the bathroom. I showered, brushed my teeth, and padded into the bedroom. Still naked, I collapsed into bed beside Sorin.

I curled into a tight ball beneath the comforter, one arm stretching out in the dark to find his hand. His fingers were as cold and still as stone when my hand wrapped around them. It took a long time, but his fingers eventually wound around mine. He gave the smallest squeeze, but it was enough to know that I wasn't alone. I closed my eyes, letting sleep roll over me.

"They won't change the date of the Summit," I heard Eyrin's voice from the bedroom as I rubbed the sleep from my eyes.

Sorin muttered something in response that was too low for me to make out, but there was obviously frustration in his voice. I rolled over and checked my phone. 6:45 p.m. The sun must've just dipped below the horizon.

Swiping into my messages, I fired off a quick reply to Victor, who was checking in, then paused on a photo from Tucker. Milo was sprawled across my niece's lap, mid-slobber, while she laughed with her whole face.

I stared at her smile, filled with light. All I could think was that the choices I made over the next few days might decide whether pictures like this would continue to reach me or stop altogether.

I dressed quickly in my faithful black turtleneck and dark jeans, then padded out into the living room. Sorin sat stiffly on the couch, his skin a touch paler than usual. Heavy bags hung under his eyes, and his cheeks looked just a little too hollow. He hadn't fed recently. Not properly, anyway.

He and Eyrin both turned as I entered.

"What did I miss?" I asked, breaking the silence.

"The Summit is still happening on Halloween," Sorin groused, clearly unhappy.

"But," Eyrin cut in, "The Second Province is willing to arrive early to observe as a non-biased party."

"You couldn't have led with that?" Sorin pinched the bridge of his nose. "Damn it, Eyrin."

"I was *getting* to it, you old bastard," Eyrin scrubbed a hand through the stubble growing on his chin.

"How's Malik?" I asked, sauntering into the kitchen,

"What will you give me if I tell you?" Eyrin batted his lashes at me, all fake innocence.

"Don't answer that," Sorin interjected, shooting Eyrin a dark glare.

Eyrin laughed. "Need your watchdog to protect you, Red?"

Malik's nickname for me on the fae's mouth made me want to stomp over there and slap that stupid look off his face.

"I don't need an ancient vampire to shove my foot so far up your ass you'll be coughin' up pixie dust for a month," I sneered.

Sorin covered his laugh with a cough, turning away from both of us. Eyrin's taunting expression slipped into mild annoyance.

"He's fine," Eyrin muttered, holding out his phone.

On the screen was a picture of Malik at dinner as proof of life. His eyes and nose scrunched in a close-lipped smile as he leaned over a plate of Indian food, posture loose and easy. He looked happy. As if someone had finally hit the "off" switch on his constant state of panic.

"Thanks," I passed the phone back, dumping fragrant heaps of coffee grounds into the coffee machine. "So, what does the council's decision mean for us?"

I hit the power switch and listened to the comforting whine and drip as it began to brew.

"It means we need to be extremely careful over the next few days," Sorin said, still rubbing the bridge of his nose. "And it means you'll need to be watched closely. Honestly, I'd prefer if you stayed inside this apartment until the Summit."

"For four days?" My heart sank. "But... what about Luke?"

"What about him?" Sorin lifted his head to look at me.

"Odessa said she doesn't even know where he is."

His brows knitted together.

"Why would Odessa know where Luke is?"

Oh. Fuck. Fuckfuckfuck.

My mouth opened. Then closed. Then opened again. Somewhere in my slow-moving brain, there was a coherent excuse, but damned if I could find it around the foot wedged firmly in my throat.

"Scarlet," Sorin said, rising from the couch and stepping in front of me. "Why would Odessa know where Luke is?"

"Well, uh... You see—" I stammered, grasping wildly for anything to save me from the steaming pile of shit I had just launched myself into.

I knew Eyrin hadn't spilled the whole story of our run-in with Odessa to Sorin. If he had, Sorin would've been breathing fire days ago. It had been a nice lie of omission to hide behind. Thanks to me, that comfortable buffer had just evaporated. The bridge I'd been avoiding was right in front of me now, and there was no way around it. Time to cross.

"Riiight," Eyrin cleared his throat as he stood. "I think I'll just—"

"Stay," Sorin ordered, pointing a finger at him without looking away from me. "We're not done yet."

"It's not important. We can talk about this later," I grasped for the coffee pot, searching for a mug to put it in.

"No." Sorin whisked the pot out of my hands. "We will talk about this now. Tell me why Odessa would know where Luke is."

I looked up at him. Took a good, long minute to study the stubborn set of his brows, the stern expression etched into every line of his face. There was no escaping this. No more stalling. I drew in a steadying breath, bracing for what was about to happen. Here it came.

"You wouldn't help me," I said quietly, "so I found someone who would."

"You... found someone," Sorin repeated hollowly.

A myriad of emotions passed across his face. Confusion, hurt, betrayal. Then, finally, anger.

"I *did* help you," his voice crackled with restrained anger. "In every way I knew how."

"It wasn't enough." I crossed my arms over my chest and looked away. "Luke was dying. I couldn't just stand there and let that happen. He was my husband."

"*Is* your husband, you mean," Sorin said in an icy tone.

I turned to face him, the sting of his words landing across my face like a slap.

"Why does that matter to you all of a sudden?" I fired back, anger burning away my guilt and reason like melting wax from a candle flame. "Because it sure as hell didn't when you had your face between my legs."

Eyrin coughed, and suddenly the wall became very interesting. Sorin's expression didn't change, but the silence that followed felt like a scream.

"Because I thought," he gritted out finally, "that you wanted to leave him behind."

His hands landed on my shoulders. "Because I thought what we had meant something more than just survival."

"It did," my voice cracked as tears welled in my eyes. "It does."

Sorin let out a bitter, broken laugh. "I have a hard time believing that."

I stepped away from him.

"I didn't want any of this."

"No, but you chose it," he spat. "You chose him when it counted. You always will."

"Because he was *dying*! Because I thought I owed him that much!" My voice trembled. "He was my *husband*, Sorin! For six fucking years!"

"And what am I?" he roared, regaining the distance between us so we were a breath apart. "What am I to you? Just a distraction? A fling? A fucking vampire novelty?!"

It was the most volatile reaction I had seen from Sorin.

"Don't you dare," I seethed. "You knew I was in a bad position, and you took advantage of it. You're the one who seduced me!"

His eyes blazed.

"And you're such an angel, always the victim. Except when you're making deals with vampire witches behind my back."

"I did what I had to do," I said, clenching my jaw so tight that it throbbed, "because you wouldn't. You're so wrapped up in your sad-boy ancient vampire bullshit that you don't care what happens to anyone else. You were too busy wallowing in your miserable, endless existence and losing touch with reality while I was begging for help."

"I was trying to protect you!" he shouted. "I have watched everyone I've ever loved die or waited until they inevitably turn on me."

His voice cracked, rage and pain bleeding together.

"What's one more to that number?"

Neither of us spoke, the hurt of old wounds too great for us to fling back at each other. Eyrin muttered something and walked into the hallway, giving us space.

Sorin's shoulders heaved with every breath. "You lied from the start."

I took a shaky step back, arms wrapped around myself to hold whatever was left of Scarlet Montgomery together. "And I'd do it again if it meant saving someone I love."

He sank to the couch like I'd knocked the air from his lungs. Silence stretched between us. Our eyes locked, but whatever was building now felt a lot less like fire and more like fractures.

"I need to get out of here." I furiously wiped at my eyes and turned for the bedroom.

Sorin's hand caught my wrist.

"Get the fuck off me!" I snarled, slamming my elbow upward to break his grip and storming into the bedroom.

"Where are you going?" Sorin demanded.

"Home!" I shouted over my shoulder, tossing clothes into my duffel bag in frantic handfuls.

"You can't go home. You have to be here for the Summit," he said flatly, following me toward the front door.

That unfeeling, uncaring mask was back on his face. It felt like the death of a man I thought I had known.

"Scarlet," He gently took my bag from my hand and set it down beside me. Straightening, he stepped close, his hands moving to my shoulders before sliding down to mine.

I didn't want to hear it. Didn't want to give him the chance to say something that might make me stay or, worse, hurt me even more. But the sincerity in his face stole the words from my tongue.

I felt it—the tug between us like an invisible rope drawn taut. I felt him pulling me in, felt the immensity of how deeply he cared. It was the sensation of a soft breeze stirring my hair when there was no wind. A little warmth that had seeded and drowned in the void within him.

He tucked a strand behind my ear with aching gentleness.

"Please—"

Eyrin burst into the room, panting, eyes nearly bulging out of his skull.

"She's here."

"Where?" Sorin asked, still staring at me, his eyes roaming my face.

"Reception floor. Dining room. The damn witch is destroying everything in sight." Eyrin leaned forward, bracing his hands on his knees. "She wants Malik back. I won't let her have him."

Sorin turned back to me, leaning in, lips brushing my cheek. The kiss was featherlight, but I felt it land like a grenade. My whole head drifted to the side from the whisper of pressure.

"Don't leave," he spoke softly against my hair. "It's dangerous. Let's discuss this more when I return."

I nodded numbly. Though my body moved, my energy was gone. It abandoned me the second my bag hit the floor. Like an artery opened too wide, the fight had bled out of me.

Eyrin and Sorin rushed from the room.

I sat. Waited. Watched the clock.

Five minutes.

Then ten.

When fifteen had passed, I picked up my bag and walked out the door.

40

SUGAR-GLASS BARRIER

Diluted strips of light filtered through the cathedral-high skylights of the glamoured apartment Eyrin had tucked Malik and me into for safekeeping. Outside, it looked like a crumbling industrial husk. I could have mistaken it for the building that Valerie had followed me into.

I hadn't ever planned on running. Forsaking the future of free humanity was not an option for me. So, I'd slipped quietly down the staircase, past the reception floor where Odessa's screams echoed into the stairwell, and stepped out into the city. The crowds surrounding Crimson & Clover made it easy to blend into the bustle and text Eyrin my location.

I sent Sorin a single message explaining where I'd gone and asking him not to contact me until the Summit. I was embarrassed, ashamed, and absolutely not equipped to deal with the fallout. My grand plan to "cross that bridge when I got to it" had turned into a spectacular belly flop into the river.

With my less-than-thrilled escort at my side, we made our way toward the apartment building. The entrance matched its body. It appeared as a peeling steel door covered in rusted sigils meant to repel the mortal gaze.   Averting my eyes, I reached forward, squeezing the warm, wooden handle. It vibrated, then gave way for me to step inside.

Massive support beams stretched high into the ceiling, hand-crafted from live wood. Their branches unfurled well above head level, each one drooping with bulbs that glowed tungsten gold. The cavernous reception room evoked the feeling that I had stepped into an ancient forest.

Shaggy green carpets sprawled across a stone floor that, in any other space, might have looked like a bad seventies movie set. But Eyrin had somehow worked them into something that resembled living moss. When I stepped onto one, my feet sank just enough to mimic the give of the forest floor. Eyrin had created an upscale apartment complex for the metaphysical, complete with an urban cathedral dressed in forest skin.

Eyrin let me drink it in, leaning lazily against one of those mammoth tree pillars. After I had finished trying to gauge the distance to the ceiling, which was well over 100 feet, he pushed off the wood and led me toward the second floor. He rattled off his plans with smug pride as we climbed the wide stairs.

"We only used natural materials, of course. Iron was only used for the framework. It's soundproofed, magic-proofed, and self-cleansing," he gave the next pillar a little pat, and a few dead leaves materialized in the air around us.

I watched as they spiraled to the ground like tiny helicopters, hit the floor, and vanished.

"I built it with expansion in mind, you know. Not all of us want to live in isolation."

He deposited me in a one-bedroom loft, where Malik greeted me with open arms and tired eyes. I collapsed onto the green couch and didn't move again for four days, except to meet basic bodily functions.

Now, I stared blankly at the exposed beams overhead. A gauzy green shimmer rippled along the walls. It was one of Eyrin's favorite illusions that he'd been showing off for Malik.

They whispered in the kitchen, voices dipping into laughter. I didn't look at them. I could practically feel the lingering touches. The loaded glances. The slow-burning heat between them. I turned over, dragging the blanket tighter around my shoulders, and buried my face in the pillow. I waited for the end of the day and maybe the end of the world as I knew it.

Footsteps creaked beside me. A cool hand brushed my hair from my forehead.

"Hey, Red," Malik said. "You doing okay?"

"I'm alive," I grunted into the pillow.

"That doesn't really answer my question." He crouched beside me. "Are you hungry?"

I was starving. But I didn't have the strength or the will to untangle myself from the cocoon of apathy I'd wrapped around my body like a death shroud. So I just shook my head.

"That's it."

Malik ripped the pillow from beneath me and rolled me off the couch. I hit the floor with a dull *thump*. Eyrin snickered from the kitchen.

"Asshole," I muttered.

"You have to get up," Malik said, stomping his foot beside me for emphasis. "We're going outside. You need fresh air."

"I would *highly* advise against that," Eyrin called out from behind a ceramic mug.

He was probably drinking blood. Possibly tea.

"What he said," I groaned, rubbing the spot on my back that had taken the brunt of the fall.

"Hush, you," Malik shot back at Eyrin. "No comments from the peanut gallery."

"Fine. But it is Halloween, you know—the day the veil between the dead and the living is thinnest. And you are hiding from a vampiric necromancer. Just saying," Eyrin said.

"All great points," I said, pushing myself up against the arm of the couch.

"You have to get up anyway," Malik gave me an encroaching look. "Tonight's the summit, and I am not taking you there smelling like a hot dumpster on the fourth of July."

I lifted my arm and took a cautious sniff. Yeah. Fair. I let the arm drop unceremoniously.

"You could go to the festival," Eyrin offered. "It's the last place they'd expect to find you. And if you're already near the Summit entrance before sundown, you'll *probably* be fine."

"Genius," Malik declared, extending a hand to me like a knight on a quest. "Go shower, Red. We'll head out as soon as you're ready."

I stared at his outstretched hand, then at his hopeful smile. Oh, hell. I couldn't say no to that. He looked like a kid begging to go to the playground after being stuck inside all week.

Grumbling under my breath, I let him pull me to my feet and trudged toward the shower. I made quick work of it. Shampoo, soap, rinse, done. Once dry, I ran a brush through my hair and pawed through the last of my clean clothes. I emerged in baggy sweats, a worn hoodie, and scuffed tennis shoes.

Eyrin looked up from his phone, one brow arched.

"Really? You're about to stand in front of the High Council at a summit that could decide the future of human freedom, and you're wearing *that*?"

"What is this? *What Not to Wear*?" I shot back defensively.

Eyrin shook his head and returned to his screen, muttering something like "hopeless."

"You are hopeless," Malik echoed and grabbed my hand again, dragging me back toward the bedroom.

Five minutes later, I was wearing the burgundy leather jacket we'd bought together, my soft heather-gray sweater, light-wash jeans, and my heeled boots. He even made me blow-dry my hair and swipe on just enough makeup to look like I hadn't been marinating in a vat of depression for the past four days.

When I finally emerged, he gave a satisfied nod.

"Now we can leave."

"Thank God."

I shoved my phone and wallet into my pocket and made for the door.

"Wait," Eyrin said, rising smoothly from his seat and stepping in front of Malik.

Malik froze. His eyes widened slightly as Eyrin raised both hands and tenderly cupped his face. A shimmer of green light passed from Malik's hairline to his boots, sliding over him like liquid moss. When it faded, the man standing before me wasn't Malik at all.

A handsome Hispanic man gazed back, his hair pulled into a neat knot at the nape of his neck. But those kind, warm eyes remained.

"What the hell?"

Malik looked down at his hands and turned them over.

"Just a glamour," Eyrin said softly as he let his hands drop. "To keep you safe."

"Oh. Uh... thanks." Malik blushed.

I turned toward the door with a little smile.

"You're on your own, Red," Eyrin called after me, already inspecting his nails. "I only do favors for the pretty ones."

Malik slapped his shoulder. Eyrin protested.

"Yeah," I stepped out of the door. "Screw you too, buddy."

At 3 p.m., the festival was already in full swing. The city had sealed off a massive park and turned it into a full-blown Halloween fever dream, complete with grinning pumpkins, giant spiderwebs, and enough sweets to send all of New York into a collective sugar coma.

Brightly colored booths zigzagged through the park in a winding, chaotic maze. Each was draped in gaudy decorations and flanked by animatronics. I watched with newfound fascination and a drop of horror as we passed the creaky witches with glowing eyes, reapers with moving scythes, and skeletons that jolted to life with poorly timed cackles.

How many of these were based on real creatures? Monsters that could quite literally be lurking around any given corner.

Jack-o-lanterns and blinking fairy lights lined every path, lit brightly enough to see even in the afternoon. Costumed performers danced through the crowd, tossing candy and waving sparklers that scribbled bright trails through the crisp autumn air. Children shrieked with joy. Teenagers laughed, momentarily setting aside their practiced angst to revel in the last dregs of their childhoods. All that golden light and fleeting wonder deserved to be immortalized on a canvas.

Against all odds, I was having a good time. I bit into a deep red candy apple, the sugar shell cracking beneath my teeth with a satisfying crunch. Bitter-sweet juice rushed over my tongue, crisp and cold.

"Red, come look at this," Malik called from a fortune teller's booth.

The deep purple tent was adorned with shimmering constellations that emitted a faint green light. It was as if they were waiting patiently for the sunset to glow radioactive. It was campy as hell and kind of charming for it. A stunning woman with dark hair flashed us a knowing smile and waved us in.

"Let's go inside," Malik grinned, tugging at my hand.

"I'm good," I slipped free but held the flap open for him. "I'll watch."

He shrugged and dropped into the chair with his palms up. The woman immediately began cooing over his lifelines.

I let my gaze drift across the fairgrounds, doing my best to ignore the dread sinking in my stomach. The last thing I wanted right now was someone to see my future, even if she was a phony. Whether I liked it or not, in just a few hours, I'd be part of deciding the fate of humanity in the United States. Maybe I could find a good luck charm instead. Something stupid and shiny like a rabbit's foot or a charm coin.

After Malik finished, we wandered deeper into the festival. It was so sprawling that it took nearly twenty minutes just to reach the far end. We passed a hall of mirrors and several haunted houses along the way. We looked at each other, shook our heads, and kept walking. No way in hell were we putting ourselves through that kind of psychological torture. Our real lives were scary enough, thanks.

At the heart of the park, a large fountain had been turned into a Halloween centerpiece. Instead of water, a cascade of amber and yellow leaves trailed down in vibrant vines. Pumpkins the size of cars clustered around the base, surrounded by a hodgepodge of gourds in every size and shade. A small plaque read: *Finalists – Annual Pumpkin Weigh-Off*.

"Oh my god, they're real," I whispered, reaching over the little graveyard fence surrounding them to touch one.

"Hey!" an attendant barked. "No touching!"

Malik and I took off, giggling breathlessly. We finally reached the far end of the park, where a faux graveyard had been built around a pop-up bar. It was one of the event's highlights, with theatrical headstones, fake fog, and eerie lighting. At the center stood a closed cathedral.

Naturally, that cathedral wasn't just for show. It was the secret entrance to where the High Council would meet for the Summit.

I stared at the gravestones, my throat constricting. If I didn't make it tonight, would I end up beneath one of them for real? Would I become another name carved into stone that no one remembered?

"Hey," Malik said gently, hooking his arm through mine. "Let's get a drink. Then we'll win one of those ridiculous prizes from the game booths."

Two orange-flavored vodka drinks in hand, served in clear plastic cups stamped with grinning black pumpkin faces, we gallivanted back into the thickening crowd.

Gorging on pumpkin pastries, we drained our drinks and chased them all with oversized, fall-flavored caffeine bombs. Buzzed from the vodka and jittery from the sugar and espresso, we stumbled, laughing through the chaos. I was determined to win a teddy bear the size of Milo.

Within the crowd, everything blurred into one long, sugar-coated haze. Malik and I moved from booth to booth, throwing darts, dodging fog machines, and chasing the prizes like it was a matter of life or death. I couldn't remember the last time I'd felt this light.

The day wore on and on. Children gave way to costumed adults, their face paint melting slightly under the afternoon sun. We stumbled out of the ring toss booth, still laughing, and I paused, blinking up at the sky. It was a rich, saturated blue. The sun hung low now, casting long shadows across the grass.

"Let's head back to the pop-up bar," Malik said, squinting up at the sun.

Just like that, the sugar-glass barrier I'd spun around myself shattered. My heart stuttered, then sped up. Nausea crawled up my throat. I wasn't ready. Not yet.

"One more booth," I blurted, spinning on my heel toward the closest stall with no line.

That alone should have been a red flag. Every other booth was swamped, but I didn't care. I crossed the path in a daze toward a faded sign painted in smeared red: Mystery Touch Boxes. I shoved a crumpled bill at the pimpled red-haired man running it. He took it without a word.

"Red, ew. No way," Malik moaned behind me.

"Oh, come on, you big baby," I teased as I plunged my hand into the first box.

Something cold and slippery squelched under my fingers, and I yelped. Malik recoiled.

"Who knows what's actually in there? I am *not* touching some sicko mystery goo box."

He stepped back, wrinkling his nose.

"I'm gonna go take a piss. Meet you back at the graveyard, okay? I think you've got like thirty minutes before you need to be at the entrance."

"Alright," I mumbled, my shoulders sagging. "See you in a few."

I stood alone beside the booth, wrist still submerged in whatever cold, wet substance the box was hiding. Fake blood or pudding, probably. Something meant to startle kids. A breath of frigid air whispered across the back of my neck, slipping under my collar and curling along my spine. I shivered, deciding to pull my hand free.

It didn't budge. It was stuck. No, not stuck. Something clammy clamped around my wrist, and my lungs seized. My entire body went rigid as terror slammed into me. Panicking, I yanked hard. The mystery box dug into the soft flesh around my wrist.

What felt like fingernails raked across the inside of my arm in a savage grip. The booth around me faded, and the sounds of the festival muffled as if I'd been dropped underwater. A guttural voice slithered out from the box, calling my name.

I clawed at my trapped wrist, gripping my elbow with my free arm, trying to wrench myself free.

"Found you," Odessa crooned from inches away.

I flinched violently with another sharp yank. The unseen hand clamped harder, and something popped in my wrist. I barely choked back a sob as the tiny bones groaned in protest.

"Where's Malik?" she asked in a voice too sweet to be anything but deadly.

When I didn't answer, her face twitched enough to show the predator underneath. The thing with fangs, barely restrained by that flawless skin, was battling to escape her. Her nostrils flared.

"I know he's here with you," she said, voice dropping an octave. "I can smell him all over you."

My stomach twisted. How was she in the sun?

She hadn't touched me yet. There were too many people around. Too many eyes. She was playing it smart, pretending we were just two strangers enjoying the festival. Two friends, maybe. But I could feel the malice radiating off her. See the tension in her hands and the set of her shoulders. I was running out of time.

"He doesn't want to see you anymore," I said, scanning the crowd for any escape, any ally. But no one was watching.

"Liar," she hissed. "I raised him. I'm practically the boy's mother."

The sheer audacity of the claim struck me. Every other thought scattered, leaving only a burning injustice.

"He knows what you did, Odessa."

Her eyes widened then narrowed as she stepped in, fangs bared and glinting in the light. That's when I smelled the faint but unmistakable stench of burnt skin. My eyes darted to her face. The bridge of her nose and the tops of her cheeks were darkening, blistering ever so slightly. Her skin looked too tight, as if it were being stretched over her bones. A sheen of sweat, or maybe something worse, gleamed across her brow. She was burning, slowly but surely, right in front of me.

I shrank away, a wave of revulsion rolling through me.

"You shouldn't be out here," I breathed through my mouth. "You're *burning*."

"Tell me where he is. Now." She inched closer, ignoring me.

My nostrils filled with the rancid stench of burnt hair.

"What are you going to do?" I bit back a gag. "Burn to death? Drain me right here? In front of all these people? All these witnesses?"

"You think that matters?" Her eyes darkened. "After tonight, after I finish with you, they'll only be cattle waiting for the slaughter."

Her hand whipped out, catching my wrist. Her fingers elongated into obsidian talons that were far darker than Sorin's. Claws pressed cruelly into my skin, breaking through the flesh in a blinding burst of agony. I clamped my mouth shut, swallowing the scream clawing up my throat. I couldn't drag anyone else into this. It was clear that Odessa had long since stopped caring about consequences or who got hurt along the way.

"You should have stayed out of this," she growled, her voice finally dropping that syrupy tone.

As I stared, her pupils stretched into vertical slits, swallowed by an enlarged, veiny yellow iris. A realization hit me then, breaking through the fear and pain.

This—this was the real Odessa all along. Her act was over. I was finally face-to-face with what she truly was. A powerful creature forged from survival and corrupted, century by century, by dark-hearted acts and the rot of unchecked power. Her mouth stretched wide. There was a wet glint on her upper fangs.

A sense of awe swept over me, and I breathed, "There you are."

"Let her go!" a voice called from behind us.

Odessa stiffened. Malik, disguised in his glamour, shoved her from behind. She staggered a step, more surprised than hurt. Her hand released my wrist, and I cradled it to my chest. A few bystanders turned to frown at him as a shimmer of green light rippled over his skin and dissolved.

Gasps erupted around us as the illusion peeled away, revealing Malik as he really was. His face was pale, jaw clenched. But he didn't look scared; he looked furious.

"She's not yours to toy with," he spoke with deadly calm. "I'm not yours anymore, either."

Odessa turned slowly, the illusion of grace deteriorating like a jack-o'-lantern left to rot on the porch.

"I raised you," she snarled, the words brittle with rage. "I made you who you are."

"No," he bared his teeth. "You murdered my mom and used me. You wanted a puppet, not a son. And if I ever have children, you'll never touch them."

"All I ever wanted was to keep you," her voice cracked with a grief so deep that it felt as if it had been festering inside her for millennia.

Her magic faltered. Whatever was gripping me snapped out of corporeal existence. I stumbled into Malik as he rushed forward and grabbed my arm.

Her face twisted, morphing into that same hideous, bestial form

Sorin had taken at Crimson & Clover. Both sets of her fangs slid free, bared in a snarl, and her eyes burned with an unnatural yellow light. As she hissed, the skin on her cheeks cracked open, revealing the raw, veined mass bubbling beneath.

"Gross," I gagged, fighting the urge to clap my hands over my eyes.

The sun had dipped just far enough to stain the sky blood-red.

We staggered backward. Malik yanked his free hand from his pocket and flung a fistful of shimmering powder into the air. Eyrin's powder, I realized in the not-lizard part of my brain that had gone into hibernation the moment Odessa had appeared. It glittered around Odessa, sticking to the places where her skin had ruptured. She froze, slack-jawed, eyes vacant.

"Run!" Malik shouted.

We bolted, shoving through the crowd towards the cemetery. The sun slipped beneath the skyline, and night spilled across the city like ink into water. We weren't playing by daylight rules anymore.

41

CLICK, CLACK

We tried to outrun the setting sun, but the speed of light was too much to contend with for two unfortunate mortals. In a straight sprint, we could've crossed the park in a few minutes. With hundreds of people packing the festival grounds, we couldn't do more than weave through them at a brisk pace.

"Damnit!" I hissed as a sweeping net of shadows swallowed the festival whole.

God, we were so screwed. All because I had to stick my hand in one more creepy-ass box. I cursed myself with every breath.

"Keep going," Malik panted, pushing through a group of masked partygoers with a frustrated grunt.

We didn't stop to apologize. Our only choice was to keep barreling forward, too panicked to care who was in costume and who might be the real deal. Screams erupted from where we had been. It could've been someone thrilled by a jump-scare animatronic. Or it could've been Odessa tearing through the crowd like fodder.

I looked up, searching over the crowd for an opening. Carmen was there. She towered above the mass, shoulders squared. It took only a second for our eyes to meet. Brows knit in determination, she started pushing forward towards us. Odessa was closing from the back. Carmen from the front.

"Malik!" I skidded to a halt.

"Don't stop, Red," he persisted, trying to drag me forward.

"No—*look!*" I pointed.

He blanched.

"We have to lose them," he said.

Back to back, we turned in frantic circles, scanning for any kind of escape. To my left, an old, tattered entrance stood crooked beneath a stuttering string of lights. There was no time to notice the faded colors or peeling paint. A sagging red curtain invited us in, flanked by two clown faces that were painted intentionally with warped eyes and smeared grins.

The hall of mirrors. I didn't give myself a second to consider. The terror rising in my chest threatened to wipe my mind clean of coherent thought.

"Over here!" I called, already moving.

We dove through the curtain, past the ticket booth and a shouting attendant we didn't bother to acknowledge. The world contorted as we ran headfirst into a maze of endless reflections, shifting lights, and false exits. Misshapen versions of ourselves stared back, multiplying with every step. It was too easy to lose our sense of direction.

"*Oof!*"

I slammed face-first into a mirror. Pain exploded across my nose. Tears spilled instantly as I staggered back, cursing.

"Fuck," I hissed, wiping at the tiny smear of blood trickling from one nostril.

Not the worst hit I'd ever taken. I pressed a hand out, leaving a faint red streak as I groped forward blindly.

"Malik," I managed, my breathing slowing just enough to get words out. "Take my hand. Watch our backs."

His trembling hand found mine.

The adrenaline was starting to fade, and with it came the crashing, choking weight of fear. We needed help. Badly.

"Malik," a husky voice called out, echoing softly through the maze. "Scarlet... it's time to come out now."

Carmen had followed us in.

"Shit, shit, shit," I whispered, dropping to my hands and knees to crawl through a low tunnel of mirrored walls and flashing lights.

"Call Sorin," Malik rasped beside me. "Scarlet, call him."

"I can hear you," Carmen called again, her voice bouncing eerily through the tunnel. "Sorin's not here. Let me help you. We can go to Odessa together, I'll talk her down for you. It's not too late for either of you."

Fuck that. My hands shook so badly that I dropped the phone twice before I could even unlock it. On the third try, Malik grabbed it from me and dialed from memory.

It picked up on the first ring.

"Scarlet," Sorin's voice lit with relief.

"Help," I gasped, cutting him off. "Help us."

I scrambled backward out of the tunnel with a startled cry as it opened into a large room.

"Where are you?" Sorin demanded. "Tell me exactly."

"Festival," I wheezed. "Odessa found us. Carmen's here too."

"Where *at* the festival?" he barked.

"H-Hall of mirrors," I stammered, yanking Malik back to his feet.

We started feeling our way forward again, blindly reaching for an exit as the walls seemed to close in. There was a shuddering impact, followed by the sound of Carmen's frustrated curses.

"It'll take me a few minutes to get there. Can you make it out of there? I'll meet you at the exit."

"I think so," I replied as we stepped into what I prayed was the final stretch of the maze.

"Then do it. I'm on my way."

He hung up. I turned to warn Malik, but he clapped a hand over my mouth, eyes wide with panic. Shaking his head, he mouthed, *listen.*

I tried to quiet my ragged breathing, lungs burning as I dragged in air. I expected to hear Carmen crawling through the tunnel. What I heard instead made my blood run cold.

Click, clack. Click, clack.

Heels. Striking the floor in quickening succession. The sound reverberated around us, impossibly close, impossibly loud. I looked for an exit, but the mirrors had gone unnaturally dark. They no longer reflected anything at all, surfaces rippling like disturbed water.

From the shifting depths, two figures sprinted toward us. Every so often, they would blur, then reappear, doubling in size as they approached. The closer they got, the more they seemed to struggle. Their steps began to drag in slow motion as though they were pushing through some invisible membrane.

One was a woman in a stained white dress, wild red hair streaming behind her. The other, my breath caught, was the spitting image of Malik. Only her mouth was torn open in a silent scream, and two bite marks oozed dark blood down her chest.

"Mom?" Malik asked hoarsely, taking a hesitant step forward. "What did she do to you?"

Valerie and Malik's mother raced toward us from opposite ends of the room, their distorted reflections stretching across the rippling glass. Valerie's eyes locked onto my very soul. I could feel her fury surging toward me with the unstoppable force of retribution.

Their voices burst forth like tangled cries through a wall of thick fabric. They were competing to be heard, to exist. Each syllable sounded like it had to claw its way through some otherworldly barrier.

Malik's mother won.

"Move, baby!" she called. Her voice drawled, and I got the impression that each syllable cost her greatly to create. "Move!"

Malik let out a strangled sob, spun on his heel, and bolted in a random direction. His mother tracked him, shifting course to follow him around a corner.

I remained transfixed. Valerie loomed, suddenly life-sized, halting just beyond the glass. Her eyes burned into mine. Then her perfect face convulsed as each of her four fangs slid free. They stretched her jaw wider, unhinging like a serpent preparing to strike.

She lifted a hand and pressed it against the mirror. It wavered—then held.

I exhaled a shaky breath. Just an illusion. Her grotesque smile faded. Then she drew back her arm and slammed her fist into the glass so hard that the room shook. Once, twice, three times.

By the fourth impact, a spiderweb crack bloomed across the surface. I stepped back, sweat trickling down my spine. My body couldn't decide if it was burning or freezing. The taste of iron filled my mouth.

On the fifth hit, the mirror exploded. A pulse of searing power launched me backward, slamming me into another wall of glass. I hit with a grunt and shattered mirror shards rained down. Something clenched deep in my stomach, but I barely registered it as I threw my arms over my head to protect myself.

What emerged from the mirror was no longer the curvaceous vixen who had seduced my husband and haunted my nightmares. A gray, decomposing corpse limped into the room. She was half-formed and rotting. The places that had taken the most damage when she fell were still in tatters. Gelatinous globs of hanging flesh and torn organs swayed as she moved.

She stumbled forward, legs trembling beneath her as if they could no longer bear her weight on those pin-prick heels. Both hands raised to her face. A deep, guttural moan slipped from her lips as her fingers tangled in the eyeball dangling from its socket.

The moan swelled into an ear-shattering, soul-splitting wail as she clutched at her festering face. It was interrupted by a flood of black bile oozing from her gaping mouth. Her one intact eye snapped open. Milky and sickeningly wide, it landed right on me. I screamed, too.

Shards crunched beneath my boots as I launched to my feet.

Valerie's corpse dragged one leg forward, her head lolling as vitriol dribbled from her chin. Her hands were outstretched like she meant to hold me in one last embrace.

"Girl, boundaries," I muttered, sprinting away.

The mirror maze twisted around me, light refracting off broken glass, footsteps slapping against polished floors. I didn't know which way was out. I just ran. Her scream echoed off every surface, chasing me like a bloodhound.

A soft surface met my outstretched hand. I burst through the curtain at the maze's entrance, nearly knocking over a little girl holding cotton candy. She shrieked in delighted laughter, and her mom pulled her a little closer.

"Are you okay?" The mom asked me as she ushered her child behind her.

I spun in place, ignoring them. The crowd had thickened. Music blared Monster Mash from a nearby speaker, and bright festival lights sparkled in Halloween colors. I still sensed her just behind the curtain. She was getting closer.

"Scarlet."

I turned and collided with a wall of black fabric and cold air. Sorin gripped my upper arm hard enough to bruise. His eyes weren't glowing, but simmered with rage as he counted every scratch across my face.

Then he looked over my shoulder and tensed. Valerie stepped out of the mirror maze. Bile glistened over her exposed cleavage; one eyeball swung like a grotesque pendulum as she stumbled forward.

A teenager in a devil costume walked by, took one look, and shouted, "Whoa. Awesome zombie costume. 10/10, lady!"

Sorin turned to him, made direct contact, and ordered, "Run away."

The kid dropped his drink and did precisely as he was told. I almost wished Sorin would use that power of suggestion to force me to calm down. I wasn't sure how much more my heart could take.

"Come," Sorin rumbled as he yanked me into the closest structure.

We rushed into a haunted house, slamming the door behind us. Inside, red lights pulsed like a heartbeat, and rubber body parts swung from the ceiling on plastic meat hooks.

Sorin turned to face the entrance, planting himself between me and whatever might follow.

"She shouldn't be walking this plane," Sorin peered through a tiny peephole where some demented employee was probably meant to jump out and scare anyone who entered. "Odessa must be near killing herself to achieve this."

I slumped against a wall, my pulse still pounding in my ears.

"You think?" I mumbled.

The taste of blood and stomach acid coated my tongue. The room tilted slightly; the lights blurred into smeared streaks. My knees buckled, and I slid down the wall, struggling to catch a full breath.

"You're bleeding," Sorin said, abandoning his post to kneel in front of me.

"The mirrors broke," I muttered, waving him off. "It's probably just a scrape."

"No. It's worse." He grasped the edge of my jacket and pulled it open.

I sucked in a sharp breath as the fabric peeled away with a wet *shlup*. Blood had soaked straight through my top. With a frown, Sorin tore back the bloodstained sweater, revealing a long shard of glass jutting from my side.

"Damn," I slurred. "That was my second favorite sweater."

"Shhh," Sorin whispered, wrapping his fingers around the shard. "This is going to hurt."

The glass came out in one brutal motion. Fire tore through my side, and white-hot stars exploded behind my eyes. I tried to scream, but his hand clamped down over my mouth. I bit down hard and tasted snow. My attention zeroed in on the little pricks of blood that washed over my tongue.

"Probably not a bad idea," he winced.

He pressed his palm to my wound, trying to slow the bleeding.

"Let me make this a little easier on both of us."

He immediately sank his fangs into the muscled curve of his forearm. Thick blood welled up, and he pressed it to my lips. I drank that ruby liquid. A moan escaped me as it slid down my throat, seeping into every crack of my body. The pain dulled. The world slowed. From the toes up, euphoria claimed me in its lulling, heady hold.

After two deep pulls, Sorin cupped my jaw between his fingers.

"That's enough, love," he said gently, though his voice carried an edge of command. "It's been a rough few days. That's all you need for now."

He wiped my mouth with his thumb. I caught his hand and drew that last drop from it with a lick. He didn't stop me.

I slumped back, chest rising and falling in deep, even breaths. My skin tingled as it stitched itself together. The fog in my head thinned as sanity returned in increments until I really saw him. Sorin was crouched before me, his arm still dripping crimson, eyes slightly unfocused. He looked... exhausted. Paler than usual. Gaunt in a way I had never seen before.

Had I done this to him?

"Sorin," I reached out to cup his face.

His skin was ice-cold. Guilt spiraled through me.

"No time for apologies," he murmured, covering my hand with his. He leaned into my touch for a breath. "We must get you to the summit. All will be well."

I shuddered as we stood together, limbs sluggish but healing.

"Okay," I said, steeling myself. "Let's do this."

42

HARBINGER

"Where's Malik?" I asked as we slipped out the back exit of the haunted house.

"Eyrin has him," Sorin replied, scanning both directions before offering me his hand.

Relieved for my friend, I took it. We wove through the crowd, heading toward the graveyard. Malik would be okay. Eyrin was one squirrelly motherfucker. Even Carmen would think twice before tangling with him. Now, I just had to worry about myself.

I glanced nervously over my shoulder. "What about Valerie?"

Sorin shook his head, eyes fixed ahead.

"It's likely Odessa reincarnated her into some form of golem. She's not truly alive, just a manifestation of a spirit that has been defiled by hatred. Your death is her only purpose."

My heart lurched. I squeezed his hand tightly to dispel some of the nervous energy racking through me.

"I'm here," he soothed as we rounded the second-to-last corner before the graveyard. "Don't worry—"

A gray blur slammed into him from the side. They hit the ground in a violent roll, sending the crowd scattering with startled shrieks. I jumped back as Sorin disappeared beneath the snarling wreckage of Valerie's half-rotted corpse.

He grappled with her, the oiliness of her decomposing flesh making it impossible to gain traction. Cracking my neck, I lunged in, ready to deliver a five-star curb-stomp that would send her straight to hell.

But a hand clamped around the back of my neck. I choked as my feet left the ground, a strangled cry escaping my lips. My hands reached helplessly behind me, trying to relieve the crushing pressure on my spine.

This was not, I repeat *not*, how I liked to be choked.

Across the pavement, Sorin finally managed to seize Valerie's head. With a savage roar, he tore it from her shoulders. Skin ripped away in ropy strands, her jaw still snapped wildly from her decapitated head. Even in the face of her second death, Valerie still went down fighting.

I had to hand it to her, she had grit. Like a roach in heels that just wouldn't quit.

Sorin raised the gnashing appendage and slammed it into the sidewalk over and over until it was nothing but pulp and twitching nerves. The crowd, silent only moments before, erupted into applause.

"This year's festival is *fucking insane!*" someone shouted.

"I can't believe they had the budget for that kind of special effects!"

Sorin looked up, breath heaving, eyes glowing red with raw aggression.

"Don't move," Carmen called from behind me. "Or I'll break her neck."

Her grip tightened, and another wheezing cry broke from my throat as pain exploded down my vertebrae.

Sorin paused, then burst into black smoke. It shot across the ground and reformed behind me in a blink. His claws tore into the arm holding me, leaving deep gouges.

Carmen cursed and dropped me in a heap, throwing her arms up to block the oncoming attack. I missed what happened next. My neck was paralyzed with pain. If I hadn't had Sorin's blood in my system, she might've actually snapped it. I pressed trembling fingers to my skin, eyes squeezed shut, jaw clenched against the ache.

By the time my body obeyed me again, the fight had vanished from view. From behind the haunted house, I heard the unmistakable sounds of fists clapping into flesh. There were grunts and cries. I couldn't tell who they belonged to. Only that someone was losing.

"It didn't have to be this way."

I looked up as Odessa stalked towards me. The crowd parted from her like water from oil. Her voice was soft, almost maternal, as she looked down at me with a demented kind of sorrow.

"You could've joined me," she said. "We could've been teammates."

"What you're doing isn't right," I gritted out, still on my knees. "Not for me. Not for Malik. Not for humanity."

Odessa peered down at me with feverish eyes. The sleeve of her blouse had lifted to her elbow, revealing a tattoo in the all too familiar shape of an inverted triangle with a line through it.

"No," she said softly, stepping closer. "But righteousness bends so easily in the wind of progress."

She crouched until we were eye to eye, her voice lowering to a reverent hiss.

"I'm not the villain here," she whispered, bending ever-so-slightly so I could see pity glimmering beneath the mania. "I'm the harbinger of a better future."

Her kick struck like a sledgehammer. I barely managed to throw my arms up, deflecting her leg just enough to save my skull. Still, the blow lifted me off the ground and flung me backward.

Most people think that when you get hit, the pain is immediate. Similar to a grenade popping off in the dark. Anyone who's actually experienced it will tell you the worst ones never register right away. It comes to you in waves, in pulses of sensation that lance your brain back into awareness. That's what this hit was like. My vision had flared white. I was conscious, but I had no idea who I was—or where.

The world seemed to blanch around me, then shimmer back in place like a glitching screen. I could hear a slight ringing, then the swooshing of my breath. A body landed beside me with a sickening thud. Sorin's face was swollen and bruised, his lips split. He lay utterly still, his eyes closed, his skin as pale as marble. None of his wounds were bleeding or healing.

"Oh God." I rolled over, crawling to him. "Oh God, Sorin. Wake up."

Odessa's smug voice squeezed into the space between us.

"He was never much of a fighter," she said, casually wrapping her arms around Carmen. "Especially not in his current state. That's why he had to partner with me, you know."

Carmen looked worse for wear. Deep gashes and purple bruises riddled her body, and a chunk of flesh was missing from her bicep. Her chest heaved as Odessa stroked her hair in a grotesque imitation of tenderness.

"Still," Odessa cooed, "you did your job, despite yourself."

She turned back to me, eyes gleaming.

"He was so torn up about you leaving. Wouldn't feed. Hasn't had a drop of blood in, what—nine days now?" She laughed like we were sharing a secret. "He even used that silly little smoke-and-mirrors trick of his. Desperation makes men reckless."

I cradled Sorin's head in my lap, brushing hair from his face with trembling fingers. Tears slipped free and splattered across his lifeless cheek.

"Sorin's real strength has always been his wits," she mused. "But you've managed to strip that away, haven't you? Really, it's quite impressive. I never imagined you two would have become so attached!"

My eyes locked on hers, and rage surged through me like fire catching dry grass. Every ounce of strength and speed Sorin's blood had given me kindled, then roared back to life. He had given me the last of his blood, I realized. I'd sucked it down without a second thought back in the haunted house.

"I'll kill you for this," I snarled.

Odessa only smiled serenely.

"No," she crooned. "You'll kill him."

"Never," I spat. The word burned in my throat.

"Never say never," she sang, clicking her tongue. Then she turned her head slightly. "Luke, come here, please."

My blood turned to ice. From the edge of the dispersing crowd, my husband stepped forward. He swaggered up beside Odessa and Carmen. He looked... perfect. Better than the man who hadn't kissed me goodbye before heading to New York that final time. His skin glowed, and his eyes were clear. When Odessa slid a hand through his thick, dark hair, he winked at her.

"Never say never," she sang, clicking her tongue. Then she turned her head slightly. "Luke, come here, please."

My blood turned to ice. From the edge of the dispersing crowd, my husband stepped forward. He swaggered up beside Odessa and Carmen. He looked... perfect. Too perfect. Better than the man who hadn't kissed me goodbye before heading to New York that final time. His skin glowed, and his eyes were clear. When Odessa slid a hand through his thick, dark hair, he winked at her.

I couldn't breathe.

"It's in your best interest to do what she says, Scarlet," he said, flashing me that same charming smile I once loved.

There was no warmth in it now.

"Get away from her, Luke," I gritted out, gently lowering Sorin's head to the ground.

"I can't do that, Scarlet." He crouched in front of me, too close. "She's going to finish what Valerie and I started. She's going to turn me."

I scoffed. There was no way that Luke could be this stupid. His eyes were lit up with that mad reverence he had when talking about Valerie, except it was directed straight at Odessa now.

"Luke, it's dangerous." My eyes darted from his face to Odessa's. "Only a few people survive that."

Uncertainty crossed his face. He turned toward Odessa with a questioning expression.

"She's lying," Odessa said smoothly. "She's jealous because she can't have you or immortality."

"That's not true!" I protested.

Carmen gave her a reproachful glance but said nothing. Luke closed his eyes and nodded.

"I'm going to do this, Scarlet," he said as he rose to his feet, brushing off his knees. "I won't let you stand in the way of my happiness anymore."

"Luke, I'm not—" My voice cracked. Fresh tears streamed down my cheeks. "Please. Don't do this. If you ever loved me, *don't do this.*"

He put his back to me, almost prancing back to the two women vampires. Odessa didn't even spare me a glance.

"The only one who can stop this is you, Scarlet," she said, releasing Carmen with a flick of her wrist.

Luke stepped forward into Odessa's waiting arms. She moved so they were chest to chest, as if they were about to kiss. Her mouth popped open as her fangs slid free.

"I'm going to live forever," Luke said giddily, allowing her arms to lace around his waist.

"Don't-"

Before I could finish, before I could *inhale*, she gripped Luke's head, yanked it to the side, and bit. He tensed, wheezed, and then went limp in her arms.

The crowd around us drew back. Someone screamed. A thick, black-red stream of blood ran down Luke's neck, soaking Odessa's front.

"I... I don't think this is fake," someone stammered.

"Someone call the police!" another voice shouted, panicked.

Watching them, I thought of our first date. Drunk and laughing, we stumbled through the soaked streets of Savannah after watching the Super Bowl at some divey sports bar. It was pouring, and we were lost, with nowhere to go because all the businesses had closed for the night. He had grabbed me around the waist, whipped me to face him, and kissed me deeply. I still remembered the heat of him pressed against me, the scent of rain on warm pavement, the soft patter of drops hitting the asphalt. And I remembered the thought that I might love this man. This handsome, quirky man, whom I'd only known for a few days.

He felt right, like the universe had built us for compatibility, thrust us together that night I was bar hopping with my girlfriends and said, "Here, Scarlet. I made this one just for you. Don't fuck it up."

My limbs ached, but righteous fury helped me push the pain aside. I rolled my shoulders back, locking eyes with her. Odessa watched, eyes rolling up to me in mad calculation.

"Fine," I planted one foot beneath me, then the other, rising painfully. "You win."

I didn't give her the satisfaction of hesitation. I lunged.

43

O VIOLENT NIGHT

Wind tore through my hair as my body became a missile of vicious retribution. Odessa didn't even have time to register the shock before my right hook collided with her face with a thunderous crack. She reeled back, her head snapping away from Luke's neck. Blood sprayed in a red-black arc, glinting under the carnival lights.

As the hot droplets spattered across my face, I thought of our wedding. That burning summer day, so full of promise, when we had said our vows and took off from the small chapel in his truck. His hand cradled the back of my neck and rolled down every window. Wind tunneled through the cab, catching my veil like a translucent sail. We laughed like we were the only two on the planet, and nothing could touch us.

Luke and Odessa broke apart, and I leaned back to load my weight to drive a kick straight into Odessa's diaphragm. Her breath burst out of her like a deflating balloon. As I stepped forward to deliver another blow, Carmen slammed into me from the side, arms locking around my waist and hurling me sideways.

I was back on my feet quicker than a heartbeat. Carmen raised her fists, and we circled each other. The chaos around us faded until it was just her, me, and the fight. My pulse drummed in my ears. Each step we took wound the tension tighter and tighter until something had to give. One of us would have to snap. Her arms were up in an old-school boxing stance—fists palm-up, ready to double jab. I raised my own guard, shielding my chin, nose, and jaw.

"I don't want to do this, Carmen," I said in a voice void of emotion. "I like you."

The world diminished into a spotlight of attention focused solely on her.

"You sound like you've already won," she glared.

We moved at the same time. Carmen had size on me. Strength too. And speed, if I was being honest. But she only used her arms. I ducked beneath her jab, fast and terrifying in its power. The air cracked beside my ear. I faked my own jab. She took the bait. That was her mistake.

I stepped in, twisting hard, and drove my knee into her liver. She folded sideways with a choked sound.

"Sorry, Carmen."

I launched a knee into her solar plexus. She flew back and hit the ground, croaking. Pouncing, I dropped on top of her and unleashed everything I had. My fists rained endlessly down into her face. When I lost feeling in my knuckles, I switched to elbows. *Hit. Hit. Hit.*

Each blow landed with a slurping *thwack*, punctuated by my grunts of effort. This was for me. For the peaceful life I had been robbed of. For Luke. For Sorin, who twitched on the ground beside us.

I raised my head, blinking away the sweat and blood stinging my eyes. Relief flooded my chest as one of Sorin's bruised eyelids fluttered open.

Wham.

A heart-stopping punch detonated into my side. I felt each rib try to hold—then snap, one by one, with a sickening chorus of *crackles.*

Consciousness danced around me, just out of reach. The world dimmed, brightened, then dimmed again. Somewhere in that in-between, I became vaguely aware of Carmen looming above me. Her hands curled around my neck as she hoisted me into the air once again.

"For the record," she panted, "I liked you too."

Breathe. I had to breathe. But I couldn't. My diaphragm was still seizing, locked tight from the catastrophic blow. My lungs refused to move. Everything felt far away except the pressure crushing my throat.

My eyes locked back on Odessa. She was on her knees, resuming draining Luke. I could only watch helplessly as every drop of blood flowed out of him and into her. She guzzled and guzzled, feasting on him until his eyes shuttered closed. There was an almost peaceful smile on his lips.

I watched him fade, thinking of all the times we curled up in bed together, whispering our dreams into the dark. I tried to remember the way he used to touch me. What did his arms feel like when they were around me as he comforted me after a difficult day or a hard conversation with my father? What had it been like again? When I had held him, weeping together after his parents had passed in a fatal car accident.

Inside, I was screaming. Begging my body to move. But all I could do was gasp in shallow breaths, feeling each shattered rib grind together as they slowly began to re-form. Sorin's blood wasn't healing me fast enough. It was far too slow to stop Odessa from draining Luke right in front of me.

Luke, who had clumsily braided my hair before my jiu-jitsu competitions, then held the water bottle up for me to drink when my hands were numb from adrenaline. Who sang terribly when he would make us breakfast. Who showed up sobbing at the hospital when I got into a fender bender because he was so scared for me. That Luke.

She sighed, content, rocking back on her heels before rising to her feet. And then she turned away.

Luke's mouth opened. A breath rattled in his throat, two words escaping.

"*I tried-*"

Whatever he meant to say died on his tongue. A ragged sob speared from my throat. What was she doing? This was the part where she was supposed to turn him. That's what she promised him.

She started to walk off.

"W–wait." The word wheezed out of me, fighting against the vice of Carmen's hold on my throat.

"You said... you'd turn him. So... turn him."

"Oh dear, that would never work," she said with a slight inflection as though speaking to an upset child. "A man as weak-willed as that would *never* survive the transformation."

She glanced back at Luke's limp body, her lip curling.

"He's not even worth the venom."

"Dess," Carmen objected quietly. "You said-"

I screamed. The sound tore from my throat like a wounded animal. My vision blurred with tears as I writhed in Carmen's grip. Grief forced my limbs to work even as the pain scorched my throat.

"You said you'd turn him! *Save him!*"

I didn't care that I was broken. I didn't care that I might not make it out alive. My hands clawed at Carmen's arms. Odessa raised a brow, unbothered.

But Carmen—Carmen looked shaken.

"He's already dead," Odessa said, nudging Luke with the tip of her boot.

He jolted just once, then stilled again. My own movements stopped with his.

"Of course," Odessa added, her burnt flesh pulling back together in grotesque, uneven chunks as she grinned, "I could always reanimate him if you've had a change of heart."

The thought of Luke returning mindless and rotten like Valerie made something in me shudder and then go berserk. The blood in my throat bubbled up and laced my sobs in copper. I screamed until I thought my lungs might rip open from the inside.

"Carmen," Odessa blew out a terse breath. "Shut her up. For good."

Carmen looked at the ground, blood running down her bruised face. She gave an extended, weary exhale before releasing me with one arm. She raised a massive fist, ready to end it.

My legs shot up, wrapping around her arm as my ankles locked together. With a harsh twist of my hips, I pulled her balance forward and locked her elbow in place. She tried to pull back, but her center had already been lost. We crashed to the ground together, her arm staying with me. I clamped my thighs together and roared, jerking my hips forward while wrenching her wrist the opposite way.

Crack.

The break was clean and complete. I relished her bellow of pain, the way her face contorted in agony. Carmen scuttled back, cradling her injured limb.

But I wasn't done. I would make her pay. Odessa *would* suffer. I would rip everything she loved right out from under her. And then that bitch would be next.

"Carmen!" Odessa cried in a warning that came too late.

I cocked my foot back and punted into Carmen's temple. Her body flew backward, flipping onto the pavement. She landed bonelessly on her side. Her broken arm was bent at a sickening angle above her head. Her broken left arm.

She didn't move. Didn't make a sound. The crowd screamed, but it was distant. Unimportant.

Stepping forward, I drew in a steady breath. My hand flattened into a blade, just like Sorin's had in the alley above Eyrin. I could do this. I had the strength to drive it clean through the delicate skin beneath her arm.

"Scarlet, no!" Sorin shouted somewhere behind me, but it was too late.

With every last ounce of fury left in me, I plunged my hand

downward. Her eyes snapped open, lips pulling to bare her fangs in a final snarl. There was almost no resistance as my fingertips sliced through flesh and sinew. As if this act of bloodshed had been preordained by the divine.

When my fingers pierced the tough outer shell of her heart and sank into the dense, ropey mass within, I splayed them wide. Her body convulsed once, twice. The light in her eyes faded, her pupils slitting and irises going dull as death claimed her. Across from me, Odessa let out a sob and dropped to her knees.

Carmen's skin began to ripple. It shuddered as if trying to hold itself together. But it couldn't. I watched with glacial, unfeeling wrath as her body seized and began to wither away. Layer by layer, her skin was stripped away, revealing muscle, tendons, and bone. Within minutes, there was nothing but a crumpled pile of ash at my feet. A gust of wind lifted Carmen's fragments into the air. Odessa lunged after them, frantically trying to catch the disintegrating remains with her bare hands.

44
____

ASHFALL

Ash spiraled around me as the October air breezed around my head, picking up strands of my blood-matted hair. Carmen's remains were slipping through Odessa's fingers like the finest dust. Her sobs turned to growls, her own anguish swelling to a frenzy.

I stood stock still, bloodied and empty-eyed. I didn't feel whole, didn't feel justified. There was no closure for me here. I was cracked, broken in a way that I didn't believe I could put back together again. I felt that yawning abyss inside of Sorin, and was at home there.

Sorin struggled to his feet, one arm cradling his ribs. His eyes still glowed faintly as they met mine. There was something unspoken between us. An apology or a reckoning. A conversation we needed to have and soon.

There was still blood to spill. A life to end that was long overdue for a reckoning. I dragged one foot in front of me, then another. Odessa was too consumed by the charred smear of her lover staining her hands to notice I was limping toward her with murder in my heart.

Two arms encircled me and pulled me against a well-muscled chest.

"No more, vita mea," Sorin pleaded into my hair and nodded in the direction of the mausoleum. "Look."

The sound of grinding stones ruptured through the night.

"Ladies and gentlemen—"

The mausoleum doors scraped open, releasing a torrent of arctic air that seemed to thrum with power. I could see it rising out of the impenetrable darkness, like the haze shimmering off the road in the middle of a summer heatwave.

Eyrin stepped forward, pretty-boy charm dialed up to eleven. His face-splitting smile gave the impression of a showman stepping into the spotlight, looking every bit the composed ringmaster.

"We thank you for attending this year's entertainment," he boomed with theatrical flair. "Our actors employed a cutting-edge blend of light and illusion to deliver the most believable performance in our capabilities. We hope to see you again next year. Enjoy your night."

He bowed as hooded figures in robes emerged from the fog rolling out from behind him. The High Council. They said nothing as they surrounded us, sealing us off from the crowd in an impenetrable circle.

A few reluctant claps rose from behind them. At Eyrin's encouragement, it grew into an ear-shattering roar of approval. I listened to them cheer on the murders of my husband and a woman who, in another life, I might have called a friend.

One of the hooded figures approached, their delicate hands separating me from Sorin. I put up a mild struggle but stopped when Sorin simply exhaled, like he'd known this was coming all along. I was too exhausted for another fight.

I allowed the woman to guide me a few feet away. Odessa howled as the last of Carmen's ashes dissipated into the wind. It was cut short when a council member clamped a hand over her mouth and silenced her grief.

My captor used the same moment on me. It was a pointless

action, though. I had no intention of screaming anymore tonight. Maybe ever.

"Hear me, Scarlet Montgomery," she spoke in a hushed, urgent voice.

Her command ripped my eyes away from Luke's lifeless body. I looked at her, surprised as I could be to see the dark-haired beauty from the fortune teller's tent.

"Do not utter a word from this point forward. There is more than your own life at risk tonight."

I felt her command bounce around my skull and sink into the marrow of my bones. A heat exuded from her palm into the plump tissue of my lips. They gripped together, and the ability to speak fled from me entirely. I opened my mouth to try and heard nothing but a ragged exhale.

"Bring them," one of the council members rasped in a voice like dust.

They dragged us into the dark, maintaining the partition between us and the crowd. The mausoleum doors slammed shut behind us. The sounds of our standing ovation, of Eyrin charming his way through the fair, faded from my ears as we descended into the dank underworld.

Down here, in the damp, crumbling belly of the dead—I knew the truth.

Freedom ended tonight. And I was the reason why.

45

THE LONGEST NIGHT

Ash clung stubbornly to my lashes as Sorin sat beside me, one arm draped protectively over my shoulders while the council debated our fate across the polished wood table of Crimson & Clover's reception floor. I wasn't listening.

My attention was glued to Odessa. She sat bound, sniveling into —of all people—Paul's shoulder. The look he was giving her could have curdled holy water. Good. At least we were on the same murderous wavelength about who nearly punched his ticket to the afterlife.

Someone argued that I had become too dangerous. They didn't even know the full body count yet, but the *method* I'd used to take down Carmen was unsettling enough to make them question whether keeping me alive was a good long-term strategy.

The one voicing concerns was the dusty-voiced relic from earlier. A senior man with skin like crumpled parchment. The geezer had a point. My hands were officially rated V for Vampire. Odessa was on my hit list, and one way or another, I planned to cross that name off.

Eyrin and Malik hovered behind me. Malik examined the injuries I'd sustained in the fight wordlessly, his face drained of color.

Once he was satisfied with what he found, my friend returned to Eyrin's side. Their fingers interlaced, though Malik angled their hands so Odessa wouldn't notice the contact.

Eyrin's eyes flicked to me, then slid away, unwilling to settle on what he saw. A woman? A monster? With as many murders as I carried under my belt, maybe I belonged at this table after all.

The dark-haired woman from the tent spoke in my defense. Because the festival had been so public, it was difficult to deny that I had been provoked. She decreed I had acted in self-preservation. Her words were undeserved.

Given half the chance, I would murder Carmen again. And the harpy weeping in the corner. But the spell remained on my lips, rendering me silent. I could not speak for myself. One council member hurled an insult at another, and the entire room burst into chaos.

"Order," rasped the ancient one, words skittering like beetles.

A gloved hand from a golden-haired fae indicated to Sorin, "You have failed to maintain the peace of your province."

"I contained a threat you saw no need to prevent."

Sorin straightened as much as his cracked ribs allowed, and I realized I was supporting most of his weight.

"Had you answered my earlier queries," he continued tightly, "this could have been avoided."

They looked to Odessa. She lifted her chin, cheeks blistered from the sun, lips split where blood dried in marbled veins. Her smile was small and close to lovely. Wrath shot through me. Sorin's fingers dug into my shoulder, preventing me from flying across the room and tearing those smug lips off her pretty face.

"I acted to remove a destabilizing influence," she said, gentle as a teacher. "Grief made me clumsy. I accept censure."

Censure. A neat little word for the slaughter of my husband. The spell on my mouth pulsed as I strained against it. My tongue burned, as if I'd drenched it in ghost peppers.

The woman's dark eyes found mine, her expression pleading. My fingers curled. Eyrin's gaze flicked to my hands, then dropped to the floor. The most imperceptible shake of his head stilled me.

Nearly an hour later, Sorin was holding me upright, and sheer exhaustion threatened to drag me into a faint. An anvil pounded behind my eyes, making the simple act of staying awake a monumental task.

"Enough. Let us vote on a verdict," the fortune teller woman sighed.

The majority of the table nodded in unison. The only thing that had been agreed upon thus far.

"Odessa of the First Province," the dust-voice intoned.

Paul dragged her to a standing position by the arm.

"All in favor of guilty?"

Hands lifted, one after another, until nearly the entire table was raised in grave consensus. A forest of pale fingers, jeweled wrists, and ink-dark claws.

"For fomenting violence and practicing necromancy beyond the sanctioned bounds, you will relinquish command of your holdings until such time as the Council restores them. You will serve under supervision. You will be bound."

A silver chain, its links fine as hair, materialized around Odessa's neck. The scent of sulfur overtook the room as it settled onto her chest. The small sense of justice I'd felt at her verdict evaporated the moment she hid a pleased smile against Paul's massive arm. Paul shuffled to the side, avoiding contact with her.

Bound, not dead. Unacceptable. I gripped Sorin's thigh until my knuckles creaked.

"Say nothing," he whispered, nodding to the old man. "Look."

Dust-voice leaned forward, his gnarled fingers tapping unrhythmically across the table. Upon his finger rested a signet ring adorned with an inverted triangle and a line running through its center.

"And your decision?" Odessa probed.

"The Winter Solstice approaches," asserted a young boy dressed entirely in white. "We cannot present ourselves to the world, divided as we are."

"We need not be divided," offered the elder.

Odessa rocked side to side, raising and lowering her head as if hearing a sermon.

The boy glared across the table, "Regardless, the experiment was compromised across all provinces."

"The Summit must proceed," insisted golden hair. "The theatrics of the first Province have forced our hand. And other clocks are moving."

Low grumbles filled the room. The chain around Odessa's throat pulled taut.

"Do you accept leash and service," the boy asked, voice soft but absolute, "for the preservation of our future?"

"I accept," Odessa purred. The chain flared, glowing like frost beneath moonlight.

The boy turned to Sorin. "Sorin Draconis, you will present your district for audit. You and the rest of the provinces will escort the petitioner to the Solstice, where we will decide on our assimilation into society. If the petitioner resists, you will persuade her. As will we all."

Petitioner. The word crawled across my skin like cold fingers. Me. And the other humans being subjugated to the experiment.

Sorin's dark eyes locked onto mine, the red receding. Nausea twisted through me at the defeat etched there.

"I will bring her," Sorin agreed.

He didn't add *if she chooses* or *unless you touch her*. He was only saying what would keep us breathing. Still, the words landed in the soft white underbelly of my already mangled emotions.

"Eyrin of the First Province," the boy went on, unblinking with those huge brown eyes. "You will coordinate the Solstice as restitution for your leadership's grievous lack of judgment."

Eyrin swept a low bow. "My pleasure, Ephrem."

Malik was saved for last, as if he were a garnish.

"The boy," the dust-voice decided. "He belongs to—"

"He belongs to himself," I snarled.

The words ripped out of me, tearing skin as it went. The spell sizzled, half-breaking in a burst of copper on my tongue. The fortune teller's head snapped toward me, eyes widening. My lips seared shut, heat welding them closed.

I felt the table's attention pour across my face like the flat of a blade laid across my cheek.

"Noted," the youth replied at last, bland as paper. "The boy is under Council protection and observation."

There was a slight tremor in Malik's hand as it dangled by his thigh. Eyrin's eyes slid over him once, then caught on me, then slipped away.

"Very well," sighed the golden-haired fae. "Let us retire. The night grows old."

Chairs scraped as the Council drained from the room, leaving only echoes and the aftertaste of injustice. The fortune teller fell in at my side and guided us toward Sorin's apartment. I chose to keep her between us.

"Scarlet." His voice was a frayed thread.

I met his eyes, throat thick with the burned edges of the spell holding back my words. I wanted to tell him I was sorry—and that I wasn't. That I loved him, even as I hated him for dragging me deeper into this nightmare. All that made it to the surface was a breath.

The fortune teller leaned close, her lips nearly brushing my ear.

"Listen carefully," she whispered. "What's coming is older than Odessa. Older than the Council itself."

"Don't speak to her," Sorin hissed, fangs in the sound.

She flicked him her middle finger without breaking stride. Maybe she wasn't so bad after all.

At his door, she paused, her tone matter-of-fact. "The spell will disperse on its own after you sleep. Tomorrow I'll return, and then we'll discuss what comes next."

"Why warn us, Seren?" Sorin asked, unlocking the door.

The three of us stood in the dim corridor, shadows stretching long across our faces.

"Come the Solstice." She lifted a hand, the air icing as it skimmed near my cheek. A shiver carved down my spine. "I will need you alive to help burn the rot festering within the Council. I've been watching you, Scarlet Montgomery. I know what you're capable of. More than even you realize."

"She will not be your tool," Sorin spat, teeth flashing.

"She has no choice," Seren whispered back, heat threading her words. "And neither will you. None of us will leave this clean. She and the other humans must be the ones to shatter the chain they'll be asked to bless."

Sorin drew me into the confines of his walls, the door whispering shut behind us. But before it could close, I jammed my foot against the frame and locked eyes with her one last time.

My brow furrowed. *Why me?*

Her gaze softened, and she shook her head in a slow, sorrowful arc.

"It is often the humble," she breathed, "who are made to bear the burden of sacrifice."

That didn't sound like it would end well for me. Martyrdom was not on my bingo card for this year. Pressing into Sorin's side, I let him absorb some of my anxiety.

"That's enough for one night," he declared with every bit of authority he had gained over two thousand years of existence.

Shame that authority hadn't been around when they were penciling me in as a Solstice sacrifice.

Seren dipped her chin, conceding. She started to turn, glancing over her shoulder for a final cryptic message.

"Remember this, Scarlet: they will dress cruelty in the guise of mercy. Do not waste your words where they will be twisted against you. Learn to listen. Listening will keep you alive."

Then she was gone. Time seemed to warp as she slipped off

Sorin's floor to wherever she would wait for the morning summit. The door clicked shut, separating me from the fortune teller.

After a long shower, I lay back on Sorin's silent bed and stared at the ceiling. He hadn't spoken since Seren left. My palms still smelled faintly of ash.

Burying my face in the pillow, I pictured Luke's face sinking into his final smile. I pictured Sorin beside me, his eyes beseeching forgiveness even as they simmered with disappointment at what I'd done tonight. I pictured Malik standing behind us because he thought he should, and Odessa somewhere in Crimson & Clover, smiling at her new piece of shiny jewelry.

In my mind, my hands closed around her throat, a stake pierced her heart, and I dragged her body into the sun for good measure. Another vision rose up of myself, naked and bleeding at a winter Solstice, silhouettes of the Council circling as my body caught fire on the pyre. An old man's grin stretched across my brain like a Cheshire cat.

I closed my eyes. I made a promise small enough to fit inside a rib and sharp enough to cut.

When the longest night came, the Solstice, there would be no blessing from me. Only breaking.

ACKNOWLEDGMENTS

To my family, thanks for surviving my wild tangents and late-night vampire rants. You deserve medals. Or at least earplugs.

To my friends, thank you for test-reading, poking holes in my plot, and reminding me that even monsters need continuity. This story would have collapsed faster than a cheap coffin without you.

To my husband, who has endured over two years of me giggling like a maniac one minute and swearing at my keyboard the next. You're still here, which means either you really love me or you're just as stubborn as I am. Either way, I love you.

And to you, the reader. Thank you for stepping into the dark with me. This debut may not be flawless, but I bled for every word (sometimes literally, thanks to caffeine and poor life choices). I'm glad you're here. Don't get too comfortable, though. The sequel, *Road to Redemption*, is coming for you.

ABOUT THE AUTHOR

R. A. Moritz is a storyteller, photographer, and U.S. military veteran. She weaves tales of resilience, temptation, and survival into dark fantasies inspired by lore, legends, and the shadows of history.

When she isn't writing, she can be found training Brazilian Jiu-Jitsu, wandering through old towns and chasing ghost stories, or losing herself in stacks of books. She lives in Virginia with her husband, dogs, and an imagination that refuses to sleep.

Want to hear more from me? Join me on social media for exclusive content, playlists, updates, and the first look at my upcoming projects.